A DEA'

A DEATH IN GREENWICH

A Joshua Dionne Mystery

By

Juri Pill

PROLOGUE

He was sure someone was in the suite. Courtney had left hours ago, and he distinctly remembered locking the door. He glanced at the alarm clock – four A.M. He breathed in slowly and exhaled quietly. Dead silence. Maybe it was a dream.

He rolled over and closed his eyes, trying to get back to sleep. Then he heard it again. It was coming from the living room – a gentle tapping, rhythmic and barely audible. He got up very quietly and started moving toward the sound. And then he saw it. The window was open, and a gentle wind was rocking the half-drawn blind back and forth, ticking the wall and creating the gentle knocking sound. He knew he had closed that window. He could feel his heart rate increasing as he reached for the light switch, but before he could get to it, he caught a slight movement in his peripheral vision, and turned quickly toward it. He saw two shadowy shapes crouching halfway across the room, and heading toward him.

Shit, he'd stumbled in here too sleepy to reach for a weapon or even his phone. And the odds — two against one — weren't good.

Years of martial arts training kicked in, and he slowed his breathing and pulse. He needed to get the adrenaline working in his favor. Within moments, his hearing and night vision sharpened. He realized that the figure on his left was bigger, heavier; the one on the right slender and fine-boned. Both were dressed in black, wearing ski masks. He had to take out the smaller one first.

With lightning movements, he grabbed a nearby chair and overturned it, striking the larger attacker and temporarily blocking his path. Then he scooped up a glass vase filled with flowers from the coffee table and hurled it at the smaller attacker. But the assailant sidestepped, and the vase crashed against a wall mirror, shattering both. He hoped someone heard it and would call the police.

And then the smaller assailant was on him. He tried to pull the guy toward him, to cut off the possibility of a strike, but the attacker's arm swept up on the diagonal, and he felt a blade slice across his arm, followed by a hard thrust into his gut. He never saw the knife.

He felt a thunderous blow to the side of his head - the bigger guy - and almost went down. The bathroom was just behind him. If he could get in there, lock them out . . .

Gasping with pain, he staggered into the bathroom. He pushed the door shut and leaned against it, turning on a light to examine his injuries. But he kept seeing the way that guy handled the knife, keeping the blade concealed, the diagonal slash, followed by the thrust. And that side fist to his head. Both of his assailants were highly trained.

He felt the door behind him pushed open. His gut was on fire and he could barely move his arm. He grabbed a towel to stop the bleeding, and they came at him. Now he saw the knife blade gleaming. He raised his bloodied arm to block the blow, and drove his other fist toward his attacker's face. His hand hit the knife. He felt nothing, but he could see his finger was gone. Then the knife slashed the muscles of his chest and he fell to his knees. He could feel his strength slowly ebbing. The needle sting in his arm was almost an afterthought, and he knew it was over. He closed his eyes and relaxed as one of them reached over and turned off the light.

CHAPTER 1

Sunday, September 7, 2008

Joshua Dionne – JD to his friends - sat tuning his Telecaster, and smiled when he saw Raji saunter into the music room, tail wagging like a metronome. Raji was a black Labrador retriever who liked western swing music, which was unusual for a dog.

Raji's master followed him in and sat down behind his drum kit. Fareed Ghanem stood about five nine, and weighed maybe one thirty, but his tempo had never failed in the fifteen years since the Charles River Playboys had first gotten together as a trio at MIT. The third member of the group, Richard Bridger, nodded as Fareed gave a few taps on the bass drum and tested the high hat. Rich was the ying to Fareed's yang. He was six four and probably two-forty, and the Fender bass looked puny in his massive frame.

Rich folded his hands and stretched them out in front of him, cracking his knuckles, and displaying the tattoo of a karate black belt on the back of his right hand. His bass hung precariously over his shoulder. "What say, we kick it off with a little 'San Antonio Rose'?"

Fareed's eyes widened as he watched the swaying neck of Rich's bass. "I think that would be a splendid idea. But please do be careful with that instrument."

JD felt the song was a little long in the tooth, but the chord progression was interesting, and it was an okay warm-up number. Fareed kicked it off, and they started in. But about halfway through, Rich stopped singing and put up his hand.

"We need to take it to a lower key, guys. I can't hit those high notes anymore."

JD tilted his head and grinned. "So get some tighter shorts."

Fareed frowned and shook his head. "That is not such a good idea. So much pain for so little gain. Why do we not attempt the song in B-flat?"

"That's easy for you to say." JD pointed at the drum kit. "All keys are the same for a drummer."

Fareed gave a little sideways glance at JD. Then he looked down and started tapping out a quiet shuffle rhythm on the snare and high hat, nodding his head to the tempo. His eyes were half-closed. JD knew he was being ignored.

Raji started growling.

Rich frowned. "Look, JD, we need it in B-flat so I can sing the damn song. My voice has changed. I'm not fucking twenty-five years old anymore. Give me a break."

JD raised his left hand from the guitar neck and flexed it. "Well, my fingers aren't what they used to be either. Let me think about this."

He felt his neck muscles tighten. Rich could never leave things alone. B-flat! But he took a deep breath, flipped his chart book to "San Antonio Rose," and made some notes. Then he started to relax a little. It could actually work.

"Okay, what the hell, I'll give it a shot. Kick it off, Dr. Drummer."

Fareed counted in the song, and JD opened with an audacious new lick leading straight into Rich's vocal. The trio hit the modulation into F, and Rich's voice was soaring. Rich finished singing the verse, and then pointed his bass at JD, who took his cue. First he worked two octaves of ascending sixteenth notes in a pattern he'd never tried before, and then a swooping series of rapid chord changes. He hit the final chord with a big grin and a shower of notes, and Fareed gave a big double kick on the bass drum as Rich moved into the second verse. When they finished the song, Raji gave a single bark of approval.

Rich put his hand up for a high five from JD. "I had no idea how you were going to land that solo. Your fingers were flying. I couldn't believe it."

Fareed gently placed his brushes on the snare. "Sometimes it is worthwhile and rewarding to try something you have never tried before. Would you not agree, Joshua?"

JD nodded. "I have no idea how I did that. But I guess that's why we've lasted fifteen years playing the same old songs. The magic's still there, somewhere."

They moved quickly through the set list for their next gig at the Sundown Saloon. When they were done, JD and Rich put their instruments on their stands and leaned back. Fareed walked over to the white and chrome '50s Frigidaire and pulled out three beers. Bridger lit up a big cigar, prompting Raji to move over to the other side of the room.

Fareed said, "Richard, please tell us about your presentation tonight. Should we attend?"

"Nothing new, so don't bother. It's about the coming crash. All those variable rate mortgages and liar loans are done like dinner. Lehman has the biggest stake in that ball game, and they're a dead man walking." Rich took a swig of his beer and looked around for an ashtray.

"Why the hell did they invite you then?" JD asked. "They've been calling you Dr. Doom for two years."

Fareed said, "Sometimes the thing that is right in front of you is not so obvious to everyone. Perhaps they have seen the light."

Rich took a long puff on his cigar, and blew three flawless smoke rings. "John Maynard Yates will be there. I haven't seen him since that plagiarism thing at Yale."

JD grinned. "A little jealous, are we? His fund is managing two billion now. Not bad for a Ph.D. dropout."

Rich glanced sharply at JD. "You know damn well Yates wasn't a dropout. And I don't think his ethics have changed. I've been looking at the returns on his fund, and they don't make sense. They're mathematically impossible."

Fareed's eyes opened very wide. "Do you think he may be running some sort of fraud?"

Rich closed his eyes and took another long puff. "I wouldn't put it past him. I've asked one of my friends at the SEC to look into it."

Rich took another long drag on his cigar, and the room was silent for a minute. The ash on the cigar was getting very long, and Fareed was looking worried about his carpets. Then Rich said, "Lehman is going to collapse, and then there's going to be a bank run. But it won't be on Main Street, like in that Jimmy Stewart picture. It's going to be on Wall Street. And we're all going to make a fucking fortune."

Fareed rushed over with an ashtray. Rich let the inch-long ash drop in the ashtray, and said, "I give it a week. All those credit default swaps will pay off."

They finished their beers, turned off the amps, and packed up the instruments.

Fareed said, "Richard, would you like to stay for dinner? Vivian is away at university, and I'm sure Heema won't mind. We can cook American."

"Thanks, but they've put me up at the Zodiac Inn, and my presentation is right there. I'm going to stop at the local dojo and get in a quick sparring practice, and then I'll get a steak at the hotel. Maybe next time."

JD said, "I hope this is just a professional meeting. No extracurricular recreation."

Bridger just smiled and did not respond.

* * *

JD slept in a little late on Monday morning. He got up and dressed without waking Annie, and went downstairs for breakfast. Their daughter had already left for school, and their son had stayed at Yale for the weekend, so the kitchen was quiet. He turned on CNBC to check the markets. The government's action in saving Fannie Mae and Freddie Mac over the weekend had caused a tidal wave of optimism, and JD wanted to see how far the tide would run. The crash was going to be delayed.

JD finished his breakfast and then walked to his office at the back of the house. JD saw a dozen emails from clients, most of them curious about the government's moves over the weekend, and its effect on their investments. It took him an hour to reply to them all, because he wanted to be thorough and detailed in the hope that there would be no more emails for a while. He had too many nervous clients. Then he picked up his guitar and worked through some chords from the new set list. When he was satisfied, he checked his watch - half past ten.

JD put down the guitar and walked over to Annie's studio on the other side of the house. She was painting when JD strolled in, and looked as if she'd been up for a while. The morning sun was low in the sky, creating an orange glow on the painting and the wall behind it. Annie was almost six feet tall, and the sun highlighted her long blond hair, startling blue eyes, and high cheekbones. Her father, a physicist at Oxford, had named her after Charles Darwin's favorite daughter. It was a lot to live up to, but JD thought she'd done all right.

She seemed to be concentrating hard on her painting. JD sat at the side and watched for a while. "I like the colors," he said. "It's very different from what you've been doing over the past year. It's much brighter."

Annie stepped back from the painting and tilted her head to look. "It's new. They were expecting more of the same. They're a little skeptical."

"I think these will sell. We're heading into the mother of all recessions, and everyone in Greenwich will be looking for something to cheer them up. Besides, I was getting worried. I wondered if you were heading somewhere really dark."

"The paintings . . . and my moods. Sometimes, I don't know which is the chicken and which is the egg. Anyway, we're into what the gallery is now calling my 'red phase'. Things are looking up. Speaking of which, would you mind getting me a cup of coffee? I can't leave this painting right now."

JD went to the kitchen and brought her back the coffee. She thanked him and was about to put another dab of orange on the canvas when her cell phone rang. She picked it up, listened for a while and then shook her head. "No, I haven't seen him. You can check with JD, he's right here."

Annie put her hand over the phone, and whispered, "It's Dot. She said Rich hasn't returned from the hotel this morning."

Rich's delay probably involved another woman, thought JD. He picked up the phone. "Hi, Dot, what's up?"

"Richard was supposed to be home an hour ago. I checked the hotel, and he hasn't signed out. There's no answer in his room, and I'm getting worried. They refuse to knock on the door. Could you please drop by and see if he's okay?"

"Of course, Dot. I'll get over there right now. He's probably involved with another client meeting. It's the Zodiac Inn, right?"

"You're an angel. Ask him to call me as soon as you find him. It's just not like him. He always calls when he's going to be late."

Yeah, thought JD, *he always has an alibi when he's cheating on her.*

JD disconnected and turned to Annie. "Looks like Rich is up to his usual tricks, and this time he didn't even bother to call Dot. I have to go over and find him."

Annie looked concerned. "He's a real piece of work, but he does always call with an excuse when he has to – quote - work late. This seems different. Dot sounded really worried."

JD sighed. "Maybe one of the husbands finally caught him in the act."

Annie's eyes narrowed in a way that JD was very familiar with. "It's not a joking matter, JD. Get up there and find out what's going on."

"I'll try him on my cell phone first. Maybe he'll answer when he sees it's me." JD punched in Rich's number, but there was no response. He left a message to call back.

Annie gave him another dark look that he didn't want to decipher. Then she turned back to her painting. JD wasn't sure whether Annie was angry with him, or with Rich, but probably both – maybe men in general. He quietly left the studio and started toward the garage.

JD jumped into his black Porsche Turbo, and wasted no time in getting to the Zodiac Inn, which was on Greenwich Harbor, just south of downtown. It had been a very rundown motel ten years earlier, but when the big hedge funds started moving onto Railroad Avenue just to the north, an international conglomerate had bought it and rebuilt it to five-star standards. As he pulled up, JD looked up at the hotel's new central module with its lobby, restaurants and meeting rooms, plus the two residential wings, one on each side, running along the harbor. A boat dock ran along the back of the hotel, usually with a few yachts and cigarette boats moored alongside. The bar and restaurant along that dock saw a lot of deal flow, with many of the principals arriving by yacht from Manhattan, across the Sound. JD had been to the bar a few times when clients insisted on it, but it was a little too look-at-me for him. He preferred the smaller restaurants on Greenwich Avenue near Fareed's office. The Zodiac Inn was more Rich's style.

JD gave the Porsche keys to the valet and walked quickly toward the entrance. As he came up to the front desk, he got the attention of one of the three desk clerks, a tall overweight man in his mid-forties. The clerk shuffled over and gave a big sigh. JD had no luggage, so he knew he was not going to get special service. The Stetson, boots and ponytail probably didn't help either. "Good morning, sir, how can I help you?"

"Good morning. I'm Doctor Joshua Dionne." JD liked to use his "doctor" title under the right circumstances. Sometimes it opened doors. "I'm a friend of Professor Richard Bridger, one of your guests. He was supposed to go home to New Haven this morning, but he didn't show up. His wife is very concerned. Have you seen him?"

"No, not that I recall, sir, but we have over a hundred guests here. Let me check his registration." The clerk made some entries on his keyboard. "I see that Professor Bridger made a presentation at a dinner meeting here last night. Let me see if he's been down for breakfast this morning." He manipulated the mouse again, and said, "No, he hasn't had breakfast. He had some room service last night, but none this morning. He's probably still asleep."

This didn't make sense to JD. Rich was always an early riser, even with a hangover. "He was supposed to be home over an hour ago. Could you please check his room?"

"Very well, sir. I shall call his room." The clerk punched in a number and waited. "No answer."

JD was starting to get worried. "Can you give me a key so I can confirm that he's all right?"

"I'm afraid I can't do that, sir. It's against policy. Only our guests have room keys."

JD's voice became louder. "So what the hell do I do? Call the damn police?"

"I'm sure that won't be necessary, sir. As I said, your friend is probably still asleep. There was quite a party here last night."

JD leaned over the desk, and glared at the clerk. "Look, I've had enough of this. Please get me the manager."

"Whatever you wish, sir." The clerk shrugged, turned around, and disappeared through a doorway behind the front desk. JD could feel his chest tightening. He hated bureaucracy, especially officious clerks, but he was more troubled by the fact that Rich was still not answering the phone. He thought of the one possible and relatively benign explanation - maybe Rich had a woman in his room. But still, why hadn't he called Dot? That was not like Rich at all. He always covered his tracks.

After a couple of minutes, the clerk returned with a second man. He was immaculately dressed: a dark blue suit, a white shirt with cufflinks, and a red silk tie. The man held out his hand to JD and smiled. "My name is Michael Powers. I'm the manager here. Steven tells me you're concerned about your friend Richard Bridger. Let's go down the hall and see if we can wake him. Professor Bridger has a large suite on the ground floor overlooking the harbor."

JD followed him out of the lobby and down the hallway to the right. They reached Rich's room, and Powers knocked on the door. There was no response, so the manager knocked again. Still no sound from the room, and he stepped back, turning to JD. "I'll have to use the key, Dr. Dionne. Please allow me go in first. There may be a need for privacy on Mr. Bridger's part."

Powers opened the door and stepped in. After looking around only a few seconds, he turned back quickly, his face ashen, and tried to stop JD from entering. JD sidestepped him and pushed his way in.

JD could feel a jolt of adrenaline as he quickly surveyed the chaos in the suite. For a few seconds, he was unable to focus, and he had to take a deep breath. A chair had been knocked over, and the mirror on the wall was shattered. Shards of glass from the mirror and a broken vase were scattered across the white carpet, interspersed with some red and yellow flowers. Next to the couch was a pool of partially-congealed blood. His eyes followed a trail of blood along the carpet, and he could see more large bloodstains on the far wall. He stumbled farther into the room, almost in a daze, and then his eyes moved toward the bathroom. He could feel Powers pulling on his arm, trying to stop him. "We have to get out of here. I have to call the police. We must not disturb anything." JD swatted away the manager's arm, and lunged into the bathroom.

He saw more blood on the bathroom floor and on the mirror. Then his eyes widened as he stared at something even more disturbing – a severed finger resting on the white tiles. Almost instinctively, he took out his handkerchief. Powers started shouting, "No, no, you mustn't touch that."

JD blocked the doorway with his back, and bent over to pick up the finger. Still almost in a trance, he examined it carefully, and felt his heart rate increasing rapidly. He saw that the bottom of the severed finger had thick calluses. Karate calluses. JD dropped the small piece of human flesh and staggered out of the bathroom. He felt the manager grab his shoulders, apparently trying to lead him out the front door into the hallway.

JD pushed the manager away abruptly, bent forward, and started vomiting violently. He could feel the cold sweat running down his face. After half a minute, he finally caught his breath and looked back toward the bathroom, wiping his mouth with his sleeve.

"That's Rich's finger," he mumbled in a toneless voice.

CHAPTER 2

JD tried to get up, but his knees buckled and he fell backwards onto the hotel room sofa. He could feel the sweat dripping off his face, but he also noticed that he was starting to shiver. The manager knelt down beside him, carefully avoiding the vomit on the carpet.

"Are you all right?" the man asked. "Should I get you a doctor?"

JD took a deep breath, trying to ease the nausea that still gripped him. "I'll be okay. Just call 9-1-1."

JD shut his eyes as the manager punched in the numbers and spoke into his cell. "This is Michael Powers, manager at the Zodiac Inn. There's been a violent incident in one of our rooms. We have blood, and . . . a severed finger. The occupant is missing. It's Room 107."

Powers was silent for a while, apparently listening to the police dispatcher, and then he said, "No, there's no sign of a body." More silence, and finally the manager said, "Okay." JD heard him disconnect, and then Powers said, "Dr. Dionne, the police are on their way. They said this is now a crime scene, and we have to leave. We cannot disturb anything, understand?"

JD glanced at the blood on the floor and shook his head. "I'm not leaving. I have to find out what happened to Rich. Maybe he's in the bedroom. We haven't checked the bedroom." He was dreading what he might find there, but he got up and started heading that way. Powers stepped in front of him to block his progress, but JD lifted him up by his armpits and set him off to one side. His adrenaline was pumping furiously. He brushed past the manager and opened the door.

The bed had seen a lot of action. An overnight suitcase lay open on the floor, strewn with clothes – underwear, a shirt, and a tie. A laptop computer lay on the writing table by the bed, still plugged in. A cell phone sat next to it. Nothing had been stolen, but there was no sign of Rich, no sign of a body. This room was clean, with no indication of violence or forced entry. But then he paused. He noticed something - a faint whiff of perfume, maybe Chanel.

JD heard the suite's front door open, and turned around. Two Greenwich Police Department patrolmen came in, followed by another hotel staffer. Powers pointed at JD. "I tried to get him out of here, but he refused to go."

One of the patrolmen looked at JD, who stared back at him defiantly. "My friend Richard Bridger was staying here, and his wife hadn't heard from him, so I came down to check it out. I'm not leaving until I find out what happened."

"That's not the way it works, sir. We'll have to ask you to wait outside."

Four more patrolmen came in, three men and a woman, plus an older uniformed officer who looked like a supervisor. He took a quick look around, and said, "Vito and Mike, set up a perimeter and start an entry list. Joe and Evangelina, start knocking on doors. Keep track of anyone coming or going, and I'll make sure forensics and the detectives are on their way." Then he turned to JD and Powers. "Anything been disturbed in here? You touched anything?"

He sniffed the air in the living room and then looked down on the tan and green puddle by the sofa. "That looks fresh. Was it there when you walked in?"

JD looked at the mess on the carpet. The sight started to make him feel sick again, but he took a deep breath and held it. The supervisor seemed to notice JD's discomfort. "Did you do that? The puke, I mean?"

JD nodded. "I was upset when I saw my friend's finger on the floor."

The supervisor's eyes narrowed. "Finger? What finger?"

JD walked toward the bathroom and pointed. "It's there."

"Did you touch it?"

"I picked it up. I wasn't thinking. And anyway, I used a handkerchief. It's Richard Bridger's finger."

The police supervisor took a deep breath and crossed his arms over his chest. "Sir, how did you know it was your friend's finger?"

"He has a second-degree black belt in karate, and that finger has a lot of calluses."

The supervisor looked down at the finger on the tile bathroom floor. "A black belt? What's your buddy do for a living?"

"He's an economics professor at Yale."

"A prof with a black belt. No shit. How big is he?"

"Big. Like a linebacker."

The cop frowned and said, almost to himself, "He put up a hell of a fight, looks like. So good chance, there was more than one perp. They probably took him out the back window there, then maybe on a boat."

He looked out the window at the dock alongside the hotel. "We gotta get the tapes from the security system."

He then turned abruptly back to JD. "Get out of here and don't touch anything. Wait for the detectives. They'll take your statement. You've been tampering with evidence at a possible homicide."

Two of the patrolmen escorted JD to the hallway, and one of the hotel staff brought some chairs. He sat down to wait. Powers sat down beside him, and one of the patrolmen stood guarding the door. JD watched as two of the other patrolmen started knocking on doors down the hall. Finally, one door opened and they disappeared into the room, carrying their notebooks. A few minutes later, three men and two women in white overalls walked down the hall and headed into Rich's room, each hefting two large aluminum cases.

The manager frowned. "Forensics. All we need now is the media. This is not going to help business."

JD did not respond. He was thinking of Rich, wondering if his friend was dead or alive. As he visualized the blood stains on the wall and floor, he started to obsess about why someone would attack and capture Rich – or maybe kill him. The most likely reason still seemed to be his friend's philandering. Probably a jealous husband, maybe that professor at Yale. But if so, he certainly had help. Rich could not have been taken by just one person.

JD saw two men in civilian clothes come walking quickly down the hallway – detectives. One was in his mid or late thirties, with wavy black hair parted on one side, dark brown eyes with prominent eyebrows, and a narrow nose. He was wearing a black Polo vest with pressed khakis, a blue button-down shirt, and brown leather work boots. JD noticed the fancy logo on the boots. Detectives must be paid okay, he thought. No rumpled raincoats here. The other man was older and heftier, with a slight paunch and a shiny bald spot. His jeans were well worn and he was wearing a black nylon Greenwich Police windbreaker. They hurried past with only a glance at JD. The patrolman guarding the room opened the door and the two detectives went inside.

* * *

The detectives came out fifteen minutes later and stopped in front of JD and Powers. The younger one with the dark hair looked down at JD. "I understand you tampered with some evidence, pal. Could we go somewhere quiet and talk about this?"

Powers said, "You can use one of the conference rooms. I'll see which ones are empty."

The detective turned toward him with a quizzical look. "And you are?"

"I'm Michael Powers, manager of the Zodiac. I opened the room for Dr. Dionne here, and we were the first ones in."

"That's good, pal. Detective Brown here will take your statement, and I'll deal with Dr. Ponytail here. Show us the way."

JD and the detectives followed Powers down two hallways, and then past the front desk to an empty conference room. The younger detective thanked the manager and waved JD into the room and pointed to a seat on the other side of a table. He closed the door and sat down opposite JD, taking out his notebook and an audio recorder. He placed the recorder on the table and turned it on. JD noticed that he sat up very straight, and he seemed thin for a police officer. JD couldn't see any gun.

"What's your name, cowboy?"

Cowboy? thought JD. This interview was not off to a great start.

"Joshua Dionne, but most people call me JD. What's yours?"

"Puccini. Detective Antonio Puccini. And I'm not here to give you a hard time, mister. I just want you to tell me what happened and what you saw."

Over the next five minutes, JD described Dot's worried phone call, driving to the hotel, and getting the manager to open the room.

"Tell me what you saw when you walked in, JD."

"The first thing was the chair on the floor and the pool of blood on the carpet. Then I saw the broken mirror and vase and the blood spatters on the wall."

"Is that when you threw up?"

"No, it was after I went in the bathroom and found Rich's finger."

"Why did you pick it up?"

"After I saw all the blood, I was in shock, kind of a stupor. I just saw Rich yesterday, and this didn't seem real. I thought I was dreaming. I wasn't thinking. I just picked it up."

"But you didn't pick it up with your bare hand. You must've been thinking a little bit. And you knew it was Bridger's finger because of the calluses, right?"

"I already told that to the other police officer."

"Yeah. And then you got sick. Threw up on the floor."

JD nodded. "I hurled. That was after I realized it was Rich's finger."

Puccini smiled slightly. "Hurled . . . you're from Canada, right? Princeton, Rhodes Scholar, Ph.D. from MIT. And Bridger was at MIT with you. Tell me a little about him. Who might've done this?"

JD felt his heart pounding. Puccini had been in that room for only fifteen minutes. JD remembered from somewhere that in a murder investigation, the person who discovered the body almost automatically became a suspect. He felt a small bead of sweat run down his back.

"How do you know all that?"

Puccini shrugged. "You're a smart guy, so I'll tell you. The uniforms ran an LPR through the parking lot before I got here, and they tracked your car registration. Nice Porsche. I had your full profile before I walked into the hotel."

"LPR? What's that?"

"License Plate Recorder. It's all digital. We identified everyone parked at the hotel within five minutes, and ran the backgrounds."

JD was starting to feel like a butterfly pinned to a board. What else did the detective know about him? JD didn't think he had anything to hide, but he was starting to wonder whether he should call a lawyer.

Puccini folded his hands in front of him. "Greenwich is a peaceful town, so when something like this happens, we pull out all the stops. We've got twelve uniformed officers working on this already, plus forensics, and we'll have ten detectives on it by this afternoon. We'll catch whoever did this. But like the lawyers say, time is of the essence. You can help us. So tell me about Professor Bridger. Who might have done this? Any enemies?"

"You've read his CV by now, I'm sure. He's an American success story. I can't imagine who would want to hurt him."

Puccini's nostrils flared and he slapped the table with an open hand. "JD, let's cut the bullshit! That perfume in the bedroom is not standard hotel décor. Your friend Bridger was playing hide-the-salami with someone in there. Who the hell was it?"

"I really don't know," JD said truthfully. "Rich is . . . a complicated individual."

"But you knew this was standard operating procedure for him. He couldn't keep his prick holstered. So he must have talked to you about it, man to man. Over a few drinks, maybe. We need it *now* if we're going to save him. Think, man."

JD was silent, considering the possibilities - the women at Yale, the one-night stands, maybe a liaison at this conference. Rich did sometimes let some details slip after a few drinks.

Puccini interrupted his thoughts. "We'll get the DNA from the bed, and we'll find out who the woman was. It's just a matter of time, but time is something we haven't got, Joshua. Professor Bridger may still be alive. So who's the woman? We find her, we find Bridger."

JD shook his head. "I don't know. A few weeks ago, he said he was seeing a married woman at Yale, but that's all I know."

"How does his wife feel about all this? Does she know?"

JD wondered how much he should disclose. But Puccini looked like he was not about to let go without getting as much information as possible. Besides, the detective would eventually find out everything anyway, and JD wanted to help find Rich - if he was still alive.

"Rich's wife knows it's happened before, and she wouldn't be too happy about it. She thought it was over."

"Not happy, huh? So how unhappy is she? Unhappy enough to do something about it? Hire some muscle, maybe?"

JD clenched his fist on the table and took a deep breath. "Detective Puccini, your implication is ridiculous. Dorothy Bridger had nothing to do with this."

"Let me tell you something, Joshua. You were the first one on the scene, and you know him. Maybe *you* had something to do with this."

"That's absurd," JD said. "Rich was one of my best friends." But JD remembered the discovered-the-body angle. He knew he had to think and speak carefully to avoid trouble.

Puccini leaned back and narrowed his eyes. "Why do you say, *was* one of your best friends? How do you know he's dead?"

JD frowned and scratched the side of his head. "Look, I don't know. Maybe you do. But finding his finger like that . . . all I know is something really bad happened to him."

Puccini leaned back and seemed to relax a little. "There's many possibilities here, JD. Maybe he was kidnapped for ransom. We need to get in touch with his wife. I have to question her as soon as possible. They have any kids? Any relatives nearby?"

JD pushed his chair back from the table. "I've said enough. I think I should call a lawyer."

Puccini finished writing and slowly looked up with a smile that was probably meant to be reassuring. "You won't need a lawyer, Dr. Dionne. I would just like your help in finding whoever did this to your friend, and more importantly, finding him alive. Could you come down to the Public Safety Complex so we can get more detail? His most recent contacts, any enemies he may have, anything you can think of?" He paused and looked serious. "We want to catch the perpetrators, and you can help us."

JD nodded thoughtfully. He did want to help, but he did not want to incriminate himself in some way he was unaware of. "I've never been through this before. Am I a suspect? What if I refuse to come down to the station?"

"You're not under arrest, so I can't force you to come. I just want a friendly chat. You've got nothing to worry about. You want to catch these guys and save your friend, right?"

A friendly chat, thought JD. The detective was bullshitting him. Maybe he should talk to a lawyer before he went for the so-called chat. "Okay, I'll come down to the station tomorrow. I need to go up to New Haven. Rich's wife is going to need some support."

Puccini frowned. "It would be better if you came down today, but suit yourself. Time's a-wasting."

JD paused. "There *is* one more thing, Detective. Years ago at Yale, Rich had a run-in with a man named John Maynard Yates. Rich got him kicked out of Yale for plagiarizing, and he told me a few days ago that he suspected Yates may be involved in some sort of financial fraud. He contacted the Securities Exchange Commission, and told them they should look into Yates's investment fund. And Yates was at this conference here at the hotel."

Puccini smiled. "You know, JD, that's the sort of stuff we need. That's very helpful. We'll look into it right away, and I'll see you tomorrow morning."

"Yes, tomorrow," JD agreed.

He left the hotel and got in his car, but then sat there for five minutes without starting the engine, staring blankly at the Marine Unit patrol boat at the dock behind the hotel. He had to think and he felt exhausted.

JD went through the day's events in his mind: the market opening, going to Annie's studio and then the call from Dot. Now Rich was missing, maybe dead. Then he realized he hadn't called Annie. His call went directly to voicemail, and he decided not to leave a message. On something this serious, he wanted to speak to her in person. Then he decided to call Fareed, and his friend picked up right away.

"Fareed, I have some bad news. Are you sitting down?"

JD heard a sharp intake of breath, and there was a momentary silence. "Yes, I am sitting down, JD. What is the bad news? Are you all right?"

"I had a call from Dot earlier today. Rich was supposed to be home this morning, and when she hadn't heard from him, she asked me to find him at the Zodiac Inn. He's not there, Fareed. He's missing from the hotel, and there were . . . signs of violence. The police are here now, and I was just questioned by one of the detectives."

There was another long pause, and JD could hear Fareed breathing deeply. "Signs of violence?"

"Some blood on the floor and on the walls, and there was something worse. A severed finger. It was Rich's finger. It had the karate calluses."

Fareed's voice became very quiet. "I cannot believe this. How could it have happened? Richard telephoned me after his presentation last night, and said it was extremely well received. I had concluded that he returned home to New Haven right after. I am very surprised that he remained at the hotel."

"I was too," JD said. "But you know Rich."

"Another woman?"

"Well, someone left a whiff of perfume in the room."

There was another silence on the phone. "That bastard. How is Dorothy? Have you told her that Richard is missing? And please pardon my language, Joshua."

"I have to go to the police station tomorrow to answer some questions. Can you think of anyone who might have done this to Rich? He's no choirboy, but this is bizarre. One possibility I thought of was John Maynard Yates. Rich mentioned him at our band practice yesterday, and that possible fraud."

"Yes, I remember. John Maynard Yates, the ABD – All But Dissertation – from Yale. But all that blood and the finger on the floor. Mr. Yates strikes me as too genteel to partake in that sort of mayhem."

"I mentioned Yates to the detective. He said they would look into it. Can you think of anyone else?"

"No, but I will give it some serious consideration, Joshua. And you say you are going to the police station tomorrow? Be careful. I'm certain that you're aware of the little charade that American police often perform, with a good officer and a bad officer taking turns in the questioning. This detective sounds like he's playing the good officer. You will meet the bad officer tomorrow. JD, I am afraid you need a solicitor. You are just a little papoose in the woods."

"I've been thinking about it. Maybe I do need some advice."

They disconnected, and JD started the car and drove home. He parked and hurried into the kitchen, where Annie was sitting quietly on one of the red plastic bar stools in front of their white granite kitchen island. She was dressed in worn jeans and a white shirt with a few yellow and red paint stains. "So what's happening? Did you find Richard? I've been on the phone with Dot for the last half hour. She's almost hysterical with worry."

JD slumped into a chair by the kitchen table. "It's not good. I'll bring you up to date . . . but first, I could use a drink." He raised his hand, and he could see it was still shaking a little.

Annie went to the living room and came back with a glass of rye whiskey with two ice cubes, and a glass of port for herself. JD took a sip of whiskey and closed his eyes. Then he brought Annie up to date on the events at the hotel. She sat very still as she listened, and then said, "I have to call Dot."

Annie dialed her phone and repeated most of what JD had told her. He could hear Dot's cries and sobs through Annie's phone. Annie said they would come up to New Haven to be with her, and then disconnected.

"She didn't take it well. We should get up there right away." She paused, and took a deep breath. "Why would someone attack Rich? It makes no sense. If they're going to kidnap someone for ransom, it wouldn't be a college professor, especially in Greenwich, with all the billionaires. But do you think . . . maybe he's dead?"

"I don't know. There was a lot of blood in that room. And one more thing. There's no need to tell Dot right now, but there was a severed finger on the floor. It was Rich's finger, because I saw the karate calluses. Whoever did this had a knife. And knew how to use it."

Annie's face turned pale. "A knife? And a severed finger?"

JD nodded. "Rich must have been badly hurt, but he put up a hell of a fight."

Annie put down her glass and looked at JD. "Could it be just a random attack?"

"I don't think so. He didn't really have much worth stealing, and if it was robbery, why would they take him and leave his laptop and phone on the desk? No, Rich was targeted. My first thought was John Maynard Yates. That's what I told the detective."

"That was over five years ago. Getting kicked out of Yale was probably the best thing that ever happened to him. Why would he go after Richard now?"

"It's not about Yale, it's about Yates's investment fund. Rich told me yesterday that Yates's running a fraud, and he'd been talking to the SEC. And Yates was at that conference with Rich. But there's one more thing. Rich had a woman with him at some point. That's probably why he stayed late. I could smell Chanel in the room."

Annie scowled and tapped her fingers on the counter. "Damn it, JD, Dot told me he had promised to change. They had quite a confrontation last week."

JD looked at her in surprise. "A confrontation?" Maybe Puccini's questions about Dot were valid. Maybe Dot's hysteria was an act, and she did have something to do with Rich's disappearance. Their relationship had always been volatile, and Rich was not always a nice guy.

Annie took a sip of her port and let out a big sigh. "Just a tiff, a squabble, nothing serious. She did put a private detective on him at one point. But you know, she still loves him."

Annie turned toward JD, her eyes narrowing. "He's been a friend of yours forever, but sometimes Richard is ass. Maybe it finally caught up with him. I'm sure he's made some enemies somewhere."

JD looked at his drink and took another sip, swirling the ice cubes slowly. He looked up at Annie. "Maybe, but he didn't deserve whatever happened to him in that hotel room. Anyway, we better get up to New Haven and see how Dot's bearing up."

Annie seemed to be a little angry, probably at JD's defense of his friend. "We should go in separate cars, because I'll probably stay up there for a while. She was very upset."

JD put down his drink. "It's not going to get any easier. The detective wants to question her."

"That's all she needs right now." Annie paused a few beats. "There's something else, JD, closer to home. I know you don't want to hear this right now, but my credit card doesn't work. I went out to Whole Foods this morning, and it was hideously embarrassing. I had a cart in the line, and I couldn't pay the bill. Are we in some sort of financial trouble? I get worried with all the talk about Lehman Brothers."

JD had to backtrack for a few seconds. His mind was so focused on Rich's disappearance, he thought he hadn't heard right. "You card didn't work?"

"They tried twice."

JD shook his head. "We're in great shape financially. Lehman is going to be a windfall for us. It's probably some mistake at the bank. I'll stop at an ATM on our way and get some cash."

They walked out to the garage. Annie got into her white SUV, and JD into his Porsche. They drove up I-95 past Bridgeport toward New Haven, and JD stopped at a bank, while Annie continued on to Dot's house.

The Bridgers lived in a two-bedroom house right on the beach, with a spectacular view of Long Island Sound. The house was over a hundred years old, but Rich and Dot had redone it in a more contemporary style, with an open plan, lots of windows and skylights, and a deck that circled three sides of the house.

JD got out of his car, and as he walked up to the house, he saw the front door open. Annie was waiting and let him in. JD could see Dot sitting on the sofa in the living room. Her blue-green eyes were red from crying, and her short red hair resembled a bird's nest. She was clutching a white handkerchief, and she almost dropped it as she stood up to greet JD. He walked over and put his arms around her in a gentle hug. He felt her shoulder trembling, and then she seemed to get hold of herself.

"Would you like a cup of coffee, JD?"

JD looked toward the kitchen. "Have you had anything to eat, Dot? I can make you something."

She wiped her eyes and took a deep breath. "I'm not hungry. I haven't had anything since this morning. I was waiting for Richard."

"That's not very good." JD tried to keep his voice light. "You need to eat something."

JD could hear the waves crashing on the beach outside as he started rummaging through the fridge and cupboards to see what he could conjure up. As he looked at the array of food, he realized he was hungry himself. It was two o'clock, and he hadn't eaten since breakfast. He finally organized a salad and some leftover cold salmon, and was about to invite Dot in to eat when the doorbell rang.

"Are you expecting anyone?" JD heard Annie ask as he walked to the front door.

JD looked out on the street through the window, and saw a grey Ford Crown Victoria parked in front of the house. It had black steel wheels and small chrome hubcaps, a government car. He opened the door.

It was Detective Puccini.

CHAPTER 3

Puccini walked in and looked around the Bridger residence. He glanced at Long Island Sound through the window and at the mid-century Scandinavian furniture in the living room. "Nice place for an economics professor. And you're getting to be a habit, Dionne. What are you doing here?"

"I could ask you the same thing, detective. Isn't this a little out of your jurisdiction?" JD held his ground by the front door. Annie and Dot watched Puccini nervously from the living room couch.

Puccini looked at JD with a slight frown, "Let me worry about that, Doc. I made a courtesy call to New Haven, and they appreciate my help. This is a much tougher town than Greenwich. They don't spend much time looking for missing professors." He then turned to Dot and the handkerchief clutched in her hand. "Mrs. Bridger, I assume? I'm Detective Antonio Puccini from the Greenwich Police Department. I'm here to help. I want to find your husband. The first forty-eight hours is critical." He then smiled at Annie. "And I take it you are the famous Annie Rutherford. I'm looking forward to your show at the Jacobs."

He never goes anywhere without doing his homework, thought JD. He not only recognized Annie; he knew about her show.

"I'd like to speak to Mrs. Bridger privately," Puccini went on. "Is there a room we could use? It won't take long. I just have few questions."

JD was skeptical. "So you drove all the way out here with just a few questions? Where's your partner? Don't you detectives usually travel in pairs?"

Puccini shrugged. "We've got a lot to do, Doc, so we spread out. Let's just get this over with and I'll be out of your ponytail."

Dot looked down at her handkerchief, and said, "It's okay, JD. I want to help. We can do the interview in Rich's office."

She got up and led the way down the hallway, followed by the detective.

* * *

Puccini looked around the office. There was a large window overlooking the beach and the Sound, and he could hear the waves crashing on the shore. He saw three sailboats a couple of miles out, making good progress in the fresh wind. He glanced at the diplomas on the wall, and focused on the big one from MIT. The desk was strewn with books and papers, and the computer keyboard was a little island in the middle of this chaos. One wall was partly covered with bookshelves, and a brown Eames chair and footstool sat in the corner. In the other corner he noticed a Fender electric bass on a stand, an amplifier, and some headphones. He looked closely at the picture of a country music band on the wall. It was Bridger, Dionne, and a third man with brown skin. The caption read Charles River Playboys, 1995. That had not been in Bridger's file.

He turned to Mrs. Bridger. "Your husband's a musician, a man of many talents?"

Her eyes started to fill. "That's how we met. A club in Boston when they were playing. He loves western swing."

Puccini pulled a notepad and pen out of his jacket. "Why don't you go sit in that fancy chair, Mrs. Bridger, and I'll sit by the desk here. You need a glass of water or anything?"

Mrs. Bridger gave the first hint of a smile. "No, but thank you for asking. I should have offered you something. I'm not a very gracious hostess today. And please call me Dot."

Puccini smiled. "You've been under a lot of strain, Mrs. Bridger . . . I mean, Dot. Your husband's disappearance must have come as quite a shock. Tell me about him. Does he have any enemies? Has anyone tried to contact you since he disappeared?"

He knew he needed to give her the softball questions first.

She rubbed the arm of the chair and shook her head. "No, he's a professor of economics at Yale, and he does some economic consulting in Greenwich. And he looks after our investments. It's a mundane life. No enemies that I know of, certainly none that would do *this* to him."

"He's got a second-degree black belt in karate. Was that for personal protection? Was he afraid of anyone specific?"

"No, Richard just enjoys it. He got the black belt long before we met, and he practices regularly, just for relaxation. He said karate gets him away from all the brain strain of his day job. Like the music."

And maybe provided protection against irate husbands – or against someone whose fraud he'd uncovered, thought Puccini. He looked at her closely. "You say he had no enemies. What about John Maynard Yates?"

Dot sat back in surprise. The surprise looked genuine, as if she hadn't thought about him for some time. "That was almost five years ago. Richard was Yates's thesis advisor at Yale, and he caught Yates plagiarizing. Yates was forced to leave Yale. But he returned to Greenwich, and an old family friend got him started in the investment business. He's done very well. But what does this have to do with Richard? That was a long time ago."

Puccini made more notes and then looked up again. This old family friend was a new angle that Dionne hadn't mentioned. "If you don't mind, Dot, I'll ask the questions for now. Who was this family friend?"

"Winthrop Harriman. I'm sure you've heard of him. But that reminds me . . . Richard mentioned just last week that he thought Harriman and Yates might be running some sort of financial fraud."

Puccini felt the blood rush to his head and a shot of adrenaline jolt his arms. *Harriman.* His kids' college fund was with Harriman. But there was no way it could be a fraud. Lots of charities and celebrities in Harriman's fund. But he wrote the name down beside Yates's, and took a deep breath. Dot was staring at him, her eyes narrowing, apparently aware that the name had somehow bothered him. He tried to regain his composure. He needed to control the interview.

"I've heard of Winthrop Harriman. His fund is over thirty billion dollars, and he's involved in a number of charity boards and museums.

He's even helped start a new stock exchange. And your husband thinks that Harriman is corrupt? That's hard to believe."

"I don't know the details. Richard doesn't talk much about his work. I do know that he had spoken to the government about investigating Yates. Maybe Harriman, too. Harriman helped Yates get started, so there could be a connection."

Puccini turned to look at Bridger's desk and his computer. "Mrs. Bridger, is this where Professor Bridger does most of his work, like maybe his investigation of Yates's fund?" Puccini paused. "And Harriman?"

"I'm not sure," Dot said. "He also has a computer in his office at Yale. That's probably where most of his work files are. He just looks after our personal investments here. And he also uses a laptop."

"There's probably some important information on this computer, Dot. Would you mind if I take it down to the station? It could help us find your husband."

Dot hesitated. "I'm not sure. Richard would hate having his privacy invaded that way. And he uses his laptop most of the time anyway."

Puccini shrugged. "That's okay. Maybe you can think about it and let me know." But he was surprised and puzzled by her response. Was there something incriminating on this computer?

He realized he'd have to get a search warrant. And he wanted all three computers. Bridger's disappearance was business, but Harriman's fund was personal. If Harriman was a fraud, Puccini had to get his money out. Bridger's computers might hold the key.

Then his thoughts drifted to Joshua Dionne – principal in a hedge fund, Ph. D. from MIT. He had the skills. But he was also a goddam suspect at this point. Puccini decided to move on with his questioning.

"Mrs. Bridger, do you think this man Yates might have something to do with your husband's disappearance? If Yates's running a fraud and your husband was investigating him, that could provide a motive."

Dot bit her lip in thought. "I don't know Yates personally, so I can't say. I suppose it's possible."

Puccini paused and took a deep breath. It was time for the money question, and he wasn't looking forward to it. "Mrs. Yates, there's one more thing I want to deal with, and I'm afraid it's not a very pleasant topic, but I have to ask you something . . . There were signs that a woman had been in Professor Bridger's room at some point. Were you aware that he was having an affair?"

Dot started to cry quietly and clutched her handkerchief again. "He said he would stop. He promised me. We had a big argument last week."

An argument – now we're getting somewhere, thought Puccini. He waited while Dot wiped her eyes. "How's your relationship? Do you get along? Do you fight sometimes?" He hesitated for effect, and looked at her intently. "Did he ever beat you?"

Dot glared back at him. "No. Rich is difficult, but he's never been violent with me." She paused and looked down. "We've had our problems . . . he wanted children, and well, that hasn't gone the way we hoped it would. We don't always agree on everything, but we love each other."

"No children then?"

Dorothy Bridger shook her head. Puccini knew he'd feel like crap when he asked his next question, but he had no choice. He had to get a clear picture of their relationship. This was one of the times that he hated his job.

"Do you and your husband sleep together?"

Dot leaned back and looked out the window. "Most of the time. But he often works late, and he's away a lot at conferences."

Puccini folded his hands and leaned toward her. "Mrs. Bridger, this is very awkward, but it's something I have to ask. Where were you last night and this morning?"

She turned back quickly from the window and faced Puccini. "I was here, working on a short story. I do a lot of writing."

Puccini leaned back and smiled. "You have quite a reputation. The *Kenyon Review* and *Antioch Review.*"

Dot sat up straight in surprise. "You've actually read some of my short stories?"

"I like good writing. Those are excellent stories, especially the one about a very difficult marriage." He paused. "Is there anyone that can verify that you were here writing?"

"No, of course not. There was no one else here. I want solitude when I'm writing. Why, am I a suspect?"

Puccini shrugged in his characteristic way, with his shoulders hunched and his open hands pointing toward the sky. "These are all standard questions, Dot, and I have to ask them, or I wouldn't be doing my job." He leaned forward. "Can you think of anyone else who might have wanted to harm your husband? Any other enemies? Anyone at Yale? Maybe back in Greenwich?"

Dot crossed her arms. "If there was a woman at the hotel, she probably had something to do with it. Maybe she was the target, and he was in the wrong place at the wrong time. Or maybe she was working with whoever took him."

Puccini nodded, wanting to keep her talking and willing to throw in a little flattery. "*La femme fatale.* That's an interesting angle. Any idea who this woman might have been?"

"In the past, it's often been married women. But Rich said he quit that. I already told you."

"Did any husbands ever find out about it?"

"I don't think so, but the affairs were mostly at Yale, so I don't know. I write and I teach high school English. I don't spend much time at Yale. . . Detective, I think we're going around in circles."

Puccini stopped to think. They lived almost separate lives, but she seemed to love him. On the other hand, she had no alibi, and she had a motive.

He got up and closed his notebook. "You've been very helpful, Mrs. Bridger. I'm going to follow up on some of your suggestions, and then I'd like to talk to you again. Would you mind coming down to the Public Safety Complex in Greenwich tomorrow?"

Dot looked down and he thought she might start crying again, but she caught herself. "I suppose so, but I've told you everything I know."

"We want to catch these people and save your husband. We have to move quickly, and sometimes it's the little things that point the way."

"Detective, do you think you'll find him?" Her voice quavered.

"I hope so," Puccini told her. "We're doing everything we can."

Dot nodded and got to her feet. Puccini followed her back to the living room.

He thanked her, and then turned to JD. "I'll see you at the station tomorrow, Dr. Dionne."

He walked out to his car, and on the drive back to Greenwich, he started obsessing about Harriman. He'd put all his eggs in the Harriman basket, and maybe the basket was cracked. He had to find out the truth, and quickly.

Then he forced himself to focus again on the case and Mrs. Bridger. *If she did it, she had help*, he concluded, *and access to a boat.* It was hard to imagine this prim high school English teacher masterminding a plot like that. But he'd seen stranger things.

* * *

Dot slumped down in her chair in the living room across from Annie and JD. "I think I need a drink. That detective thinks I had something to do with Richard's disappearance. And he wanted to take Richard's computer – without a warrant. He must think I just tumbled off a hay-wagon."

JD felt a jolt somewhere in his neck. This was something new in Dot - real anger, and maybe some deviousness. Why wouldn't she give Puccini the computer? Annie looked at JD with a frown, but Dot didn't seem to notice JD's reaction. Dot got up and walked to the liquor cabinet. "I have some Sazerac. Would anyone like some?" She smiled at JD and put two ice cubes in a glass, adding two shots of the rye before handing it to him. Then she poured a glass of port for Annie, and finally prepared a Manhattan for herself. As she plopped the maraschino cherry in the glass, she proposed a toast. "Here's to Detective Puccini, who leaves no rock unturned. He asked me where I was yesterday and this morning. I was by myself, right here, writing. Which means I don't have an alibi, right? Maybe I should get a lawyer." She took a big sip of the Manhattan.

JD nodded. "Maybe you do need a lawyer."

Annie looked at JD with a frown. "I think we should take more of an initiative ourselves here, JD, maybe look into Yates, see if Richard was right about the fraud. You have the skills to do that, and I'm not sure the police do. The lawyers certainly don't."

JD ran his hand through his ponytail. "Yeah, the police might miss some things. And Yates is definitely the best lead we have. Rich would not have mentioned him unless he was a hundred percent certain. It's probably all on his computer." He turned toward Dot. "Do you have the password, Dot?"

Dot's face turned a little pale. "No, Richard never shared those sorts of things with me. And I'm not really computer literate, except for using Word on my laptop."

JD looked carefully at her reaction to the question, and then shook his head. She wasn't going to give him the password. Something was going on. "Then it would take me too long to get into his computer. It's probably encrypted, with a firewall, and I'd need to come back with a random word generator and a lot of other software. I'm sure Rich has very secure passwords. It would be quicker if I investigate Yates on my own. I have some ideas about how Rich might have discovered this fraud, and I can probably get to the bottom of this in half the time it would take the police."

Annie said, "I'll stay here tonight and help Dot. I'll be home in the morning. And please remember to look into my credit card." She looked at Dot with a wan smile. "The bank fouled up, and my card doesn't work."

"Thanks for reminding me." JD reached into his pocket and handed Annie an envelope. "This should get you through the day and get you home. I'll get it fixed as soon as possible."

JD went over to Dot and gave her a hug. "It'll be okay. We should get some news soon if he's showed up at a hospital." But he had his doubts.

Dot gave a weak smile. "I hope so. Thanks for your support."

JD gave Annie a quick kiss and walked out to his car. As he started the engine, he realized that even after all these years, maybe he'd never really known his friend's wife.

* * *

Back at home, JD went directly to his office. He did most of his work there, and he'd laid it out efficiently with all the latest equipment. On one side of the room stood a small white birch conference table, square in shape, flanked by four black leather high-back chairs. In the far corner of the room was his L-shaped desk, almost ten feet wide. Sitting at one end of the L, he could look out the wide window toward the trees behind the house – his contemplative view. At the other side of the table, he had his two computer monitors and a keyboard, with a large bookshelf up above. There was a white leather sofa against the third wall, and the far wall was mostly covered by an erasable white board for jotting down numbers and ideas.

He turned on the new program he'd developed to monitor his family's accounts and investments, and went directly to the joint checking account. He saw that there had been a small withdrawal, about $35, from a very strange IP address. He followed the trail, tracing it to a site in Stockholm. The trail then led to Sydney, Toronto, and finally Greenwich. Someone right in town had hacked into their account using a very circuitous route. It was a small withdrawal, but he knew it might be a probe to confirm the connection before cleaning out the whole account. He was relieved that the bank had shut down the account before the hackers could take that final step.

He used another special program to hack the culprit's email, and then sent the following message:

"Dear sir or madam, what you are doing constitutes financial fraud, punishable by lengthy incarceration. The authorities have been notified."

The answer came back within a minute:

"Lighten up, Dad. It was just a practice run with some of my friends. I tried to put the money back in your account, but it was frozen. Love, Junior."

JD smiled despite himself. He was proud of his own hacking skills, but Junior, no doubt with some help, was catching up. He emailed back:

I should charge you interest. Be careful, though, or you could end up in jail. What you did is illegal. Seriously! Love, Dad.

The answer came back:

Dad, everyone's doing it. I'm more likely to get a job offer from the bank than go to jail.

JD realized he needed a serious discussion with Junior. Telling her about Rich's abduction would now have to wait. He sent back one more email: *Let's talk.*

Moments later, the door to JD's office opened and his daughter bounced in. Junior was seventeen, and shorter than her mother, about the same height as JD. But she had Annie's blond hair, blue eyes, and long legs. She also had the same first name as her mother — Annie — which was why the family called her Junior. This morning she was dressed in jeans, an Obama 2008 t-shirt, and black Converse All Stars, no socks. A white iPod was sticking out of her back pocket, with the ear buds hanging off the side.

She smiled brightly and said, "What's up? And where's Mom?"

"Mom's up in New Haven visiting Dot. And what's up, sweetheart, is that I hope you have a good lawyer."

Junior thrust her head forward and squinted hard. "What *are* you talking about?"

JD looked down at the floor and ran his hand back over his long black hair. "It's about the hacking. Your hack into our bank account."

"No worries, Dad. I'm part of a hacker group now. We're fighting for open web access, and making the Library of Congress Library free for everyone. It belongs to the people, and we shouldn't have to pay to download something we own."

"Hacking banks is different. That's a felony. I know about hacking, but never banks."

Junior looked at JD quizzically. "You're telling me you're a hacker too?"

JD shrugged. "Look, Junior, banks get upset, and they have political connections. Plus lawyers and top IT guys."

Junior leaned back and crossed her arms. "They do have some IT people, but they're second rate. If the bank catches me, they'll offer me a job."

"You're referring to that fifteen-year-old who wanted a Honda and a *Playboy* subscription as a signing bonus to work for the software company he hacked. It never happened. The writer made it up."

Junior's eyes grew very cold, and she said in a carefully controlled tone, "Chris Porter, seventeen, hired by Facebook. Michael Molroney, nineteen, hired by ezSoft. Peter Hillier, twenty-two, hired by Apple. Adrian Lerner, twenty, hired by the FBI. I could give you a dozen more. Maybe they got warnings or suspended sentences, but they all got hired. It's a career path, Dad."

JD looked at her and sighed deeply. "Junior, that was in the past. The government is cracking down. There's a hacker at MIT who's facing thirty-five years in prison."

Junior stared back defiantly. "Those are just scare stories. I've read them all. There's nothing to worry about. Nothing."

"It's not just about you. They come after the parents too. The whole family could be liable for damages."

Junior's voice increased a few decibels. "So that's it. You're worried about your little nest egg. I can't wait to get out of this place and get to college." A single tear trickled down her cheek, and she hurried from the office, head down, slamming the door as she left.

JD's head was starting to hurt. He'd had a rough day, and it wasn't over. Junior needed some time to cool down, and then they'd continue the conversation. Annie usually acted as buffer and peace-maker in these situations, but he was on his own here. And he hadn't even told Junior about Rich's disappearance yet. But first things first - he had to call the bank and clear up Annie's credit card problem. It took many frustrating minutes on hold, but after a long discussion, it was done. Both he and the bank refrained from any mention of the hacking.

JD then went downstairs and got his bottle of Sazerac, plus an ice bucket, and then strolled back to his office. He poured himself a large drink and pulled out a photo album from the MIT days. There was a picture from 1994 when the three couples were out celebrating Fareed's thirtieth birthday, all looking very young and happy. As he turned more pages, he stopped abruptly. He stared at a picture of John Maynard Yates and his beautiful blond wife at a Yale party for graduate students, with Rich and Dot standing beside them smiling - the mentor and the cheating protégé.

He turned to a picture of the Charles River Playboys on stage at the club where Dot had met Rich. Maybe Dot had taken the picture. JD went to the stereo and put on one of the band's CDs. The first cut was the Playboys' rendition of Hank William's "Howlin' At The Moon" - with Raji's soulful baying in the background. Raji, Fareed's beautiful black Lab, was even listed on the CD, and that made JD smile.

JD could finally sense the tension draining as he listened to the music. The door opened quietly, and Junior walked in. Her expression indicated that she was no longer angry, and JD reached over and turned down the music.

Junior sat down on the white leather sofa, and said, "I'm sorry I got so upset. We won't do it again. Banks are off limits. But where's Mom? What's going on?"

JD was relieved the storm had passed. He took a deep breath. "We've got a big problem, Junior. Our friend Professor Bridger has disappeared, and Mom is up in New Haven helping Dot."

Junior leaned forward abruptly, her eyes open wide. "Disappeared? What do you mean? People don't just disappear."

"Rich was supposed to be home in New Haven this morning from a conference here in Greenwich, and he didn't show up. Dot asked me to go check at the hotel, but he wasn't there. Someone had taken him away. There were signs of a struggle in the room. The police are investigating."

Junior's frown deepened. "Were there any clues?"

JD pictured the severed finger in his mind, but decided not to mention that. "The forensics people were there. They'll let us know if they find anything."

"I'm so, so sorry. I hope he's okay. Have you told B?"

JD knew he had forgotten something. "No, but he's busy at school."

"I'll send him an email. He's going to want to know."

"I'll give him a call later. Let's go have some dinner."

* * *

After dinner, JD went back to his office and sat down to think about his next steps. His thoughts were interrupted by the fiddle break from "San Antonio Rose," and he picked up his cell phone. It was Fareed.

"JD, have you received any further word about the whereabouts of our friend Richard?"

"Nothing. Annie and I went up to see Dot in New Haven, and the detective came up to question her, but no further news."

"Did you retain the services of a barrister, as I suggested?"

JD smiled to himself. Fareed was always worried about him. "No, I don't need one. I can take care of myself. All I have to do is tell the truth. And besides, I'm going to start doing some financial forensics on John Maynard Yates. That qualification in forensic accounting will be useful once again. I think I can help the police in their investigation."

"I think that is an excellent idea. However, JD, you must be careful. To use your sports vernacular, Mr. Yates seems to play hard ball, if our suspicion about him is correct."

"The difference is that I *know* he plays hard ball, and Rich didn't. I can keep my head up. Annie and I still have those guns we bought in Boston. Anyway, I have no choice here. I *have* to investigate Yates. The police know fingerprints and firearms, but they don't know finance and forensic accounting."

JD could hear Fareed's deep sigh on the phone. "Joshua, sometimes it seems to me that you missed your calling. I think that you would like to become a detective."

JD paused. "Maybe, if that's the only way to save Rich."

There was silence on the phone. Then Fareed said, "I am very concerned about you, JD. Could we have lunch tomorrow to discuss this further?"

"That would be a pleasure. How about d'Allessandro's at noon?"

They agreed to meet the next day, and disconnected. JD then called Annie to see how Dot was holding up.

"She's doing better. The Manhattans seem to help," Annie reported. "But you sound funny. Have you been drinking?"

"I had a little rye. I've been reminiscing, looking at the old pictures and listening to our music. Rich has his rough edges, but I miss him."

"Well, don't give up hope yet. He may still turn up."

"Maybe. But there's some news on the home front. I found the problem with your credit card. Junior's crew hacked your account, and the bank shut it down. It's fixed now, and I had a heart-to-heart with the perpetrator."

There was silence on the phone for a few seconds. "Junior? Did you at least ground her for a month? Sometimes that girl . . ." Annie gave a big sigh. "But Dot's all I can handle right now. We'll talk when I get home."

"Get some sleep. I love you."

"I love you. See you tomorrow."

JD went to bed. He had a fitful sleep, with nightmares involving blood and severed fingers.

CHAPTER 4

Tuesday, September 9, 2008

JD woke up a little groggy. His head was throbbing and he could hardly open his eyes. Maybe he'd had more rye than he remembered. He had a quick shower and felt a little better, and as he stumbled downstairs he could smell fresh coffee brewing. Junior was already in the kitchen, and as usual, CNBC's *Squawk Box* was on full blast. He poured himself a big cup and sat down to watch the show with her. The news was not good. The commentators were discussing Lehman Brothers, and there were rumors that Nomura was not pleased with what they had seen in their due diligence on Lehman's books. After the previous day's euphoria about the Fannie and Freddie rescue, market futures were down.

Junior continued to stare at the screen while sipping her coffee, transfixed, and finally turned to JD. "Looks like that crash you've been predicting is here. Or almost here." Her eyes widened. "And whoa . . . you look awful, Dad. Did you get any sleep?"

"Not much, a few nightmares. And maybe a bit too much to drink last night. I was reminiscing about Rich." Junior's chair scraped on the floor as she turned around completely to face JD, and he winced in pain from the sound. He said, "Let this be a lesson to you. Don't start drinking. I'll cook us some breakfast. Maybe that will make me feel better."

JD took some eggs, fresh vegetables and cheese from the fridge, and started cooking two omelets on the gas cooktop, along with some Canadian back bacon. When the first side was done, he expertly flipped the omelets and added some mozzarella before folding them over on white plates alongside the sizzling bacon. He added some oregano and pepper, and they sat down to eat, continuing to watch *Squawk Box*. There was a new development. The London Stock Exchange had crashed due to some software problem, and trading in Barclays bank and GlaxoSmithKline had been suspended for six hours.

Junior finished her breakfast and said, “I have to get to school, Dad. What are you up to today?”

“I have to make some trades, and then respond to some of my clients. They’re getting nervous. Some days they’re euphoric, some days they just want to take their money and run. And then I have to meet Detective Puccini down at the police station. He wants to do an official interview and take my statement about Rich’s disappearance.”

Junior looked worried. “I thought you already talked to them. And why down at the police station? That sounds creepy.”

“This particular detective is very thorough. But I think the interview is just a formality. After that, I’m having lunch with Fareed downtown.” JD was trying to sound more optimistic than he really felt.

“Dad, are you a suspect? Is that why the detective wants to talk to you again?”

“Everyone’s a suspect until they’re crossed off the list. He just wants to cross me off. That’s part of his job.”

“I hope you’re right,” she said, and went upstairs to get ready for school. JD went to his office to check his emails, and answered five new ones from clients. There was an email from B, and he was about to answer it when the land line rang. It was Annie.

“How are you feeling this morning, dear?”

“A little rough, but I had a pleasant breakfast with Junior. Have you heard from B? I was just about to answer his email.”

“He called me last night, worried about you. He wanted to hear what was going on before he spoke to you.”

“I’ll give him a call. Are you coming back to Greenwich this morning with Dot? She’s supposed to go to the police station. Maybe we can go together.”

"She's not up yet, too many Manhattans last night. She's probably feeling worse than you. We'll come down later."

"Okay, I'm off to see Mr. Puccini. Love you."

JD hung up and called B. There was no answer, so he sent him an email, assuring him that he was fine. Then he walked back to the garage, and fired up the Porsche.

He turned onto Perryridge Road, passing Greenwich Hospital on the right. The doctors' parking lot was about half full, and he could see a few bleary-eyed residents and interns leaving after the night shift. He turned down Lafayette Place and as he reached Greenwich Avenue, there was less traffic and he briefly pushed his foot down as the Porsche squirted through the intersection. He braked hard when he saw the traffic cop further down the block, waving cars through the next intersection just south of the police station. He almost missed the turn to Bruce Place, but he made a sharp left and saw the new Public Safety Complex. It was hard to miss. He remembered reading about it, how it had cost $60 million, and it showed.

The entryway to the new building was a two- story glass-and-steel structure. The building itself was three stories high, with a textured concrete and brick facing, and large rectangular windows framed in an angular geometric pattern. He parked the car in one of the public spaces behind the building, and walked back to the front entrance, passing through the high glass entrance doors into an atrium.

On the right side of the atrium was a police motorcycle on display – a chrome Harley Davidson trimmed in black and blue – with signs for a police charity. On the left was a closed door with a small wired window, and beside it was the desk officer's cubicle, enclosed in glass – or more likely bullet-proof Lexan.

JD approached the cubicle, and the officer looked up from his computer and pointed at the small stainless steel cylinder installed in the glass. The officer's mouth moved and a voice in the cylinder said, "How can I help you? Please speak into the microphone."

JD leaned toward the microphone. "I'm here to see Detective Puccini. He's expecting me. My name is Joshua Dionne."

The officer picked up a phone and said something, then hung up and went back to working on his computer. There was no place to sit in the atrium, so JD continued standing at the cubicle. A few minutes later, the door on the left opened and a middle-aged man walked out. JD recognized him from the Zodiac Inn as Brown, the detective who had accompanied Puccini to the crime scene. He was still dressed in his ragged blue jeans and black GPD windbreaker.

The detective kept the door open and gestured to JD to proceed. "Nice to see you again. Come on upstairs, Detective Puccini is on the phone."

The door closed behind them and JD could see a wide staircase with a skylight above. "Nice place you have here," JD said.

Brown paused on the landing and looked back at him. "The PSC just opened. You should have seen the hell-hole we were in before. Freezing in the winter and sweating in the summer. Twenty years in that place was enough."

They continued up the stairs to the second floor and reached a long hallway with doors on either side. Brown pulled a card off his belt and opened one of the doors. They stepped into an open area filled with partitions and work stations. Each work station had two computer monitors, an L-shaped desk, and bookshelves. The room was carpeted, and very quiet despite half a dozen individuals working at their desks. JD saw Detective Puccini. The detective made one final punch on his keyboard and got up to meet them.

"Good morning, Dr. Dionne. Thank you for coming down so early. Let's go to the Case Cracker room." He thanked Brown, and then led JD to another door along the back wall and opened it. JD saw a small room. Inside was a square table with a chair on either side. On the wall behind each chair, a small camera lens was pointed at the chair on the opposite side of the table.

Puccini pulled out the chair on the left and asked JD to sit down, and then sat in the other chair, placing his open notepad and a large file on the table, with his cell phone and laptop beside it.

He leaned back and smiled. "I guess you've never been here before. It's all new. All the latest technology. It's called Case Cracker. Everything is recorded in high definition. Garry Brown is monitoring from another room. We don't use one-way mirrors anymore. It's all gone digital."

JD looked up at the camera lens in the wall behind Puccini. "Are you going to read me my rights now? I feel like an animal at the zoo."

Puccini shrugged. "Everyone has a lawyer now, and we have to be careful. What all this gadgetry does is keep it simple. Everything is recorded. Don't worry about it, it's for your own protection. And you're not under arrest, so there's no need for Miranda. You're here voluntarily, helping us catch the criminals who abducted your friend Richard Bridger. Let's start by having you tell us a little bit about yourself."

It was clear to JD that Puccini was speaking to the camera, not to him, and the whole performance was starting to irritate him. "You already know all about me. Why should I repeat it now?"

"We just want it on the record as background. Where were you born?"

"I was born on Christian Island, which is a First Nations reserve on Lake Huron in Canada. My mother is Ojibway and my father is Quebecois, but he left when I was very young. But what's this have to do with Richard Bridger's disappearance?"

"You went to Princeton on a scholarship and were a varsity swimmer, then a Rhodes Scholar. That's a long, long way from Christian Island. Please connect the dots. How did you get from there to here? I'm curious."

For a long moment, JD stared at Puccini in disbelief. This seemed like a total waste of time. Then with a sigh of resignation, he said, "All right, you asked for it, so here goes. I used to swim and canoe from Christian Island to the mainland, and I worked at a marina. This banker from Toronto went out in a major storm after I warned him, and I had to rescue him after his boat sank. He got me admitted to the University of Toronto Schools. That led to Princeton, and the varsity swimming just came naturally. That's all there is to it. Can we talk about Rich now?"

"What about the Rhodes Scholarship?"

"The Rhodes committee likes athletes. I was a swimmer. It's not a big deal." JD knew he'd been lucky, and was reluctant to talk about his achievements.

"And then you came back to America. Why didn't you go back to Canada after MIT?"

"I guess the main reasons were Fareed Ghanem and Richard Bridger. We became friends. And after Annie and I spent four years in Boston, we realized we really liked America."

"It's people like you that make America great, Dr. Dionne."

JD couldn't tell if Puccini was being sarcastic or trying to flatter him. He was often still confused by Americans' overwhelming camaraderie.

Puccini glanced at the file again. "I see that in addition to your doctorate in mathematical finance from MIT, you have a certification in forensic accounting. That's an unusual combination. How did that come about?"

"I had a partner in my first investment fund who turned out to be an embezzler. He took off for Hong Kong when I figured it out, and I had to do a lot of forensic research to get him extradited and jailed. Then I vowed that I would never allow that to happen again. I learned how to recognize fraudulent balance sheets and financial statements." JD decided not to mention his finely-honed hacking skills.

Puccini smiled slightly. "So you have a nose for financial fraud."

"I'm trained to find it, but what's your point, detective? Where's this heading? You haven't even mentioned Richard Bridger."

"I'm coming to that, Dr. Dionne, and you were right. It appears that the motive for Professor Bridger's disappearance may be connected to his discovery of a financial fraud perpetrated by the person you mentioned yesterday, John Maynard Yates. What do you know about Yates and his relationship with Professor Bridger?"

"I've already told you. Richard was Yates's advisor on Yates's doctoral thesis, and Rich discovered some flagrant plagiarism. Yates was suspended from graduate school. Since then, he's done very well running an investment fund here in Greenwich. A couple of days ago . . . just before he went to that conference at the Zodiac . . . Rich told us that he thought Yates's investment fund was fraudulent."

"What made Professor Bridger look into Yates's fund? That incident at Yale was over five years ago."

"I don't know, he never told us. Maybe it was professional jealousy, trying to figure out how Yates was getting those outsized returns. If we find him, we can ask him."

Puccini ignored the sarcasm. "What evidence did Professor Bridger have about this alleged fraud?"

"I don't know. He mentioned it only once, and he didn't provide any detail."

Then Puccini asked a question totally out of left field. "What about Winthrop Harriman?"

JD sat back in surprise. "What about him? He helped Yates set up his fund after Yates got kicked out of Yale. Harriman is old guard northeast establishment, and runs one of the biggest funds around. He's on half a dozen charity boards, on the board of the stock exchange, active at the Securities Exchange Commission, and hangs around with Hollywood stars. What's your point?"

"I heard there's a connection between Yates and Harriman. And there could be a connection to Bridger's disappearance."

JD just stared at him. "You think Harriman's connected to that bloody scene in the hotel? That's ridiculous. Harriman is running over thirty billion in assets. Yates is small time, more in my league."

"So you don't see any connection between Yates and Harriman?"

"No, nothing connected to Rich's disappearance. That doesn't make any sense."

"Okay, thank you, that will be all, Dr. Dionne."

"That's it? That's what you dragged me down here for?"

Puccini paused. "Oh, I almost forgot. There *is* one more thing I wanted you to look at."

JD smiled. "Maybe what you forgot is your unlit cigar and beat-up raincoat. This 'just one more thing' routine is straight out of *Columbo*. You're trying to throw me off balance, right?"

Puccini smiled. "I love that show. I have all the episodes at home on DVD."

Puccini leaned forward and opened his laptop on the table. He manipulated the touchpad and then moved the screen over to the side so that JD could see it. "Here's what I'm talking about, JD. We checked the security cameras, and we think we have an image of the woman who was in Bridger's room."

JD noticed that Puccini was now addressing him by his nickname, not his formal title. Probably trying to get JD to let down his guard. Or did he actually need JD's help in some way?

The video showed a woman walking quickly past the front desk at the hotel. She had dark hair, complemented by stylish white sunglasses, and she was fashionably dressed in a black skirt and a white top. The video was grainy and did not show much detail.

"Anyone you know?"

JD stared at the video closely. "Run it again. She does look familiar."

Puccini ran the clip again. JD said, "Stop it right there." He pulled the laptop toward him and focused on the image. "I know her from somewhere, maybe something to do with MIT, but I can't place her. Could I have a copy of this?"

"I'll email it to you. Let me know if you come up with something."

JD was lost in thought, and then finally looked up. "Run it again, please." He watched the video intently for a third time. "It's the walk and something about her face," he mused. "I'll show it to Annie. Maybe she'll know."

"Your wife is good at recognizing people?" Puccini asked.

"She's an artist, very visual. She notices things about people . . . things that go right past me."

"Well, then show it to her," Puccini said. He got to his feet. "Let me take you downstairs."

Puccini opened the door, and JD followed him down to the lobby. As they entered the atrium, Puccini turned to JD and said, "There's something else I wanted to discuss with you, and it's kind of personal. Could I buy you a cup of coffee? There's a Starbucks just down the street."

JD was taken aback. First the detective had summarized JD's life story, and now he wanted to be JD's buddy. What the hell was going on?

"I really should be getting back home," JD said, wanting to end this weird exchange. "The markets are moving, and I have to make some trades."

Puccini frowned. "What's your hurry, pal? And the markets – that's what I want to talk to you about. C'mon, I'll buy you a cappuccino and maybe a biscotti. It's just down the street. You like cappuccinos?"

JD hesitated. "I have to put some money in the meter."

"Ahh, don't worry about it. Just give me the ticket if you get one, I'll take care of it. Let's go."

JD's eyes narrowed. "As far as I can tell, I'm still a suspect. And now you want to buy me a cup of coffee . . . off the record. What's going on here?"

Puccini gave his special shrug, maybe a little exaggerated this time. "Look, JD, don't take it personally. It's like this. Your friend Bridger's disappearance is still an open case. So I can't officially rule out any suspects just yet. The Captain would be very unhappy. He's got twelve detectives working on it, and he doesn't want anyone jumping to conclusions. But just between you and me, you're not at the top of my list."

JD finally gave in, deciding it wasn't worth fighting. They walked a block down to the Starbucks at the corner of Greenwich and Havemeyer, and Puccini ordered a cappuccino and biscotti for JD and a triple espresso for himself. "Let's sit down in the corner over there. It's a lot quieter."

They sat down, and JD said, "Okay, here we are. First you imply that I'm a suspect in my friend's kidnapping and possible murder, and now you want to buy me a cappuccino. What the hell is this all about, Puccini? Are you still recording me? Or are you playing 'good cop' now?"

Puccini did his little shrug and took a sip of his espresso. The shrug was becoming annoying. "No recording. You can pat me down. This is personal. I'm worried about something, and I think maybe you can help me. It's about my investments. My wife was killed in a car accident, a fucking drunk driver, three years ago. That's why I left Manhattan and came here, trying to raise two kids in a friendlier neighborhood. We live up in Milford. I got a nice settlement from the accident, and I invested it with Harriman. I'm worried about that investment after I heard some rumors, JD."

Puccini took another sip of his espresso and waited for a response. JD rubbed his forehead in confusion. "This is nuts. You're investigating

Rich's disappearance and think I'm a suspect, and now you want my investment advice."

"Hey, I'm a cop, and I'm trying to do my job, but I also have a life. I don't know many people with a Ph. D. in mathematical economics and a qualification in forensic accounting. And hey, you know what? You happen to be the only one, sport. So you want to help me or not? There are probably ways I can make your life easier too, if you think about it."

JD's voice became quiet. "Well, I'm very sorry about your wife. That's tragic. How old are your kids?"

"Isabella's four and Angelo's six. You have kids?"

JD thought about B and Junior, and what it would have been like to raise them without Annie. "Yes, I do. They're a little older."

He realized that Puccini was mostly making conversation – he probably knew all the details of JD's family already. But the detective's approach was working. JD was developing some sympathy for the Puccini's concerns. And he *had* heard some rumors about Harriman, crazy as it seemed.

Puccini was looking at him expectantly, and JD finally asked, "Well okay, so how can I help?"

Puccini visibly relaxed. "I have a friend at the TSA who does favors for me sometimes. I can get access to almost everything except financial data. Wall Street has a wall around it. That's where you come in. You help me, I help you, that's how it works."

JD thought about it for a long moment. Wall Street certainly had a wall around it, but he'd gotten through it in the past, and could probably do it again. And it might help find Rich, if Yates was involved.

"What specifically do you want me to do?"

"I want you to check out Harriman for me. And I mean, really check him out. There's been rumors about him, and the Securities Exchange Commission has supposedly dug into it, but they got nothing. I have a gut feeling about this, and you're a smart guy. And maybe there's a connection to Yates and your friend Bridger, so in a way you could be helping find him. What do you say?"

JD stirred his cappuccino with the biscotti, and took a bite. He was still thinking. He was about to start investigating Yates anyway, but if Harriman was connected somehow, it could be a natural fit.

"Okay, I'll start looking into Harriman. But no guarantees. And if I have to do something a little over the edge, are you with me? I'm sure Harriman has some powerful friends."

Puccini smiled. "No guarantees from my end, but I'll do my best. If you cut some corners, don't tell me about it, and we're okay." He raised his cup in a mock salute. "Here's to forensic accounting." He wrote down his cell phone number and his private email and handed it to JD. "Keep me posted."

JD said, "There's one more thing. I'll need all your quarterly reports and transaction records from Harriman's fund."

"Transaction records? I don't think I ever got any. But I'll check."

"Harriman buys and sells securities to make his returns. He has to report any major transactions."

"I'll send you what I have, but it's not much. And thanks . . . I really appreciate this."

"I may not find anything."

"Just give it your best shot, sport. That's all I ask. Maybe Harriman's clean. End of story."

They walked back up Greenwich Avenue to the PSC and shook hands. Puccini went back upstairs and JD walked to the parking lot behind the building. It was too early for lunch with Ghanem, so he started the Porsche and headed back home.

CHAPTER 5

The house was quiet, and JD went back to his office to check the markets. It was almost noon, and he was starting to feel hungry.

The Dow had dropped 137 points, and Lehman was down 28 percent. The nervousness was palpable. The indices were bouncing around, but with a very definite downtrend. The bond-rating agencies that had helped cause the crisis were now looking at a possible downgrade of Lehman's debt.

They're finally closing the barn door, thought JD, *but the damn horse is gone.* Where the hell were they when they had a chance to stop the madness? Getting fat off the fees from over-rating those crap real estate bonds.

JD reviewed a few nervous emails from his investors, and he assured them that his strategy was still on track. Most of them were locked in for another year, so he didn't waste much time on it.

He heard the door open downstairs and saw Annie's SUV parked beside his Porsche on the driveway. He sent one final email and went downstairs. Annie and Dot were sitting in the kitchen. JD still had a strange feeling about Dot, that she was keeping something from them.

Annie smiled. "I missed you last night, JD. How was Detective Puccini this morning?"

"There were a few surprises. He's a lot smarter than he looks. He likes to be underestimated." JD turned to Dot. "And how are you doing, Dot? Are you feeling a little better?"

Dot's eyes were still red, and she slouched as she spoke. "I'm okay, I guess. I didn't get much sleep, and I'm not looking forward to sitting down with that creepy detective again, especially at the police station. I already told him everything I know."

"You look like you could do with some coffee. Cappuccino?"

Dot nodded. As JD turned on the cappuccino machine, he noticed Annie tapping her fingers on the counter. She'd probably been listening to Dot's stories all morning, and was getting impatient. "You mentioned some surprises, JD. What happened?"

"Puccini didn't really ask me much about Rich," JD began. "He seemed more interested in my education and degrees. It was a little strange. At the end of the interview, he took me over to Starbucks and wanted some personal investment advice. He thinks Winthrop Harriman may be running a fraud, and asked me to look into it because he's invested with him. The whole thing seems kind of odd, considering I'd just met him."

Dot became very interested. "That's what Richard thought, that Harriman was some kind of mentor to Yates, and probably involved in the fraud. That's what I told the detective."

JD handed a cappuccino to Dot. "So that's where Puccini got the idea and connected Harriman and Yates. If Rich was onto them, it would certainly provide a motive."

JD's iPhone pinged with a reminder, and he looked at the screen. "You'll have to pardon me, ladies. I'm having lunch with Fareed downtown in fifteen minutes, and I don't want to be late."

He kissed Annie goodbye, grabbed his laptop, and left for downtown. He passed the police station and the Starbucks at the north end of Greenwich Avenue, and continued two blocks farther south down the wide one-way boulevard, passing the designer boutiques, art galleries and restaurants that lined the avenue. He found a parking spot just north of d'Allessandro's.

JD saw Fareed at his regular corner table when he entered, checking his cell phone. The restaurant was done in a nautical theme, with blocks and ropes along the walls, and small white sails behind the tables. The *maitre d'* and owner, Michael d'Allessandro, greeted JD and walked him over to the table.

"José will tell you about the specials today and take good care of you."

JD nodded at Fareed, and sat down. Fareed smiled and put away his cell phone. "It's a very interesting day in the markets, JD. It reminds me of that ancient Chinese curse: *May you live in interesting times.* How was your meeting with Detective Puccini?"

"As I told Annie, it was a little strange. He didn't talk much about Rich's disappearance. His main interest was in whether Yates and Winthrop Harriman are running a fraud. He wants me to look into it for him."

Fareed seemed lost in thought as he absent-mindedly broke off a piece of bread. "Richard told us about Yates, but Mr. Harriman is a bit of a surprise, don't you think? He is running one of the biggest independent investment funds in the world. It seems implausible that he would be involved in something illegal."

"You're probably right, but I did agree to look into it. I'll use my forensic accounting, with maybe a little hacking on the side. Let's order some food. I had too much coffee this morning."

Fareed beckoned to José, who came quickly to the table. "The fish is truly excellent today, sir," he began, and then reeled off a list of daily specials. Fareed ordered hidden fjord salmon with grilled asparagus, and JD ordered wild striped bass with mango and fig salad. José took their orders and said, "And may I assume the usual wines? A gavi di gavi for Dr. Ghanem and a pinot grigio for Dr. Dionne, with a large bottle of San Pelegrino?"

Fareed nodded. "That would be just splendid, José. Thank you very much." He turned to JD. "Hacking, you say? That is not legal, Joshua."

"Fareed, you fret too much. It's for a good cause. It might help me save Rich . . . if he's still alive."

"It has been almost two days now. Have there been any further developments?"

"That's why I brought the laptop. The police have the video from the security cameras at the hotel, and it includes the woman they think visited Rich in his room. Here, let me show you."

JD put his laptop on the table and started the video. Fareed watched it intently. "I cannot discern much due to her large sunglasses, but the features remind me of someone I have seen here in Greenwich, perhaps at one of the hedge fund receptions at the yacht club. Please show it to me again."

They looked at it a second time but still could not pin down the woman's identity. The food arrived along with the wine, and Fareed proposed a toast. "To our friend Richard, may our prayers be with you. Do not give up, no matter where you are."

They ate silently for a while, thinking about Rich. Fareed took a sip of wine, savored it slowly, and then took a drink of the San Pelegrino. "I still cannot quite believe it. I expect Richard to walk through that door and join us at this table, as he did a week ago."

"I miss him too," JD said. "But the most important thing right now is to help the police find him. I'm going to focus on Yates and Harriman."

Fareed frowned. "If they were party to Rich's abduction, then they are dangerous. Maybe we should let the public safety professionals handle it, Joshua."

"I can't let go, Fareed. And I think I can do a better job than th police."

Fareed paused for a few seconds. "I understand, but do be careful. And know you will be busy, but I have a small favor to ask of you. Do you hav any firm commitments on your schedule for this coming weekend, aside from your research on Yates and Harriman?"

"B will be home from Yale, and we were hoping to do a little family sailing on *Ojibwa* if there's a decent wind. The season is almost over. We were planning to have a picnic on one of the islands. What did you have in mind?"

"As you say, JD, the sailing season is almost over, and the club championship is coming down to the wire. My regular foredeck hand has to attend a wedding in Boston, and I was wondering if you would mind crewing for me in the big race, maybe along with B. Vivian will be sailing with me as usual, and it will be a very pleasant experience, I can assure you. It would be a great favor to me if you could find the time."

"Always the competitor, eh, Fareed? My family sails for fresh air and sunshine, and you're after the silver mugs." This reminded him of Fareed's dramatic history with the yacht club. "But how are the other members treating you now?"

Fareed took a bite of his salmon. "Time heals most wounds. It has been over five years since we settled the lawsuit, and quite a few more people of color have joined the club. I even had a very pleasant lunch with the vice commodore last week. But I must say that this history is a large part of my motivation for trying to win the championship."

"Fareed, you opened the door for us all to join the club, and I'm very thankful."

Fareed took a sip of his wine and savored it for a moment. "What was it that your President Teddy Roosevelt once said? Speak softly and carry a big stick." He paused. "I just like to keep my big stick out of sight until I need it."

JD smiled. "You're all bite and no bark, Fareed. A pit bull." He raised his glass and offered a toast. "Here's to our boy from Bangalore. May he cross the finish line first on Saturday."

Fareed clicked JD's glass. "Those are very kind words, JD, but I must point out that you have not answered my question. My chances of winning will be considerably enhanced if you and B will crew for me."

"Of course. I'll be there bright and early, and I'll make sure that B comes as well. It won't take much convincing if Vivian is part of the crew."

"Thank you, JD." Fareed became serious again. "I wish that Richard were here to join us."

They ate in silence for a few minutes, and then Fareed's cell phone rang. The ring tone was the guitar break to "Faded Love". Fareed picked up the phone, and as he listened carefully, his face started to become pinched. His eyes narrowed, almost closing. Finally, he said, "Mortimer, this is completely and absolutely unacceptable. We had reached an agreement, sir, and I expect you to fulfill it. That is what gentlemen do."

Fareed was silent for a few more seconds, and then his voice became louder. "No, no, no, Mortimer. I am going to buy that piece for the price we agreed on. I do not care who offered you more. I must say, I am very disappointed that your word is not your bond."

José came up to the table and gave Fareed a disapproving look. Other customers were staring in their direction. Fareed waved the waiter away as he continued. "No, Mortimer, it is not okay. I do not want you [illegible] substitute a different sculpture. I want the one we agreed on . . . No, Mortimer, please listen to me. I want to make myself very, very clear. This is unacceptable, and I shall bloody well see you in court. You will be receiving a writ from my solicitor before the sun has set. Good-bye." Fareed put the phone back in his pocket and looked at JD. His jaw was set, and his chest was heaving. As he took a large gulp of wine, his hand shook. Fareed sat up straight, continued his deep breathing for a few more seconds, and finally seemed to calm down.

JD studied him for a moment. "It sounds as if someone else thought you were a pushover. Now they're meeting the real you."

"That was the artist Mortimer, who makes those large ceramic sculptures. Heema and I fell in love with one particular piece because of the colors. Mortimer calls it *Tricolor One.* It's saffron, white and green, which are the colors of the Indian flag. The saffron symbolizes Hinduism, green stands for Islam, and white represents the peace between them. It would be a perfect fit and highlight for the foyer in our home, and would remind us of our native country. Now Mortimer wants to sell it to someone who has offered him more money."

"Can't you just choose another piece and avoid the lawyers?" Fareed seemed to be taking this to an extreme – as usual.

"This piece is unique, and I must have it. Furthermore, it is the principle. This is America, a land ruled by laws that apply equally to everyone. I hate to be discourteous, Joshua, but I simply must speak to my solicitor right away."

Fareed punched in a number, and left a voicemail for his lawyer to call as soon as possible. "He is probably at court," said Fareed. They started eating again, but the lawyer called back within minutes. Fareed took the call, and said, "I had agreed to purchase a work of art from the artist Mortimer, and he is now reneging on our agreement. I would like to start proceedings immediately to sue him for breach of contract." He listened for half a minute, and then muted the phone as he turned to JD. "This conversation could be of significant duration, JD, so you may wish to leave, and I will take care of the invoice."

JD was getting frustrated with his friend. "Fareed, I think you're going too far with this. It's only a piece of art. And you know American courts. The rule of law is fine in theory, but in practice it can be a random walk. You could waste a small fortune on legal fees, and still have no guarantee of how it'll turn out."

"No, I have to do this, Joshua. I will not be a pushover. They think I am just a little man from India, and that I will not fight. I have to teach this artist a lesson." He went back to his cell phone and continued talking to the lawyer. JD shook his head as he got up and walked out.

As he sat down in his car, JD felt a twinge of concern. Fareed could be very stubborn, and JD had a bad gut feeling about the conversation he had just overheard. Was his friend going too far, maybe messing with the wrong person? There was violence in the air. He shook his head and started the car.

CHAPTER 6

Moments after JD returned home from his lunch with Fareed, Annie tiptoed down the stairs, with a finger to her lips. When she reached the bottom step, she whispered, "Dot's finally asleep. Please don't wake her. She really needs the rest."

JD closed the door quietly and gave Annie a hug. She pointed toward the kitchen island and said, "There's a package for you. A taxi dropped it off."

"That's probably from Puccini - his investment reports from Harriman. I should take a look at them right away."

He hurried down the hall to his office and opened the package. He read it all carefully. There were five annual investment reports showing rock steady returns of almost exactly ten percent each year, and transaction records indicating stock purchases and sales over the same period.

The amazingly consistent returns instantly set off alarm bells. In JD's experience, investment returns always bounced around a little, and the charts should have looked like a squiggle, not a straight line. There was always some randomness in real-world returns. He decided to check for consistency between the returns shown in the investment reports, and the actual transactions that resulted in these returns. Did the stock purchases and sales actually produce the returns that Harriman was showing?

JD entered all of the purchases and sales of stocks from Harriman's transaction records into his proprietary investment program, and ran the numbers. To his great surprise, they all checked out. The buying and selling of the stocks shown in the transaction reports produced the returns indicated in the annual investment reports. But he was still not convinced.

He decided to calculate the probability of such consistent ten percent returns for five years in a row.

He assumed a Gaussian probability distribution, and based the standard deviation on the Dow Jones index over the same five years. Then he entered the numbers into his mathematical model, and looked at the answer. The probability of any investment fund returning exactly ten percent for five years in a row was about *one in four million.*

These returns were basically impossible, JD realized. Puccini was right – and maybe this was somehow related to Rich's disappearance. Rich had stumbled onto some dangerous information.

JD Googled Harriman's fund and started doing more detailed due diligence. Harriman had started Winthrop B. Harriman Investment Securities LLC in 1962, with some capital from his father-in-law, and at first had specialized as a "market maker," someone who helped set the price of a stock by posting the prices at which he would be willing to buy or sell. JD knew that this was a respected and necessary function in the market, and Harriman's firm had developed some innovative computer technology to disseminate their stock quotes. All reviews of this part of the business seemed positive, and made a great deal of sense. Harriman's innovative technology had helped start a new electronic stock exchange, which was now competing with the New York Stock Exchange for listings.

But Harriman also had an investment advisory business on the side, and its track record was more problematic. The first signs of trouble seemed to be in 1993, right after the 1991 recession, when two clients complained to the Securities Exchange Commission about one of Harriman's funds. Few public details were available, and a private settlement was reached. Harriman returned the money to the investors and the SEC closed the case. Harriman was very active in the Securities Industry and Financial Markets Association, and he seemed to have very close ties to the SEC as well. He had been investigated by the SEC on three other occasions in the nineties, but had been cleared each time.

JD couldn't quite make sense of what he was seeing. Harriman's investment fund was now managing over thirty billion dollars in assets. How could such a huge fund be crooked? That seemed to be way too big for a Ponzi. Somebody would have figured it out by now, and he would be in jail. But if it actually was a Ponzi, the coming recession would expose him. When the market nosedived, investors would get very nervous and would want to see their profits. If Harriman had actually spent the money instead of investing it, his whole scheme – if it was a scheme – would blow up in his face.

JD knew what his next step had to be – he would confirm whether the stock trades supposedly documented in Harriman's investment reports had actually taken place. They would be listed at the Depository Trust Company. He was certain that the Securities Exchange Commission had already done this in their investigations, but then he remembered his mother's dictum: *Believe none of what you hear, and half of what you see.*

The only way into the DTC records would be via a major and very dangerous hack. If JD started down this path, there would be no turning back. He closed his eyes, and visualized the last band practice with Rich and Fareed - Raji wagging his tail, and Rich singing his heart out. JD shook his head, opened his eyes, and turned toward his special computer array – the one with three of the latest graphic processor units, some additional cutting edge software that was not publicly available, and a ghost connection to an untraceable server.

He had become aware long before that the hacking community was divided into two parts: the White Hats – those who helped increase the security of computer systems by finding weaknesses and fixing them; and the Black Hats – those who invaded computer systems in order to simply wreak havoc or to steal money and secrets. JD was still receiving help and advice on occasion from some of his White Hat colleagues at MIT. He considered himself to be very much on their side - even though he was about to do something highly illegal.

JD's first goal was to get access to the Harriman's records at the Depository Trust Company to determine if Puccini's reported transactions had actually occurred, and the only way to do it was to hack into the DTC's system.

First, JD decided to carry out a weakness analysis on the DTC computer network to see where he could attack. He set up his vulnerability scanner program, and had the layout of the network mapped within an hour. He located the storage module for the transaction records, but he had to get access. He found three possible entry points using a port scanner, and then set about determining the passwords he needed for entry. Using a password cracking program that he had developed with some help from his MIT colleagues, he started the attack. He first tried a brute-force tool, but after an hour, it was clear that the password was too robust for this technique, even at a hundred million password tests per second. He added a cracking dictionary, but again was unable to break through. Then he put the three graphic processor units in parallel to bring the computing power to another level, and increased the test rate to three trillion per second. It took another hour, but that did it. He found the password and got into the system. But there was an additional firewall, and he was running out of options.

He stopped, and took a deep breath. He knew he had to be very careful, and concentrate fully. If he left any trace, they'd be able to track him, and he'd end up in jail. He wiped the sweat from his brow with his sleeve, and turned back to the keyboard.

His last resort was an SQL-injection attack. He started looking for any vulnerability in the software applications on the site's backend Structured Query Language databases, and he finally found a flaw after another two hours of probing. That opening then became the access point for a multi-layered pivot into the stock transaction records he was looking for. The mental effort of monitoring all the programs while avoiding detection was exhausting, and JD took a brief break to prepare a cappuccino and consider his next step.

So far, so good, he mused as he took a sip. Now he just had to find Harriman and get out.

Once he was into the Depository Trust Company transaction storage module, he used the layout map to probe the likely locations for the records of Winthrop B. Harriman Investment Securities LLC. He could find none. He checked once more, because he couldn't believe that there was absolutely no record of thirty billion dollars in transactions. On his third attempt, his hand shaking a little, he came close to spilling his cappuccino on the keyboard. He could feel beads of sweat rolling down his back, and he had to push his chair back to catch his breath.

"Holy shit," he whispered to himself. The transaction records simply didn't exist. There were absolutely no records of any transactions, no trace of Harriman anywhere in the DTC. Harriman had simply kept the money, and maybe divvied some of it out to a few select friends. How the hell was he getting away with this?

JD took a few minutes to calm down, and took another sip of the cappuccino. He grimaced – the cappuccino was cold. He was losing track of time. He closed his eyes and concentrated. What other tests could he do? Maybe he was missing something, and the transactions were there somewhere. Or maybe his software was wonky.

Then he realized how he could test his software - he would check the records of his own investment fund in the DTC. It took a little while to find his small fund, but he confirmed that all the records were there in full detail. He then checked Fareed's fund, and all the records were there as well. There was no problem with the software.

So that was it. Harriman's transaction records were all faked. He'd never bought or sold any stocks. This was a classic Ponzi scheme. Harriman took the money from his investors and simply put it in his own bank account. When a few investors wanted to withdraw their funds along with their earnings, he wrote them a check from that bank account. *He never invested it.* When stock markets were climbing, not many wanted to withdraw their money, so the scheme worked like a well-oiled machine. But in the coming crash, everyone would run for safety – out of stocks and into government bonds. But Harriman would not have the money when his investors came calling.

What was Harriman's exit plan? And what about the banks he dealt with? Wouldn't they have been suspicious? They had to be, JD reasoned, but then he thought about the gargantuan banking fees on that thirty billion. Just like the bond-rating agencies, the banks would go along to get along. It was all about the fees. Everyone just looked the other way.

JD carefully withdrew his digital probe from the Depository Trust Company records, and removed all traces of his hacking. When he was satisfied that all was secure and no digital evidence had been left behind, he called Puccini on his cell phone.

"You were one hundred percent right about Harriman, detective. Let me buy you a coffee and I'll give you the whole story. Can we meet at Starbuck's in half an hour?"

"Make it an hour. I'm waiting on some DNA results." Still the detective, thought JD, even when his life savings were at risk.

JD's neck and back were very tense, and he needed a break from all the mental stress. He picked up one of his guitars, plugged it into the amp, and worked through some standard chord changes. It had been a couple of days since he had thought about his music, and as his fingers worked up and down the fretboard, he could feel some of the tension drain away. As he played some of the old familiar chords, his mind drifted back to the last rehearsal of the Charles River Playboys. That brought back the memory of Dot's phone call asking him to check on Rich at the hotel, and suddenly the mental imprint of the blood in that room overwhelmed his music. He just couldn't get away from it. JD sighed, put down the guitar, and went back to the living room. Annie was on the sofa, reading a book. She looked exhausted.

JD walked over and gave her a kiss. "You look like you need some sleep. How's Dot?"

"She's upstairs, totally passed out. That's where I should be, but I want to be here when she wakes up. What's happening? You were in the office a long time."

"I was checking into Puccini's investments, and it doesn't look good. It's a fraud."

Annie frowned. "I hope you didn't do anything illegal."

JD shrugged. "If it gets Puccini on our side, it's worth it. I have to go see him again now."

"Again? I thought you were no longer a suspect."

"He says I'm not at the top of his list, whatever that means. Anyway, it's about Harriman. I have to preserve Puccini's life savings."

Annie's voice became very calm. "I want to find out more about Junior's hacking. You could both end up in jail."

"Don't worry about it. She's too smart to get caught."

"And what about you, JD?"

"I'll see you later. Puccini's waiting."

* * *

Starbucks was busy, and Puccini was nowhere in sight. JD bought two cappuccinos but couldn't find an empty table. As he was standing there, awkwardly juggling his laptop case and the coffees, Puccini walked in and nodded hello. He strolled over to his favorite corner table at the back, where a young well-dressed man was hunched over a laptop. The man's coffee cup was empty, and Puccini said something to him very quietly. The man looked at Puccini, got up, took his laptop, and walked out. Puccini beckoned JD to come and sit down.

"Nothing but your favorite table, eh?" JD said. He put down the cappuccinos, and put his laptop on the table.

Puccini did his little shrug. "Hey, he was finished his coffee, plus I'm in a hurry. What do we have here, JD?" He took a sip of his cappuccino. "Did you know that in Italy we never have a cappuccino after eleven in the morning? We should be having espressos. The cappuccino is a breakfast drink."

JD sighed. "So you want an espresso instead?'

Puccini smiled. "I'll let it go this time, partner. So what do you have?"

"You were right. Harriman is running a Ponzi. You should get your money out as soon as possible."

Puccini's face turned pale, and he was silent for a few long seconds. "Are you absolutely one-hundred percent positive? The SEC has investigated him five times and found nothing. How the fuck can you get away with kiting thirty billion?"

"I'll show you. The transactions in his reports never happened. I've got it all here on the spreadsheet. The probability that --"

"I don't need to see that shit," Puccini interrupted quietly. "I won't understand it anyway. The way I deal with people is, I trust them until I find I can't. Life is much easier that way. I trust you, pal, so I'll just follow your advice. I'll put my life savings in your hands."

"Does that mean you believe me when I say I had nothing to do with Rich's death?"

Puccini gave him a hard stare. "Yeah, I guess I do."

JD tried to hide a smile. "Good."

Puccini picked up his phone and pushed a name on his speed-dial list. "Hello, I'd like to speak to Mr. Harriman, please." Puccini tapped his fingers loudly on the table. "Hi, Grinny, is Bucky there? No? Well, here's the deal, Grinny. I've found a better place to invest my money, and I'd like to withdraw all my funds." Puccini certainly wasted no time getting to the point. He listened for a while, looking intently at JD and shaking his head. "Tomorrow? What time?" Another pause. "Okay, see you then. I'll bring along my financial adviser." He hung up.

Puccini took another sip of his cappuccino. "Bucky wasn't there - that's Winthrop Buckminster Harriman to us common folk - so I spoke to his son Peregrine. Tell me something, JD . . . would you want to go through life being called Peregrine? He goes mostly by Grinny, which is even worse. Almost as bad as Bucky." Puccini paused, as if to punctuate the ridiculousness of the names. "Anyway, he won't do anything over the phone, wants to sit down with me, show me why my money's safe. It's on for tomorrow morning, and I'd like you to come with me, pal. That way he can't bullshit me. You can put the squeeze on him with all your fancy spreadsheets and get my money out."

"What about the connection to Rich? Have you forgotten about that? Harriman may be involved somehow. Aren't you getting your personal affairs mixed up with a possible murder case?"

"Don't worry about it, JD, we've still got those twelve detectives working on it. That's what the DNA was about. We're pulling it all together. We'll nail those bastards. If Harriman's part of it, he'll get caught in the net. And Yates, too. Don't worry, I haven't forgotten about Yates. So what about it? Are you in?"

JD pondered for a moment, wondering how much leverage he had. "Okay, I'll come with you tomorrow on one condition. You interview Dorothy Bridger at our house rather than the police station." That would make Annie happy, he knew.

Puccini frowned. "I guess I can do that, but there's something you should know, even though you're close to her and everything. Maybe especially because you're so close to her. I think she's hiding something.

There was some evidence on Bridger's laptop that points to her . . . and before you even ask, I can't tell you what it is."

JD felt that familiar shiver down his back. Maybe his gut feeling about Dot was correct.

* * *

JD reached the house first, and after a quick kiss, brought Annie up to date on his conversation with Puccini.

Annie shook her head. "I still can't believe it. How can Harriman fool that many people for so long? And you said he's on the SEC compliance committee. That's like having the wolf guarding the sheep."

"I'm afraid the sheep are about to be sheared in a very big way. We'll see what Harriman has to say when we meet him tomorrow. And maybe there's a connection to Yates. By the way, how's Dot? Puccini's on his way over here. He agreed to do his questioning here instead of grilling her downtown. That was the quid pro quo when I said I would help him with Harriman."

"She's out on the deck reading. She's feeling better . . . but she's fragile. I'm not sure she's ready for another interrogation."

"I don't think she has much choice," JD said as he saw Puccini's Crown Vic pulling up in the driveway.

Puccini came into the house carrying a large briefcase. Annie went out on the deck to get Dot, and they both came in a few minutes later. She turned to JD. "I explained to Dot that she wouldn't have to go downtown for the interview. Maybe the best place would be your office."

Dot looked well-rested, and her eyes were no longer puffy and red-rimmed. She glared at Puccini. "I'm not looking forward to this, detective. I think it's a waste of time. I have nothing to add to what I've already told you. You should be out there harassing John Maynard Yates instead of me."

Puccini sighed. "Look, Mrs. Bridger, it's my job. It won't take long."

JD led Puccini and Dot to his office at the rear of the house. As they walked into the large room, Puccini paused, glancing at the three guitars hanging on the far wall. "That looks like a Gibson L-5, an old one. Very nice axe. And that looks like a 'fifties Telecaster."

JD smiled. "I see you know your guitars. Do you play as well?"

"I fool around a little. I played bass in a rock band in high school. Not much time now with the kids and all."

Dot stepped into the middle of the room and crossed her arms, looking at Puccini and JD with a frown. "Can we get on with this interview now? I didn't come here for a damn guitar seminar."

Puccini smiled and put down his briefcase. "My apologies, ma'am." He nodded at JD, who quietly left the room and closed the door.

* * *

"Please sit down, Mrs. Bridger. There've been some new developments I'd like to discuss with you." Puccini pulled out an audio recorder and turned it on. "I'd like to record this, if you don't mind." She nodded slightly, and he pulled a laptop out of his briefcase and placed it on the desk. "Does this laptop look familiar, Mrs. Bridger?"

She leaned forward and looked at it closely. "It looks like the computer Richard travels with, but I'm not sure. They all look alike to me."

Puccini turned on the computer, scrolled down a few items, and opened one of the files. "This laptop was in Professor Bridger's hotel room. Getting it running took us quite a while. We had to call in the FBI, and it took her half a day. Come take a look at what we found."

He turned the screen around so that she could read the document. He watched closely to see her reaction, but she just shrugged her shoulders, and said, "That's our prenup."

She was being very cool about this, thought Puccini. It was time to put on a little squeeze. "Your prenuptial agreement with Professor Bridger is very one-sided. It leaves you with almost nothing if you were to divorce him."

Dot shook her head. "I didn't read it very closely when I signed it thirteen years ago, and I haven't looked at it since. To me, marriage is forever, in sickness and in health and all that. I never thought about divorce, so this agreement didn't mean anything to me. Richard wanted it, so I said okay."

Puccini turned the computer around to face himself again. "I'd like to ask you about the argument you had with Professor Bridger last week. You mentioned it when we talked yesterday. What was it about?"

Dot looked exhausted. "That feels like it happened a year ago, detective. I can't remember exactly, but it must have been my suspicions about another affair. He'd promised."

"Mrs. Bridger, do you know any members of Professor Bridger's karate group?"

"I've met a few of them. Sometimes we go out for drinks or dinner, but they mostly talk about karate, and it's extremely boring. They're very narrow in their interests."

Puccini turned to the computer again and brought a picture to the screen. It was time for the money shot. He turned it around to show her. "Who's that in the picture, Mrs. Bridger? You look like you're having a good time on that cabin cruiser."

She looked at the picture and smiled. "That's Clint Houston, one of Richard's regular sparring partners. So what?"

"Does he have a black belt?"

"Yes, I think so. Otherwise he wouldn't be sparring with Richard, would he? Don't they have to be at a similar skill level?"

"And is that his yacht in the picture?"

"Yes, but what's your point? I went out for a ride on his boat. Richard was there as well."

Puccini leaned back and took a deep breath. He'd rehearsed the questions in his mind, but the next one was awkward. "Mrs. Bridger, I know that Professor Bridger had many affairs, and it must have been frustrating and difficult for you. Were you ever tempted to have an affair of your own?"

Dorothy Bridger's face started to turn red, but Puccini couldn't tell whether it was from embarrassment - or anger. He soon found out.

"What kind of fucking stupid question is that? Of course I haven't had any affairs. Clint is Richard's friend and my friend, if that's what you're getting at. But that's all there is to it. Just a friend. Who the hell do you think you are, anyway? My husband is gone, maybe dead, and all you want to do is harass me?"

Puccini closed the laptop and put it in the briefcase, and then turned off the audio recorder. He finally said, "You don't have an alibi, Mrs. Bridger, and you have a possible motive, namely money. Professor Bridger has done well with his investments, and you wouldn't get anything out of a divorce. The only way you get that money is if he dies. I think you should stay in town, and maybe talk to a lawyer."

The look Dorothy Bridger fixed him with was cold and furious. "You're wasting your time, detective. I love my husband despite everything. I'm not the one you're looking for."

Puccini left her sitting there and went back to the living room, where JD and Annie waited. "Don't forget," he said to JD. "Ten o'clock tomorrow at Harriman's house in Belle Plains. I'll pick you up at nine-thirty."

Annie looked back toward JD's office and then at Puccini. "Where's Dot?"

Puccini shrugged. "She's back there. I think she's a little upset with me."

Puccini walked out to his car, and as he put the briefcase on the seat beside him in the Crown Vic, he looked back at the house. He'd set the trap, and now he just had to wait.

* * *

Annie and JD went to JD's office to see how Dot was doing after the questioning. She was sitting in the chair beside the desk, looking out the window.

"That detective is useless," she told them. "They're never going to catch the people who took Richard. Puccini thinks I'm having an affair, and that I hired my lover to get rid of Richard. Or something like that. It's absolutely surreal."

Annie sat down beside her. "I'd like to hear about it. I can drive you back to New Haven and stay overnight again."

"I'll stay here and look after Junior," JD offered. His cell phone rang, and he saw that it was Fareed. He excused himself and went back to the living room to take the call.

"I just had a very interesting visitor at my house," Fareed began. "A man named John Smith. I think he threatened me."

"Threatened you? What did he do?"

"First, he's a big man. Very big. And he stood very close to me. He said he was worried about my health, and he'd like to see me continue to have good health. He talked about accidents, how one has to be very careful these days."

JD smiled. "Was he an insurance salesman?'

"No, no, JD, this is serious. He talked about Mortimer's sculpture. He said I should let it go to the new buyer, that it would be good for my health. The new owner is very unhappy that I have started a lawsuit."

"Did this big guy actually threaten you?"

"No, not in so many words. In fact, he was very careful and precise in his choice of words. The threat was implied, but never stated explicitly."

"Have you talked to your lawyer about it?"

"Yes. He said there's nothing to be done. I let Mr. Smith come into my home, and he gave me some advice. It was all hypothetical, expressed in the subjunctive. Could you please talk to your detective friend about this incident?"

"He's not exactly my friend, Fareed. But maybe you should forget the lawsuit."

"No, I will not be intimidated." JD heard a familiar *woof* in the background, and then heard Fareed say, "In a minute, Raji. You must be patient. Please bring me the leash." Then Fareed was back talking to JD. "Raji is anxious for his evening walk, JD, so I must go. Could we talk about this tomorrow? I am a little worried."

"Sure, let's talk tomorrow. Maybe Puccini can find out more about this John Smith person, if that's his real name." JD hung up.

He found Annie in the living room, putting a book into a tote bag. "Dot's upstairs, getting her things together. I'll drive her home, and come back tomorrow morning. You know, she's very upset with Puccini. He seems to be going a little overboard."

"He said he found something on Rich's laptop. That's probably why he's being so harsh."

"You keep defending him, JD. I think he plays head games. There was no need to abuse Dot. Anyway, what was that phone call about?"

"It was Fareed . . . being Fareed. He's suing that artist Mortimer over a sculpture sale that fell through, and one of Mortimer's goons paid him a visit."

"Fareed loves the lawyers too much. Someday he's going to poke the wrong wasp's nest." She gave JD a curious look. "Wait a minute. You said 'one of Mortimer's goons.' Are you sure this person works for Mortimer? To me, that doesn't ring true. Mortimer is an artist. I'd look to the client who actually bought that sculpture that Fareed is so concerned about."

JD thought for a moment. "Maybe you're right. Fareed said the thug told him the new buyer was upset about the lawsuit. Anyway, Fareed wants me to speak to Puccini about this guy. His name supposedly is John Smith."

Dot came downstairs with her overnight bag. "Did someone mention Puccini? I don't trust that man. I think he's incompetent."

JD did not respond. Dot's comments were becoming tiresome. He kissed Annie at the door as she and Dot left for New Haven. Then he returned to his office. Junior came in very quietly, and said, "Have you heard the news? Lehman is going to release their quarterly earnings tomorrow, a week ahead of schedule."

JD sighed. "They're just rearranging the deck chairs on the *Titanic.*"

He continued working on Harriman. He found nothing new, but started wondering about Fareed's threatening visitor. Was it somehow connected to Rich's disappearance? And what did Puccini find on Rich's laptop? Was it something that implicated Dot?

CHAPTER 7

Wednesday, September 10, 2008

Junior already had the coffee perking and was watching CNBC when JD came downstairs. It was her turn to prepare breakfast, and he saw two bowls of granola with yogurt and berries. JD poured himself a cup of coffee and sat down to eat. "What's happening this morning?"

"The Dow fell another 280 points yesterday, but is seems to be recovering. Not much else."

"It's all a waiting game at this point. The calm before the storm."

They watched quietly and finished their breakfast. Junior went upstairs to get ready for school, and JD called Annie in New Haven. JD knew that with each passing hour, the chances of finding Rich alive were declining. The statistics were very clear on this. And if it was a matter of ransom, there would have been a demand within the first few hours. But he decided not discuss this with Annie yet. "How's Dot this morning?" he asked.

"She had a good sleep, but she's still angry with Puccini."

"He's just being a pro, looking at all the angles." JD paused, wondering whether now was the time, but he decided to go ahead. "Annie, I know she's one of your best friends, but do you think there's any possibility that Dot *is* somehow involved? That Puccini may be onto something?"

There was a long, silent pause. "JD, don't be ridiculous. I'll be back later today." She disconnected.

JD told himself that Annie was right. They'd known Dot for over a decade. Puccini was barking up the wrong tree.

He was checking the markets again when he heard Puccini's Crown Vic in front of the house. He grabbed his laptop and went out to the car.

As they pulled away, Puccini said, "I've put in a lot of overtime on the Bridger case, so I was able to get a couple of hours of PT this morning. We'll see if Harriman agrees to return my money when you give him the third degree."

"Has there been any progress on Bridger? I understand that the first forty-eight hours are critical."

"That's a myth. You never know. We're still working on it. Something will turn up."

JD couldn't tell whether Puccini was telling the truth or just trying to reassure him. He decided to change the subject. "I'm sure when Harriman sees your squad car in the driveway he'll want to make nice. The last thing he needs is an unhappy detective complaining to the SEC."

"Maybe. But he lives in a different world. You ever been inside Belle Plains?"

"I don't know anyone there, so I've never had the opportunity." JD had heard about it, of course. Everyone in Greenwich knew that Belle Plains was a privately owned enclave on a small peninsula jutting into Long Island Sound. It was one of the oldest and most elite communities in the country.

Puccini continued. "It's like a separate country. We have no idea what goes on in there, because they have their own security staff, a gatehouse, and a private road system. Someone could commit murder in there and we'd never hear about it. As someone once said, the rich are different from you and me. It's only a hundred and twenty homes, and it's been around for over a hundred years."

Puccini turned right onto East Putnam Avenue and then left onto Field Point Road, passing under the Connecticut Turnpike and then onto Belle Plains peninsula. They reached the gatehouse leading into the Belle Plains Land Association, and Puccini rolled down his window.

The guard looked at the dusty and beat-up Crown Victoria. "And whom might you be visiting this morning, sir?"

Puccini pulled out his GPD badge and showed it to the guard. The guard was not impressed. "That's very nice, thank you. Whom are you visiting? I cannot let you in unless you have an appointment with a resident of the Association."

Puccini smiled, and said, "We have an appointment with Mr. Winthrop Buckminster Harriman on Harbor Drive. My name is Antonio Puccini, and the gentleman on my right is Dr. Joshua Dionne."

The guard checked his computer screen for a few seconds, and then opened the gate. "Have a very pleasant day, sir."

Puccini drove slowly into the enclave. The street was as smooth as glass, and there were mature trees on both sides, some over a hundred feet tall. Each house had a lot the size of a football field, and some of the gardens could have been shipped over from Versailles. JD could see Long Island Sound and Greenwich Harbor through breaks in the trees, creating spectacular vistas. The designs of the houses varied, with some Victorians interspersed among white clapboard colonials. There was one house that looked like a slightly scaled-down French chateau, finished in reclaimed brick and stone. Many of the homes did look a century old, and a few of them probably were. Each one was immaculate, ready for a star turn in *Architectural Digest*.

JD looked out at the towering trees and Long Island Sound to the left. "So this is where the one percent of the one percent live."

Puccini pulled into a circular driveway in front of a very large white clapboard colonial-style home. There were carefully trimmed trees to the side, and a small green island in the middle of the circular drive, covered by a lush rolling lawn and an intricate pattern of perennials. Clearly, Harriman had put some of his investors' money into landscaping.

Puccini rang the doorbell, and a young dark-haired maid dressed in grey and white opened the door. She asked them in, and led them through a two-story entry hall and art gallery. JD stopped to admire the vaulted ceiling and skylights. Then he noticed that under one of the skylights, bathed in the morning sun reflecting off the far white wall, was a spectacular ceramic sculpture. It was about eight feet tall, with sensuous shapes and brilliant colors. The main body of the sculpture was red with an overlay of light blue, and the two smaller pieces connected to it were a high-gloss black. He looked closely at the brass plaque on a pedestal beside the sculpture. It read, *Opus 9, Red and Black – Mortimer.*

The maid waited patiently while JD walked around the sculpture. Finally Puccini said, "Enough, JD. We've got a meeting with Harriman. Let's go."

JD quickly caught up to Puccini. "That's a Mortimer. I don't know much about art, but it *is* pretty spectacular." He could almost see why Fareed was so obsessed with one of Mortimer's pieces.

The maid proceeded down a corridor leading to the right. She opened a large double glass door and led them to a stone terrace overlooking Long Island Sound. "Would you like some coffee while you're waiting for Mr. Harriman? A cappuccino and some biscotti, perhaps?"

Puccini smiled and said, "Yes, please," and the maid left. They sat down on a blue sectional sofa. JD put his laptop on the table. There was a gentle breeze off the Sound, and they could see the Cos Cob Yacht Club across the harbor. There were two sailboats beating into the wind, and Calf Island and Shore Island were still resplendent in their September greenery. It wouldn't be long before they would display a spectacular array of autumn oranges and yellows.

JD smiled and looked at Puccini. "I could get used to this."

"Enjoy the view, but be careful what you say. You can bet that we're being monitored and recorded."

The maid brought in the cappuccinos and biscotti. JD started sipping his coffee. Five minutes stretched into fifteen, and still no sign of Harriman. Finally a young man sauntered in. His white deck shoes, white linen trousers, and navy blue blazer with silk shirt resonated with the ambiance of the spectacular terrace.

The young man smiled, and drawled nasally, "Good morning, Tony. I'm awfully sorry we kept you waiting, but we absolutely had to catch Lehman's conference call this morning. I'm afraid it wasn't very good news. Did you, by chance, have the opportunity to listen in? But of course not . . . Maria should have given you the password to our wi-fi. My sincere apologies."

Puccini stood up. "Hi, Grinny, it's nice to see you again. This is Dr. Joshua Dionne. I brought him along to keep us on the straight and narrow."

Grinny's head tilted back slightly as he looked at JD, a frown momentarily creasing his face. JD offered his hand, and said, "I understand that you work for your father in the investment fund. I have a few questions."

Grinny eyes narrowed and he shook JD's hand quickly. "We always welcome questions. Research is very important to us. Skip is here as well, so why don't we wait until he and Bucky can join us? Bucky's doing some media interviews about the Lehman conference call, and then he'll be right down."

JD looked at his laptop. "What's the wi-fi password? I can catch up on Lehman while we're waiting."

"It's '33bigwuns,' but I can bring you up to date on the conference call if you wish. Lehman is looking for a buyer, and they need a few billion - from somewhere - to shore up their balance sheet. Their stock fell twenty percent while the conference call was under way. They are in deep doo-doo. The Feds will have to step in."

"I don't think that's likely," muttered JD as he punched in the password.

Grinny frowned. "Bucky has the word from on high. The administration won't let Lehman collapse. Too much collateral damage." He paused. "I better see what's happening upstairs." He left, and the maid brought more cappuccinos.

JD took a sip. "Tony, you may have to switch to espressos soon if this goes on much longer. It'll be after eleven o'clock. They don't seem to have much time for you."

Puccini scowled, looking out on the Sound as he took a bite of biscotti. The wind had picked up a bit, and there were now whitecaps on the water. The two sailboats were heeling over, and moving much faster. They waited another ten minutes, and finally a tall silver-haired patrician gentleman walked in, followed by Grinny and another young man carrying a laptop and a large file folder. JD recognized Winthrop Harriman from numerous media reports and appearances on CNBC. He looked the very model of a New England financier, the bluest of blue-chip money managers.

Harriman smiled broadly as he held out his hand to Puccini. "Tony, it's so great to see you. Please accept my apologies for keeping you waiting, but the *Journal* called for a quote after the Lehman call, and you know how reporters can be."

Puccini shook hands and said, "No problem." Then he looked toward JD. "This is the financial whiz I told you about, Dr. Joshua Dionne."

Harriman extended his hand to JD. "It's wonderful to meet you, Dr. Dionne. I checked on your fund, and you've been doing very well. I brought along my son Skip, with his spreadsheets and formulas. If you have any questions, Skip has all the answers."

"This won't take much time," Puccini began. "As I mentioned on the phone, I'd like to withdraw my money from your fund and invest it elsewhere."

Harriman kept smiling. "Of course, of course. But you know, you're making a very, very big mistake, Tony. Look at how you've built up your capital by leaving it all in the fund since day one. I really can't imagine how you could do as well anywhere else."

"To be very blunt, Bucky, I'm worried about your fund." Puccini turned toward JD expectantly.

JD looked up from his laptop. "It looks as if Lehman is going under, and there's going to be a lot of market turmoil. How will your fund get through that chaos?"

Harriman's smile did not waver. "I have it on the best authority . . . right from the top, in fact . . . that the government will step in. There's nothing to worry about. Tony's money is as safe as houses."

"Yes, safe as houses. And that's the problem. Houses are not safe. Their prices are declining, and all those mortgage bonds are going to implode."

Harriman turned to Skip. "Show Dr. Dionne how we're hedged against a housing collapse."

Before Skip could respond, JD interrupted him. "There's also the question of the amazing consistency of your returns. They're mathematically impossible."

Harriman's demeanor changed completely. The smile vanished, and his piercing blue eyes peered intently at JD. "The SEC has reviewed my fund five times, and we received a clean bill of health each time. We have over thirty billion in assets under management, and we've been around for thirty years. Skip has some very sophisticated proprietary models for arbitrage and high-speed trading. That's how we make those steady returns that you say are impossible. I understand you run a fund as well, Mr. Dionne. Perhaps your concern is based on professional jealousy?"

"I'd like to see those models, if I may," JD said.

Harriman started smiling again. "They're proprietary. If we showed them to you, we'd have to kill you."

The smile was absolutely relentless.

"But I'll tell you what. . ." He turned toward Puccini. "Tony, I can see that you're very concerned about your investments, even though in my opinion your concerns are totally baseless. Since you've been a faithful client for three years, I'm willing to return all your funds plus all of your earnings, right here and now. Would that be acceptable? Skip can calculate your net return to date, and I will write you a check for the full amount. Our last quarter has been outstanding. I know you'll regret withdrawing from the fund, but I'd rather retain your friendship than have an unhappy client."

Puccini said, "I'd like to see the amount, and then I'll decide."

He was negotiating for all he could get, thought JD. Smart move.

Harriman shrugged. "Skip, please calculate what we owe Detective Puccini." He turned to Puccini and JD, and swept his arm in an expansive gesture toward the back gardens and the Sound. "I'll give these gentlemen a tour of the grounds while you're working." Skip nodded and got to work on his laptop.

JD and Puccini followed Harriman along a flagstone path down to the dock behind the house. The carefully manicured miniature trees and the bright autumn flowers made it a very pleasant walk. Tied to the dock were a sleek red and white cigarette boat and a large cabin cruiser. "If we had more time, I'd take you out on a tour of the Sound. The islands out there are remarkably wild and natural."

JD said, "I noticed that you have one of Mortimer's ceramic sculptures in the entry hall. Do you have other pieces by him?"

"Yes, I have five of them. I'm one of his most active patrons. Mortimer's a magnificent artist, and also a friend and neighbor. His house is on the other side of the peninsula, right on the water. You can also see his island studio way out there, that little dot on the horizon. That's where he creates his sculptures. He's also a big investor in our fund."

"He seems to live remarkably well for an artist," JD remarked. "A house in Belle Plains, and his own private island."

Harriman smiled. "At the top level, art can be remarkably lucrative. Damien Hirst is holding an auction at Sotheby's in London next week, and he expects to clear over $150 million."

I hope he's not invested with you, thought JD.

They returned to the terrace, and Skip showed his calculations to Harriman. Harriman wrote it down and showed it to Puccini. "I still think you should leave it in the fund. But if you insist, I'll write you a check for this amount right here and now – no hard feelings."

Puccini looked at the number and did a little double take. He turned toward JD, who nodded yes. "I think I'll take the check. As you say, these are outstanding returns, and I really appreciate it. No hard feelings, Bucky."

Harriman excused himself, and came back five minutes later with a check for the amount agreed to. He shook hands with Puccini and JD, and said, "Grinny will show you out. Good luck, and keep your powder dry. And I take it there's no more need for your very capable friend to do any more analysis of our fund."

* * *

As they were driving back toward downtown, Puccini handed the check over to JD for inspection. "Not too bad, huh?"

JD glanced at the check. "Well done. But I assume you noticed that he didn't sell any securities. Any legitimate investment fund would have to sell some assets to get this much cash. Even money market funds are not instantly liquid, and no fund would leave this much capital in a bank account. He simply wrote you a check, and that's a dead giveaway. You received some cash that someone else just invested in the fund, and it's basically hush money. He didn't like the questions I was asking and wanted you to go away quietly."

Puccini took back the check. "I guess I should feel guilty, but I have to look out for my kids and their college fund. I'll talk to my friends at the FBI. Maybe they can get at him. And by the way, where should I invest this money now?"

"Just deposit it immediately to make sure the check is good, and then call your broker and put it all in Treasury bonds. That's where everyone will be fleeing in a few weeks when the panic hits. Right now Treasuries are cheap. Stay away from stocks for at least six months, maybe longer. When you want to get back into stocks, give me a call. There will be some bargains around when the dust settles."

"You think the sons are in on it?"

"It's hard to say. Grinny's not the sharpest knife in the drawer, but Skip knows his way around financial software."

Puccini continued driving, and as they approached Greenwich Avenue, he said, "How about some lunch? I have a little more personal time. I'll be working late tonight."

"Who looks after your kids? How can you work such long shifts?"

"I have a live-in nanny. Lucia's parents are helping with the finances. He's a partner in a Wall Street law firm, and they love their grandkids. Lucia would be very happy to see how well Isabella and Angelo are doing." Puccini was silent for a few seconds. "I still miss her."

Puccini parked the car in front of d'Allessandro's. "I can't really afford this place, but this is a special occasion. Let's celebrate."

They went in. Michael d'Allessandro was busy overseeing the seating arrangements and chatting with a few regular customers. He saw JD and said, "Welcome, Dr. Dionne. Would you like your regular table? Will Dr. Ghanem be joining you as well?"

"Yes, please, Michael, my regular table, and it will be just the two of us. I'd like you to meet Detective Antonio Puccini."

D'Allessandro smiled. "A detective from Italy? I hope we're not under investigation."

Puccini grinned a little at the weak joke. "Actually, I'm with the Greenwich police, and this isn't a work visit. Nice place you've got here."

As they sat down at the corner table, Puccini said, "So this is where you investor types hang out. The owner acted like he was your long-lost buddy."

"I come here once a week with my friend Fareed Ghanem. His office is just down the street, on the other side of Greenwich Avenue." JD pointed toward Fareed's office. "In fact, I'd like to talk to you about Fareed. And it has to do with Mortimer, that artist I discussed with Harriman. Fareed agreed to buy one of Mortimer's pieces, and Mortimer reneged when he got a better offer. Now Fareed is suing him, and this is where things start to get complicated."

"So I hope he likes to spend money. Lawsuits can go off the rails quickly. And over a piece of art?" Puccini almost sneered at the idea.

"It looks like Mortimer doesn't like being sued. He sent a very intimidating associate to try to convince Fareed to drop the suit."

Puccini pursed his lips in thought. "Intimidating, huh? But did he actually mention Mortimer by name? Maybe it wasn't Mortimer. Maybe the new buyer sent him."

"That could be. That's what my wife thinks."

Puccini smiled. "Smart wife, keeps an open mind. Now, did this associate threaten . . . Fareed? . . . Did I get that name right?"

"Not explicitly. It was all implied. 'It would be terrible if your family had an accident' . . . that sort of thing."

"Sounds like a pro who knows the law. There's not much we can do unless he makes a real threat. But if Fareed has a good description, maybe we can at least identify him. Does your friend have a security system with cameras?"

"Yes, he does. Maybe you could meet with Fareed to check this guy out?"

Puccini shrugged. "He could just drop the lawsuit and buy something else. End of story."

"You don't know Fareed. Once he makes up his mind, he never backs down. That's probably why he's been so successful in investment management."

"Then maybe I should invest with him. But you know, there's something else I wanted to talk about. In fact, that's why I wanted to have lunch. I really appreciate the help you gave me in getting my money out from Harriman. I was thinking . . . maybe we could use your skills elsewhere."

The waiter came to the table and asked if they'd had a chance to look at the menu. Puccini ordered a steak, medium rare, plus a diet Coke, and JD ordered seared tuna with a small bottle of San Pellegrino.

JD said, "Use my skills elsewhere? What do you have in mind? Are some of the other detectives invested with Harriman?"

"I think the Chief is, and I've got to talk to him. But I'm thinking of something else. There's a lot of financial fraud in Greenwich, because there's so much money floating around. But we don't really have the tools to get at it. The FBI can help us, but they're not always available. That's where you come in. You've got the forensic accounting, so you could dig out the evidence and be a credible expert witness in court. You could help us catch these cheating bastards, make the world a better place."

"It's not easy to catch crooks in good suits. Money talks, and it also makes people reluctant to talk. Plus it pays for first-class lawyers."

"I think you could take them on, JD. I watched you handle Harriman."

JD leaned back and smiled. "Now you're bullshitting me again, detective."

"You can call me Tony," Puccini said, "and no, I'm not. I think you could help us catch scum like Harriman. So what about it? You want to help us?"

JD hesitated. "To get at Harriman, I might have to play by his rules. I'm not sure I can do that. And if I did, you wouldn't want to know about it."

"So I don't have to know. Don't want to know. What's the big deal? Just give me plausible deniability. But are you in or out?"

"Maybe . . . I'll think about it. I may shut down the fund when we cash in all those credit default swaps. My clients are unhappy with my strategy, and I'm tired of holding their hands. And if my big bet pays off, I won't need any more money."

"I've never heard anyone say *that* before . . . not needing any more money."

"The family's looked after, my mother on Christian Island is good, and I have the house, three guitars, a nice Porsche, and a big boat. What more could I want?"

"Your lack of greed is really commendable but very weird, Joshua. Anyway, consider my offer. Not much money, but lots of satisfaction."

"Okay, I'll think about it. By the way, I hear you unlocked Rich's laptop. Could I borrow it for a day or so? I'd like to see what he was working on." *Especially concerning Yates,* JD added silently.

"I can't do that right now. It's evidence and it's locked up tight."

"I see," JD said coldly, suddenly losing enthusiasm for Puccini's idea.

Puccini's eyes narrowed. "What's the problem, pal?"

"If I agree to work with you, it'd be like this, wouldn't it? I'd always be on the outside looking in?"

"That's how it is. You're not a cop. Not much I can do about that."

JD nodded, unsurprised but still wanting to get all the information he could out of Puccini. "I hear you gave Dorothy Bridger a really hard time."

"I can't talk about that, JD. Sorry."

"Do you really think she had something to do with it?

"The evidence will lead us wherever it leads. That's all I can say."

The food came, and they ate quietly, mostly making small talk. After lunch, Puccini drove JD home. He stepped out to admire the Porsche Turbo in JD's driveway. "That's quite the car. Roll cage, racing seats, a cut-off switch. You must get a lot of tickets." Puccini smiled.

JD couldn't help smiling back at Puccini. *If you only knew,* thought JD to himself. "Last one I got was ten years ago. I do my driving on a proper racetrack with the Porsche Club. Lime Rock, Watkins Glen, Mosport. That's my relaxation."

"Well, be careful. That's a tricky car. They call it the widow-maker. And thanks again for helping me with Harriman. Think about my offer. We'd make a great team. Your brains and my . . . whatever."

"Except when you have to be a cop."

Puccini grinned and pulled away.

* * *

Annie was finally back in the studio, painting. JD watched for a while as the reds and yellows joined the patch of blue on one side and the dark purple at the bottom. "Are you still angry with me for that comment about Dot?"

Annie continued painting. "We've known Dot for a long time. How could you believe a cop you just met against the word of one of our best friends?"

JD sat down. "I'm sorry. Puccini can be quite convincing. He said he found something on Rich's computer."

Annie turned toward JD. "Do you actually think that Dot might be involved somehow?"

"No, I'm sure she's not. Can we please just move on now?" JD was still skeptical about Dot - after all, being married to Rich might push any woman over the edge - but he knew there was no point in discussing it with Annie. He'd have to deal with it on his own.

Annie seemed satisfied, and started mixing a new shade of orange on her palette. "How was the meeting with Harriman?"

"Quite bizarre. I met the whole family. Bucky, Grinny and Skip. The patriarch and his two sons, but it sounds more like three chipmunks. And it was in Belle Plains, which was an experience. It felt like the Roaring Twenties with air conditioning and wi-fi. But Puccini got his money back, and he treated me to lunch at d'Allessandro's. He wants me to work with him on financial fraud cases."

"That sounds interesting. Why don't you try that? You seem bored, and your clients can be very frustrating."

"I said I'd think about it, Annie . . . yeah, think about it." He sat back and looked out the window. "And how *is* Dot, by the way?"

"She's calmed down a little. But she's worried sick about Rich, and it doesn't help that Puccini is harassing her."

"I'm still trying to place that woman in the security video at the hotel."

"Maybe Dot has some pictures from Yale that will jog your memory. I'll ask her."

"Also ask her if there are any reports in Rich's office about Yates's fund. He might have left a paper trail, and that would be a big help. Puccini wouldn't let me borrow Rich's laptop, and he wouldn't say anything about Dot's interrogation."

"So your new buddy keeps things close to the vest."

"He's a cop. They're a very tight bunch."

JD went back to his office and started work on Yates's fund. There wasn't much public information, and all the media reports were positive. In sharp contrast to Harriman's fund, he saw no reports of any SEC investigation. And JD had no investment reports or transaction reports as he had for Harriman. This investigation would be more difficult.

JD's cell phone rang, and he saw it was Fareed.

JD answered, but at first there was no sound. Then he could hear some faint breathing, and what sounded like a sob. After about ten seconds, Fareed finally spoke.

"They killed Raji."

"What? How? What happened?"

"They slit his throat. Someone snuck into the back yard and slit Raji's throat. He's dead."

CHAPTER 8

JD couldn't quite believe it. Raji, Fareed's beautiful black Labrador retriever, was dead. He'd been brutally killed by a backyard intruder, his throat slashed

He remembered how Fareed and his daughter Vivian had gone to the breeder to select that puppy almost ten years ago, and how Fareed had bonded almost instantly with the little black furball. Fareed had never had a dog before, but Vivian had insisted on getting one, and Fareed soon became a convert, a true dog lover. And Raji became an honorary member of their band, an integral part of every practice. And now he was gone.

"I'm so sorry, Fareed," JD said on the phone. He wished he could be more eloquent, but he was too upset. Fareed was still almost unable to speak. JD could hear his quiet sobbing. "Do you want me to come over?" JD asked.

JD could hear Fareed blowing his nose, and then his friend finally spoke. "Raji was such a beautiful dog. He loved everyone. How could they do this?"

"I don't know. It doesn't make sense." JD's mind was racing. Rich's disappearance had been a shock, and the graphic evidence in the hotel room was still seared in his memory. Another violent event so soon was almost overwhelming. He was starting to feel queasy. But he knew Fareed was even more devastated, so he tried to keep his voice steady. "Is Heema there? Do you need some help?"

"Yes, she's here. I wrapped Raji in a blanket and carried him inside. I didn't want her to see him like this."

"Have you called the police?"

"I called them, but they referred me to Animal Control. I told them that this was a deliberate act of intimidation, but they were not interested." Fareed paused to blow his nose again. "I think this is tied to John Smith's visit. They left a picture of Mortimer's sculpture next to Raji's body. Could you please discuss this with Detective Puccini? I am now afraid for my family."

"Raji *was* part of your family, Fareed. I'll call Puccini right now. Please don't touch that picture. It might have fingerprints."

JD hung up and called Puccini's cell phone, but the call went directly to voicemail. He walked over to Annie's studio, where she was still working on the red and yellow painting. He watched her for a while, not wanting to disturb her, until she finally turned and looked at him. When she saw JD's face, she put down her brush.

"You look like death warmed over," she said. "What's wrong?"

JD dropped into a chair and held his head in his hands. "It's about Fareed. Someone killed Raji."

Annie took a deep breath and sat down across from JD. She gently put her hand on his knee. "What happened? Was he hit by a car?"

"No, it was very deliberate. Raji was in the backyard. Someone slit his throat."

Annie was silent for a moment, and her face turned pale. Then she tilted her head forward and closed her eyes tight. A tear trickled down her cheek. "That is really, really sick. I can't believe it. Who would kill an innocent dog like that? And in such a brutal way."

"They left a picture of Mortimer's sculpture next to Raji. It's intimidation."

Annie opened her. "Are the police involved?"

"Fareed called them, but they fobbed him off to Animal Control. They weren't interested. I've called Puccini to see if he can help."

"I think we're dealing with a crazy person. This could be a psychopath."

"Maybe. Or maybe it's just a callous way of doing business. Someone wants that sculpture and will go to any lengths to get it. Or maybe Mortimer doesn't like paying lawyers."

"Do you think this may be tied somehow to Rich's disappearance? We've now had two violent incidents just a few days apart, aimed at two people who are good friends. That seems like an odd coincidence, especially in a place like Greenwich."

JD paused. "It's possible. But if Rich was abducted because he was on to Yates, tying it to Raji's death is a bit of a stretch. Yates's fraud and Mortimer's sculpture don't seem to have anything in common."

Then he remembered something. "But Harriman also had one of Mortimer's sculptures. He says he's a good friend of Mortimer. And Harriman got Yates started in the investment fund business. So Yates and Mortimer have only one degree of separation. They're both connected to Harriman."

Annie seemed lost in thought. "I think there's a common thread. It's just a gut feeling."

JD was silent for a few seconds as he contemplated the probabilities in his mind. Maybe Rich's disappearance and the killing of Fareed's dog *were* linked somehow. JD had gone for decades – in fact, since that mugging in Boston - without being personally affected by violence, and now two good friends had suffered violent incidents within a week. Was it just coincidence? Not very likely. And there was another common factor. Both attacks involved a knife. "I think you may be right," he finally said. "These two attacks may be related. They're not random."

His cell phone rang, and it was Puccini. "So what's up?" the detective asked.

JD got right to the point. "Fareed's dog was deliberately killed in his backyard just now, and we think it's tied to that sculpture I told you about." JD paused, and took a deep breath. He could visualize Raji with his throat slashed. "And Fareed called 9-1-1, but they said to take it to Animal Control. I think it's more serious than that. Do you think you could look into it?"

Puccini sighed heavily. "We're kind of overloaded right now. Tell me exactly what happened."

"Fareed called me half an hour ago. His dog was a beautiful black Lab, and someone slit its throat. Then they left a photo of that sculpture beside the dog's body." JD had to steady himself to continue. "It seems to be connected to John Smith's visit and those threats. Have you had a chance to look into Smith?"

"Not yet. I told you, we're kind of busy. We're trying to figure out what happened to your friend Bridger."

"I know, and I appreciate that, but Fareed's very upset, and he's afraid his family could be next. Could you do me a big favor and meet with him? This could get worse. Isn't killing animals how serial killers get started?"

"Maybe. Or maybe someone got tired of a dog barking all night. Wouldn't be the first time. But okay, a knife in broad daylight is not your typical MO. So we can have a short meeting tomorrow. But I warn you, it's just a formality. There's not much I can do. The Chief would go ape-shit if he found out I'm dealing with a dog case when we've got half the department working on Bridger."

"What about that picture of the sculpture? Doesn't that paint a different scenario?"

"I don't have much time for scenarios right now, but bring it along. I'll see you both tomorrow at ten."

JD hung up and looked at Annie, shaking his head. Then he called Fareed and briefed him on the conversation with Puccini. They agreed that JD would pick up Fareed at nine-thirty the next morning, and they'd meet with the detective at the PSC.

* * *

Breakfast next morning was somber. It was September 11th, and much of the morning news coverage dealt with the seventh anniversary of the World Trade Center tragedy. JD, Junior, and Annie watched mostly in silence. There was nothing to say as they watched the image of the two burning towers, with black smoke billowing into the clear blue sky. JD thought about two friends from MIT who perished that day. And now it had been three days since Rich had disappeared. The tragic memories of the World Trade Tower heightened his worries about Rich. The blood and severed finger floated by his mind's eye and combined slowly with images of people jumping off that tower. JD had to walk over to the window to clear his mind. He looked at the oak trees swaying in the backyard and felt a little better.

After breakfast, JD walked down the hall to his office. He took a deep breath to clear his head of the awful images he had seen, and started work again on digging into Yates's fund. He first used public sources, examining the overall returns of the fund as shown in Yates's marketing material. The returns were good, but not outstanding, and they bounced up and down a little. They did not look as contrived as Harriman's. So either Rich was wrong about Yates, or Yates had covered his tracks much better than Harriman. JD considered it carefully. Yates was a plagiarist, but he'd been smart enough to get into the Ph.D. program at Yale. He was very intelligent and knew a lot about statistics, which meant he could have set up his fake returns to be statistically credible. JD would have to get into his transaction reports to get the whole story.

He glanced at the time on the screen– nine o'clock. It was time to pick up Fareed and meet with Puccini. He'd have to drop his investigation for now.

He fired up the Porsche and headed back south through downtown, then onto the Turnpike, and over to Riverside where Fareed lived. He knocked on the front door, and Heema answered. She was still dressed in her housecoat, and her eyes were red and puffy, almost the same color as her bindi, the little red mark on her forehead. She was short and stocky, with dark brown eyes, and her black hair was pulled back in a wavy ponytail.

Heema clutched the collar of her housecoat tightly. "Come in, please, JD, and sit down. Fareed has taken Raji to the veterinarian to have him cremated. We both said our good-byes this morning."

JD sat down in the living room. The house seemed very quiet, almost ghostly, without the dog. He half expected Raji to come running around the corner, tail wagging furiously, and bounding over to lick his hand.

Heema seemed to sense what he was thinking. "I miss him too, Joshua. Could I offer you some coffee while you are waiting?"

JD said, "Yes, thank you," and Heema went to the kitchen. A few minutes later Fareed came in the front door. He looked like he hadn't slept much. "It wasn't a very pleasant task, but I wanted to take care of it right away. When we receive Raji's ashes, I will spread them in his favorite spot near the shore. He loved the water."

JD looked at his friend. "I'm so sorry. I missed him as soon as I walked in, but for you it must feel terrible. He was part of your life for a long time."

Fareed sat down heavily. "It was a wonderful ten years, and I will never forget him. I loved him very much. He was part of the family in every way."

Fareed and JD sat silently for a minute. Then Fareed's face turned a little colder. "I miss him, Joshua, but we must move on. We need to catch the people who did this." He got up with a determined look on his face. "Let me show you where it happened."

Fareed led JD to the backyard. The yard was almost fifty yards deep, with a fenced-in swimming pool on the left side, and large maple trees at the back. There was a hedge on the right side, and the grass was carefully manicured. Fareed walked about halfway down the yard to a dark spot on the lawn. "This is where they killed Raji. They must have come through those big trees at the back."

"Have you checked with the neighbors? Did anyone see anything?"

"No. I would expect the police to do that."

JD fought back a stab of impatience. He was now looking at the world in a new way, and assumed that Fareed should be doing the same – paying attention to details. Someone might have seen the intruders, and could provide a description. But he sensed that this wasn't the time to tell his friend.

"Then we should go downtown and talk to Puccini right away. Where's the picture they left behind?"

They went back inside the house, where two coffees were waiting in the kitchen. Fareed ignored them and went back to his office. He returned with the photograph of the Mortimer sculpture, encased in a clear plastic zip-lock bag. He pulled on latex gloves and removed the picture from the bag, placing it on the table. The photo was small, only postcard size, and looked like it had been printed off a computer. There was no caption, and no visible marks of any kind except two dark spots that looked like dried blood.

JD examined it carefully. "There's not much there. But we'll take it along to show Puccini."

Fareed frowned. "On the contrary, I think this picture is very significant. It shows the motivation for Raji's murder."

"I agree that there's a message here about possible motivation, Fareed. I just meant there may not be anything on it to identify who killed Raji. We have to start thinking in terms of proof and evidence. Let's take it downtown and see what we have."

* * *

In the police station JD introduced Fareed to Puccini, who then led them to a small interrogation room, one without cameras. The detective put his notebook and laptop on the table and asked them to sit down. "I'm very sorry about your dog, Dr. Ghanem. I've had a chance to check up on a few possible John Smiths, and I'd like you to look at some pictures."

Puccini opened his laptop and turned it sideways so that Fareed and JD could see the screen. He started scrolling slowly through some portraits of what looked like football players or professional wrestlers. As he got to the fourth picture, Fareed said loudly, "That is he. That is John Smith."

Puccini scrolled to the left so they could read Smith's bio. "He works as head of security for Stuart Cole of Cole Strategic Investments. Former Army Ranger, served in Iraq in Desert Storm. Seven confirmed sniper kills. He tried police work after the army, but it didn't work out. Insubordination and excessive use of force. He's been with Cole for three years. No criminal record." Puccini paused and looked at JD. "And it's an odd coincidence that we have an investment fund involved again here. First we had Yates's fund and Bridger, and now it's Cole with this intimidation. Hedge funds are supposed to be paper pushers, not the Mafia."

JD shook his head. "There are about three hundred hedge funds around Greenwich, and most of them use heavy security. And there's no doubt that a few of them cut corners. It's the nature of the business, and there's always the threat of kidnapping. So the security doesn't surprise me."

Fareed was still staring intently at the picture. “I remember that face very well. I had assumed that Smith worked for Mortimer when he came for that first visit.” He rubbed his chin, deep in thought. “But it is becoming clear to me now. My lawyer hired a private investigator, and he discovered that Stuart Cole is the one who actually offered Mortimer more money for the sculpture after I had bought it. And now you say that Smith works for Cole. That connection to Stuart Cole proves that killing Raji was about the sculpture, and that Smith did it. Would you not agree, detective?”

Puccini shook his head. “I’m afraid it proves nothing. To use a fancy economics term, all you have is a hypothesis. You have a possible motive, but that’s just the start. This guy’s a war hero. You need physical evidence or a witness, preferably both.”

Fareed reached into his briefcase and pulled out the photo of Mortimer’s sculpture. “This is the picture I found beside Raji’s body.” He placed it on the table, still protected by the plastic bag. “That is physical evidence.”

Puccini picked up the bag and examined the picture inside. “Looks like it has some blood on it. I’ll give it to forensics and have it checked out. This guy’s Smith is a pro, so we probably won’t find anything. And please keep this quiet. I don’t want the Captain to find out I’m using our forensics lab for a canine case.”

JD said, “And what about Stuart Cole? Smith is connected to him, and Cole is connected to the sculpture. Maybe you should talk to him. I know Cole’s hedge fund. He’s a big shooter, running almost a billion.”

“Look, JD, I appreciate what you’ve done for me with Harriman, but there’s a limit to what I can do in return. We’ve got everyone working on Bridger, and I have to account for my hours. And I have some news on Bridger. I got it classified as a homicide, and I’ve opened a Homicide Book on the case. It brings the whole investigation up a notch, and – ”

“Excuse me, detective, are you saying that Richard is dead?” interrupted Fareed.

Puccini shook his head. “No, we don’t know that. It’s only been three days. There’s still hope. But by opening the Book, it kicks the whole investigation up a notch, and we can get more cooperation from the FBI. If he *is* still alive, it increases our chances of finding him.”

"So in a sense it's good news," JD said.

"Yeah, and believe me, getting it reclassified wasn't easy. The Captain and the Chief said this case is taking up too much of my time. There's another big one about to break. We've had someone undercover for two years."

Fareed scratched his head. "What is a Homicide Book? It is a very odd title."

"It's a file with every report and every test result on the case, from the beginning," Puccini explained. "It makes the case highest priority, much more important than a missing person."

"Are there any further leads?" JD asked.

"We have lots. We're checking alibis and motives, matching DNA and fingerprints. We're making progress. We have a number of suspects."

"Anyone we know?"

"JD, you know I can't talk about that."

Fareed pointed at the picture on the table. "And what about this? When can we see the results?"

Puccini put the photo on top of his notebook. "It'll take a few days. I'll let you know as soon as I've got it. Give me your cell number."

Fareed looked anxious. "And what about Stuart Cole and John Smith? Will you interrogate them?"

Puccini shrugged. "I'll try to sit down with Cole and Smith. But I have nothing on them except that social visit, so they may just tell me to get lost. I'll see how it goes, try to push them a bit." He glanced down at the picture on his laptop. "This Smith character looks interesting. I'd like to find out more about him, get a feel for what he's like. No criminal record, but that doesn't mean he's clean."

Fareed nodded. "Speaking of John Smith, I am very worried about my family. Killing Raji might be just the start. Can you provide us with some protection?"

"I can try to send a patrol car out through your neighborhood to check on your house once in a while."

"I appreciate that, detective, but an occasional patrol car does not provide me with much security."

"That's all I can do, and believe me, even that won't come easy. I'll have to embellish the dog story a little. But why don't you hire a professional bodyguard if you're nervous? I know some retired detectives who could do that for you."

JD said, "Fareed, maybe you should think about that before Smith comes for a second . . . or third . . . visit."

Fareed looked skeptical. "How would that work, detective? Would he come and live with us?"

"You can make any arrangement you want. It's mostly a matter of how much you want to pay. You want me to give you some names?"

"Yes, please. A bodyguard sounds like a splendid idea."

Puccini tilted his head and paused. "My real advice to you, Dr. Ghanem . . . the way you could probably make this all go away? Drop that lawsuit against Mortimer."

A muscle in Fareed's neck started twitching. "Detective, I'm afraid you don't understand. This has now become a matter of principle. I cannot lose face. I will hire a bodyguard. Please send me those names."

JD sighed, resigned to his friend's stubbornness, and then turned toward Puccini. "Thank you for making the extra effort, and for opening the Homicide Book. Just one more thing . . . do you think there's a connection between Rich's disappearance and Fareed's dog?"

"I'm not going to speculate. Without evidence, it's academic. And this is all I can do for you now. I have to get back to work."

Puccini got up, and Fareed and JD followed him out. A younger detective took them downstairs, and JD drove Fareed back to Riverside. As he was leaving Fareed's house to return home, the "check engine" light on the dashboard of the Porsche came on.

"Great," JD muttered. "That's all I need right now – car trouble."

CHAPTER 9

The CEL – Check Engine Light – on the dashboard of JD's Porsche Turbo was glowing bright red. There was a problem with the engine. The only way to get a proper diagnosis was to take it to his mechanic, but he knew of one possible cause that did not require a complicated computer plug-in -- carbon build-up in the secondary air injection ports. It reminded him of the problems he'd had with the old Alfa Romeo Spider he and Annie had driven in England when he was at Oxford. That Alfa had Weber carburetors, and if the car wasn't driven aggressively, the spark plugs would foul, and the car would stumble and run rough. The way to clear the plugs was to do an "Italian tune-up," which consisted of taking the Alfa out on a high-speed motorway and driving it very hard for half an hour. That always did the trick, as the plugs would clear, and the car would run smoothly until the next time he was stuck in traffic.

He decided to try his old Italian tune-up trick, and he knew just the right place. Before he had started taking his car to Lime Rock, Watkins Glen and other racetracks for track days, he had done his own private laps around certain suitable roads right in Greenwich. He would only do it occasionally, using the latest radar and laser detectors to avoid the speed traps, and he would do only one lap at a time in case the very wealthy neighbors along his special route became anxious and called the police - or put their security staff on him. He called it his One Lap of Greenwich, an allusion to the notorious and highly illegal road race called One Lap of America, which had run from New York to Santa Monica back in the seventies.

JD had stumbled on these perfect test roads up in northern Greenwich, the land of ten-acre lots, long driveways, and lots of hills and curves. The houses were set so far back that most of them could not be seen from the road, and there was almost no traffic. JD turned on his radar detector and started north toward the Merritt Parkway to do his One Lap of Greenwich.

The Merritt Parkway had opened in 1940, and it was one of the oldest divided highways in the nation. Lined with mature trees, it had two lanes in each direction, passing under elegant Art Deco bridges designed by a prominent architect of the day. Unlike modern limited-access highways, the merge lanes on the entrance ramps were very short, making merging difficult for slower cars. The speed limit on the Parkway was only fifty-five miles an hour, except for two sharp curves near Putnam Lake, where the speed dropped to forty-five. When JD did his One Lap of Greenwich, he entered those sharp curves at ninety miles an hour – twice the speed limit.

JD headed up Glenville Road toward the Parkway, passing elegant houses on large lots set well back from the road. He settled in behind a silver Mercedes driving barely above the speed limit. There was no point in trying to pass on this winding road, so he relaxed and focused on the events of the past week.

JD knew that the most likely suspect in Rich's disappearance was Yates, but he still wondered about Dot. Puccini seemed to think that she might be involved somehow. JD was very aware that Dot was one of Annie's best friends, and Annie was totally convinced that Dot was innocent. Okay, but . . . maybe Annie was too close to see the truth. JD knew that Rich and Dot had had a big argument the week before. Had Rich asked for a divorce? That could be a motive. And something about the way Dot had been behaving since Rich disappeared seemed off. She was certainly upset, but she almost seemed more upset by Puccini's questioning. Of course, everyone knew that the spouse was always the first suspect, so maybe that's why she was so hostile. And yet, if she had nothing to hide, why would she be so defensive? Was it possible that Puccini was getting too close to the truth? JD shook his head. The way he saw it, Yates had a much stronger motive to hurt Rich. And maybe Puccini was just doing his job, having to check out Dot as a suspect.

He glanced at the turbo boost gauge, and all was well. The Mercedes was still dawdling, so as they trundled along, JD's thoughts turned again to the other case - Fareed's dog. As he had said to Annie, Greenwich was a quiet place, and having two violent events less than a week apart – happening to two friends - was off the charts in terms of low probabilities. And what did the two incidents have in common? Well, both Rich and Fareed had seriously pissed off powerful people – Yates in Rich's case, and Cole in Fareed's. He started wondering again if Yates and Cole were connected somehow. They both ran investment funds, but you couldn't swing a cat in Greenwich without hitting a dozen hedge funds, so that wasn't much of a coincidence. But was there another link between them? School? Art collecting? Greenwich was a small town, so Cole and Yates probably knew each other. Maybe Smith was involved in kidnapping Rich. He certainly had the skills.

The silver Mercedes in front of him turned left along Glen Ridge, and JD had to focus his attention back on the road. JD turned right, heading up Riversville toward the Parkway. He speeded up a little once the Mercedes was gone, but stayed close to the speed limit. There were too many houses close to the road here to open up the Porsche quite yet.

JD's thoughts were interrupted by a glance in his rearview mirror. Two black SUVs were driving right behind him, almost on his bumper. He was certain they hadn't been there earlier. Where had they come from? He felt a jolt of adrenaline course down his arms.

He decided to speed up slightly as he came to a left hand bend in the road, to see how the two SUVs responded. The Porsche accelerated sharply, sputtering just a little as the turbocharger spooled up, and he looked in the mirror again. The two SUVs had also speeded up. Something was going on. As they closed in again, he could see they were Cadillacs. He felt a small bead of sweat start down his back. But he knew that if those two drivers wanted to give him any trouble, his four-hundred-horsepower Porsche would take care of business as soon as he hit the Parkway. He'd be long gone.

JD reached the entrance ramp to the Parkway. The short merging lane was clear, traffic was light, and he floored the accelerator. Within a quarter mile, he was moving at over a hundred miles an hour. He had to maneuver sharply to avoid two slower cars, but then the highway ahead was clear and he accelerated to a hundred and thirty. The Parkway turned gently to the right, and as he passed under the bridge at Round Hill Road without slowing down, he looked in his rearview mirror.

Both black SUVs were still right behind him. At a hundred and thirty miles per hour.

Sweat started to trickle down his forehead, and he could feel his heart pounding.

Holy shit. Those trucks are fucking fast.

There was another gentle bend to the right after the bridge, and JD had to brake slightly as the Porsche started drifting into the left lane. The two SUVs behind him slowed. There was no way they could keep pace through this curve at a hundred and ten, and a sharper bend was coming up, just before the exit to North Street. JD could hear the Porsche's tires screaming in protest as he took that next sharp bend at ninety, and the Porsche started to rotate slowly into a spin. He remembered his track training and feathered the throttle, just on the edge of spinning, with the car heading down the highway sideways at ninety miles an hour. He very gently counter-steered the Porsche back into a straight line, hit the brakes hard, and took the exit ramp to North Street.

Fuck, that was way too close. I almost bought the farm back there.

He glanced in the mirror, and saw no sign of the black SUVs. He took a deep breath. His hands were shaking and sweaty, and his neck was so tight he could hardly move it.

He slowed down to the speed limit, heading for home. He didn't want to take a direct route in case they were still following him, so he turned right at Clapboard Ridge and headed toward Round Hill, part of his regular One Lap of Greenwich. He came to the stop sign at Lake Avenue and downshifted, rolling to a stop. He could see the red "Check Engine" light still glowing, but dealing with that was now the last thing on his mind. He wanted to get home safely. He instinctively checked his rearview mirror as he came to the intersection.

The two black SUVs were right behind him again.

Where the hell did they come from? I know damn well I lost them on the Parkway.

He turned left at the stop sign to head south, and started to accelerate hard to get away again, but the lead SUV drove right through the stop sign, and accelerated even harder. JD was momentarily distracted when he saw the big vehicle in his side mirror, and the Porsche started fishtailing as the rear tires lost traction. The SUV passed him on the left, and then the second SUV pulled up behind him. He could now hear their engines, and they had the slightly muffled rumble of turbochargers. These were not everyday Cadillac SUVs - they squatted much lower than standard on their oversized tires, and their engines were clearly not showroom stock.

They've got at least six hundred horsepower, he realized, *and they sure as hell know how to use them all.*

JD was now boxed in. The lead SUV started speeding up, and the one behind him also speeded up and started nudging his bumper. They were soon going eighty miles an hour down that hilly and winding two-lane road. And then JD remembered. About halfway down Round Hill Road, there was a sharp curve bordered by a fifty foot drop-off, and there were no safety barriers. In this fancy neighborhood, aesthetics were far more important than safety. That's where they were pushing him – toward that drop. His roll cage would be useless if the Porsche careened fifty feet into those trees at eighty miles an hour.

That's it. They want to see if this Porsche can fucking fly.

Then JD heard a new sound over the roar of the three engines - a sharp *Crack!* And a hole appeared in his windshield, a foot to the right of his head. Then there were two more gun reports, and another hole in his windshield. He couldn't stay boxed in where he was, or he'd be dead.

He slowed slightly to get a gap from the vehicle in front, and then accelerated hard as he turned the steering wheel sharply to the left in an attempt to pass the front SUV. But the SUV anticipated his move and also moved to the left, blocking him. He touched the brakes and moved back into the right lane again. He had one option left in his bag of tricks. His hands were slippery and his heart was pounding, but it was his last chance. The drop-off was coming up fast.

I have to try a bootlegger turn. It's now or never.

He turned the wheel sharply left, and simultaneously pulled the handbrake as hard as he could, locking the rear wheels.

It's all about the timing. I have to get this right.

The Porsche started to rotate counterclockwise, and as soon as the car had made a half-turn, he released the handbrake and slammed on the foot brake. The car kept sliding straight backwards in a cloud of tire smoke in the left lane as the rear SUV passed him, still going south in the right lane. As soon as the Porsche had stopped sliding backwards, JD stepped on the gas, heading north, away from the SUVs. The whole maneuver had taken less than ten seconds. He checked his rearview mirror. Both SUVs had stopped. They would have to make three-point turns to follow him, and by that time, he'd be out of sight. He continued to the closest intersection and turned downtown on Lake Avenue. There was more traffic there, and he felt safe. Even if the SUVs found him again, there were now too many witnesses.

He slowed down with the traffic and wiped his forehead with his sleeve. The sweat was rolling into his eyes and he could hardly see. He looked at the two gunshot holes in the windshield, and then he glanced at the dashboard, because something was different. The "Check Engine" light was no longer red. He patted the top of the dashboard in a gesture of thanks and took a deep breath.

How the hell did they know where he was going? He had lost them on the Parkway, and then they were right behind again. It was a very close call. He had to talk to Puccini to figure out what had just happened. Who was trying to kill him? And why?

JD continued down Lake Avenue to downtown, and parked behind the Public Safety Complex on Bruce Place. When he stopped, he realized he was almost in shock. He had to sit in the car for a few minutes, trying to bring his heart rate down - and to stop shivering as the sweat continued to pour down his back. His head was pounding. Then finally, his thinking started to clear a little. The only thing he could see in his mind's eye was Harriman. JD had threatened to expose Harriman's financial fraud, and the consequences had almost been fatal. *It's got to be Harriman.*

His breathing was finally becoming normal, so he picked up his cell phone and called Puccini. "Someone just tried to kill me, detective. They shot at me, and tried to run me off the road. I need to talk to you. I'm just outside in the parking lot. Can I come up?"

"Shot at you? Are you sure?"

"I'm looking at two bullet holes in my windshield. They almost parted my hair. I felt like a twelve-point buck on the first day of hunting season."

"In broad daylight? Where did it happen?"

"On Round Hill Road. They tried to run me off that big drop into the trees."

"The rich folks' playground. What were you doing up there?"

JD sighed. "It's a long story. Can I come up and talk about it?"

"Okay, I'll see what I can do. Give me a few minutes, and I'll meet you downstairs."

JD got out of the car and saw two more bullet holes in the rear window. The engine was making crackling and pinging noises as it cooled down, and he could see another bullet hole in the engine cover, just below the spoiler. He opened the cover to see if there was any damage, but the bullet had not hit any vital parts, and there were no obvious oil leaks. He checked under the engine for damage, but everything looked okay. Then he saw something new. It was a small black metallic box, less than an inch square, stuck to the bottom of a steel bumper support. He took out his handkerchief to cover his fingers and pulled on the box. It came right off. He turned the little box upside down, and saw that it had been held in place by a magnet.

So that's how they followed me. This must be some sort of tracking device.

He wrapped it in the handkerchief, put it in his pocket, and headed to the front desk. Puccini was waiting for him.

He took in JD with an appraising glance. "You're sweating like a quarter-horse. Looks like you really pissed somebody off. Let's go upstairs. You need a coffee?" He paused. "Or a glass of water? You look like hell."

Puccini led JD upstairs and they sat down in one of the interview rooms. Puccini left and came back with a cup of coffee and a bottle of water, juggling them as he held his laptop under his arm. He also had a small white towel draped over his shoulder. He opened the water bottle and gave it to JD, and then offered him the towel. "Here, wipe your face, pal. You'll ruin the furniture."

JD took the towel and wiped his face and neck, and then took a sip of water. "Thanks, Tony, I needed that."

"Tell me what happened."

JD took another sip, and then pulled the small metal box out of his pocket and put it on the table. "This is how they followed me. It was stuck to the bottom of my car."

"We had a couple of calls from Round Hill Road about possible gunshots. We sent a patrol car up there, and we'll see if they find anything."

"It was two black Cadillac SUVs. They were really low to the ground, good tires, and lots of power. The drivers knew their way around apexes and braking zones."

Puccini ran a hand through his hair. "It doesn't make sense. It's broad daylight, lots of traffic. There are easier ways to get you."

"This was probably not their first rodeo. Round Hill Road is deserted most of the time, the houses are out of sight. No one was around, there were no witnesses. They knew I was going over there. I lost them on the Parkway, but they knew exactly where to find me."

"Did you get a look at the drivers? Any license numbers?"

"The windows were blacked out, so I couldn't see them, and I didn't get their license plates. I was kind of busy staying alive."

"You should've called me as soon as you got away. We might've caught them."

JD felt a rising sense of irritation. "Look, as I said, I was too busy trying to avoid getting killed. This is all new to me. I'm a nerd in finance. I won't be able to sleep for a week, so don't push me." JD's voice softened. "I need your help."

Puccini took a sip of his coffee and started tapping his fingers on the table. "There's probably a hundred black Cadillac SUVs in this county, so that's not much to go on." He looked up at JD. "Any other thoughts? The obvious suspect is Harriman. He wasn't very happy about your questions. But he'd never do this sort of thing himself. He'd hire pros."

"These guys were pros, all right."

"We need to question Harriman, but I'm sure he'll have all the right answers. The main thing now is to keep you alive."

"That's an excellent idea, detective. Can you provide me with some sort of protection?"

Puccini shrugged. "No can do. We're stretched too thin. The best thing is to get a bodyguard, like Ghanem. I gave him some names, and he's interviewing them today."

JD shook his head. "I don't want a bodyguard. I can take care of myself. A bodyguard wouldn't have been much help today anyway."

"Maybe not. But think about it. In the meantime, you could get a concealed carry permit and a gun. You're defenseless right now. I can print off the forms, and get the waiting period waived. Just get yourself a nice Glock. You know how to shoot, right?"

"Annie and I already have guns and permits. Ever since Boston. And we know how to use them. We still go to the range every year."

"Actually, I knew that. I sort of forgot. But you might still want a bodyguard."

JD realized that Puccini had done a full background check on Annie as well. He wasn't sure how he felt about that. But he decided to move on.

"Maybe, but I think we have the skills to take care of ourselves. Right now, I have to take the car in for repair and get a rental car, so I should get going. Thanks for listening to me . . . even though there doesn't seem to be much you can do." Then JD had another thought. "By the way, did you want to see the car, maybe for forensics?"

Puccini nodded. "Yeah, I think we should give it the once-over downstairs. Leave it with us for a few days. We might find something. And you'll want our report for the insurance anyway. They might have some questions about the bullet holes, ask you if you were going around robbing banks."

JD handed the Porsche keys to Puccini. "Okay, thanks, but take it easy on any test drives. The 'check engine' light was on for a while. I'll just take a cab to the car rental place."

Just as JD was about to get up and leave, Puccini said, "There's just one more thing – I've got some pictures I want to show you. As a cop, I know I shouldn't do this, but I wanted to give you a heads-up." Puccini opened his laptop on the table and scrolled through some photos. When he came to the one he wanted, he turned the screen to face JD. "These were taken last night by a stake-out keeping tabs on Mrs. Bridger."

JD stared at a picture of Dot sitting in a restaurant with a man.

"That's Clint Houston, one of Professor Bridger's sparring partners. Mrs. Bridger and Mr. Houston look pretty friendly, don't you think?"

JD felt his stomach start churning. It was clear that Dot had not been telling Annie the whole truth. But then he calmed down. Maybe it was just two friends having dinner. "So what? They're just having dinner. She's upset and needed someone to talk to."

"Maybe. Nothing illegal about that, but it makes you think, right? She ever tell you Bridger made her sign a prenup when they married? If they get divorced, she gets nothing. And there's something else . . . this guy Houston's a black belt, too. Some of the pieces of this puzzle are starting to fit."

JD's eyes narrowed. "What are you going to do with this?"

"Nothing right now. We're still working in it. But I wanted you to see it."

JD thought about that for a moment. Why had Puccini wanted him to see it? The answer wasn't pretty. *He's testing me to see if I can keep my mouth shut.*

JD thanked Puccini, and one of the other detectives escorted him downstairs.

* * *

JD called a taxi, and instructed the driver to take him to a specific car rental agency that specialized in exotic automobiles. He rented a silver Mercedes C63 AMG–a car with 451 horsepower.

In case I run into those black Cadillacs again, he told himself.

He pulled into the driveway at home fifteen minutes later, and parked the Mercedes. As he walked in, Annie was standing in the living room staring at the new car, a look of surprise on her face. "Well, that was precipitous. You hadn't even mentioned getting new wheels. I thought you loved that Porsche. And a Mercedes? That's an old man's car."

"It's nice to see you too, dear. I've had a helluva day." JD sat down on the sofa.

Annie turned and inspected him more closely. "You do look worn out, JD." She sat down beside him and took his hand. "What happened?"

"It's been a crazy day. Two SUVs tried to run me off that cliff on Round Hill Road, and they took some shots at me." He shook his head, unable to believe his own words. "Someone tried to kill me. I was lucky to get away. There were some bullet holes in the car, and I left it downtown for forensics. The Mercedes is a rental."

Annie gasped. "Kill you? Who was it? Are you hurt?"

"No, they missed, and I used some of my track techniques to get away. I don't know who it was. But my guess is that it had to do with Harriman. I asked him some tough questions about his fund, and he wasn't very happy about that. I stopped off to see Puccini, but he says there's very little hope of catching whoever did this."

"What if these thugs come back? They're still out there somewhere."

"Puccini said he can't protect us much. He suggested a professional bodyguard."

"A bodyguard, here in the house? I'm not sure I could live with that." Annie bit her lip. "I want my life back. I don't want some stranger looking over my shoulder while I paint."

JD saw the anguish on her face. "I know. It's tough to deal with. But we got through it in Boston. We've seen violence before. I have my Glock and you have your Sig."

"I don't know, JD. We had them, but we never had to use them. This is different. It's not random muggings. We're being targeted."

Annie's cell phone rang. She glanced at it, and said, "It's Dot. I should answer this. She's still having a rough time." She excused herself and went to the kitchen. JD let his head rest on the back of the sofa and closed his eyes. He was starting to feel relaxed for the first time in hours, and then he remembered the picture of Dot and Houston that Puccini had showed him. He'd have to decide whether to tell Annie about it, and he could feel the muscles in his neck tightening again. His mouth suddenly felt very dry.

Annie came back from the kitchen a few minutes later, and said, "Dot sounded worried about something, and she wasn't very talkative. But she emailed me a link to those pictures of Yale faculty and students I had asked for, and I forwarded those to you. Maybe they'll give you some clues about that mystery woman who visited Richard at the hotel."

JD didn't respond, and Annie looked at him quizzically. "What's the matter?"

"Nothing. I was just resting. I'm really tired."

Annie put her hands on her hips. "Come on, JD. I can see it in your face. What's bothering you? It's something about Dot, isn't it?"

JD lowered his gaze. "It's about Dot, but I can't talk about it. Puccini would nail me."

"What? You don't trust me all of a sudden?"

"Sometimes you're better off not knowing."

Annie crossed her arms. A pink flush was moving up her cheeks as she said in a very slow, calm voice, "Joshua, this would probably be the first time you've kept something from me. We've always trusted each other completely. What the hell is going on here?"

JD stared down at the floor. "I just can't tell you. I'm sorry."

"Fine. You suddenly don't trust me. Well, let me ask you this. When have I ever broken that trust? Hey, that's an easy one, Joshua. The answer is . . . bloomin' never." She paused. "I suppose it's all relative, though. At least you're not lying to me." Annie glared at him silently. A muscle in her neck was twitching.

JD mulled it over for a few seconds. He had to make a decision, and quickly. "Okay, I'll tell you . . . but you're not going to like it. Puccini showed me some pictures the cops took last night at a restaurant. Dot was having dinner with Clint Houston, one of Rich's sparring partners. He has a black belt."

"So the goddam police were spying on her?" Annie was furious. "Shite, what kind of bloody country is this?"

"Annie, did you hear what I said? Dot hasn't been totally open with us, and Puccini thinks there's more to it. Especially the black belt part."

Annie crossed her arms and took some deep breaths, apparently trying to calm down. "So she was having dinner with someone. That's a lot better than sitting at home drinking and crying, don't you think? And Clint is Rich's friend. Why wouldn't she have dinner with him?"

"Puccini thinks it's suspicious."

"Puccini, Puccini, goddam Puccini. That's all I hear about now." She got up. "I'm going to the studio. You can make your own lunch." And she walked out.

JD felt bone-tired. And he knew he was in the danger-zone now with Annie. Maybe he shouldn't have told her. But they had always been honest with each other, and he wasn't ready to rip a hole in his marriage that couldn't be repaired. He had to tell her, Puccini be damned. But he still wasn't sure about Dot. The prenuptial agreement Puccini had mentioned put a new slant on things - a possible motive.

JD had no appetite for lunch after their argument, so he went back to his office to review the photographs that Annie had sent him. He opened her email and followed a link to a photo storage site, and there were hundreds of pictures from Yale, with captions and dates. Dot had been helpful - maybe trying to deflect suspicion? But maybe also trying to find out what had happened to her husband, JD reminded himself.

He started sorting through the pictures, looking closely at the women. One particular photo stopped him. There was something about the woman in the picture that looked familiar. But this woman was blond, and the woman at the hotel had dark hair. He printed the picture, and used a marker to darken the woman's hair. Then he opened the security photo from the hotel, and printed off that picture. He put the two pictures side by side.

It was the same woman

He went back to check the caption on the Yale photo. The woman in the picture was Courtney Yates, John Maynard Yates's wife. She was a few years younger in the Yale picture, but there was no doubt. JD pushed back his chair from the computer and ran his hand through his hair.

So Rich had been having an affair with Yates's wife. That would have provided an additional motive for Yates to hurt Rich. Or maybe, JD thought, Yates and his wife were working together. He had to get this to Puccini. The planets were aligning.

JD called Puccini, but his call went directly to voicemail. JD left a message saying he had figured out who the mystery woman was, and asking Puccini to call him right back. He returned to his computer and took another look at the picture. He started scrolling through the file to see if there were any other useful pictures.

He was still looking through them when Annie walked in. She sat down in one of the chairs, and rubbed her knees with her hands. At first she didn't say a word. She looked out the window, and then finally at JD. "I've had a chance to think about it, JD. Thank you for telling me about Dot's picture with Houston. It must have been difficult, breaking your word to Puccini."

"You were right. We have to trust each other."

"I'm not convinced Puccini is right. I think they were just having dinner. But it makes me wonder if there were other things . . . things she didn't want me to know about." Annie seemed lost in thought.

"I know I don't have to repeat this, but please don't let on that I've told you about the photo."

"You know I'll do my best, but you also know I'm not a very good liar." Annie gave him a wry smile. "I can't start avoiding her all of a sudden, not now when she's having such a rough time . . . Tell me something, Joshua. Do you think Dot *was* involved in Richard's murder?"

JD took a breath and sighed. "I don't know."

"Did Puccini say anything else about Clint Houston? We've met him, but I hardly remember him."

"No, but I'm guessing Puccini has questioned him already. Puccini doesn't disclose much. I think he told me about Dot and Houston to see if I could keep my mouth shut." JD paused and gazed up at Annie. "I haven't done too well on that score, have I?"

Annie smiled. "Don't worry, dear. Your secret is safe with me. It will be awkward, but I can do it."

JD turned toward the computer screen. "Speaking of pictures, I just had a major breakthrough. Come take a look at these." He placed the printout of the Yale picture with the retouched blond woman next to the hotel picture of the mystery woman from the hotel. Annie looked at them for about ten seconds, and said, "It's the same person, isn't it? Who is she?"

"It's Courtney Yates, John Maynard Yates's wife. She's the woman who was at the hotel with Rich."

Annie was silent for a few seconds. "That's a surprise, but then nothing Richard does really surprises me anymore."

JD nodded. "This opens up some complications on the case. Dot may be a suspect in Puccini's mind, but Yates also has an obvious motive. And his wife may be part of the motive . . . or part of the crime."

Annie got up and gave JD a kiss. "I've done enough thinking for one day. I hear some yellow and red pigment calling me." After she left, JD got back on his computer. He still had to figure out whether Yates's fund was fraudulent. Maybe Rich had been wrong about that, and Yates's main motive – if he *was* the one behind the attack – had to do with his wife's affair.

JD had just opened the website for Yates's fund when his cell phone rang. It was Puccini. "How's it going, JD? Your message said that you identified the woman who was at the hotel with Bridger."

"Yes, I found some old pictures from Yale and made a match with the hotel photo. It took a little retouching, because she's changed her hair color, but it's Courtney Yates, John Maynard Yates's wife. That's who's in the picture at the hotel."

"You're absolutely right, JD. We've already questioned her three times."

"What? You've already questioned her? Why didn't you tell me?"

"She's no longer a suspect. She was at the hotel on Sunday night, but she left before Bridger was taken, and she had a bullet-proof alibi for the rest of the night."

"Alibi? What kind of alibi?"

"Her husband. She was at home in Greenwich with John Maynard Yates."

"But if his wife was having an affair with Rich, wouldn't that be a motive for Yates to hurt him?"

"Maybe, but Yates has an alibi – his wife. So neither one could have done it. Or at least we can't prove it. We can't even check the DNA, because with the alibis, we can't get probable cause."

"That doesn't make sense. Maybe they were both involved, and they're covering for each other."

“Welcome to police work. If there’s no evidence, it didn’t happen.”

CHAPTER 10

JD sat in his office, thinking about the conversation he'd just had with Puccini. He still couldn't quite believe that Puccini had kept him in the dark about Courtney Yates. Puccini had already questioned her three times but had never mentioned it, and had already dismissed her as a suspect. And he'd eliminated Yates as well – or so he said.

It was like peeling away the layers of an onion. The deeper JD got, the more there was to it. He wanted to help catch whoever took Rich. But Puccini always seemed to be two damn steps ahead of him. What else was he keeping from JD? Did he actually know who took Rich? And where did Dot fit in? This was all very different from economic research, and JD was getting frustrated. In order to get more information from Puccini, it was becoming clear that he needed something to trade. He had to get ahead of Puccini's investigation in some area, and the best place to do it was in his own field of expertise – finance and economics. Maybe he could take a more mathematical approach to the puzzle. He freed his ponytail from his collar and started thinking about which techniques he could use.

Then his cell phone rang, and he saw that it was Fareed. "JD, I have good news. We now have a professional bodyguard. His name is Patrick Riley. He was a Navy SEAL before he became a security specialist. Heema is very pleased."

"That was quick. Where has he worked before? Did he have good references?"

"He was head of security for a major corporate executive up in Armonk, but they had a disagreement about his duties. He refused to tend bar at a party, but fortunately I have no need for a bartender. He will be staying at our house as long as necessary."

"I'm actually starting to wonder if *we* need a bodyguard," JD admitted. "Someone just tried to kill me this morning."

There was a pause on the phone. "Joshua, did you say someone tried to kill you? How? What happened?"

"Two SUVs tried to run me off that cliff on Round Hill Road, and they took some shots at me. I had to do a bootlegger turn to get away from them. I'm lucky to be alive."

"You have reported this to the police?"

"I talked to Puccini, but there's not much he can do. At least Annie and I have our guns."

"In my opinion, a professional bodyguard would be preferable. You are not on Christian Island anymore."

"I know." JD wanted to change the subject. "Listen, I figured out who that mystery woman was at the hotel. It was John Maynard Yates's wife."

There was a pause again as Fareed digested this new information. "Yates's wife? That complicates matters, does it not? It provides an additional motive for Yates."

"Yes, it does, but both Yates and his wife have alibis for the time when Rich was attacked. They were supposedly together at home. Puccini has already questioned them, though he didn't bother to tell me. "

JD heard footsteps behind him, and looked around to see Annie walk in and sit down. He said, "I'll call you later, Fareed. Annie just came in, and we need to talk." He disconnected.

Annie looked angry. "Did I just hear you say that Puccini knew all along that the woman in the picture was Yates's wife—and he never told you?"

"He's a cop and I'm a civilian, and that's how it's going to be. He was doing his job, and he doesn't want leaks."

"Why are you defending him? He should have told you, saved you all that effort. It's the least he could do after you got his life savings away from that fraudster."

"That was personal. This is business. Maybe he'll learn to trust me more as he gets to know me."

Annie shook her head. "He's using you. Maybe you should keep your distance from him. You're becoming a little obsessed with this detective business."

"But how else am I going to help find Rich's kidnappers? And track down whoever's trying to kill me?"

"Why don't you use the skills you have? As someone once said, follow the money. What about Yates's money?"

JD started to say something but realized that he was getting defensive. Annie had a point. "You're right. I need to figure out what Yates is up to, where he gets his capital. That's something Puccini can't do. He couldn't even figure out what Harriman was involved in, and neither could the SEC or the FBI."

Annie relaxed a little. "That would be a good start. By the way, how is Fareed doing? Is he starting to recover from Raji's death?"

"He seems okay. They've hired a bodyguard, a former Navy SEAL. Have you had a chance to think about that, whether we should get a bodyguard?"

"I have, and I don't want one. It seems like . . . pardon the pun . . . overkill. We have an alarm system, and we have our guns. Having a stranger wandering around would make me self-conscious about my painting. I'd rather look out for myself and have my privacy."

"Okay, if you're sure about that. We can still change our minds."

Annie got up and left for her studio. JD turned to his computer to start probing Yates's investment fund. What he needed to do was somehow recreate whatever the hell it was that Rich did to uncover Yates's fraud. But he didn't have access to any of Rich's computers, and he didn't have any client investment reports or transaction records. He would have to start from another angle. The best starting point again seemed to be a review of the Depository Trust Company records to determine whether Yates's fund had been doing any transactions. If there was no record of buying and selling stocks, the situation would be identical to Harriman's fund – a pure Ponzi scheme.

JD had already found an entry point to the DTC system in his investigation of Harriman, so he repeated his steps carefully, making sure that there was no sign that his earlier probe had been discovered. There was little doubt that the password had been changed since his last visit, so he used his password cracking program again. He knew from his last attempt that the brute-forcing tool and the cracking dictionary would be too primitive to break the password, so he went directly to the final step he had used previously – the three graphic processor units in parallel. These units were originally designed for high-definition computer animation, and three of them in parallel provided state-of-the-art speed in generating trillions of random password combinations. This time it took only half an hour, and he had the password. Then he had to get through the firewall. He started the SQL-injection attack and in another hour, he found an opening and was into the system. He pushed back his chair to take a break.

It had been a little easier this time, but he couldn't get cocky. He had to concentrate fully at each step. One wrong move, and he'd be looking for Annie to pay his bail after giving up his passport.

He took a deep breath and started searching the transaction files, looking for the Yates Alpha Fund, and he soon found it. *There were thousands of transactions in the file.* It appeared that Yates had actually been buying and selling stocks, doing real investing. But Rich had found something indicating fraud, so JD knew he had to dig deeper.

He had to stop and think. How could Yates be running a Ponzi if the transactions actually existed? One easy check was to see if the transaction flow added up to the assets under management – that is, whether the money that the investors had put into the fund equaled the total cost of the stocks that Yates had purchased. Yates's marketing materials claimed that the total assets were about two billion dollars, so JD just needed to add up the value of the stocks Yates had purchased and compare that total to that overall fund value that Yates claimed. JD quickly set up a program to tally the cumulative "buy" transactions in the Yates Alpha Fund. The total came to just over a billion dollars.

This meant that Yates had invested only *half* the money he got directly from investors. So Yates was running a "half-Ponzi," JD realized. It was quite clever, more sophisticated than Harriman's approach. It looked as if the student had surpassed the master. The SEC would have to dig deeper to catch Yates, and since they hadn't caught Harriman with his much more obvious fraud, they were unlikely to catch Yates. It was no wonder that Yates probably went ballistic when Rich discovered his scam.

JD now had what he needed. He carefully backtracked through the firewall, and checked twice to ensure that he had left no evidence of the intrusion. Once he was satisfied, he went out to the kitchen to prepare a cappuccino and think about his next step. That would be to call Puccini. This would definitely be news to him, and maybe would buy more confidence and trust from the detective - and maybe more information about the investigation.

He tapped Puccini's number on his speed-dial, and to his surprise, Puccini picked up right away. "What's happening, JD? Anything new?"

"I found something interesting. Rich was right. Yates is running a Ponzi, but it's different from Harriman's. More intricate."

There was silence for a few seconds. "How do you know that? We've been checking with the SEC and the FBI, and they say Yates is clean. We thought Bridger must be wrong about Yates. That's why we started looking into Bridger's wife."

JD smiled. "I'm sorry, but I can't tell you how I found out. You'll have to trust me on this one. And maybe when you do trust me, you can share more of *your* information. I wasted my time trying to figure out who that woman was. Why didn't you just tell me?"

"There are a lot of things I haven't told you," Puccini admitted, "things that only the perp might know. I have to be careful, and believe me, it's not personal. One slip can blow up a case like this when it gets to court. Anyway, tell me more about Yates."

"He's running what I would characterize as a half-Ponzi. He actually does invest half the money he gets from clients, and probably keeps the other half in a bank account for his own use and to pay off redemptions. He skims off less than Harriman, but he runs less risk as well. He actually does some investing."

"When he gets caught, he won't go to half-jail. But tell me, how did you find out about all this?"

"Believe me, you don't want to know. You said you want plausible deniability, so this conversation never took place."

"Yes, it did, pal. You're on a cell phone with a police officer, remember? So don't say anything more." JD could hear Puccini's sigh.

"You've got a lot to learn, JD. But thanks for letting me know. That's useful for motive, even if it can never be used in court."

"There's a crash coming when Lehman collapses, and then the motive will be obvious. Yates's fund will blow up, just like Harriman's. Everyone will know it's a fraud when they can't get their money out. And anyway, all the evidence you need is on Rich's laptop." JD paused to let that sink in. "All you need is someone to figure that out for you."

JD knew he didn't need Rich's laptop anymore. He'd already reverse engineered everything Rich had done, and gone well beyond. But he couldn't resist tweaking Puccini for keeping him out of the loop.

"All right, point taken. I'll try to keep you informed, and maybe I can get that laptop freed up for you to do your thing. I'll look into it."

"What about Rich's home computer?" JD asked. "Did you ever take it from Dot's house?"

Puccini hesitated. "Yeah. And it took us a while to get into that one, too. But there was nothing relevant on it."

"Then why was Dot so reluctant to let you have it?"

"You'll have to ask her that," Puccini said. "I have to go now. I've got an appointment with Cole and Smith. I'll be in touch."

* * *

Puccini had mixed feelings about JD. His skills in forensic accounting could be very helpful, but Puccini was sensing that maybe JD wanted to play detective, thinking he could solve the Bridger puzzle. That could be a problem, because JD didn't know enough about the unwritten rules in Puccini's line of work - or even the written ones. JD could get in the way.

The puzzle was becoming more complex, with the death of Ghanem's dog and the attempt to run JD off the road. Were these events related somehow? And what about the Harriman and Mortimer connection? The Bridger disappearance was still front and center, and to him, it was now murder. There had been no ransom demands or any sign of Bridger, and five days had passed - enough time to convince Puccini that there was now very little hope of finding Bridger alive. Puccini figured that the most likely killer was John Maynard Yates, and that his wife's alibi was one of convenience. Courtney Yates liked her current lifestyle, and although she also seemed to like a little spice on the side, she probably did not want her husband in jail – so she gave him an alibi. Love, or whatever you call their arrangement, can be strange. Just look at Bridger and *his* wife. And that was the other possibility – Dorothy Bridger and Clint Houston. And then there was Cole and Smith. Where did they fit in? He had maybe half of what he needed to figure it out.

As Puccini was ruminating over the pieces of the puzzle, Lieutenant Jim Argus walked into his cubicle. Argus was tall with light brown hair streaked with a few strands of grey. He always looked good in the TV interviews when a big case hit the media. He'd come up through the ranks, and paid his dues, but he now played the political game with a lot of skill.

Argus put his coffee cup on the corner of Puccini's desk. "You've been spending a lot of time on that dog case. The Captain's wondering what that's about." Argus crossed his arms. "We have to focus on the Bridger homicide. Why don't you let Animal Control take over on the dog? And in case you're forgotten, we're also preparing for that big drug raid, and we need all hands on deck for that."

"Don't worry, Jim, I'll be ready. But something else is going on here. We've got three victims who know each other, all involved in violent incidents over less than a week. Don't you think there's a pattern there? And this guy Dionne says that John Maynard Yates is running a fraud, same as Harriman."

Argus frowned. "Look, Puccini, I admire your imagination, but that's not what you're paid for. I checked out Harriman, and the SEC has cleared him on all counts. Those rumors about financial fraud are bullshit. I even told the Chief. If they were true, Harriman would be in jail. So watch yourself. He's got powerful friends."

Argus took another sip of his coffee and waited for a response. Puccini sighed, and said in a low voice, "There's something there, and I'm going to find it."

Argus turned to leave. "I've put you on notice, Puccini. Get your priorities straight, or you'll be lecturing elementary school kids on why the policeman is your friend." Argus walked back to his office without looking back.

Puccini returned to his computer and his background check of Stuart Cole. He had less than an hour before he had to leave for their meeting, and he wanted to figure out what made the guy tick.

Stuart Cole had been born rich. His father came from old New England money, and was CEO of one of the big New York banks. Cole had gone to prep school at Coates Academy, not far from Greenwich, and then done a BA at Yale and an MBA at Wharton. His father had been married three times, and Cole had two younger brothers who had also gone to Coates. One was now an architect in France, and the other an actor in Los Angeles. Stuart Cole had never married.

Puccini double-checked the address and took a look at the house on Google Maps. Cole's house was set on about ten acres of the most desirable real estate on Round Hill Road. He'd done more than all right for himself, thought Puccini.

He dug a little deeper into Cole's education, and as he scrolled through the Coates Academy website, he noticed something interesting – one of the smaller campus buildings was named the Harriman Building. As he probed further, he saw that Bucky Harriman and his two sons were also Coates alumni, and Harriman had made a twenty-million dollar grant to the school. So Cole and Harriman might be connected.

Puccini looked at the time. It was almost two o'clock, and he realized he had to leave for his appointment on Round Hill Road. He turned to Garry Brown in the next cubicle. "You want to come with me for this meeting with Cole?"

Brown looked up. "No, I'm still working on my report for the homicide book on Bridger. That's what you should be doing."

Puccini smiled. "I guess you heard Argus ream me out about that dead dog. I'll do the paperwork later. But I've got a hunch about the Bridger case, so do me a favor. Don't tell Argus about this meeting with Cole."

* * *

Puccini was both frustrated and intrigued when he returned to the squad room from his meeting with Cole and Smith. They had politely given him zero information. He had no evidence, but his instinct now indicated they were involved in killing Ghanem's dog. Smith had visited Ghanem first to give him an opportunity to back off on his lawsuit, and when Ghanem refused, Smith had taken the next step – he killed Ghanem's dog and left that picture. And then there was Tracy Alder, Cole's girlfriend. She was probably in on it too. And given the Coates Academy connection between Harriman and Cole, Puccini decided he should get JD to look at Cole's fund. Maybe Harriman had mentored more than one Coates alumnus in Ponzi 101.

Garry Brown interrupted his train of thought. "You better get to work on that Bridger report before Argus comes back."

Puccini opened the report template on his computer and started typing, grumbling under his breath. It took him an hour to finish it. He pushed his chair back to think some more about the meeting with Cole and Smith. Then he realized he probably should call JD about the meeting. After all, JD had saved his kids' college fund, so he did owe him one or two favors. He dialed JD's number. "Hi, JD, how's it going? I wanted to let you know, I just went to see Cole and Smith. I can't prove anything, but my gut says they killed the dog. I don't think there's much of a mystery there."

"What's Smith like?"

"Everything you expect in someone with seven sniper kills. He wouldn't think twice about cutting a dog's throat. But there's something else. Cole went to Coates Academy, and so did Harriman. Harriman's got a building named after him at Coates."

There was a pause on the phone. "I know. I found that out yesterday. But here's the really interesting part – they both belonged to the same secret society at Yale."

Puccini smiled despite himself. JD was starting to make some interesting moves. "You and I have to talk."

"Maybe later. I'm trying out some new ideas to crack this case."

"Okay, partner. Stay in touch."

* * *

JD was sitting in his office after the call from Puccini, trying to figure out what to do next. He realized that he'd have to take a different approach from Puccini. Systems theory and mathematics were more in his wheelhouse than trying to sift through clues like a detective. He didn't have to take it to court. He just had to figure out the truth.

Some of those techniques were a little hazy now– it had been almost twenty years since he'd studied math and physics at Princeton. He knew that there was a high probability of a connection among the three violent incidents of the past week, and he needed a way to structure it, to look at it from different points of view to see where the links might be.

He started thinking about a visual approach to the problem – a chart. He decided on a Venn diagram, a series of circles showing where the overlaps were between different parts of the puzzle. He stepped up to the white-board, and slowly drew a circle for Cole and another one for Harriman with a slight overlap. He colored in the area of overlap and wrote in *Coates Academy,* and then added *Yale Secret Society.* He added a number of other overlapping circles. He couldn't see any patterns yet, but that would take time.

JD realized that the Venn diagram was helpful, but it had one flaw. It did not show the *timing* of the events. He needed a flow chart, showing the chronology. He started sketching out a flow chart on the top half of the white-board wall. First, the events at the hotel when Rich disappeared. Then, Fareed's visit from Smith and Raji's death. And finally, JD's visit to Harriman and the car chase this morning when his Porsche had almost been run off the road. That was the sequence.

He stepped back and sat down, turning his chair to look at the wall. There was a connection between Raji's death and the car chase, and it ran through Coates Academy and Yale. The likely perpetrators in each case probably knew each another. But what was the significance? Were they partners in crime? Did they help one another in carrying out these violent acts, or did they hire someone to do their dirty work? Where did Smith fit in? Did he just go after Raji, or was he also involved in the car chase? Was Smith the one who did the dirty work for Harriman as well?

And, JD wondered, did that mean a trained sniper was now coming after him?

* * *

After dinner that evening, JD cleaned up the dishes and went out on the back deck where Annie was already sitting. It was getting cooler, so he put on his down vest.

Annie took his hand. "Well, this was quite a day. I'm afraid Junior didn't take the news about Raji very well." Junior had left the dinner table in tears.

"None of us did," JD said. "But I'm glad we didn't also hit her with my incident on Round Hill Road."

"We're going to have to tell her about that, too," Annie said. "She needs to understand what's going on. I'm just glad you got through it okay."

JD took a sip of his rye. "It's funny how things work out. I had all that driver training for fun, and today it saved my life."

Annie shuddered. "I don't want to think about it. We almost lost you."

JD took a deep breath of the night air. "I'm glad I'm still around. But it's not over."

CHAPTER 11

Friday, September 12, 2008

JD heard the twin fiddle strains of Bob Wills' "Take Me Back to Tulsa" from his alarm, and he rolled over to look at the time. Six o'clock. He glanced over at Annie sleeping peacefully, and closed his eyes again. He was very tired. He'd had two nightmares about car chases, and both times the dreams had culminated in a flight off that cliff into the trees. He'd woken up with a start each time, drenched in sweat, and had taken a long time to get back to sleep. He turned off the alarm, and thought about maybe getting a gentler wake-up sound. Those twin fiddles could be harsh, first thing in the morning. He finally drifted back to sleep peacefully. The next thing he felt was Annie's hand on his shoulder, shaking him gently. "It's almost eight o'clock, dear. Time to get up."

JD yawned and stretched, had a shower, got dressed, and then went down to the kitchen, where Junior and Annie were already preparing breakfast. He poured himself a large cup of black coffee and sat down to watch coverage of the financial markets. Lehman Brothers was down 77 percent for the week, and the pain was spreading. Merrill Lynch had dropped 30 percent, and AIG, the insurance company loaded with those sketchy credit default swaps, was also falling fast. Junior was looking at the television report with rapt concentration as she fried their peameal bacon for breakfast. "Do you think the government will step in like they did for Bear Stearns last spring?"

JD took a sip of his coffee. "No, I don't think it's politically possible. Next week is going to be interesting. There are a lot of dominos lined up, and Lehman is first in line."

Annie flipped the eggs over easy, and started buttering toast. She looked up at JD. "And how are you feeling this morning? That was quite an adventure yesterday."

"Tired. I didn't get much sleep, too many nightmares."

Junior put the bacon on three plates and added the eggs. "I had some nightmares too, about Raji. That's just awful. I still can't believe it."

They sat down, and Annie turned to Junior. "We haven't told you the whole story. We didn't want you to worry too much last night. There's more to it. Someone tried to force Dad off the road yesterday up on Round Hill Road."

Junior put down her knife and fork. "Force him off the road? You mean like a crazy driver or something?"

Annie bit her lip. "It's worse than that. It was two black SUVs. They had guns, and took some shots at him."

Junior's mouth fell open. "Shots? Oh my God!" She spilled some of her coffee on the table. "Are you okay, Dad?"

JD nodded. "I'm fine, but we're going to have to protect ourselves. Someone was definitely after me, and it may be connected to Rich's disappearance and Raji's death."

"But why didn't you tell me yesterday? You should have told me."

Annie said, "We didn't want you to be too upset by giving you all the bad news at once."

Junior's face reddened slightly. "Well, please upset me when something like this happens. I can take it. I want to know the truth right away." She crossed her arms. "I'm not a kid anymore. I'm seventeen years old."

JD sighed, and lowered his voice. "Our lives are changing, Junior. We've done a lot of thinking. We're looking into getting bodyguards. The police can't be everywhere. And Mom and I are going to start carrying our guns again."

"Guns? Are you kidding me?" Junior shook her head, and then her eyes widened. "And what about me? Will they come after me?"

"It's possible. We may have to get you a bodyguard. I'm sorry. I should drive you to school today."

Junior stood up. "I can't eat right now. I'm not hungry anymore. And I'll get to school by myself, thank you." She left the table hurriedly and went upstairs.

"Well, that went about as well as I expected," JD said.

Annie smiled a little. "She'll calm down. We'll have to bring B up to date when he gets home tonight. I don't know how he'll react to all this."

They heard the door slam as Junior left for school without saying good-bye.

Annie went to her studio, and JD headed for his office. He had just started to work on his wall charts when his cell phone rang. It was Fareed.

"Good morning, JD. I am calling to confirm our sailboat race tomorrow. I fully expect that we shall win that race and the club championship."

JD had to stop and think for a moment. He'd forgotten about the race in the midst of all the turmoil. And it was strange - Fareed sounded almost cheerful. He seemed to have either gotten over Raji's death or was covering up his grief.

JD said, "So you're still going ahead with the race, after all that's happened?"

"Yes. It will help me get my mind off Raji . . . and Richard. And the bodyguard says nothing can happen to us on the water." He paused. "It does not look good for Richard, does it, Joshua?"

"No, it's been almost a week. If it were a ransom situation, we'd have heard something by now."

There was a silence on the phone, then Fareed said, "But life must go on. I will race tomorrow. Richard would understand."

JD hesitated, but he knew he couldn't let his friend down. "Okay. B and I will be there. So how's the bodyguard working out?"

"He is truly excellent. We feel very secure. Would you like me to ask him for a reference to one of his colleagues?"

"No, we've decided against it." As he said it, JD reminded himself that he and Annie had to start carrying those guns regularly now, and they needed some practice. It had been a long time.

"I think that is foolhardy, but it is your decision." Fareed hesitated another moment, and then said, in a quiet voice, "We shall see you tomorrow, bright and early, at the yacht club. The forecast is for sunny skies and gentle winds. A perfect autumn day. Vivian will be joining us."

"How is Vivian handling Raji's death? She must be very upset."

"She came home from Yale at once. Her heart is breaking. I am hoping that being out on the water will help her, too, but it will take us all a long time to recover."

"Of course," JD said. "I'm glad Vivian's coming with us." He paused, thinking again of Raji. "We'll see you in the morning. What time should we meet? I want to keep an eye on Lehman over the weekend. I've almost lost track of the markets."

"Let us make it eight o'clock, JD. Perhaps we can discuss our investment strategies in the afternoon after the race."

"It's a deal. See you then."

JD disconnected and went back to work on his wall chart. He kept coming back to the connection between Cole and Harriman through Coates Academy and Yale. Then he looked over at the circle representing Yates. Was there any overlap there? He needed to find out about Yates's early schooling, and he went online to investigate. After a few minutes, he confirmed that Yates had also graduated from Coates, although he had gone to Harvard as an undergraduate, not Yale. However, he had gone to Yale for graduate school – until Rich had expelled him for plagiarism. And JD knew that Harriman had been Yates's mentor, helping him establish his first investment fund, and quite possibly teaching him the finer points of running a Ponzi. The next question was whether Cole was also running a Ponzi. Determining that should be straightforward.

JD spent the next three hours examining Cole's fund, but he found no evidence of fraud. It looked as if Cole was actually just an astute investment manager. His returns were excellent but plausible, mostly in insurance and housing construction. Unfortunately, he held a very large position in AIG, the largest insurance firm in the world. JD knew that AIG was in serious trouble, so Cole's investors would soon be very upset if AIG tanked. But JD was now even more perplexed about Cole. Why did he need a goon like Smith around if he wasn't involved in fraud?

Then JD noticed an email from one of his old MIT friends now working at a Wall Street investment bank. Apparently a dozen black limousines were parked in front of the Federal Reserve building in Manhattan. The big banks had been summoned to a conference with the government about the Lehman Brothers situation.

JD thoughts drifted back to his discussion with Fareed about the guns. He hadn't touched his Glock in six months, since the last time he and Annie had been to the pistol range. Annie had grown up with shotguns in England, and she still enjoyed the target practice with her Sig Sauer pistol, even though she hadn't used it for protection since their days in Boston.

JD walked over to the small gun safe attached to the wall in the middle of his oak bookshelf. He twirled the combination, and removed the two pistols. He ejected the magazines and inspected the actions and barrels. Both pistols looked ready for action, so he found the holsters, took a box of ammunition from the safe, and headed for Annie's studio.

Annie was sitting in front of the easel, contemplating a half-finished painting, and JD sat down beside her, holding the two holstered pistols on his knee. "Time to fish or cut bait," he said. "If we're not getting a bodyguard, we need to get used to these again. We need to go to the range."

Annie put down her brush. "I'm ready. Let's go."

* * *

When they arrived home from the range, Annie placed their two paper targets on the kitchen counter with a satisfied grin. Her shots had mostly been through and around the bull's eye, while JD's pattern was a little more scattered. She turned to JD, and said, "I haven't lost much in six months. I can still beat you, dear."

JD shrugged and looked closely at his target. "It's good enough. We can both take care of ourselves. But paper doesn't shoot back."

Annie's smile disappeared, and she started preparing dinner. JD went to his office to check on the markets. Despite all the volatility, the Dow Jones was up two percent over the week. But all the signs pointed to big trouble over the weekend. The limos were still sitting in front of the Federal Reserve building.

He turned to his wall charts on the three criminal cases, but aside from the Coates connection, made no further progress. He was getting very frustrated, so he gave up and went back to the kitchen, where he started helping cut some vegetables for dinner. He was wearing his Glock tucked under his belt in the concealed-carry holster.

B would be home from Yale soon, so JD added an extra plate. "I wonder how he's enjoying his new Winchester. He had a free day on Wednesday, and he took it to the thousand-yard range for the first time."

Annie put the sea bass in the oven and sat down, swirling her wine in the glass before she took a sip. "Maybe we should hire him as a bodyguard." She took a deep breath. "JD, do you think maybe we should get some bullet-proof vests?"

The door opened and B walked in, dropping his backpack on the floor. B's full name was Balthazar, named after a character in one of JD's favorite books, J.P Donleavy's *The Beastly Beatitudes of Balthazar B.* Junior had trouble saying Balthazar when she was little, and she just started calling her big brother "B". The nickname stuck, and now his family almost never called him by his full name – unless they were really, really angry.

B stood a head taller than his father, and he had light brown skin, not as dark as JD's. His black hair was cut short, his eyes were dark brown, and his eyebrows reached almost across the top of his nose. He had scars above his lip and on his left cheek from hockey. Junior said all the girls thought her big brother was very cool. He was a junior at Yale, and often came home for weekends.

As he sat down at the kitchen island, B shook his head. "I hear you've had quite the week. A dead dog, a car chase, and now you're into concealed carry again?" He looked keenly at his parents. "Seriously, what's going on?"

Annie raised her sweatshirt slightly to expose the Sig under her waistband. "Greenwich is becoming dangerous . . . for us, at least. We went to the range this afternoon to freshen up. Someone tried to kill Dad."

Junior walked in and saw the pistol in Annie's waistband. "So you did it, Mom. I can't believe it. I'm ashamed to be part of this family."

B smiled slightly at Junior's comment, and she became furious. "It's not funny, B, and you know it. I still can't believe we have handguns in the house. And now you're actually carrying them around like some wild-west characters."

B kept smiling. "It's even worse than you thought, Junior. I finally got to take my new Winchester .308 to the thousand-yard range, and it's bitchin'."

Junior frowned at B's comment, got up, and went to sit at the dining room table by herself, conspicuously turning up the volume on her iPod.

B glanced in her direction with a deliberate smile. "And you know what? It's not really a thousand-yard gun. I was hitting maybe one out of ten at that distance. If I'm going to get serious about this long-range shooting, I'll need something more powerful."

Junior glanced up quickly, and then averted her eyes again. Apparently she could still hear their conversation despite the iPod earbuds.

JD's eyes widened. "More powerful than a .308? What are we talking about? I thought the .308 was the standard-issue long distance rifle."

B grinned a very big grin. "Not anymore. Now you need a .50 BMG or a .338 Lapua Magnum. I saw one of each at the range, with two shooters who couldn't miss . . . even at a thousand yards. It was amazing. They hit the gong every time. And here's the thing . . . one of them was a woman, if you can believe it. The one shooting the Lapua. The guy shooting the BMG was no slouch either. He looked like a boot camp drill sergeant, or maybe a linebacker. They were quite the pair. They stuck to themselves, never talked to anybody."

"Sounds like you better stay out of their way."

JD got up and asked everyone to sit down at the dinner table with Junior. She removed her earbuds. As JD took his seat, he said, "Junior, we didn't do this to spite you. We're in danger, and it's for protection. Honestly, I'd feel better if you had one, too."

Junior's eyes widened in disbelief. "No way. I'd rather die."

JD looked at Annie, and neither could think of a response. B came to their rescue, asking, "And how are the markets doing? What's happening with Lehman?"

They continued in quiet conversation over dinner, and Junior eventually joined the discussion. After dinner, JD reminded B about the race the next day, and the two of them cleared the table.

It was getting too cold to sit out on the deck, so JD and Annie had their nightcap in her studio. Annie took a sip of her port. "Well, at least we're not defenseless now."

"I hope we can make it count if and when the time comes. Shooting at the real thing is very different from targets."

Annie put her hand on JD's arm. "I hope we never have to find out."

CHAPTER 12

Saturday, September 13, 2008

JD reached over to shut off the alarm quickly. He didn't want to waken Annie. She wasn't going sailing with them, so there was no reason to disturb her. He went down to the kitchen. B was already there, savoring a cappuccino. B nodded toward a second cup sitting on the counter. "All set for you, Dad. I thought you'd need a wake-up shot after yesterday."

All the ingredients for egg-white omelets were sitting on the kitchen island, waiting for JD's deft touch. The Saturday omelets had been a family tradition for many years, and JD got to work. He saw on the TV that CNBC was running a special report on Lehman, and he turned up the sound. The reporting was all speculative at this point, because the government was being very quiet about their discussions. Videos from the previous day showed the limos arriving at the Fed building in New York, obviously for a big meeting. But a cone of silence had descended on the discussions.

B turned to JD with a quizzical expression. "Are we going to be okay financially? I know we have those credit default swaps, but my economics professor says there's no crisis, and those swaps will be worthless."

JD added some cheese to the omelets and carefully folded them over. "Your professor is wrong. It's like those generals who are always fighting the last war, refusing to see that things have changed. We'll do well." JD put the omelets on the plates. "So anyway, what's happening with Vivian? You've been spending a lot of time with her lately. Is it getting serious?"

B's face flushed slightly, and he took a bite of his omelet. "We're just friends, same as we've always been. I help her with math sometimes. And she's all torn up over Raji's death, so I tried to comfort her." He looked like he wanted to change the subject.

JD nodded and took a sip of his cappuccino. "Aside from that idiot economics prof, how were your classes this week?"

B relaxed visibly. "They were fine, not too busy. I even had a chance to shoot with the rifle club, but after the .308, the .22 was sort of boring. By the way, can I take the *Ojibway* out for a picnic on one of the islands? It's almost end of the season, and the weather's supposed to be good."

"Of course, but you'll need a crew. Who's going with you? You want me to tag along?"

B hesitated, and his face creased in a sheepish grin. "Vivian. She thought it would be a nice break, some relaxation after today's race. Her dad can get a little intense in competition."

JD smiled. So B and Vivian *were* getting serious. "That's fine. You both know the charts and can handle the boat, so have a good time. But we better get going. We have a race to win today. Could you clean up? I have to check the weather reports before the race."

B started clearing the table as JD went to his office. He checked a number of weather sites on his computer, and printed off some maps showing the probable direction of the low pressure system moving in later that day. As he was compiling the printouts and making some notations, B walked in. He stopped abruptly, and stared at JD's charts on the wall showing the violent events of the last week. He sat down in one of the chairs without taking his eyes off the charts. He studied them for a long moment, then said. "You want to solve this all by yourself, don't you? Shouldn't you leave it to the police? You're dealing with some nasty people."

"I'm helping the police. I've gotten to know one of the detectives, and we're working together."

B looked again at the wall chart, and stood up to move a little closer. His eyes followed some of the lines and circles. "Have you shown these to the detective?"

"No, I'm just using it to structure my own thinking. I'm trying to see where the connections are among those three events – Rich's disappearance, Raji's death, and my car chase. Detective Puccini thinks that John Smith, this former army sniper who threatened Fareed, may be involved in all three." JD got up and traced the connection on the chart.

B's eyes narrowed. "Former army sniper?"

"That's what Puccini said. He works for Stuart Cole, which is another long story."

B sat down again, sprawling in his chair. "Dad, no offense, but I think you're in over your head. And you say this guy's name is John Smith? As if."

JD frowned. He didn't need B's attitude right then. He got up abruptly, and jammed the weather printouts into his briefcase. "Let's get going. Fareed won't be happy if we're late. Nor will Vivian." He took one last look at Rich's box on the chart, and shook his head. He missed that dumb ox. Rich would probably have been sailing with them in the race that morning, and then joining them for band practice on Sunday.

* * *

JD parked the Mercedes at the Cos Cob Yacht Club, and he and B walked toward the clubhouse. The club had been founded in the late nineteenth century when Greenwich was a summer getaway for rich New Yorkers, and the town had grown around it as the year-round population increased. The new clubhouse had been built in the 1920s, and expanded and renovated numerous times. It was done in colonial style using white clapboard, with large windows overlooking the yachts, and a broad promenade in front. The lawns were carefully manicured, and the sailing activities were complemented by eight tennis courts and a large swimming pool. Over a hundred and fifty yachts of various sizes and pedigrees were moored at long jetties jutting into the harbor, and along the other side of the grounds, dozens of smaller racing dinghies sat on dollies, ready for action.

The clubhouse was busy with members preparing for the regatta, having breakfast and shooting the breeze. JD and B greeted a few friends as they went to the locker room to change, and then headed out to the jetties where the yachts were moored. JD smiled as they passed the *Ojibway*, the Fisher 32 that the family had enjoyed since the kids were little. It wasn't a racing boat, but a very sturdy motor-sailor, powered by a small diesel engine. JD had arranged for all the sail controls to run to the pilot-house, so it could be managed by a crew of two. Mounted to the stern was a set of davits supporting a Zodiac inflatable dinghy with a small outboard motor, so the *Ojibway* was the perfect boat for a family cruise on a sunny weekend. They could anchor it and take the dinghy ashore to have picnics and explore the small islands in Long Island Sound. Both B and Junior had been through the junior sailing program at the club, and had also studied navigation and diesel engine basics, but as they became teenagers, they lost interest in the family picnics. Now the *Ojibway* often sat idle. As they walked by it, JD said, "I'm glad that you're taking her out tomorrow, B. She's been sitting for a couple of weeks, and she needs some exercise."

They walked a little farther, and as they neared Fareed's boat, JD could see Vivian working on the foredeck, checking the jib sheets. When she saw them, she smiled and jumped off the boat onto the jetty. "Good morning, sailors. Isn't it an awesome day?" She walked up to B and gave him a hug. Fareed was in the cockpit, and he looked up and waved. B gave Vivian a tentative half-hug and pulled away, a little embarrassed. Vivian laughed and jumped over the lifelines back onto the boat. She was dressed in white cotton pants and a tight blue parka that showed off her slim waist; her long black hair was tied back in a ponytail that stuck through the back of her yellow baseball cap. JD could see that she was determined to have a good time despite the loss of Raji.

Fareed's boat was named *Damini*, which meant lightning. She was a J/33, a racer/cruiser that was perfect for Fareed, who used it mainly for racing.

As JD prepared to step aboard, he noticed a third person on the boat. A large man in blue jeans and a grey hoodie stepped up from the cockpit. JD climbed aboard, and Fareed said, "JD, I'd like you to meet Patrick Riley, our bodyguard." They shook hands. "Patrick is not a sailor, so he will not be joining us for the race. He will stay ashore, and then he will drive me home safely."

Riley folded his muscular arms across his chest and tilted his head back. "Maybe I should go back to your house and look after Mrs. Ghanem. There's not much I can do sitting in that fancy clubhouse up there."

JD looked up at the clubhouse and then at Riley. He knew Riley's blue jeans were a contravention of the club dress code, which could become an issue if Riley stayed. Fareed was not the most popular member of the club after his lawsuit, and that feeling could extend to Riley. The members might ask him to leave.

Fareed shrugged. "That will be fine, Mr. Riley. I shall give you a call when we have finished the race, and you can meet us when we tie up at the dock." Fareed gave his car keys to Riley, and Riley left. Fareed turned to JD and said, "Perhaps it is better that he is home looking after Heema. She is very nervous alone in the house."

JD stepped down into the cabin and pulled out his weather charts. He laid them out on a table, and Fareed joined him for a discussion of the likely wind patterns over the next few hours. The wind was very gentle this early in the morning, and the harbor was almost glassy calm, with just a few catspaws rippling across the surface.

JD said, "I think the wind will pick up and shift. We should use the smaller jib so we don't get overpowered."

Fareed looked at the weather chart and JD's notes. "I am not certain about that. We need the larger jib for power when the wind is gentle, and we can flatten the main when the wind increases."

JD started picking up his weather charts. "Okay, skipper, it's your boat and your race. Maybe we should wait and see."

They returned to the cockpit, and saw that the wind was picking up. B and Vivian had checked the folded spinnakers, and they were ready to cast off. They hauled up the mainsail and unfurled the jib, and Fareed looked up at the sails as they started to flutter in the gentle breeze. B jumped back on the jetty to untie the mooring lines, leaped back on, and they were underway as Vivian and JD pulled in the sheets to tighten the sails.

Damini started moving slowly into the harbor along with two dozen other boats, all heading for the starting line three miles out in the Sound. The wind picked up slightly, and it was from astern, so Fareed gave the order to hoist the spinnaker. He didn't want to be late for the start.

They all started to relax as the boat picked up speed. The wind was steady, so the boat almost sailed itself. Fareed kept a gentle hand on the tiller, and they had a chance to discuss the markets. Every few minutes, their conversation was interrupted by corporate jets taking off from Westchester County Airport.

JD looked up at one of the jets. "Looks like some of the hedge fund guys are heading to Washington this weekend for that big Republican fundraiser."

Fareed kept his eyes on the spinnaker. "Yes, my friend, but the hosts better cash those checks today. On Monday, the accounts might have insufficient funds."

B and Vivian were sitting very close to each other, up on the windward side, leaning against the lifelines, looking relaxed and happy. JD turned to Fareed and nodded toward the young couple. Fareed stuck up his thumb in an all's-good gesture, and smiled.

It took another half hour to reach the starting line, and Fareed decided to tack partway up the first leg to check out the wind. They heard the ten-minute gun and saw the puff of white smoke from the committee boat, and JD started his stopwatch.

Fareed said, 'It is time to get serious. Please take your places." Fareed sailed along the line for a minute and said, "The line is fair. There is no advantage to either end. We shall just aim for hitting the middle of the line at full speed when the gun goes off."

It was getting crowded downwind of the starting line, as over twenty yachts maneuvered for the start. There were near collisions, and shouts of "Starboard!" rang out as these two- or three-ton vessels passed within a few feet of each other. The five-minute gun went off, and the countdown continued. JD shouted out each minute as Fareed started his run for the starting line. At thirty seconds, Fareed ordered everyone to pull in the sheets for full power, and the boat accelerated toward the line, along with two dozen other boats above and below, all heading toward the line.

It was apparent that the boat just above them had started its run too early, and had to ease her sails to avoid going over the line before the gun. With ten seconds showing on the stopwatch, JD started a verbal countdown, and as he shouted "Three, two, one, *go,*" the gun sounded and they crossed the line at full speed. There was no time to celebrate the good start, because five other boats had done just as well, and were beating to windward above and below them. There was total silence on all the boats as each crew concentrated on the task at hand, keeping each sail just short of luffing to maintain maximum speed. A gain or loss of a few feet at this point could mean the difference between first or sixth at the first mark.

Damini rounded the first mark in third place. There were two boats ahead of them, so at that point JD knew the club championship was very much up in the air. They had to pass those two boats.

Over the next two hours, they sailed the course without closing the gap. JD could see that Fareed was becoming very frustrated – he hated losing. The boat rounded the last downwind mark and headed upwind again on the last leg of the race. JD could see the committee boat at the finish line two miles away.

The two leading boats had tacked over to the left side of the course, still battling each other and not paying much attention to *Damini.* The wind was picking up, and JD could see a few whitecaps. He looked up at the sky and studied the cloud patterns. "Fareed, I think we should head toward the right side. There's a big wind shift coming."

Fareed kept looking at the jib as he steered upwind, glancing occasionally at the two leading boats. "How do you know?"

"It's something I learned on Christian Island. It's the clouds. I can't exactly explain it."

Vivian and B looked back briefly over their shoulders as they watched the discussion. Fareed seemed to be lost in thought as he looked upwind toward the finish line. "Those two up ahead are staying on the left side. We would be taking a big chance if we go to the right."

"We can't catch them on this tack. It's our only hope. We have to play the shift." The wind was increasing.

Fareed looked up at the shape of the mainsail momentarily. "JD, please tighten the backstay to flatten the mainsail. We do not want to be overpowered." He seemed to be buying time before making a decision.

JD asked B to take over the mainsheet winch and started pumping the backstay adjuster. He watched the sail shape change, and then said, "How's it look, Fareed? You want it flatter?"

Fareed looked up briefly. "That is excellent. Thank you."

JD could see that his friend was still trying to decide about taking the gamble. After two more frustrating minutes, he heard Fareed finally give the order to tack. As they headed toward the right side of the course, he saw the two leading boats still heading left, moving farther and farther away to the other side of the course.

Five minutes later, the wind shifted sharply clockwise. The two leading boats were now caught on the wrong side of the course, and would have to sail a much longer route to the finish. If this new wind held, *Damini* would cross the line first, well clear of the other two boats.

The crew concentrated on trimming the sails, and Fareed kept the boat close to the wind. They all sat on the windward gunwale to help balance the boat as it knifed through the whitecaps. No one spoke.

The wind held to the finish, and they all cheered as they heard the gun and saw the puff of smoke from the committee boat.

Fareed turned to JD with a big grin. "We did it, thanks to you, JD. I should hire you as my navigator for all my races next year."

JD looked up at the sky, where another jet was leaving Westchester Airport. "You can't afford me, Fareed. Just treat me to a good rye when we get to the clubhouse."

They started heading back to the club, making good speed now. They didn't bother putting up the spinnaker. There was no hurry. It was time to savor the victory and relax after the intense two and half hours of total concentration.

They could see Duck Island on the left, and Fareed steered toward it to avoid the shallower water on the right. One of the other sailboats at the club had run aground there the previous year, and there was no point in taking chances at the speed they were now making. The club was about two miles away, and Fareed said, "JD, could you please take over the tiller? I should call Mr.Riley to ask him to meet us at the clubhouse now."

JD smiled. "Maybe you should wait. You may want to celebrate your victory a little, have a good time. You deserve it. And I think Vivian and B would enjoy that."

"Do you think it would be appropriate? A celebration --

Fareed was interrupted by a jet taking off overhead, and JD looked up, annoyed at the interruption. *Off to Washington*, he thought. *Politics again - what a waste of time.* The *Damini* hit a big wave and bobbed sharply up and down, and JD had to grab a lifeline to keep from falling. He glanced down, and saw that Fareed had fallen when the wave hit. As the boat stabilized, he reached over to help his friend to his feet, but stopped abruptly. Fareed's face was ashen, and his brow was furrowed in surprise. And then JD saw the red stain spreading on Fareed's right shoulder. He was dripping dark red blood onto the white deck.

Vivian gave a piercing scream, and ran over to her father. The boat started heeling as it turned abruptly upwind with no one at the tiller, and JD grabbed it to get them back on course. B looked over from his perch on the windward side, his eyes very wide, and eased the mainsail to stabilize the boat. Vivian was holding her father's head in her hands. His eyes were closed, and his breathing was shallow and rapid. JD saw his lips move, but couldn't tell what his friend was saying.

JD shouted to Vivian, "Come and take over the tiller. I'll help Fareed."

Vivian wouldn't move, so B eased off both sails to slow the boat, and then came back to take over the tiller. There was now a small pool of blood on the deck next to Fareed. JD knelt down beside him and took a closer look at Fareed's shoulder. "I think you've been shot, Fareed. We have to get you to the hospital ASAP." He pulled out his cell phone, but there was only a half bar of reception, and he couldn't reach 9-1-1. JD took off his parka and then his shirt, rolled the shirt into a ball, and then pulled open Fareed's parka gently to look at his shoulder. Vivian turned away and closed her eyes at the sight of torn flesh and white bone. JD pressed the rolled-up shirt against Fareed's bleeding shoulder. To JD it looked as if no vital organs had been hit, but the bleeding was a problem. He pressed the compress against the wound, and Fareed winced in pain. JD turned to Vivian. "Here, press this and hold it. I need to call 9-1-1." Vivian wiped away some tears and took over from JD. The bleeding seemed to subside a little.

As B steered the boat toward the club, JD finally got a full bar of reception on his cell phone. He dialed 9-1-1, and shouted into his phone. "We have an emergency on the water. Our skipper's been shot, and he's bleeding badly. We need medical help right away." The dispatcher determined their location via JD's cell phone, and said they would send out the marine unit as quickly as possible. JD was starting to shiver, and he grabbed a life jacket to try to keep warm.

A few minutes later, he saw a black-and-white cabin cruiser speeding toward them from the harbor. As the cruiser pulled closer, he could see the POLICE insignia on the side. It was a large shallow-draft jet boat with three officers aboard, and within a few minutes they were tied up alongside *Damini.* One of the officers jumped aboard, and after taking one look at Fareed, motioned for another officer to join him. They passed a yellow plastic basket stretcher on board, and gently placed Fareed inside, strapping him in for safety. Then they lifted the stretcher onto the police boat. Fareed smiled weakly, and the officer said, "There's an ambulance waiting on shore. We'll get you to the hospital as quickly as possible." One of the officers untied the police boat from *Damini,* and it sped away. The whole process had taken about three minutes.

JD was still shaking, but he started some deep breathing to calm down. B had been a trooper through the whole incident, and was now steering toward the club with total concentration. Vivian was sitting in the cockpit, and it looked to JD as if she might be going into shock. She had her arms around her shoulders, her head was down on her chest, and she was shivering vigorously. JD gently rubbed her shoulder. "Please get up, Vivian. We need you on the jib. I'll take the main. We need to get back to the club. Your dad is in good hands, and he'll be okay." Vivian got up, her teeth chattering, and took over the winch for the main sheet, turning the handle to keep the mainsail drawing. JD took over the jib sheet, and the only sound was the hissing of the hull slicing through the waves as they headed for shore. No one spoke.

* * *

Half an hour later, they tied up at their berth. Detective Puccini was waiting for them, along with his partner and two uniformed officers.

Puccini climbed aboard. "Your friend Ghanem made it to the hospital, and he'll be okay. Lost a lot of blood, but he'll be okay."

JD sat down in the cockpit and put his head in his hands. He was still shivering. "It happened so fast. One minute we were celebrating our victory, and the next minute he was on the deck, bleeding." B and Vivian were sitting on the opposite side of the cockpit, still looking stunned. Puccini motioned for Brown and the two officers to come aboard. "We'll have to set up a perimeter here. The boat is a crime scene, and we'll take each of your statements separately. Maybe we can do that in the clubhouse so you won't have to come downtown." He paused. "We haven't called his wife yet. I thought you might want to do that yourself."

The uniformed officers started putting yellow crime scene ribbon around the *Damini's* lifelines, and Puccini and Brown accompanied JD, B, and Vivian up to the clubhouse. A crowd had gathered on the front lawn, gawking at the police presence and the yellow tape on the yacht. Puccini pushed his way through and asked for the manager, who quickly led them to three rooms at the rear of the clubhouse to get them away from the crowd. Puccini asked JD to go into the first room, and Brown went into the second room with Vivian. B was to wait in the third room while JD and Vivian made their statements.

JD eased himself into a seat. The room was some sort of office, with a desk, chairs, and bookshelves. It reminded him of the room where he had waited when Rich had disappeared at the hotel. There were sailing pictures on the wall, some of them very old, and a few model yachts in glass cases. Puccini came in and sat down. "I need to ask you what happened. But maybe you should call Ghanem's wife first, tell her about her husband. He's at Greenwich Hospital, in good hands."

JD dialed Fareed's home number, and a man answered. Riley, he thought. JD asked for Heema – no point in going through it with Riley first. Heema got on the phone. "Hi, JD, did you win? Where is Fareed?"

"I'm afraid I have some bad news, Heema. Are you sitting down?"

There was silence on the phone. "I am sitting down now, JD. Has something happened to Fareed?"

"He's hurt, and he was taken to the hospital. He'll be okay, but I wanted to let you know as soon as possible."

"He is hurt? What happened? Did something break on the boat?"

"No, it looks like he was shot. The police are here now."

There was another long silence on the phone, and then a loud moan. "Shot? He was shot? Who could have a gun in a sailboat race?" She was silent for a few seconds. "Joshua, did you have your gun with you? Is that what happened?"

JD sighed. "No, the shot came from far away. The police will have to investigate."

"Where are you now? Are you at the club? I will come right down there."

"No, Heema, there's nothing you can do here. We'll come and get you, and you can go to the hospital with us. He's at Greenwich Hospital."

There was another pause. "I will go to the hospital right now. Fareed needs me. I shall see you there." She disconnected.

JD looked up at Puccini. "She's going to the hospital. I should get up there as well."

Puccini shrugged. "There's not much you can do. He's probably in surgery, and you'll just be sitting around. Anyway, I need to take your statement while it's fresh. Tell me what happened."

JD described the events on the boat as Puccini took notes on the statement form. When JD had finished, Puccini said, "It sounds like a sniper, probably from Duck Island. We'll send someone out there to take a look. The jet must have covered up the sound of the shot. And hitting that wave probably saved Ghanem's life."

Puccini asked JD to sign the statement form, and then Puccini went to take B's statement. JD called Annie to let her know what happened. Annie answered the phone on the second ring.

"So did you win?"

"We won, but things are pretty rough here. We had another incident."

JD could hear a sharp intake of breath. "Incident? What sort of incident?"

"Fareed was shot. Probably a sniper. He'll be okay, but he's at Greenwich Hospital."

Annie did not respond immediately. "Shot? This is getting crazy. It's as if we're at war or something." She paused to catch her breath. "But he'll be okay?"

"We're going to see him at the hospital when Puccini's finished with us. Heema's on her way there already." JD paused to look over at the other interview room. "Could you go and give Heema some support? We could be here a while. The police are still interviewing B and Vivian."

"I'll get up there as soon as I can. And maybe I should bring Junior."

"Yeah, that makes sense. She'll be nervous when she hears about this."

JD disconnected, and sat down to wait. Puccini came back in, and said, "You're free to go. We have all your statements, and we've sent a forensics team out to Duck Island. I'll let you know if we find anything. I see John Smith's hand in this." He touched JD's shoulder briefly. "I have to get going. The media's here, and I have to feed the beast."

B and Vivian were waiting in the hallway. Vivian looked a little calmer, although her mascara was streaked from crying. They all got in the Mercedes and headed for the hospital, passing two television trucks as they left the parking lot.

* * *

The waiting room in the intensive care unit at Greenwich Hospital was crowded. Heema was already there. Vivian ran up to her and they hugged each other.

"I wanted to see him," Heema said, "but they would not let me. The doctor said they need to stabilize him for surgery. His shoulder is shattered."

They sat down to wait, and then JD noticed something. "Heema, where's your bodyguard? Patrick Riley?"

Heema scowled. "I fired him. He did not do his job. He provided bad advice. Fareed should not have been racing today."

JD had some sympathy for Riley. Trying to stop Fareed from racing today would have been like trying to keep a bull away from a heifer in heat.

One of the doctors approached Heema and had a quiet conversation with her. "Fareed is stable," Heema soon told the others. "They will start surgery in the next hour. I shall be able to see him after he comes out of surgery."

Annie and Junior arrived, and there were hugs all around. They all sat down to wait. Half an hour later, the doctor came back in and had another discussion with Heema in the hallway. When she came back to her seat, her expression had changed. Her face was taut, on the verge of tears, and her lower lip quavered. "Fareed may lose his arm," she said.

CHAPTER 13

Heema stood facing them, seemingly paralyzed by the doctor's prognosis. There wasn't much to say, but Annie put an arm around her and helped her into a chair. They sat in silence for a few minutes. Vivian looked stunned by the news, and B held her hand as she sobbed quietly. JD saw one of the doctors checking a chart at the nursing station, and decided to see if he could get more information.

He approached the doctor, a tall woman in her mid-thirties with dark hair. She had a surgical mask hanging under her chin, and her eyes narrowed as JD approached. "Yes, can I help you?"

"I'm a friend of Fareed Ghanem, the man who was shot in the shoulder. Apparently he's going into surgery and may lose his arm. Is there any way to avoid that?"

She looked at him closely, as if unsure whether to trust him. Then she glanced over at Heema, who was now crying in her daughter's arms. "We'll do our best. The bullet tumbled when it hit bone, and shattered the end of the humerus. The scapula is severely damaged, along with the rotator cuff. We'll know more when I open him up. We'll have the answer in a few hours. Please excuse me, I have to go now. He's prepped."

She signed an order on the counter and walked down the hall without looking back. JD went back and sat down. "There's still hope," he said to Heema. "Let's wait and see." He almost believed it when he said it.

Heema wiped her eyes and straightened up. She gave JD a weak smile. "Thank you, Joshua."

Vivian put her hand on her mother's. "Would you like me to get you anything? A coffee or some food?"

“Yes, that would be nice. Maybe we can go to the cafeteria. We will be here for a while.” She looked at JD. “You should all go home and come back later. I will call you when Fareed comes out of surgery.”

JD thought for a moment. “No, I’d like to stay. I need to know whether they saved his arm.”

Junior frowned a little and looked down at the floor. Annie noticed, and said, “I can take you home, Junior. You look tired.”

Junior nodded, and as they got up to leave, she said, “I hope Fareed will be okay. It was terrible what happened today.” Heema gave a weak smile of thanks, and Junior followed Annie out the door. The rest of the group went down to the cafeteria, had a light dinner of hospital food, and came back to wait.

* * *

They had waited two hours, but still no word. “Maybe it is worse than we thought,” Heema said. “They are taking a long time.”

JD rubbed his hands on his knees and got up to look out the window. It was getting dark outside. He turned back to Heema. “No, that’s probably good news. They’re working very hard on Fareed, and that’s a positive sign.” He knew an amputation would probably take a lot less time. They waited another hour, and finally the surgeon appeared. It was impossible to discern the outcome from her expression. She approached Heema and asked her to follow to the nursing station. They talked quietly for a few minutes, and Heema started crying again. The surgeon left, and Heema came back to join Vivian, B, and JD. She sat down heavily, and said, “They have saved Fareed’s arm. He may not be able to move it much, but they have saved his right arm.”

Vivian started crying and put her arms around her mother. JD waited a few minutes until Heema looked a little calmer, and then asked, “Can we see him now?”

Heema shook her head. “He will be in recovery, and it will be a few hours. And then it will be family only. You may be able to visit him tomorrow morning, Joshua.”

JD looked over at B. "Then I think I'll head for home with B, and come back tomorrow. But could you please call if Fareed can see me tonight, Heema?"

B looked back at his father, and then sat down beside Vivian. "I think I'll stay here, Dad, and go with the Ghanems tonight." Vivian took his hand and smiled.

JD thought about it for a few seconds. "Okay then, you may need this." He reached under his jacket, took out his Glock and holster, and gave both to B. The nurse at the station glanced over quickly, narrowed her eyes, and then resumed her work on the computer. Vivian and Heema both frowned, but did not comment. B put the pistol and holster under his belt. "I don't have a concealed carry permit. But thanks. I'll look after it."

JD got up to drive home. He had a lot to think about.

* * *

Annie was back in her studio, painting, when JD walked in. He knew it was her way of dealing with stress, and he sat down to watch. It was the first time he had relaxed a little since the *Damini* had bounced on that big wave and Fareed had fallen on the deck. Annie was concentrating on a grey and yellow painting, which was not quite as cheery as her other recent efforts. It was clear that the tension was getting to her. She paused and looked up at JD. "I'm hungry. Could we just order a pizza tonight? Junior went out with some friends." She looked toward the door. "Where's B?"

"He stayed with Heema and Vivian. Mostly with Vivian, I think. He's the man of the house for tonight at the Ghanems, so I gave him my Glock."

"Is that a good idea? He doesn't have a permit."

"It's just for tonight. He knows how to use it."

Annie shrugged and went back to her painting, while JD went to the kitchen to order a pizza. Then he poured a glass of port for Annie and a large rye for himself, and took them back to the studio. He handed the port to Annie. "They saved Fareed's arm. I have a feeling that the surgeon was very good."

She put down her brush and clinked glasses with JD. "That's a blessing. Thank God." They both took a sip, and Annie sat down. "And how are *you* doing, JD? It's been another crazy day."

JD put his glass down and rubbed his eyes. "I am really, really tired. As in, rode hard and put away wet."

She tilted her head and frowned. "JD, tell me something . . . do you think they were aiming at you instead of Fareed?"

He thought about it for a moment. "No, Puccini said that Fareed was the target, and he survived only because the boat hit that wave just before the bullet hit him. They were aiming at his heart. If I'd been the target, they would have taken another shot. I was still standing there after the first shot. So it must have been Fareed."

"But why would they take a chance like that - using a sniper, I mean? That seems to involve a lot of risk."

JD took another sip of his rye, and closed his eyes to think. "Maybe because of the bodyguard. After Fareed hired the bodyguard, they couldn't get close to him. They had to try it from three hundred yards away."

"*Who* had to try it? Who wanted to kill Fareed? And why?"

"Puccini thinks it was John Smith, working for Cole, and it was about that damn sculpture. That thing is cursed. The next thing you know – "

They were interrupted by the doorbell, and JD went to get the pizza. He brought it back to the studio with two plates, and Annie said, "I think that's all the painting for tonight. I need to clean up, and we can go eat in the kitchen."

JD had just opened the pizza box when Junior walked in. "Oh, wow, pizza, I am *so* hungry. Can I have a piece?" She sat down and grabbed a slice, wolfing it down quickly, and then pulled a soft drink from the fridge to wash it down. Annie came in and watched her briefly. "I guess I forgot to feed you, Junior. Welcome home." Junior reached for another piece as JD smiled, and said, "Maybe I should've ordered more." Junior finished her second piece, and then seemed to remember the day's events. "How is Fareed?"

"The surgeon was able to save his arm. His career as a drummer may be over, but he can still be a hedge fund mogul."

Later, when the rest of the pizza was gone and Junior and Annie had both gone up to bed, JD returned to his office. He couldn't sleep. He had to try to figure out what was happening. He sat down in the swivel chair at his desk and turned to look at the flow chart on the wall. It seemed like a year ago that he had stumbled into Rich's hotel room and almost passed out when he saw that finger on the floor. He knew something inside him had changed since then. He hadn't panicked when he saw Fareed bleeding on the deck; his ancient Ojibway instincts seemed to have taken over. The veneer of nerdiness from Princeton, Oxford, and MIT had dropped away, and he had discovered that the warrior from Christian Island was still in there somewhere.

His cell phone rang. Puccini. It was very late for a call, so he figured it must be important. He picked up, and Puccini got right to the point.

"Hi, sport, I shouldn't be doing this, but I thought I'd give you an update. Keep this to yourself, but we found gunpowder traces over on Duck Island. The shot came from there, no question. But we didn't find anything else. No shell casing, no tracks. These guys were pros. Witnesses saw a white powerboat leaving the island, two people aboard, very fast. No description, except one person was smaller. I'd bet on Smith and Cole."

"Smith certainly has the skills to do it," JD mused. "But would Cole be directly involved in this sort of dirty work. . . be out there when the bullets start flying?"

Puccini seemed to think that over. "Well . . . maybe not Cole himself. But Smith for sure, and someone else, maybe another body guard. Or even Cole's girlfriend."

"Do you have enough to go after them?"

"No, but I'm working on a warrant. It won't be easy, not much probable cause, but I'm going to give it a shot. I'll try to interview Ghanem tomorrow, though he likely won't have much to add. And we don't have the bullet. It went through and through. There wasn't even enough to determine the caliber. The shot was less than a quarter of a mile, so it could've been a number of possible loads and rifles. And the jet covered up the report, so no one heard it."

JD paused as he mulled over the events of the past week. "I think there's got to be a link among these four incidents – Rich's disappearance, Raji's death, my car chase, and now Fareed getting shot. It can't be random. There has to be a pattern. I'm working on some ideas."

Puccini was silent for a moment, and JD could almost sense his skepticism over the phone. "Some ideas, huh? Well, be sure to keep me posted." It sounded like Puccini was taking a swig of coffee and chewing on a donut. "Maybe I'll see you over at the hospital tomorrow."

"Thanks for the call. It's much appreciated."

JD disconnected and returned to contemplate his wall chart again. He added a large new circle for Fareed's shooting, and added the sniper on Duck Island. If the four incidents were connected, and if Cole was the common element, there had to be a connection between Cole and Rich's disappearance. But what was it? Rich didn't collect art, and he hadn't gone to Coates. As far as JD could remember, Rich had never mentioned Cole in conversation. Maybe if JD could get hold of Rich's laptop, he might find some evidence of a connection. Or was the connection through Yates? And if Dot had been involved in Rich's disappearance, how did that connect to the other events? That didn't seem plausible. JD couldn't see Dot going after Fareed or himself. He started to get a headache.

He went to the kitchen and poured himself another tumbler of Sazerac, and then returned to his office. He dropped into his chair, taking a big cowboy gulp of the rye. He put his boots up on the desk, and closed his eyes. The day's events started streaming through his consciousness, and he was soon fast asleep. The tumbler rolled from his lap and shattered on the hardwood floor.

* * *

JD awoke with a start. Annie was shaking his shoulder. "Wake up, JD. Come up to bed. You need some sleep. And be careful. Don't step on the glass." He followed her up the stairs groggily, and tumbled into bed without taking off his boots.

He was asleep before his head hit the pillow.

CHAPTER 14

Sunday, September 14, 2008

JD was still dressed, but his boots were on the floor. He couldn't remember much after his phone call with Puccini the night before. Annie was nowhere in sight, and he stripped off his clothes and stepped into the shower. The hot water started to get his blood circulating, and he shaved and got dressed.

Downstairs, Annie had breakfast ready. "Junior's still sleeping, so let's be quiet. And you had a rough night. You were tossing and turning like crazy."

"I don't remember anything. I think my nervous system just collapsed last night, or maybe it was the rye. Puccini called. He said they found traces of gunpowder on Duck Island. It was definitely a sniper."

"I saw the charts you're working on. Could we look at them together? I'd like to understand them."

"Sure, but let's have breakfast first. Junior ate most of that pizza last night, and I'm starved."

They finished their breakfast, and then went to JD's office. Annie studied the flow chart on the wall. "There's something missing there. I can't put my finger on it, but it just doesn't look right. And that reminds me . . . I found out more about Mortimer. You should have him in that chart."

JD scratched his head. "Mortimer is just an artist. Why would he fit up there?"

Annie folded her arms. “I like the way you say ‘just an artist.’ I could say that you’re ‘just an economist,’ but you know that’s not the whole picture. I asked some of my artist friends about Mortimer, and there are some very strange rumors.”

JD backpedaled. “Okay, tell me about Mortimer. Why should I care about him?”

“Well, first off, how is he selling multi-million dollar pieces in Greenwich? Why isn’t he in New York or London? Those are the real global art centers, and he’s based here in an artistic backwater. But his pieces still sell in the millions. It doesn’t compute.”

“You could say the same thing about hedge funds. Why are so many of them in Greenwich rather than in New York or London? And maybe that’s why Mortimer is here. He has lots of wealthy potential clients in this area. Like Harriman. Or maybe he just likes living here.”

“Maybe. But there’s also the question of his wealth. He has a house in Bell Haven, which I can understand. His art could pay for that. But he also owns a big island out in the Sound, and that’s where he keeps his studio. He’s living beyond his means.”

JD looked up at the chart again. “Maybe you’re right. I’ll add Mortimer. And I’ll take a closer look at his assets, see if the numbers make sense.”

“Good. And you know . . . there’s something else. They say Mortimer has this mysterious assistant, but no one’s ever seen him. He lives out on the island, and never appears in public.”

JD sighed. “Maybe this assistant is just shy. That’s not illegal. But anyway, I’ll look into it.” He glanced down at his cell phone. “Have you heard from the hospital or from B?”

“B called early this morning, and said that Fareed came through the night okay. Heema was able to see him for a few minutes last night in the recovery room. He’s out on a regular ward now. You might be able to talk to him.”

“I have to get down there. I’ll call you as soon as I know how he’s doing. And maybe B wants to come home.”

Annie smiled. “If Vivian will let him.”

* * *

At the hospital, JD found Heema, Vivian, and B in the waiting room by the fourth floor ward. "Fareed is asleep now," Heema told him. "The nurses will let me know when he wakes up."

They sat down to wait, and JD bought a cup of coffee from the vending machine. After an hour and two more cups of mediocre coffee, JD finally saw the nurse walk toward them.

"Mr. Ghanem can see visitors now," she began, "but only very briefly, maybe two or three minutes. And you'll have to go in one at a time." She looked at the group waiting expectantly. "Who would like to be first?"

Heema said, "Maybe you should go in now, Joshua. I saw him earlier, and I know he really wants to see you."

JD followed the nurse down the hall into Fareed's room. The back of the bed had been tilted up about forty-five degrees, and Fareed could see JD without having to raise his head. An intravenous bottle was dripping slowly into his left arm, and his right arm and shoulder were swathed in white bandages, partly covered by his grey hospital gown. Fareed gave a very weak smile, and said, "Did you pick up the trophy, JD?" Then he grimaced and coughed, closing his eyes. JD could see that Fareed's right arm was tightly bound to his chest.

JD waited until Fareed recovered from his coughing fit. "I'm sure the trophy is safe and sound, Fareed. We'll have a big celebration when you pick it up."

Fareed looked at JD. "This is very serious now, Joshua. We must be careful."

JD smiled. "I know. You need a bodyguard."

Fareed turned his head slightly. "Heema fired him." He gave a little wheezing laugh, but then winced in pain.

The nurse came in, and said, "That's enough for now. Mr. Ghanem needs his rest." Fareed was now breathing steadily again, and JD nodded and smiled. "I'll be back." Then he followed the nurse out to the waiting room.

B stood up. "I'm ready to go home. Vivian and Heema will be all right, and I still have some work to do before class tomorrow."

Heema nodded. "You have been very helpful, Balthazar. Thank you."

Vivian came over and kissed B on the cheek. "Can you drive me back to Yale tonight?" she asked, holding his hand.

"No problem," B told her, and then joined JD on the way out to the car. Inside the Mercedes, B handed over the Glock and the holster. "Thanks, Dad. I'm glad I didn't need it."

They were home in a few minutes. JD realized he hadn't checked the markets since Saturday morning—since before the boat race. Now, he went onto three financial websites to see if there was any news about the status of Lehman Brothers. There was nothing. The Federal Reserve had put a very tight lid on the rescue negotiations. He called two of his sources in New York, and the only bit of intelligence he could glean was that a British bank was in the discussions. The Fed and the Treasury Department usually made their rescue announcements on Monday before the markets opened, so whatever the negotiations were, the parties at the table were running into a deadline. A decision was imminent. Either the government would save Lehman, creating political problems about taxpayer billions paying off fat-cat bankers, or they would let it go down, leading to financial chaos. JD had already placed his bets on some chaos.

There was nothing further to learn about the Lehman situation, so JD went back to the wall chart. He had added Mortimer as Annie had suggested, and connected him to Harriman - Mortimer was one of Harriman's clients - and to Cole because of *Tricolor One*, the piece that Fareed had sued him about. And that was the connection between Mortimer and Fareed as well. He'd almost forgotten about that, because Puccini was concentrating so strongly on Cole. JD drew a very visible link between Mortimer and Fareed. He looked at the circle containing Yates, and then at Mortimer, but after thinking about it for a few minutes, he couldn't see any connection - unless Yates also owned some of Mortimer's art. He continued working on the flow chart for another half hour, but had no more insights. He decided he wasn't quite ready to show it to Puccini.

* * *

That evening, after they'd had dinner and B had left to drive back to school, Annie came into JD's office. She sat down, again staring at the chart. "I see you've added Mortimer. And the connection to Fareed." She paused, rubbing a finger across her lower lip. "I can't believe I'm even suggesting this, but . . . do you think Mortimer might be involved in shooting Fareed? Maybe he's more than a sculptor. After all, he's the one that Fareed was actually suing."

JD tilted back his head and looked intently at the chart. He got up and ran his finger along one of the lines. "No, I think it's Cole and Smith. Smith threatened Fareed, and probably killed Raji. Puccini is going after Cole. That's the direct line. Mortimer is an artist, not a killer." JD turned toward Annie. "Remember, Fareed was shot from a quarter of a mile away, and Smith was a sniper in Iraq. Seven kills."

Annie nodded. "I suppose that does make more sense. Still . . ."

Junior popped her head in. "Bye, folks, I'm going to a party. I won't be very late."

Annie stared at her in surprise. "A party? On a Sunday night?"

"It's a surprise party for Kevin. It's his birthday today."

JD smiled. "Well, have a good time, and don't be late. You have school tomorrow."

"I won't. Bye." And she was gone.

Annie turned back to the chart on the wall. "I still think there's more to Mortimer. Maybe he's involved in Harriman's fraud somehow. Maybe that's how he has so much money."

JD sighed. "Okay, okay. I'll start digging into Mortimer's finances right now, see what I can find."

"Thank you, dear. It can't hurt to check him out."

JD turned toward his desk and started Googling Mortimer. Annie came up behind him to watch the monitor. "It's been a rough week, hasn't it?" She started rubbing his back gently. "Your neck is v-e-r-y tense. You need to relax." She started massaging the back of his neck, and then his shoulders. JD took his hand off the computer mouse and tilted his head back. "O-o-h-h, that feels good."

One thing led to another, and they had a very pleasant night.

CHAPTER 15

Monday, September 15, 2008

It had been a very fulfilling evening with Annie, and JD had been quite relaxed when he'd finally fallen asleep. But partway through the night, he started tossing and turning. He was having a very vivid nightmare about a sniper trying to kill him as he was swimming from Christian Island over to Penetanguishene. The bullets were flying all around him, and as he dove underwater to escape, he could see the trails of bubbles to the left and to the right, not missing him by much. JD swam as far as he could beneath the waves, holding his breath until he thought his lungs would burst, and then suddenly felt someone shaking him.

He opened his eyes. It was Junior. He glanced over at the alarm clock - 1:45 A.M. Annie was still sleeping peacefully beside him.

JD rubbed his eyes. "What's going on here, Junior? It's the middle of the night. What's wrong?"

"I'm sorry to wake you, Dad, but I thought you'd like to know. Lehman Brothers just declared bankruptcy."

"How do you know that? And why are you awake at this hour?"

"I got back from the party and couldn't sleep, so I checked my computer for messages. I get email notices from Bloomberg and CNBC, and they both sent out a special bulletin. Lehman is bankrupt. The CEO issued a statement. The government didn't rescue them."

JD sat deep in thought for a few seconds, trying to digest the news and shake off the last remnants of sleep. Annie stirred on the bed beside him, and rolled over without waking up.

"We'd better be quiet," JD said, and got up to put on his bathrobe. They went downstairs to the kitchen and turned on the TV. The BBC newscast from London was covering the story, and it was true. Lehman Brothers, founded in 1850, was gone. And Merrill Lynch, famous for its "thundering herd" sales force dealing in stocks and bonds, had been bought out for $50 billion by Bank of America to save it from a similar fate. Bank of America and Barclays of England had both looked into buying Lehman over the weekend, which would have prevented its bankruptcy, but the US government refused to make the potential buyers whole against any possible losses. Lehman's 25,000 employees were now in limbo.

JD said, "I guess the Treasury and the Feds just couldn't do it. Too much political damage from saving the fat cats."

Junior looked worried. "Are we going to be all right?"

"We'll be fine. I knew this was coming. Let's get some sleep now. We'll get the details in the morning. It's going to be an interesting week."

Junior and JD went back upstairs, and Junior went to her room. When JD got to his bed, Annie was still dozing away peacefully, and he set his alarm for 5:30 A.M. He fell asleep quickly, and his dreams were more pleasant this time, mostly about cashing in all those credit default swaps.

* * *

JD woke up as soon as the alarm went off. He was groggy, but he didn't want to miss what was about to happen. Rich, Fareed and JD had seen this coming for a year, and JD had endured a lot of criticism from his clients. Many of them had wanted to withdraw their money, but their funds were locked in. Some had even threatened legal action. Human nature being what it is, JD was expecting no kudos from these clients when they finally saw their windfall profits from his strategy.

But there could still be a problem, JD realized. If the dominos kept falling, the whole financial system could collapse, as it had in the 1930s. The government now had to step in at some point. Lehman was only one domino, and if other banks started failing, the result could be another Great Depression, and all bets would be off. More specifically, he knew that for his credit default swaps to pay off, the counterparties – the banks and insurance companies that had sold him the swaps – had to survive. If *they* also went bankrupt, his swaps would be worthless. It would be as if your house burned down on the same day your insurance company went bankrupt. You'd be out of luck.

He got dressed, went downstairs, and brewed a pot of coffee. Then he turned on CNBC's *Squawk Box* and sat down to watch. There was a balancing act going on. The commentators were trying to convince themselves that it would be business as usual today, but he could see the glimmer of fear in their eyes. They were trying to reassure themselves as much as to reassure the audience that all would be well. Their tone seemed to be, "Maybe a little hiccup, but no reason to panic." JD wished he could call Rich and Fareed to share the news, maybe get together for a celebratory breakfast.

Then he saw that AIG was in trouble - the largest insurance company in the world, and the most avid issuer of credit default swaps. He remembered his dreams of the night before about cashing in the credit default swaps. Would the government let AIG collapse? For the first time since the three of them had conceived their strategy, JD started to worry that things might still go completely sideways. Letting Lehman fail was political expediency, but it was also the right thing to do. The bankers involved had done some dumb things with their clients' money, and they deserved to crash and burn. It was tough love, and a lesson to the markets. But this could all go too far.

JD ruminated on this possibility for a while, and then was jerked back into the present when his stomach started growling. He suddenly realized he was very hungry, probably from all the nightmares and the news in the middle of the night. He started cooking his breakfast, just some simple bacon and eggs. The aroma from his cooking must have wafted upstairs, because five minutes later, Junior came slowly trudging down the hallway. Her eyes were half-closed as she sat down at the kitchen island and poured herself a cup of coffee. She looked at the TV screen. "So what's happening with our credit default swaps now?"

JD chose the positive approach. "They'll pay off, and we'll be rich."

JD finished cooking another order of bacon and eggs, and Junior started eating. She was quiet for a while, focused attentively on the TV screen. She and JD turned as Annie walked in. Annie looked like she had showered, and was already dressed in her painting jeans and blue long-sleeved shirt, with her hair pinned back. "You're up early, Junior. How was the party last night?"

"It was sort of okay. The surprise was spoiled. I think Kevin had figured it out, and was just playing along. He's not a very good actor."

Junior went upstairs, and Annie looked at the TV screen intently. "So Lehman is bankrupt. Are we going to be okay? Financially, I mean?"

JD smiled. "I've been expecting this for a long time. This is what we used to talk about at our band practices. We're fully hedged, no matter what happens." He didn't want to worry her about the prospect of AIG going bankrupt.

Annie walked over and gently kissed the top of JD's head. "That's good to know, Doctor Genius Smarty-Pants."

"I wish Rich were around to share it with us." He looked out the window at the woods behind the house as gathering daylight gradually brought the trees into focus. "That reminds me . . . what's happening with Dot? Have you heard from her at all?"

"She called yesterday, wanted to talk about Fareed. She'd seen the news, and knew he was in that race. I brought her up to date. She's sick with fear for Rich, but she didn't mention Houston, or anything more about being questioned by Puccini."

"Did she mention the fact that Puccini took Rich's home computer?" JD asked.

"She did, actually," Annie admitted.

"Do you know why she didn't want them to take it?"

Annie smiled. "Dot and Rich weren't always at odds. Rich had some old photos of her stored on it . . . photos that were . . . personal."

"Personal? Oh, I see . . . *that* kind of personal," JD said. They heard the front door close as Junior left for school. Annie went to her studio, and JD headed to his office to check on the markets. The futures were well down, and he called two of his contacts in Manhattan. There were many rumors about AIG, but all he could do now was wait.

He checked his client emails, and as expected, they were mostly negative. Many of them still did not understand the money-making link between the current market crash and his credit default swaps.

JD decided to compose a detailed explanation of his strategy – for the fourth time – to his clients. There were a few more emails as he was writing his report, and there was even one positive one from a fellow MIT alumnus. He did answer that one, and then sent out his strategic summary to his full client list. He felt better after he clicked the "Send" button.

He turned away from his desk to look at his wall charts. With the turmoil in the markets during the morning, he had almost forgotten about Fareed, and he decided to call Heema, to see if there was any further news.

"Fareed is feeling better," Heema told him. "They are cutting back on the morphine, so he feels more pain, but he can also think more clearly. He is more like his old self, and that is truly a blessing. You will be able to see him again today, and for more than a few minutes. And I think he will have a surprise for you."

"A surprise?" JD paused. "What kind of surprise?"

"I am afraid you will have to wait until Fareed tells you, or it would not be a surprise."

"Okay, I can wait. It sounds like good news. And how are you doing yourself, Heema? And how is Vivian?"

"We are persevering. That is how Fareed would like us to behave. But I must admit that I am nervous. Perhaps I should not have terminated our bodyguard so precipitously."

"We can find you another one. Would you like me to speak to Detective Puccini?"

"Yes, please. Vivian has returned to college, and I am on my own now. I spend most of my time here at the hospital, of course, but when I am in that big house at night . . . I am afraid, Joshua. Very afraid."

Especially with Raji gone, thought JD. "Maybe you should come stay with us, Heema."

There was silence on the phone for a few seconds. "You are very kind, Joshua. Perhaps we can discuss it when you visit Fareed tonight. And there is one more thing I should mention. I have asked the lawyers to cancel the lawsuit against Mortimer. It is not something we should be concerned with right now. But please don't tell Fareed."

JD paused. That was a bit of a surprise. Fareed would certainly have proceeded with the suit, but Heema was correct. This was not the time. "It was the right thing to do, Heema. And don't worry, I won't tell him."

JD disconnected, and went back to reviewing his Venn diagram and flow chart. After following the various links and lines for a few minutes, he could see a gap. Cole, Harriman, and Yates had all received their schooling at Coates Academy, plus Cole and Harriman were connected to Mortimer through Mortimer's art. But there was still nothing obvious tying Yates and Mortimer.

Yates to Mortimer – that was the missing link, JD realized. And if he found it, Dot would probably be in the clear.

He returned to his desk and started a more detailed examination of Mortimer. The first step was to confirm Mortimer's property ownership. First, JD looked at the public property records for Mortimer's house in Belle Plains. Mortimer had owned the house outright for over ten years, and its current assessed value was $5.7 million. There had been a series of permits issued for major renovations and a deep-water dock. It was clear that Mortimer had been doing well financially for a long time. Or else, like Harriman, he had started with inherited wealth.

JD next tried to find information on Mortimer's private island out in Long Island Sound. After some research, he found what he was looking for in *Art World*, a contemporary art magazine. It was a four-page spread on *Ceramic Heaven*, Mortimer's island and studio. It was impressive. The island itself was five miles off-shore from Greenwich, just across from three smaller uninhabited islands. JD remembered picnicking with the family on one of those small islands when the kids were little, and he had wondered at the time about that bigger island. The *Art World* article showed a large house in contemporary style, grounds that were mostly wild, with a few small patches of lawn, and pathways leading around the island. One side of the island was fairly low, and a large dock and boathouse hugged that shoreline. The other side of the island was much higher, and was bordered by a cliff. But to JD the most interesting parts of the article were the descriptions of Mortimer's large ceramic kiln, and the barge he used to transport his huge ceramic pieces back to the mainland after firing. According to the article, the kiln was one of only three of such huge size in the country, and transporting and assembling it had been a major project. The kiln was over ten years old, which meant Mortimer had owned the island at least as long as his house in Belle Plains.

JD wanted to confirm that Mortimer actually owned the island, but he could find nothing in the public record about ownership except the name of a corporation. He traced the chairman of the corporation to a small accounting office in Stamford, Connecticut, named Richards Burnett LLC. Their website was very crude, and they seemed to have only four employees. JD thought it quite odd that such a small accounting firm would be looking after Mortimer's millions. He also noticed a lawyer on the board of this small corporation, and he traced the lawyer to one of the largest international law firms in New York. He checked out their website; this firm had offices in London, Tokyo, and Munich. But what stopped him dead in his tracks was their two smaller offices - one in Zurich and one in the Cayman Islands. He knew these were perfect locations for quiet and confidential bank accounts, safe from prying U.S. government eyes. And Mortimer's island was assessed at $25.6 million for tax purposes. Not many artists could afford that.

JD would have liked to get more detail on Mortimer's finances, but he knew that determining the actual dollar amounts in those off-shore accounts was far beyond his hacking skills. He could probably identify the banks in Zurich and the Caymans, and maybe hack into their systems, but he was certain the accounts would have no names on them – only identifying numbers – and without the list linking the account numbers to names, all his hacking efforts would be meaningless. And he had no way to get that list. It would not have been digitized, but would have been recorded in the pre-computer manner – on paper, with ink. And paper and ink could not be hacked.

Wanting to share what he had found with Annie, JD walked over to her studio. He sat down and waited until Annie put down her brush, and said, "You may be right about Mortimer. His house is worth nearly $6 million. And that island is worth over $25 million. Plus he's probably parked some money in Switzerland and the Caymans."

Annie's eyes widened. "Are you sure about those numbers? I had my suspicions, but that's beyond anything I imagined. He works out of Greenwich, for goodness' sake, and you're saying he has at least $30 million in assets? I had no idea the island was worth that much. Do you think maybe he inherited his wealth - or at least the real estate?"

JD shrugged. "I have to do more research, but if it's inherited, you would expect the media would include that in his biographies. No one seems to know much about his background. I haven't even been able to find his full name. His only income seems to be his art. We need to figure out his cash flow, and compare it to his assets."

"What do you mean 'cash flow'?"

"How much money he makes by selling his art. Is there a record somewhere of all his sales and prices? We could add them all up, estimate his expenses, and get a sense of his net income. I can't believe it would be enough to pay for all those assets."

Annie shook her head. "Those numbers are not easy to come by. Initial sales for living artists are through private galleries, and they don't always publicize their figures. And the commissions can be obscure and negotiable, so you don't know how much the artist actually gets. Prominent artists pay a lower commission."

"But what about those Picassos and van Goghs that sell for a hundred million? That's all public."

"Those are all resales, not initial sales, and they're at auction. So the artist never sees that money. And in most of those cases, the artist is dead. Damien Hirst is trying to change that. He's taking two hundred original works that have never been sold before directly to auction. In fact, that auction is on today and tomorrow in London. Sales are expected to be almost $200 million."

"Hirst may not sell anything today, given what's happening in the financial markets. It's chaos and panic."

"Oh, I don't know. There's still some smart money around. Look at you, dear. You should be over in London right now, bidding."

"I don't think so. I know nothing about art. But I do want to find out more about Mortimer."

Annie started cleaning her brushes. "I'll see what I can find out about Mortimer's sales. Maybe I'll call a few friends who know the sculpture market. And we could go visit his gallery. By the way, where did Mortimer go to school? I know he went to Pratt for sculpture at one point, but that was a post-graduate fellowship. And we do need to find his full name. Is Mortimer his first name or his last name, or a made-up name?"

JD nodded. "I'll check into that. And a tour of Mortimer's gallery should definitely be on our to-do list."

"Maybe we can buy one of his pieces now that your ship is coming in."

JD winced. "Buying one of his works seems to be bad karma. But maybe we can just pretend that we're interested, put on a bit of a show."

JD walked over to his office and sat down at the desk to do more research. He ignored a dozen new emails from clients, and was just getting started again on Mortimer when his phone rang. It was Puccini.

"Hi, sport, I'm glad I caught you. What's happening with the markets? That's all anyone's talking about in the squad room . . . the Lehman bankruptcy. Are my funds okay? Everyone's in a panic." For the first time that JD could recall, Puccini sounded a little nervous.

JD paused. "Let me ask you something – did you put all your money in Treasury bonds, as I suggested?"

"Yeah, I did. I had to argue with my broker. He said Lehman was a screaming deal, they would get bought out or rescued by the government and I'd make a lot of money. I had to get real loud, but he finally heard me, so I'm in government bonds. All of it."

"Then you're golden. By the end of the week, everyone will be scrambling into Treasuries, and their prices will skyrocket. That's my hedge, too. If AIG goes under, the only safe haven will be the government. The government can't go broke, because they're the ones who print the money."

JD heard a sigh of relief. "That's what I wanted to hear, pal."

"So just sit tight, and do nothing for six months. Then you can look around. When the market hits bottom, there'll be some bargains."

There was silence for a few seconds. "This is the second time you're saved my bacon . . . and my kids' college fund. And what happens to Harriman now?"

"His fund is on a death watch, and he'd better start practicing his perp walk. And speaking of Harriman, I've been doing some research on his favorite artist, Mortimer. He seems to be living way beyond his means."

"Huh? What's that mean? Like, he's borrowing money?"

"Maybe, but more likely he's getting a lot of money from something other than his art sales. His island out in the Sound is worth over $25 million, and I suspect he has a lot hidden in Switzerland and the Cayman Islands."

"Well, I can't help you on that. You know fraud's not my area, and besides, all the brainpower we have on our side still hasn't caught Harriman. And maybe Harriman might be pushing a few favors Mortimer's way, letting him dip into the honey pot. Maybe that's where Mortimer gets his money."

JD thought about this for a few seconds. "That might explain it. Harriman wouldn't keep all the Ponzi money for himself. That's not the way it works. He'd spread some of it around, to show that his clients can actually withdraw their winnings if they want. Those fake redemptions are part of his marketing program. But why would he favor Mortimer?"

"Don't have a clue. Financial fraud is your area, buddy. Anyway, I'm not going to worry about some artist getting too rich. Not my problem. I've got to zero in on Smith and Cole for attempted murder. I should get my search warrant in the next twenty-four hours."

"What do you expect to find?"

"I want to get Smith's Tac-50 and his sniper equipment. I can't place it at the scene yet, but it'll look good in court. Very graphic. And when I get that rifle, we may have enough circumstantial evidence to make an arrest."

"Well, that's good news. But do you have anything new on Richard Bridger? That's where this whole thing started. Was Smith involved in that? He certainly has the skill. And have you found any connection between Cole and Bridger? Everything you're doing seems to be about Cole."

"I haven't forgotten about Bridger." Puccini sounded annoyed. "No links with Cole that I can see, but we're still looking. And we're still looking into Mrs. Bridger. I don't really see much connection between the Bridger case and this new Ghanem shooting, if you want to know the truth."

"And what are Fareed's views on all this? Have you talked to him?"

"No, he was too weak yesterday. The docs say maybe later today."

"I saw him for about two minutes yesterday. His wife fired their bodyguard, saying he should have protected Fareed."

"That's not a smart move. She should get someone else until we get Smith behind bars."

"Do you have any suggestions?"

Puccini was silent for a few seconds. "No, not off the bat. If she fired Riley, she's probably burned my sources in the bodyguard business. Word gets around, so I'll have to get back to you on that. I'll be in touch."

Puccini disconnected.

JD turned back to his computer. The Dow Jones was down another 300 points, and still plunging. No word on AIG, but their stock was being dumped. There were twenty more emails from clients, and he scanned them quickly. There was nothing to do but wait, so he decided not to respond.

He turned to continue his research on Mortimer. His next goal was to find out more about Mortimer's schooling. None of the various bios indicated where he had gone to high school. The *Art World* spread on his island studio mentioned Pratt Institute, but nothing else. The newspaper archives did not go back that far in digital format, and the search engines didn't help much. He started laboriously going through the Pratt Institute alumni magazine on their website, and two hour later, he finally found what he was looking for.

Mortimer had graduated from Coates Academy.

CHAPTER 16

Mortimer's alma mater, Coates Academy, was the same prep school near Greenwich attended by Cole, Yates, and Harriman. JD decided to dig a little deeper. It took him less than fifteen minutes to hack into the Coates website, and he started examining their yearbooks, which had all been digitally remastered and were fully searchable. Then he realized that he didn't know Mortimer's full name.

He first assumed that Mortimer was the artist's last name, not his given name. There were fifteen Coates graduates over the years with Mortimer as a surname, and he started examining the ones whose graduation year was consistent with Mortimer's probable age, which he guessed as being between thirty and fifty. So he examined the Mortimers that had graduated from Coates between 1976 and 1996. There were six on that list, and since he had never seen Mortimer, he couldn't recognize his picture by sight. He Googled Mortimer the current artist, examined his picture, and then compared it to the six Mortimers he had found in the Coates yearbooks. It wasn't easy to make a match, because the hairstyles varied considerably from decade to decade, and Mortimer's hair was now black, fairly short and spiky. JD finally zeroed in on one particular student who graduated in 1981. His hair was long, but it was black, and he had been a member of the Arts Club. His ambition at the time, as expressed in his yearbook caption, was to become a major artist. And he could now see why Mortimer had decided to shorten his name to one word.

This student's full name was Yelberton Abraham Mortimer. Poor guy, thought JD. Mortimer's parents had apparently named him after Y.A.

Tittle, the New York Giants Hall-of-Fame quarterback from 1961 to 1963. His classmates might have called him Y.A. – but probably something much worse.

JD continued looking through the 1981 yearbook, and then stopped abruptly. A sudden chill ran down his spine. *Stuart Cole and Mortimer had been classmates.* They were standing next to each other in a group photo of the Arts Club in 1981.

The dots were getting connected.

He went over to Annie's studio to bring her up to date. Annie had finally finished the grey and yellow painting, which was sitting on an easel in the corner. She had started a new one, with much brighter colors – yellow and red, with a touch of blue. She looked relaxed. "So what have you found?" she asked.

"Well, first off, Mortimer also went to Coates Academy, same as those other three. Don't you think it's odd for an artist to graduate from a prep school?"

"Not if you're from Greenwich. If you don't go to prep school, you're considered a drop-out here. But it's an interesting coincidence."

"It's not a coincidence. Stuart Cole and Yelberton Abraham Mortimer were classmates, and both belonged to the Arts Club."

Annie squinted in confusion. "Yelberton . . . what?"

"Yelberton Abraham Mortimer. That's probably why he shortened it to Mortimer. He must have interesting parents."

Annie continued painting. "So they're all connected. Yates, Harriman, Cole . . . and Mortimer?"

"And Smith. Don't forget Smith. He's part of the network."

"Don't tell me he went to Coates as well."

"No, he's from Kentucky, doesn't quite have that Coates pedigree."

Annie put a wide slash of orange on her painting. JD said, "Your outlook seems to more positive. This painting is much brighter."

"I had to force myself. Maybe my mood will follow my painting."

JD watched her mixing some yellow, and could see that she was moving well on this piece. But he was now anxious to follow up on Mortimer.

"I know this will break your creative flow, but I think we need to do more research on Mortimer, and I need your help. We should go down to his gallery and see what we can find. Something may click."

Annie put down her brush, and looked at JD. "Then we should do it right away. I have a bad feeling about Mortimer."

"His dealer's name is Ivan Kosnowski, and his gallery is on Greenwich Avenue, down the street from D'Allessandro's. Fareed showed me. You need an appointment to get in. Do you know Kosnowski?"

Annie started cleaning her brushes. "I know him, and I also know you need a thick wallet to get through that door. But I'll give him a call. He knows my dealer and he knows me, even though I'm at a different price point. I'll tell him we may be interested in buying one of Mortimer's big sculptures."

"Would that be credible?"

"I'm sure he'll do some research on you before we get there, and once he checks out your hedge fund, he'll give us the royal tour."

Annie called Kosnowski's gallery and got them an appointment an hour later.

JD went back to his office to check on the markets, but he got a shock. They had hardly moved. The collapse he had expected was nowhere in sight. It didn't make sense. He saw almost twenty more emails from clients, but he ignored them again. He would have to wait, to see whether the market finally reacted the way he expected.

* * *

Promptly at 10 A.M., JD and Annie were standing outside Kosnowski's gallery. The building was two stories high, with a large window to the left of the glass door in front. The window had discreet gold lettering that simply said Kosnowski Gallery. JD peered inside. The room he could see was small, with only a few small paintings on the walls. A fancy designer desk sat to one side, and he saw a door leading to the back. There were two security cameras on the far wall.

Annie pushed the button on the intercom next to the door. Moments later, a large man dressed in grey slacks, a blue blazer, and a black turtleneck opened the door and invited them inside.

Annie and JD were ushered past the front room into a large office. The man behind the desk was about fifty years old, tall and slim, and his blond hair was flecked with grey. He was dressed in an expensive designer suit with an open-neck silk shirt. He got up, took Annie's hand, kissed it gently, and said in an eastern European accent, "A-a-h-h, it is the wondrous Madame Rutherford. I am so looking forward to your new show. I've been following your work for quite some time now." He turned to JD. "And you must be Dr. Dionne, the hedge fund king from the wilds of Ontario." He chuckled as he shook JD's hand. Kosnowski had obviously done his research. "And what can we do for you today? I am at your service."

"Ivan, we are here to look at some Mortimers," Annie said. "The word is that you have some spectacular new pieces. We are renovating our house, and I'm thinking one of them might be perfect for our new atrium."

Kosnowski folded his arms and frowned dramatically. "You must realize that these pieces are very big . . . almost monumental. You need a very, very large vista to give them proper breathing space."

Annie's mouth turned down at the corner and she narrowed her eyes. "We can send you the architectural renderings. Our renovations were designed by Hayakawa and Horvath, and I assure you the atrium is spacious enough for several Mortimers."

JD smiled at Annie's imaginative response, and Kosnowski backed down, saying, "Hayakawa and Horvath, you say? Very well, let us go in and see what you might like. However, Mortimer will still have the final say. It is in his contract. He is very particular about who buys his works." JD thought this odd. As long as someone paid full price, why would he care?

Kosnowski opened the door at the back by punching a code into the security pad on the wall. Bowing deeply, he beckoned them to enter. The room was very big, a full two stories in height, and at least fifty feet square. The floors were white marble, and the walls were also painted white, with numerous skylights above. In each quadrant of the room sat a Mortimer ceramic sculpture bathed in natural light. Annie and JD were both silent as they walked around the four enormous pieces. Kosnowski stood off to one side and watched, with his arms crossed and a wide smile on his face.

Annie stopped in front of one of the sculptures and looked at JD. "I think this is the one." It was yellow and red, with a touch of grey and black. Kosnowski moved closer and looked up at the shimmering colors. "This is one of Mortimer's latest pieces. He named it *Blood and Bone.*"

JD took a deep breath. "And what sort of numbers are we talking here?"

Kosnowski looked very serious. "Well, sir, if you have to ask, then perhaps you cannot afford it." He chortled, and then smiled. "I was . . . how you say? . . . pulling your leg. It is three and a half million dollars."

Annie looked at JD. "Can we buy it, dear? It would look perfect in the atrium."

JD peered at the sculpture for a few seconds. "Of course, love, if you think it will complement our new renovations." JD turned toward Kosnwoski. "Annie is the artist in the family. I trust her judgment completely."

Annie smiled. "Thank you, dear. Let's -- "

They were interrupted by the opening of the door. The guard in the blazer ushered in a big man with black spiky hair. His neck was very wide, and he looked like a weight-lifter in his black t-shirt and artfully tattered designer jeans. JD recognized him from his recent research. It was Mortimer.

The guard made a hasty exit. Mortimer stood by the door, his piercing blue eyes scanning the room. He glanced at JD and Annie, and then glared at Kosnowski.

"I'm having a very bad day, Ivan. What's going on? Why did you ask me to come down here?"

Looking a little anxious, Kosnowski forced a smile. "These are two very important clients, Mortimer. This is Anne Rutherford, the artist, and this is Doctor Joshua Dionne, a well-known and successful hedge fund manager. They are interested in purchasing *Blood and Bone*." Annie and JD moved forward to shake Mortimer's hand, but Mortimer did not make any move to reciprocate, so they stepped back. JD could see that the situation was becoming awkward.

Mortimer turned to Kosnowski. "Lehman Brothers declared bankruptcy this morning, Ivan, and the markets are imploding. Someone told me that AIG may be next. I'm worried about my sales, and I'm worried about my investments. I may have to take these pieces off the market until the world settles down. Art prices are going to collapse."

Kosnowski sighed dramatically in apparent relief. "Is *that* your concern, Mortimer? I can assure you there is no need to worry about your prices. Damien Hirst's auction in London today was a roaring success. He grossed over eighty million on the first day, with more to come tomorrow. All the pieces sold, and most of the selling prices were well above Sotheby's estimates. His clients . . . and *your* clients . . . are not affected by something as mundane as the stock market." Kosnowski paused and looked at JD. "Take Doctor Dionne here. He is about to put down three million for *Blood and Bone.* He is certainly not worried about the markets."

JD tilted his head back and tried to look smug. "That's three *and a half* million, Ivan."

Mortimer turned and looked at JD, and his face softened a little. "So you're running a hedge fund. And you're not worried about the market implosion?"

"The smart money is never surprised by anything. This turmoil today was inevitable. I saw it coming a year ago."

Mortimer nodded slightly. "That's what my investment manager said this morning . . . that there's nothing to worry about. I've tripled my money over the last ten years, so he knows what he's doing. But I still worry. I may want take some profits." Mortimer's lips curved into a slight smile, and then the shadow came back over him quickly. "How have *your* returns been, Doctor Dionne?"

"They've been good, comparable to yours. But the big payoff will come over the next few weeks. I went very short, and loaded up on credit default swaps."

Mortimer paused. "Credit default swaps? What the fuck is that?"

"They're insurance policies that pay off in a financial collapse."

Mortimer rubbed his chin. "That sounds interesting. I should talk to my investment manager."

"I'm afraid it's a little late. No one will sell you fire insurance when they see flames. By the way, who is your investment manager?" JD knew the answer, but he wanted to determine whether Mortimer had any idea that Harriman's fund was a fraud.

"Winthrop Harriman. Maybe you've heard of him."

Kownowksi smiled and interjected, "Bucky Harriman is one of Mortimer's biggest patrons. They're neighbors in Belle Plains."

"Harriman's done well by me," Mortimer said. "He runs a very tight ship. We have the same accounting firm, so I always know what's going on."

That was the accounting firm with only four employees, JD remembered. And so Harriman used them as well, he realized. It was strange enough that someone with Mortimer's assets would use such a small firm - but Harriman? How could a thirty billion dollar fund have only four part-time accountants looking after its books? And then JD realized why – Harriman didn't have any books, just a very large bank account. And it was clear that Mortimer had no idea that Harriman was running a Ponzi.

Annie interrupted JD's train of thought. She stepped forward and folded her arms. "All right, boys, that's quite enough finance for now." She turned to JD. "We came here to buy some art and I, for one, would like to get back to that instead of discussing credit fault whatevers."

JD looked sideways at Mortimer, shrugged in surrender and turned to Annie. "You're absolutely right, dear. Let's deal with something far more important."

Annie looked up at *Blood and Bone* raptly. "That one is perfect. It's almost as if it had been commissioned for our atrium. It has a great deal of inherent tension." She paused, not taking her eyes off the sculpture. "The grey is fighting the yellow for dominance. The yin and the yang, one might say."

Mortimer steepled his fingers and nodded. His voice became very quiet, almost seductive. "You have an excellent eye, Ms. Rutherford. Most of my pieces involve harmony rather than discord, but I sought a little more conflict in this one. I finished it only two days ago. It was a very difficult piece to get right. I had to use some new interesting materials."

Annie turned to Mortimer with an innocent smile, full of curiosity. "These are very big pieces, Mr. Mortimer. May I ask you how you fire them? It must be a very complex process to get the texture and the colors just right on this massive scale. One mistake, and you've ruined a couple of tons of clay."

"A good question. As a matter of fact, I have one of the biggest ceramic kilns in the world. There are only two others in the country of this scale, and they're both smaller than mine."

Annie turned to JD. "Can we buy it, dear?" JD thought she was about to bat her eyelashes.

"I'm not sure. I know you like that piece very much, but we should consider it carefully. We do have a few other options for the atrium."

Kosnowski stepped forward. "We could do the necessary paperwork right here to hold the piece for you. My feeling is that it will sell quickly, especially when the news of the Hirst auction hits the hedge fund community. This would be an excellent investment, as well as a piece that you will enjoy for decades."

Annie looked at JD. "I think Ivan is one hundred percent correct. This is a very unusual piece. It would be absolutely dreadful if we missed this opportunity." She turned to look up at it again. "And besides, as Ivan says, it's an excellent investment."

Don't overplay it, Annie, JD thought. "All right, dear, if you're sure that's what you want. I need to move some accounts around. It'll take a day or two to free up three and a half million in cash."

Kosnowski smiled, obviously pleased with the sale. "One of Mortimer's regular clients is having a party tonight to celebrate the acquisition of a new piece called *Tricolor One.* You might enjoy it, and meet some fellow Mortimer collectors. His name is Stuart Cole. Maybe you know him from the hedge fund community?"

"No, we haven't met," JD said, hoping that neither Kosnowski nor Mortimer could see his sharp intake of breath on hearing the name. *Tricolor* One was the sculpture that Ghanem had wanted to buy. So now that Heema had dropped the lawsuit, Cole's offer to purchase the piece must have gone through, and Cole now owned the sculpture.

Annie nudged JD on the elbow, and JD popped back into the present. "That sounds wonderful. We'll be there."

Kosnowski smiled again. "Splendid. I shall make certain that you are added to the guest list. It is at seven o'clock at Stuart's home on Round Hill Road. I shall see you there."

* * *

Annie and JD were soon back home, preparing lunch in the kitchen. Annie cut some tomatoes and cucumbers and added them to the salad. "So what did you think of Mortimer?" she asked.

"He's a little weird, but he's an artist, so that's part of the package. And he seems to know about finance. What was your impression?"

Annie paused before answering. "I'm not sure. Something was off about his mannerisms. I can't quite put my finger on it, but he made me very uncomfortable. Maybe it was his eyes. They were so amazingly intense. He was angry when he arrived, and then he became friendlier, but his eyes never changed." Annie put the salad bowl on the table, and they sat down to eat. "Maybe we'll find out more about him tonight at Cole's party."

JD nodded. "And I should visit Fareed before we go to the party, maybe this afternoon."

"Are you going to tell him that Cole has his sculpture . . . and that we're going to Cole's party?"

"No," JD said quickly. "It'll just upset him. He needs his rest more than information right now, and we don't have anything concrete yet. But I should call Puccini to tell him about Mortimer's connection to Coates Academy." JD thought a moment. "There's a good chance that most of the suspects on my wall chart are going to be there tonight: Cole, his man Smith, Harriman, and maybe even Yates."

"Plus Mortimer, of course," Annie murmured. She looked up at him. "Why don't you wait to call Puccini? We need to dig into this a little more, see what we can learn at the party."

JD smiled. "You're becoming a great little detective, Miss Marple."

"And you're not so bad yourself, Mr. Holmes."

CHAPTER 17

Annie and JD had just finished lunch, and it was now almost two o'clock. JD was thinking about Cole's party as he walked back to his office. In a few hours they'd be driving up Round Hill Road again. He still had vivid memories of his last time there – of the two black Cadillac SUVs closing in on him, pushing him toward the cliff and the trees below. He took a few deep breaths to clear his mind of the vision, and sat down at his desk to check the markets, but there was little change. The collapse of Lehman seemed to have been taken in stride, and the stock indices had declined only slightly. He was starting to get a little nervous about his strategy. What if the markets recovered? What if he was wrong?

He realized he was grinding his teeth with the tension, so he switched off the market report, pushed his chair back, and turned to look at his Venn diagrams. There were now four people up there connected through Coates Academy, and three of them – Yates, Cole and Harriman – had motivation for the three violent incidents over the past week. He looked at the listing on the wall again:

- Yates was a suspect in Rich's disappearance because Rich had discovered that Yates was running a financial fraud.
- John Smith, acting for Cole, was a suspect in Fareed's shooting because Fareed had tied up Cole's purchase of *Tricolor One* in a lawsuit.
- Harriman was a suspect in the attempt to run JD off the road because JD had evidence that Harriman was also running a financial fraud.

But one thought still nagged at JD. Was it possible that the three events were coincidental, three separate incidents involving three individuals who just happened to have gone to the same school? All three had grown up on Greenwich, so all three would have been expected to go to Coates Academy or a similar prep school. Maybe the school issue was just a red herring. He decided to do some quick probability calculations. If the three incidents *were* unrelated and random, but the perpetrators had all grown up in Greenwich, what was the probability that all three would have gone to Coates Academy? With a little research, he found that about twenty-two percent of upper-middle-class students in Greenwich actually went to Coates – almost one in five. Then he considered a hypothetical situation. If three traffic accidents were to occur in Greenwich within a week, involving former preppies in high-end cars, what was the probability that all three drivers were Coates alumni? JD did a quick calculation. *The chance of this sort of random coincidence was only one percent.* By analogy, he concluded that the three violent events over the past week were not random at all, but were connected somehow. The probability that they were unconnected was only one in a hundred.

And where did Mortimer fit in, if at all? There was now a more direct connection between Cole and Mortimer, because they had known each other at Coates. In his traffic-accident scenario, they might even have been in the same car. They had the school connection, and Cole was in the exclusive circle of Mortimer collectors. Was that all there was to it? JD couldn't help wondering if the two old school friends also shared a hit man, namely John Smith. Maybe tonight, he and Annie would come closer to fitting the pieces of the puzzle.

JD then turned to Bloomberg to check on the markets again. The stock indices had dropped a little but were remarkably stable despite all the angst a few hours earlier. He turned on CNBC. There was a report about this remarkable resiliency, and the talking heads looked almost cheerful. It seemed bizarre, thought JD, like whistling past a graveyard. But all this cheerfulness was starting to worry him. He decided to calculate what would happen to his fund if the markets did recover.

It took him over an hour to analyze the potential impacts in detail, and he realized that his fund would actually lose money. Many of his clients would probably pull out their capital at the first opportunity, and his fund would have to fold. And all those experts he'd been disparaging for so long would turn out to be right. He took a deep breath and closed the program.

Greatly worried after this analysis, JD went back to Bloomberg to check the markets again. At first he felt some relief. Reality was sinking in. AIG had plummeted 60 percent, and there was now a lot of serious concern about its survival. And after the apparent calm of an hour earlier, a wave of selling had suddenly engulfed the market. The Dow was down 504 points, the biggest single-day drop in six years. But now he was hoping it wouldn't go too far. He needed a crisis, not a disaster.

JD felt a headache coming on. He took a deep breath, and shut down the computer. He'd had enough bad news for the day, and it was getting late – time to get down to the hospital to see how Fareed was doing. That would at least take his mind off the markets.

* * *

JD got into the Mercedes. Traffic was light, and ten minutes later he was at the hospital. He stopped at the small gift shop on the first floor, bought a book of Dilbert cartoons to cheer up Fareed, and went up to his room.

Fareed was lying in his bed fast asleep when JD entered, with the IV bottle dripping silently into his arm. JD could see the bandages bulging out of the hospital gown around Fareed's right shoulder as his friend breathed steadily and peacefully. JD sat down beside the bed and opened the Dilbert book. One of the cartoons was too close to home, and JD let out a loud laugh. He caught himself and looked up, and saw that Fareed had stirred at the sound.

Fareed slowly opened his eyes, and when he saw JD, his face lit up with a smile. "Hello, Joshua. It is so wonderful to see you."

"I brought you a little present." JD handed Fareed the Dilbert book.

Fareed laid it on the table beside him with a sigh. "I shall read it later, Joshua. I am a Dilbert fanatic, but unfortunately, it hurts when I laugh." Fareed pushed a button on the side of the bed, rose to a sitting position, and picked up a small cylinder connected to the IV bottle. "This is my morphine pump, and it is a Godsend." He took a long, steadying breath. "Heema told me that Lehman declared bankruptcy this morning. I had requested a laptop to follow the markets, but the doctors said no, it would upset me too much. They looked worried, so they must be long the market. I told them I had been expecting this for a year, but they still would not allow me to have a laptop."

JD chuckled. Fareed had nearly died two days ago but was now quintessentially himself again. "The Dow fell over five hundred points today," JD said. "It's happening, Fareed. All our bets are going to pay off." JD decided not to mention AIG, afraid it would upset Fareed too much. But Fareed was well ahead of him.

"What about AIG? They are the next domino in the queue."

JD realized that he had to tell his friend the truth. "I really don't know. The Fed has to rescue them, or it'll be chaos. You know what the problem is . . . the other big investment banks are all counterparties to AIG's swaps, and they could face collapse if AIG goes under."

Fareed closed his eyes, smiling a little. The morphine seemed to be having its effect. He opened them after a few seconds. "I think the Federal Reserve and the Treasury Department will rescue AIG, Joshua. There is nothing to worry about. In any case, we have placed our bets and must live with the consequences."

JD breathed a sigh of relief, glad that Fareed did not seem upset by the news. He decided to change the subject. "And how's your shoulder coming along? How long will you have to stay in the hospital?"

Fareed smiled. "Joshua, my shoulder is destroyed. The humerus, the scapula, and the rotator cuff are all seriously damaged. However, here is the good news. Doctor Craig will provide me with a brand-new shoulder. She will install a reverse shoulder replacement. I shall become a bionic man and set off all the alarms at the airport security machines. She said I will even be able to play the drums again."

JD sat back to digest this positive news. "Reverse shoulder replacement? Will you have to play the drums behind your back, then?"

Fareed laughed - and then winced in pain. "No, no, Joshua. It just means the new socket will be in the humerus bone, and the ball will be in my scapula. It shall be the reverse of what you and I have naturally, but Doctor Craig assures me that this is the superior surgical approach."

JD tried to imagine the new configuration but quickly gave up. His friend seemed happy with the prospect of a new metallic shoulder, and that was good enough for him. He looked over at the book on the bedside table. "Well, enjoy Dilbert, Fareed. You'll soon be back at work. Enjoy your rest, and I'll see you tomorrow."

"Thank you for coming, and don't worry about AIG. But Joshua, has there been any word on Richard?"

JD shook his head. "Not yet." He got up, gently shook Fareed's left hand, and walked out. As he drove home, he started thinking again about the shooting on the sailboat. Fareed had shown no desire to raise the topic, and was probably doing his best to forget the trauma he had been through. But after seeing his friend and the damage that had been done, JD was even more focused on determining what had happened. All the evidence seemed to point to Smith and Cole, but he still had a gnawing feeling that he was overlooking something. It was something hiding in plain sight, but he couldn't put his finger on it.

CHAPTER 18

Just after eight that night, JD and Annie got into the Mercedes. She was wearing a bright, blue silk dress with a yellow shawl, and JD had his white Mark Twain suit, complemented by black Tony Lama boots and a white Stetson with two eagle feathers. They both had their guns in concealed holsters. JD took off his Stetson and put it on the backseat. Then they set off for Stuart Cole's house. He couldn't help instinctively checking for black Cadillac SUVs, but he saw only a white car going in the other direction as he turned onto Round Hill Road. He drove slowly, checking the numbers on the signposts, and finally found Cole's property.

Cole's driveway weaved back and forth for about a quarter of a mile up a hill, and then finally ended at a black wrought-iron fence with a wide security gate. JD saw a camera mounted on the narrow metal arch above the gate, and as the Mercedes approached, the gate slowly opened. JD drove into a large courtyard brightly lit by elevated floodlights.

There were about two dozen cars already parked in the huge courtyard. JD noticed two Ferraris, two Bentleys, three Rolls Royces, and a few Mercedes. He spotted a black SUV parked at the far end, and he thought about walking over to see whether it was a Cadillac, but finally decided that he was just being paranoid. It was probably just another Mercedes. Annie grabbed his arm, and they walked up toward the house, which was bathed in floodlights. It was very large, maybe two hundred feet wide, done in an odd combination of architectural styles.

"Well, that's certainly idiosyncratic," Annie said. "It's a blend of American colonial and Greek classical." JD looked at the semi-circular portico in front, supported by Doric columns, with a dome-shaped skylight.

It was quite a contrast with the white clapboard walls and blue-trimmed windows. JD thought it was kind of ugly.

As they headed toward the massive oak front door, a large man in a tuxedo opened it and ushered them in. "Welcome. The party is right through there." He pointed toward the center hall, just past an archway. JD looked around the large entry hall. It had limestone walls, a cove ceiling, and an elevator off to the side. Annie looked down at the off-white floor. "That's Bourgogne limestone."

They could hear the noise of the party guests in the center hall, and they started walking that way, pausing to admire some of the artwork on the walls. "There's a Basquiat. Cole must have quite a collection if he puts a Basquiat in the entry hall."

They entered the center hall, where two dozen people were milling around a very large ceramic sculpture. The skylight JD had seen outside was now overhead, and the room was very spacious, two stories high and at least a hundred feet wide. There was a staircase on the right side up to a mezzanine floor, and on the left side, JD could see a hallway leading to the back of the house. At the back of the room, the windows reached up two full stories. Peering through them, JD could see a floodlit garden, a swimming pool, and a tennis court.

A striking blond woman sauntered over and introduced herself. She was dressed in a classic black sheath dress showing plenty of cleavage. "Welcome to *C'est Si Bon.* I'm Tracy Alder. And by the look of your hat and boots, you must be the famous Joshua Dionne. And Anne Rutherford, I presume. Come, let me show you around. How do you like our house?"

Annie looked around the room. "It's striking. I really like the combination of styles. It's unusual, but it works. And the Basquiat. You must have quite a collection."

"Thank you. Stuart and I designed the house ourselves. And we have many other pieces along the hallway back there, including a Rothko. But what we're most proud of is our new Mortimer."

She led them over to the ceramic sculpture in the atrium. The other guests were drinking champagne, and talking in small groups. No one noticed them as they approached. JD saw Cole holding forth with Harriman and a few others. John Maynard Yates was part of the group, laughing at something Cole said. This proved JD's hypothesis: the three Coates graduates were friends, and the three violent incidents had to be related. But how? And who was the perpetrator?

Then he saw John Smith standing off to the side, towering above the crowd. JD glanced back at the three Coates alumni friends, and then realized that Smith must know all three of them. If he knew them all, did he maybe work for them all?

JD's thoughts were interrupted when Annie nudged him on the elbow. One of the tux-clad waiters was offering them flutes of champagne. Tracy Alder was still standing there with a smile. "Dom Perignon Special Reserve. Enjoy."

JD turned to the waiter. "Would it be possible to get a splash of Sazerac rye with two ice cubes?"

The waiter looked at Alder, and she nodded. "Of course. Please bring Dr. Dionne some Sazerac." She turned to JD. "It's my favorite rye whiskey, the essential ingredient for a Manhattan."

"I like mine straight."

Alder smiled politely and moved on, and JD turned to Annie. "Look over there," he said in a low voice. "That's John Maynard Yates with Cole and Harriman, acting like their best buddy. Those three all know one another. And Smith knows them all."

"Which one is Smith?"

JD realized she hadn't seen the headshot that Puccini had shown him and Ghanem. "The guy over there who's built like a linebacker."

Annie glanced over at the three men briefly, and then over at Smith. "Do you think Smith works for all of them?"

"I think it's likely. He's probably the only one of them with the skills to kidnap Rich."

"But what would be his motive?"

"The usual . . . follow the money. They can all afford to pay him well for his services. And I'm sure Cole wouldn't mind farming him out. They're all friends."

"I suppose that's all perfectly logical, but you're forgetting about Mortimer. Where does he fit in? I still think there's something very odd about him."

"You really think he was involved in kidnapping Rich? Why would an artist get mixed up in that?" JD shook his head. "I agree he's eccentric, but I just can't picture it. Even if Mortimer had a knife, Rich would have taken him easily. Rich is bigger, and he's a second-degree black belt."

Annie smiled and took JD's hand. "Maybe you're right, dear. But let's leave the detective work for now and spend some time with Mortimer's sculpture. That's what we came for, and we have to look as if we care about it."

The waiter brought JD his Sazerac, and they walked over to the sculpture. *Tricolor One* was bathed in an array of spotlights, and the colors shimmered and reflected as Annie and JD slowly moved around it. Annie stopped and turned to JD. "That saffron is really striking in its contrast to the green and white. And the glaze is applied in a very subtle way. The technique is amazing. I can see why Fareed loved this piece so much. Mortimer really is an outstanding artist. He should be showing in New York and London."

JD shrugged. "It's nice, but I still don't get it. Is it nice enough to get shot over?"

They were interrupted when Ivan Kosnowski walked over. He nodded to JD and then dramatically kissed Annie's hand. "I am so pleased that you were able to join this celebration. And it is indeed a celebration. Nine of Mortimer's most important collectors are here, one from England and three from the Continent. And I'm sure you know Charles Whitson and Murray Benoit from Greenwich. They each have important pieces from Mortimer."

JD was familiar with the local residents that Kosnowski mentioned, but not from his knowledge of the art world. Both individuals were billionaires, and were regularly profiled in *Fortune* and the *Financial Times.*

Kosnowski continued. "And of course you must know Winthrop Harriman. He's over there with Stuart and John Maynard Yates. Please make yourselves comfortable and enjoy the food and wine. Stuart will be making a brief speech shortly. And Mortimer will be here. He likes his entrances to be dramatic."

Kosnowski wandered away to glad-hand other clients, and JD said, "I see a lot of familiar faces in here . . . money faces. Cole has a lot of very influential friends."

"And Mortimer has quite the list of collectors," Annie added. For a second, JD wondered if she was jealous of Mortimer's success. Annie's art had always sold well, but her pieces had never commanded the sort of money that Mortimer was clearly getting for his. Maybe that's why she was so negative about him.

JD saw Harriman still talking animatedly to Cole and Yates. Harriman was with a tall, elegant woman with silver-streaked black hair, who JD assumed was his wife. JD noticed that Yates's wife was a blonde again.

Harriman turned and glanced over at JD and Annie. He smiled his broad smile, and beckoned them over. "Doctor Dionne, so nice to see you here. I understand you may be acquiring one of Mortimer's sculptures. An excellent choice. I'd like you to meet my wife, Patricia."

JD shook hands with Harriman, and smiled at Mrs. Harriman, who seemed a little nervous and worried as she shook hands. JD turned to Annie. "Annie, I'd like you to meet Winthrop and Patricia Harriman."

Harriman turned back to JD. "And how is our friend, Detective Puccini?" At the mention of Puccini, JD saw Cole turn sharply toward Harriman.

Harriman continued, "I think he made a big mistake by leaving my fund. We're doing very well."

JD smiled with some effort, thinking about the Ponzi that was about to implode. "I'm glad to hear that. It's been a difficult day in the markets."

Cole joined the conversation. "It's just a blip, a one-day-wonder. The markets will be back on track tomorrow."

"Absolutely," Yates agreed. "Everyone's in a panic over nothing."

JD noticed that Mrs. Harriman seemed to flinch at these comments, as if she disagreed - or didn't believe their optimism. Something was obviously bothering her.

Yates was a little older than he had looked in JD's photographs. He was probably in his mid-thirties, a little overweight, and not athletic. His tight-fitting tux made him look slightly pear-shaped. Cole was quite a contrast to Yates - a little shorter but stockier. His trapezius muscles stood well clear of his white formal shirt, and he had no belly bulge. He looked like he worked out a lot – and maybe trained in martial arts. JD looked for calluses on his hands, but couldn't really tell.

Cole smiled and raised his glass. "Ivan tells me that you're thinking of buying one of Mortimer's pieces. How do you like *Tricolor One*?"

Annie looked back at the sculpture. "It's brilliant. I love the colors. I wonder how he achieved that particular yellow. And your display is spectacular. You and Tracy must have spent a long time designing the lighting."

Cole looked pleased. "You have a very good eye. You really should take home one of Mortimer's new works." Cole turned to JD. "And how do you like the sculpture, Dr. Dionne?"

JD couldn't think of much to say, so he mumbled, "I think it's great." He was trying to come up with a more articulate comment when, to his relief, they were interrupted by Mortimer entering the room. A hush fell over the crowd. Cole excused himself and went over to escort the artist to a spot in front of the sculpture, directly under one of the spotlights. Mortimer was dressed completely in black, and his spiky black hair shimmered in the reflections off *Tricolor One.*

"Good evening, everyone," Cole began. "Though many of you already know him, it is my great honor to introduce the world's greatest living artist. Mortimer has been a friend of mine for over ten years, and he just keeps getting better and better. Don't you all agree?"

The crowd applauded enthusiastically in response, and then quieted down again, waiting for the great man himself to say a few words. Mortimer looked very serious as he started to speak.

"Art is a mystery to all of us. It calls each of us in a different way. My journey started on the day when I was ten years old and saw my first Picasso. I had started drawing and painting at the age of four, and I did realistic portraits of my parents when I was nine. Those still hang at their home. But Picasso made me realize that imagination is at least as important as what you see, and that changed my life. I began to experiment. And then I discovered sculpture through Barbara Hepworth, who famously said, 'I rarely draw what I see. I draw what I feel in my body.' When I was in my teens I was exposed to the sculptures of Peter Voulkos, who kept crocodiles in his studio, and later, I was influenced by the great Henry Moore. As you can see, whatever minor progress I have made, it's been by standing on the shoulders of the giants who preceded me. It took me twenty years to discover my own vision, and it is in the clay, color, and fire that you see before you. But I take very little credit for it. Ideas belong to us all, and I reach for the stars and occasionally find one. *Tricolor One* is one of the stars I was able to pull down from the firmament. My hope is that it will instill in you a respect for the unknown, and a feeling for the infinite wisdom of the universe."

There was thunderous applause, and the guests wandered closer to the sculpture, gazing up in awe. "That was quite a speech," JD murmured.

"It was," Annie agreed, sounding troubled. "I still feel uneasy about Mortimer, but I have to admit, he's really an exceptional artist. And articulate and charming, as well."

JD frowned. "Uneasy? Why do you feel uneasy? What is going on?"

Annie glanced over at Mortimer. "I told you . . . I just can't put it into words. It's a gut feeling. There's something about his face when he's talking, something not quite . . . real. But his art is very real, genius-level, in fact, so it's confusing."

"What was it that article in the *Times* said . . . that some artists have *personas*? The image they project to the public is as deliberate and carefully crafted as any painting or sculpture."

"That article was about Andy Warhol," Annie reminded him. "Besides, I know many artists, and this is different. It's not about Mortimer's art or his outfit or even his speech."

JD wasn't sure what Annie was referring to, but he tried to understand her concern. He knew she often had a sixth sense about these things, and usually turned out to be right, even if she could never explain precisely why. It was something she was not willing – or able – to discuss. So he decided he should pay closer attention to Mortimer, to try to see what she had noticed about him.

They went over to the bar to get more champagne and Sazerac, and then wandered over to a table covered with oysters, cheese, and a variety of hors d'oeuvres. The party was still going strong. Cole was talking animatedly to his girl-friend Tracy Alder, and the nine billionaires were off in their own corner, not mingling much.

The front door opened. Someone had arrived late and missed the ceremonies. But it wasn't a guest. It was Detective Puccini, accompanied by Detective Brown and four uniformed patrolmen. The party became silent again as the tuxedoed greeter stopped the police entourage at the door and looked for Cole. The crowd started to buzz again, and John Smith walked over to the door. Cole joined him, and there was brief huddle with Puccini, who pulled out a document and showed it to Cole. *So Puccini got the search warrant,* thought JD. Cole did not raise his voice, but he got very close to Puccini's face as he talked to him. Puccini waited impassively for Cole to finish and then beckoned his crew to follow him to the back of the house, with Tracy Alder and John Smith following. Puccini did not acknowledge JD's presence, for which JD was thankful.

Cole finally rejoined the party, his face now showing some reddish splotches. "My apologies for the interruption. There's been a misunderstanding, nothing to worry about. Waiter, more champagne for everyone."

But the buzz in the party had been deflated. The discussions were quieter, and they were not about art. Mortimer had disappeared into one of the back rooms, and Harriman seemed nervous about the police presence. He was in an animated conversation with two people who looked vaguely familiar.

"Puccini certainly knows how to make a grand entrance," Annie observed. "Why couldn't he have waited until the party was over?"

JD thought about that. "It looks like Puccini had the papers and he had the posse. He was not going to turn around and go home. I think he's rather enjoying this."

Puccini returned from the back of the house wearing latex gloves, and ostentatiously carrying a very large rifle. Brown was following him with a telescope on a tripod and some aluminum boxes that probably contained sniper equipment and ammunition.

JD said, "That must be Smith's rifle."

"Do you still think Smith shot Fareed?"

"I do. And I'm starting to think that maybe Smith did more than shoot Fareed. He was involved in Rich's disappearance."

Annie looked over at Smith, who was staring at them. "I'm getting a little nervous, JD," she said quietly. "We should leave. Maybe we could follow Puccini out of here." JD noticed that she brushed her hand down her side, probably to confirm that her Sig was still there.

The crowd murmured as the six police officers walked out the front door with their prizes. Cole was over talking to the billionaires, and Mortimer came back from the rear of the house and joined Cole.

Kosnowski was doing another round of the room, and came over to JD and Annie with a reassuring smile. "A little adventure, nothing to worry about. Have you had a chance to think about *Blood and Bone*? Should I complete the paperwork?"

JD frowned. "I'm afraid we've changed our minds, Ivan. Trouble seems to follow Mortimer. We're thinking about maybe a Damien Hirst. What was that police raid about? It makes us nervous."

Kosnowski's smile was bulletproof. "Probably a case of mistaken identity. Stuart's lawyers are on the case as we speak. It is a storm in a beer stein."

Annie smiled. "Joshua, dear, I think we should be going. Thank you for inviting us to the party, Ivan. I'm sure *Blood and Bone* will find a suitable home. It's a very interesting piece, but unfortunately not for us."

Annie and JD walked over to thank Cole, but he was still in a very intense discussion, so they nodded to the tux-clad man at the door and strolled out to their car. Annie looked back nervously to see whether anyone was following them. As they got into the Mercedes, the procession of three police cars was just leaving the courtyard. JD followed them down Round Hill Road at a leisurely pace, and checked his mirror to confirm that no one was behind them. He took a right turn off Deer Park Drive onto Glen Road as the police procession continued downtown, and five minutes later they were home.

CHAPTER 19

Tuesday, September 16, 2008

Puccini arrived at his cubicle very early that morning. The Tac-50 and the sniper equipment they had confiscated were being processed in the forensics lab, and he felt a certain satisfaction that he had finally taken some concrete action on the Fareed Ghanem case. Garry Brown was typing the report on "items found" in their execution of the warrant at Cole's party. Puccini's challenge now was to put the pieces of the puzzle in the right order, and to construct a case that could lead to an arrest. He pulled out the report he had written for probable cause in obtaining the search warrant. He scanned the criteria he had listed:

- Fareed Ghanem was shot by a sniper from at least a quarter of a mile away while Ghanem was on a moving sailboat.
- Executing this shot took special skill and experience.
- John Smith had been a military sniper in Iraq, with seven confirmed kills.
- Smith owned a Tac-50 and associated sniper equipment.
- John Smith had threatened Fareed Ghanem over a lawsuit that Ghanem had filed involving Smith's boss, Stuart Cole.
- Ghanem's dog was deliberately killed in a very violent manner, and a photo of the sculpture involved in the lawsuit was left by the dog's body.

- Smith was the prime suspect in the killing of Ghanem's dog, due to the previous threat.
- Smith worked for Stuart Cole, so Cole would have had knowledge of Smith's activities, and probably directed them.

Puccini sat back and considered his list carefully. He knew he was missing two important items – the bullet and the shell casing. He'd had enough for the search warrant, but probably not enough for an indictment.

He showed the list to Brown. "What do you think, Garry?"

Brown took a quick look. "It's all circumstantial. It'll never stick."

"But maybe it's enough for an arrest. We can hold Smith overnight, and who knows? Maybe he'll say something. I want to get him in the room."

"Tony, what's with this burr under your saddle? Just step back. It's not enough."

Puccini walked over to the coffee machine and poured himself a cup. He knew Brown was right. He'd pushed very hard to get the search warrant, and unless forensics found something on the rifle and scope, he was stuck. He was convinced that Smith was the shooter, but there was no way to prove it. The witnesses who had seen the white speedboat leave the island after the shooting couldn't identify the two people aboard, or provide even a rudimentary description beyond saying one was bigger than the other. As for the get-away boat itself, there were at least a hundred white speedboats around Greenwich.

Puccini needed more evidence, a breakthrough of some sort. He gave up for the moment, and went back to sifting through the Bridger case. On that one, at least they had physical evidence – the blood sample and DNA. He had focused completely on Yates, but what if Smith was also involved in the Bridger kidnapping? He couldn't see any obvious motive, aside from a performance fee, but Smith certainly had the strength and skill to take out Bridger. All Puccini needed was a DNA sample from Smith to test his hunch.

He was sketching out a probable cause for getting a sample from Smith, when he saw Lieutenant Argus walk out of his office toward his cubicle. He was striding quickly, and his face was grim.

Argus stopped in front of Puccini's desk, arms crossed. "Well, dammit, Puccini, you screwed the pooch again. The Commissioner came down on the Chief for your raid on Stuart Cole's house last night. It's become an international incident. There were four heavy hitters from Europe at that party. The German consulate got involved, and the French probably aren't far behind. What the fuck were you thinking?"

Puccini was puzzled. Why would those heavy hitters go political? Did Cole put them up to it? But Argus was his more immediate problem, so Puccini turned to Brown with a hint of a smile, looking for support. Brown had his head down, busily and deliberately working on his report. Puccini looked up at Argus and shrugged. "It took me a while to get the warrant, and as soon as we got it, I served it. How was I supposed to know there was a party going on?"

"You saw it when you got there. You didn't have to go in."

"We already had six officers on overtime. I read the directive on the departmental budget, and I don't want to waste resources. We were there, so we went in."

Argus looked as if he couldn't decide whether to get angrier at the hint of insubordination, or back off. After a few deep breaths, he seemed to calm down. "All right, I'll see if I can get the Chief to turn down his burners. What did you find?"

"Everything listed on the warrant. A Tac-50, a spotting scope, lots of ammunition, and trajectory software. I'm building a case."

Argus looked over at Brown, who was still busy typing his report. "I know you were part of it too, Brown. Next time, pull the plug if your dumb partner won't. We don't need this shit."

Argus got up and walked back to his office. Brown finally looked up. "Business as usual. Nothing but politics."

Puccini nodded. He was about to explain his new idea of getting a warrant for Smith's DNA to tie him to the Bridger case, when his desk phone rang. It was the Chief's office. Puccini listened, hung up and turned back to Brown. "I've got to get upstairs. I think what Argus gave me was just the preliminaries. This thing's not over yet. Keep the coffee hot. I may be a while."

Puccini took the elevator up to the fourth floor, and the Chief's assistant led him right into the office. Puccini was expecting a major dressing-down, but the Chief was actually smiling.

"Take a seat, Tony. I owe you some thanks."

Puccini dropped into the chair in front of the Chief's desk, and waited.

"I heard from Argus that you were convinced that Winthrop Harriman was running a Ponzi scheme," the Chief continued. "I had some investments with him, and I thought I'd check it out with one of our pension-fund board members. He told me the rumors were probably true, that none of the big funds would invest with Harriman. So I pulled out my money last week. It wasn't easy. Harriman gave me a hard time, said I'd regret it. But I got it out. So thank you."

Puccini was almost too stunned to speak, but finally found his tongue. "Anything I can do for a brother, Chief." He wondered if there was more to come, and there was.

The Chief looked down at a piece of paper on his desk, and turned it to face Puccini. "Here, take a look at this. Came in fifteen minutes ago. Winthrop Harriman has disappeared. His wife called it in. No signs of violence, so he may have just skipped town. I want you to take this, find out what happened."

Puccini knew that the Chief had totally ignored the chain of command in summoning him upstairs without Argus. He wondered what was going on, why he had been anointed. As far as he could tell, this was a missing person case. But the Chief was ahead of him again, almost reading his mind. "I bypassed the Captain and Lieutenant on this, Puccini, but don't worry about it. I want you off the Cole and Smith case. It's too hot. This will give you something to keep you busy. The Cole thing has too much hair on it right now.

He's got a lot of influential friends, and they've been calling the Commissioner. So let it be and move on."

Puccini was still trying to figure out what the Chief's agenda was. "I thought cops weren't supposed to play politics. Cole is a bad dude."

The Chief paused, looking as if he was trying to decide how much to tell Puccini. "Maybe, but trust me, this is not the time. Anyway, this Harriman thing could be very big, if you're right about the Ponzi. The uniforms are already out there, so take Brown and see what's going on. Keep it quiet for now, and report directly to me. Any questions?"

"What's Harriman's address?"

The Chief's smile disappeared. "Don't try to bullshit me, Puccini. You know damn well what his fucking address is. You were out there withdrawing your own funds last week. I didn't just fall off a turnip truck, pal. I've got my own sources. Get the fuck out there and find out where Harriman is."

Puccini scratched his head and shrugged. He picked up the sheet of paper, and left the room. When he reached his desk, he briefed Brown. Brown looked toward Argus's office. "You going to tell the LT?"

Puccini shook his head. "Let's get the hell over to Belle Plains. The Chief said to keep it quiet." As he was getting up from his desk, Puccini noticed an email from Joshua Dionne. He opened it and read it, still standing, and then he smiled. It was about AIG.

Puccini said, "The Feds came through and saved AIG. The world is not about to fall apart."

Brown nodded. He seemed to know better than to ask for an explanation. That could take half an hour.

* * *

Puccini and Brown were at the Belle Plains gatehouse within twenty minutes. They stopped at the gate, and Puccini rolled down his window, showing the security guard his badge. The guard said, "You're going to the Harriman house, no doubt."

"Yeah, we are. Word travels fast around here."

"Your colleagues in a patrol car preceded you, and you are welcome to proceed as well. I do hope that Mr. Harriman has done nothing untoward."

As they drove by the open gate, Brown looked back. "Quite the place. Even their rent-a-cops went to Harvard."

They arrived in front of Harriman's large colonial-style home. A black-and-white was already parked in the wide circular driveway in front. Puccini knocked on the door. One of the uniformed officers opened the door, and said, "The wife's in the living room. She's barely holding it together. It's down the hallway to your right."

Puccini and Brown walked quickly down the hallway and into the living room.

Puccini remembered Patricia Harriman from Cole's party the previous night. Then she had looked very elegant, almost regal. The woman sitting on the couch was slouched over, wearing a housecoat, and her long black hair with its grey streaks hung loosely to her shoulders, partly covering her face. A female uniformed officer, who was sitting in a chair opposite Mrs. Harriman, got up as Puccini and Brown entered the room.

The officer said, "Mrs. Harriman can give you more details, but it's pretty simple. They went to bed last night after they attended a party, and when she woke up this morning, he was gone. No sign of violence, no note, just gone."

Mrs. Harriman looked up. "Disappeared," she said. Then with a start, she seemed to recognize Puccini and Brown from the search warrant incident at Cole's the night before. She straightened up and brushed the hair away from her face. Puccini could see that her eyes were red and slightly puffy; she'd been crying.

Puccini thanked the officer, who left the room. Puccini and Brown sat down directly in front of Mrs. Harriman. Puccini nodded to her sympathetically. "I'm Detective Puccini, Mrs. Harriman, and this is Detective Brown. We're here to help find your husband." He paused, waiting for a reaction, but there was none. "I can see it's been a rough morning. A real shock. Did your husband do or say anything unusual last night?"

"One unusual thing was your extremely rude visit to Stuart Cole last night, Detective Puccini. Did you find whatever you were looking for?"

Puccini shrugged. "It's just part of my job, Mrs. Harriman, no fun for anyone. But tell me what happened last night."

"But I already told the whole story to the other officer."

Brown smiled, and said, "We know you did, but maybe you'll remember something new. Some important detail. We want to find your husband, and you can help us."

Mrs. Harriman sighed. "We got home fairly late. It was nearly one, and I went straight to bed. Bucky went to his home office, and I don't remember when he came to bed." She paused and took a deep breath. "He didn't want me to worry, but I think he was very concerned about the stock market. He had many angry phone calls yesterday, some from Los Angeles, and a lot of emails."

"You say he was worried about the stock market? What did he say?" Brown asked. "How could you tell?"

Mrs. Harriman raised her chin, and Puccini could see that she was working hard to maintain her composure. "Bucky does not wear his heart on his sleeve, you know, but after almost forty years, a wife can sense it. He became even more cheerful than usual. I knew there was something serious going on."

"Who called from Los Angeles?" Puccini asked.

"One of the calls was Stephen Beaton. I know because I took the call. I don't know who the other caller was, but they were on the phone for a long time."

"Stephen Beaton, the director? Do you know why he was calling?"

"It had something to do with Bucky's investment fund. Bucky said he had to do a lot of hand-holding. There are a lot of . . .

well, high-profile clients in the fund, and they can be quite demanding."

"I see. So he deals with a lot of celebrities." Puccini wrote something in his notebook. "And how was he at the party last night?"

"He had a lot to drink, and later on, he became the life of the party. Then Willy Manners and Michael Cartwright sort of cornered him, and their voices got quite loud. Bucky seemed a little subdued after that, but he didn't want to leave."

"Manners and Cartwright? That's the Jets' quarterback and the writer? I remember them from last night. Do you know what they were talking about?"

"Bucky wouldn't tell me, but I think it was about the fund. Everyone seemed to be talking about the stock market last night. There was some sort of problem. Something about bankruptcy maybe?"

Puccini leaned forward and touched his forehead with his fingertips. JD's predictions about Harriman's fund were correct. It was blowing up, and his clients were not happy. "Tell me, Mrs. Harriman, do you think anyone threatened your husband in some way? Either at the party or on the phone?"

"No, of course not," she said. "Why would anyone threaten him? He's made a lot of money for them. And we're talking about some very famous people. They all loved him."

It was clear to Puccini that Harriman had kept his wife totally in the dark about his Ponzi scheme – or else she was an exceptionally gifted actor. But this was not something worth pursuing at the moment, so he decided to change the subject.

"What was your husband wearing when he left this morning? Are any of his clothes missing? And is his car gone? Did he take a suitcase?"

"His car is gone. That was the first thing I checked when I couldn't find him. And his blue suit is gone. But I didn't check for a suitcase. I was upset."

"Why don't we go and see what's missing? That would – "

Puccini stopped and turned. Skip and Grinny Harriman, Bucky Harriman's two sons, had just walked in. They quickly crossed the room and sat down on either side of their mother, each son taking one of her hands. Skip turned to her, and said, "We got here as soon as we could, Mother. How are you holding up?"

"It's been terrible," she said, her voice shaking. "I don't know what's happened to him. Why would he leave without telling me? He's never done anything like this before."

Skip got to his feet and turned to Puccini and Brown. "Would you mind giving us some privacy? We have to discuss something with our mother, and it can't wait."

Puccini knew that at the moment he was a guest in the house, and there was no evidence yet of a crime having been committed.

"No problem." He nodded to Brown. "We'll wait outside in the hall."

Puccini and Brown went into the hall and closed the door. The female officer stood by the front door with her partner, and the two detectives walked over to touch base with them as they waited. A few minutes later, they heard a muffled scream from the living room. Puccini ran down the hall and opened the door. Mrs. Harriman was sitting on the couch with her head in her hands, sobbing uncontrollably. Skip Harriman put his finger to his lips and motioned for Puccini to leave. Puccini hesitated for a moment, but after determining that Mrs. Harriman was in no immediate danger, withdrew again, closing the door behind him.

"So what happened?" Brown asked.

"I think the sons finally clued her in about their daddy."

They waited for another fifteen minutes, and finally Skip came out and said they could come back to the living room, adding, "We think we know why Father left."

Puccini and Brown followed Skip to the living room. Mrs. Harriman was calm again, sitting on the couch taking deep breaths. Her hands were balled into fists, and she was rocking back and forth very slowly. Grinny was perched on a chair at the side of the room.

Skip gave a big sigh. "Okay, here goes. Dad called us early this morning, asked us both to come down to the office. He said he couldn't sleep and he needed to talk to us."

"We've never seen him so upset," Grinny interjected. "He could hardly speak. He told us that Winthrop B. Harriman Investment Securities was broke. His clients were clamoring for redemptions after the crash yesterday, and there was no money left to pay them."

Skip shook his head. "It's a thirty billion dollar fund, and he said the money's gone."

Puccini looked very closely at the two brothers. It didn't seem possible that they could be ignorant about the scam, especially Skip. After all, he did the goddam spreadsheets. But Puccini decided to nudge rather than confront. He'd check with JD later to determine whether it was possible for the brothers to really be in the dark about the Ponzi, or whether they were trying to bullshit him. At the moment, his gut feeling was for the bullshit option, at least for Skip. Grinny seemed to be a few grapes short of a full vineyard, so he might have been outside the circle of fraud.

Puccini turned to Skip. "Are you saying that your father was running a Ponzi scheme, and you didn't know?"

Skip raised his hands in an I-had-no-idea gesture. "All the books were in order. We saw the annual reports, and all the transaction reports. These were sent to the clients. It all looked great. There were no problems. None."

Puccini looked down at his notebook. "Who did the accounting?"

"Steven Burnett. He and Dad went to school together. He's one of Dad's best friends. He's a big investor in the fund."

Puccini leaned back and let out a sigh. Burnett had probably been paid off. Big time. "It sounds like your father is in very serious trouble. You are all now persons of interest, and I would like to request that you not leave the house for now. Financial fraud is not my area, so I have to go out and make some calls. I'll get the right people here, and they'll take your formal statements. Please relax, and I'll be right back."

Skip was frowning. "Hey, we're just trying to help here. You can't put us under house arrest, or whatever it is you're doing. We need to call our lawyers."

"Then I would suggest you do that. But the more you cooperate, the easier it will be. You're not suspects yet, but your decisions in the next few minutes could affect the rest of your lives, so think about it very carefully. I'll be right back after I make a couple of calls."

Puccini and Brown went into the hallway again and closed the door. Brown asked, "You going to call the Chief?"

"Yeah, I'll call him . . . but I've got to think this through first." Puccini looked at his notes. "We're talking about inter-state financial fraud, maybe international. I don't think that's something for the GPD. It's thirty billion dollars, maybe the biggest Ponzi of all time. I think this is something for the Bureau."

Brown shook his head. "The Chief will be pissed. He wants to be in the loop."

"The SEC investigated this guy four times and found zip. I want someone on this who knows what they're doing and has the balls to finish it. Besides, the Chief has some inside sources. He knew I'd pulled my money from Harriman."

"Argus knew that. He probably told the Chief."

"Whatever. I'm calling Delvecchio up in New Haven. And you can go back to HQ if you want deniability. No hard feelings if you do."

Brown hesitated. "No, I'll stay here and look after mom and the kids. Do what you have to do. We can send the uniforms home."

Puccini punched in a number on his cell, and Delvecchio picked up on the second ring. "What's up, Tony? You want to make another contribution to the FBI Benevolent Poker Fund? We've got a game Wednesday night, regular time."

"No, I gave at the office. It's about Winthrop Harriman. Remember how I said this hedge fund guy got my money out? Well, it looks like Harriman's Ponzi has finally gone tits up. He confessed to his sons, and now he's disappeared."

"Confessed? No shit. We've been trying to nail him for five years, but he's got too many friends. Somebody kept pulling the plug whenever we got close. I always knew he was dirty."

"Thanks again for warning me about him. I want to return the favor. I'm at Harriman's house right now. Brown and I can wait until you get here and take statements from his wife and his two sons. They're going to lawyer up, so you better get here fast."

"I'm on my way, right after I round up some agents. Thanks, Tony."

They disconnected, and Puccini called the Chief to bring him up to date. "Harriman's sons say Harriman confessed to them this morning about his Ponzi scheme. I brought in the FBI. It's a Federal case. Harriman has inter-state clients all the way out to California, and we're talking over thirty billion."

There was a long pause. "Fuck that, Puccini. You should have brought it to me first."

"No time, Chief. Skip and Grinny are ready to bolt, and we had to act fast. Why don't you call Washington, and give them a heads up? And the Commish."

The Chief's voice became a little softer. "I'll get the word out. Give me all the details soon as you get back. I'll put out an APB on Harriman. The media will be on it very quickly. This will blow up very big."

Puccini disconnected and sat down to wait for Delvecchio. As he thought about where Harriman might have gone, he realized he should call JD to give him the news. It wasn't strictly protocol to call while he was in the middle of a case, but he owed JD. He dialed his land line, but it was busy, so he left a message.

As he disconnected, Puccini saw a black Mercedes pull up and park on the driveway. The lawyers were here.

* * *

JD had received five responses to the three-page email he'd sent his clients explaining how his strategy had finally succeeded, but the subject lines indicated that three of them were probably negative. He went to the kitchen to make another cappuccino. He wanted to clear his head so he could respond. The final step of his year-long plan was about to fall into place, but it had been a close call. If AIG had gone under, all bets would have been off. He brought his cappuccino back to the keyboard, and opened the first email, but the land line rang before he could read it. He looked at the Caller ID. The name was blocked. He picked up.

"Hello?"

"Good morning, Doctor Dionne. We had a little excitement last night, and I didn't have a chance to talk to you. Do you have a minute?"

JD didn't recognize the voice. Was it Cole? Why would he be calling? "I'm sorry, but what excitement are you referring to? And who is this?"

"It's Mortimer, your favorite artist. You were interested in *Blood and Bone*, and we had a little discussion about investment over at Kosnowski's gallery yesterday. That's what I'm calling about. Investment. I'd like you to manage some of my money. I was very, very impressed with your strategy."

JD paused, more than a little surprised. "Invest with me? But what about Harriman?"

"After our discussion, I became . . . concerned, and I redeemed some of my investment from him. It was a little awkward, because he's a good friend. But business is business."

The story didn't ring true to JD - Harriman had no funds left for redemptions, according to his sons. So he decided to play it a little coy. "My current fund is closed to new investors, but I may be starting a new one. The credit default swaps have run their course, and I need to develop a new strategy. Right now, Treasury bonds are probably your best option. You should keep your money safe until the market hits bottom next year, and then move back in."

"That sounds like a very clever approach. Could we talk about it in a little more detail? I could write you a substantial check to get started. Say ten million?"

JD had to catch his breath at the number. But he wanted to sound calm when he answered, not too eager. "Ten million? Yes, I could sit down and discuss that. How about early next week, say Monday or Tuesday?"

"I was thinking more like today, say in an hour or so. I want to move on this quickly."

JD's phone line clicked, indicating there was another call on the line. He let it go to voice mail. He'd never been able to figure out how to use "call waiting" without losing one call or the other.

Mortimer continued. "What do you say? Ten million up front."

JD looked at the Venn diagram. Mortimer was up there, front and center. Rich had been missing nine days now. If meeting with Mortimer could provide information that would help unravel the connections up on that wall, he couldn't refuse. And that ten million had certainly gotten his attention. "Okay, I can do that. What's your address?"

Mortimer gave JD the address, and they disconnected. JD already knew the address from his research. It was in one of the most exclusive parts of Bellle Haven, overlooking the Sound.

JD leaned back and mulled over what had just happened. Maybe Harriman *had* actually let Mortimer take out some of his so-called earnings the previous day. After all, Puccini had been able to do the same earlier, although it had taken more than a little effort. How many of Harriman's clients had called to withdraw their funds, JD wondered. And how many, besides Puccini, had actually been paid?

JD walked over to Annie's studio, but she wasn't there. He found her sitting in a lounge chair on the back deck. She looked like she'd been sitting there for quite a while.

"I just couldn't paint," she said as he came out onto the deck. "All this is getting to me. I didn't realize until this morning how close you were to losing your fund."

JD put his hand on Annie's shoulder. "It's all fine. The government saved AIG. Would you like a coffee or something? It's cold out here."

"Thanks, I'm okay. What are you up to?"

"I just had a weird call from Mortimer. He wants me to come over to his house to talk investments. He's ready to place ten million in a new fund."

"Ten million? And a new fund?" Annie looked keenly at JD for a few seconds. "I thought this was your last fund, because your clients never appreciate what you've done for them."

JD ran a hand through his hair. "It's hard to say no to ten million. At least without talking to him. And it might lead to something much bigger. Remember those European art collectors at Cole's party? Mortimer knows a number of billionaires."

"Well, be careful. You know I have a bad feeling about Mortimer."

JD was starting to get impatient. "I know about your feelings. You don't like Mortimer . . . okay. But I've got these two words that keep running through my head . . . the words *ten million*, as in dollars. With maybe a lot more to come."

Annie frowned. "Those *are* just words at this point, dear. You haven't actually seen the ten million. And I think maybe you're becoming a little greedy. That's not like you. It might be a trap of some sort. And are you sure that Mortimer actually has that ten million?"

JD hesitated. Annie had a point. They didn't really need any more money now. And he also had to remind himself of Mortimer's place on his wall chart. He was on the periphery of all the recent violence, connected in some way JD had yet to understand.

"Maybe you're right. I'll be careful. And I have my Glock."

"Okay, good . . . and watch your back. By the way, I think there's a message on the land line. It's probably for you. You should check it before you go."

"I'll check it when I get back. I've had enough with the clients today."

"Do you think maybe it was Detective Puccini?"

"If it was, he probably wanted to hear about the markets. I sent him an email earlier that AIG pulled through." JD glanced at his watch. "Anyway, I have to get going over to Belle Plains. I'll be home for lunch."

JD headed for the garage. As he pulled out in the Mercedes, he could see Annie standing at the front window.

She looked worried.

CHAPTER 20

JD pulled up to the guardhouse at the Belle Plains gate, and rolled down his window. The guard rose from his computer monitor and stood in the doorway. "What is your name, sir, and whom would you be visiting this afternoon?"

"Joshua Dionne. I have an appointment with Mr. Mortimer, the artist. He lives off Quarry Point."

"Very good, sir. You should also be aware that one of Mortimer's neighbors had a visit from the police, but if you do see a patrol car, there is no cause for alarm. Everything is under control. Have a wonderful day."

JD was puzzled by the police presence and thought about asking for more detail. He looked up at the guard, but the man seemed to be in no mood to expand on his statement. The gate opened, and JD followed the road down to Quarry Point. When he was about halfway there, he passed Winthrop Harriman's house, and saw a GPD patrol car and a grey Crown Victoria parked in the circular drive in front. He slowed down and stopped, but he could see no movement in the house. Obviously something was going on. Maybe there had been a burglary, although with the tight security in this exclusive enclave, that seemed unlikely. Then he remembered Puccini's comment about Belle Plains – that someone could commit a murder in there and the police might never hear about it. He felt a chill down his spine as he looked at the house, and he wondered whether the grey Crown Vic might be Puccini's. Maybe they were finally interrogating Harriman about the attempt to run JD off the road. But why the additional patrol car? Two detectives wouldn't need uniformed officers along just to question a suspect. Something wasn't right.

JD decided to call Puccini. He pulled over and hit Puccini's number. The phone rang six times, but there was no response. JD left a voicemail. "I'm sitting in front of Harriman's house in Belle Plains, and there are two police cars in front. I thought you might know what's going on. Please give me a call."

JD put the phone away and took one final look at Harriman's house. He saw a uniformed officer staring out the window at him, and slowly eased away from the curb. If it *had* been a burglary or a robbery, he didn't want to get involved. He had an appointment with Mortimer about a ten million dollar investment.

JD started driving slowly toward Mortimer's address. The houses and gardens were becoming even more opulent as he proceeded down the meandering roadway. When he reached the address, he had to check his notes to make sure it was correct. The property in front of him had over three hundred feet of frontage, and was surrounded by a six-foot stone wall. JD could see the pale red tiles of a roof, but most of the house was hidden by tall oaks and maples. There was a very wide two-panel gate in the opening of the wall, made of thick wooden beams in an X-pattern, with an intercom beside it on an angled metal post, and a camera next to it on the wall.

He drove up to the opening in the wall, and could now see the mansion through the beams of the gate. As he scanned all this grandeur, he thought back on his discussion with Annie about Mortimer's finances, and his own research on the topic. Reviewing Mortimer's assets on a computer was one thing, but seeing this bricks-and mortar totem to his wealth made it very real.

JD's thoughts were interrupted by a muffled male voice on the intercom. He rolled down the window and looked at the camera. "I'm here for a meeting with Mortimer. My name is Joshua Dionne." The gate opened, and he drove up a wide stone driveway toward the house.

The house was bigger than Harriman's, done in a contemporary style, yellow in color, with a red tile roof. JD saw a wide circular drive in front, and a second driveway leading around the right side of the house. A stairway shaped like a truncated half-pyramid led to a wide double front door. JD parked in front, grabbed his briefcase, and started climbing the stairs.

The front door opened, and Mortimer stood there smiling. "Welcome, Doctor Dionne. Please do come in. I'm looking forward to our discussion."

"Thank you. I have my presentation deck right here," said JD, pointing to his briefcase.

JD was a little taken aback by Mortimer's appearance. He was dressed in a dark blue pinstripe banker suit complemented by a green silk tie and looked completely different from the black-clad bohemian that JD had seen the previous day. His spiky 'do was gone, and his black hair was slicked back. He was now more financier than artist. Maybe this new image was more appropriate for a discussion about a possible ten-million dollar investment, but JD started to wonder who the real Mortimer was. He started to get a little nervous, thinking again about Annie's warning. Mortimer seemed to be a chameleon, changing his appearance for whatever his current role demanded.

JD was also surprised to be personally greeted by Mortimer himself. Looking at the size of the house and property, he had expected a maid or some other servant to open the door.

JD stepped into the house, and Mortimer led him into the foyer. The inside of the house was even more impressive than the outside. It had an open plan in the middle beneath a high vaulted ceiling. A two-sided red brick fireplace stood in the center of the open space. To the right of the fireplace, he saw a contemporary living room, with black leather couches and chairs and two large white marble coffee tables. To the left, he glanced at an open kitchen and a dining table that would probably seat twenty.

Mortimer motioned JD toward the couches and marble coffee tables. "Let's sit down. Would you like a drink? Sazerac, I believe?"

JD sat back in surprise when Mortimer mentioned Sazerac. How did he know? And what else did Mortimer know about him?

Mortimer must have noticed JD's reaction. "Is something wrong? Have I offended you somehow?"

"It's nothing. Sazerac is fine. But how did you know that's my favorite?"

Mortimer looked at JD with a steady gaze. "I'm an artist, and I observe. You ordered Sazerac at Stuart's party last night. Not many people drink Sazerac rye, especially neat. Besides, if I'm going to invest ten million, I need to know all about you." He hesitated and smiled a little. "For instance, I know you like to visit Lime Rock and Watkins Glen, and that you're an excellent track driver."

JD's feeling of unease started to increase. On the one hand, the reference to his driving ability might be a result of Mortimer's research on him as a potential investment manager. JD had been active in the Porsche Club at one time, and that would have been easy to track down in a Google search. But Mortimer's comment could also be an oblique reference to the attempt on JD's life back on Round Hill Road. Did Mortimer also know about that? JD's thoughts were starting to bounce between paranoia and reason. Was Mortimer playing some sort of weird mind game? Annie's concerns about him started to resonate again.

Mortimer walked over to the bar at the side of the room, and took out a bottle of Sazerac, along with some Laphroaig for himself. While Mortimer was concentrating on preparing the drinks, JD had a chance to look around. He saw sunlight coming in the floor-to-ceiling windows overlooking Long Island Sound, and stared at the wide lawn running down to the water, with two long docks jutting out from the shore. One dock had a large grey cabin cruiser tied up next to it, and the other had a small white speedboat. A drop of sweat trickled down JD's back as he stared at the white speedboat, thinking of Fareed. He shifted his leg to make sure the Glock was still there and accessible. Then he took a deep breath, and tried to move his thought patterns back to the present. After all, there were many white speedboats in Greenwich. It was a coincidence, nothing more. And he was here for a very specific purpose - to maybe add ten million to his new fund. He had to focus on the presentation he was going to make to Mortimer. It was something he'd done hundreds of times before, but it had been a long time since he'd made this particular pitch. He had to be sharp.

He turned around and scanned the other side of the room. That's when he noticed the artwork on the wall near the front entrance. He hadn't noticed these pieces when he walked in, and then he realized that they were probably placed there to protect them from sunlight. He recognized an Andy Warhol and a Picasso. There were many millions hanging on that wall.

Mortimer gave JD the rye, and then raised his own glass. "Here's to stellar returns in your new fund." They both took a sip, and Mortimer noticed JD looking over at the wall with the Picasso and the Warhol. "Would you like to take a closer look at my collection?"

JD got up and followed Mortimer to gaze at the dozen paintings on the wall. "I recognized one of Warhol's *Marilyns*, and the Picasso. I don't really know the other ones here. I'm sure my wife would know them all."

Mortimer pointed at one particular painting, almost cartoon-like, depicting a woman crying. "That's one of my favorites, a Lichtenstein."

JD looked at it without comment. To him, it looked like something done by a Disney cartoonist. Mortimer was looking at him expectantly. Finally, JD said, "Interesting. But you don't have any of your own pieces on display here."

Mortimer frowned. "Showing one's own work at home is gauche, in my opinion. I do have a small private gallery at the back of the house, with some very special pieces, but they're for my own private viewing and pleasure. I don't put them on display. Perhaps I can show them to you later, if you're interested. But for now, why don't we get down to business? I'd like to hear more about your investment approach."

Mortimer motioned JD toward the black leather couch, and then sat down in the chair next to him. JD opened his laptop and started his presentation. His first slide was a chart showing the history of inflation-adjusted median house prices in the US since 1900.

"This is where my investment approach started. It's a graph based on the work of Professor Shiller at Yale, who predicted both the dot-com bubble and the housing crash. Here, take a look. What do you see?"

Mortimer looked at the chart. "House prices were flat from about 1950 to 2000, and then they went up in a straight line from 2000 to 2008. The real prices doubled over eight years. But so what? What does that mean for your investment fund?"

"First, and I admit it's very obvious, the only way to make money on stocks is to buy low and sell high. Most investors do the opposite. They buy when everyone's excited about something, and sell when everyone's in a panic. That's a perfect recipe for losing money. Second, in my experience, only five percent of experts actually know what they're talking about. Most experts simply parrot things they've heard from other so-called experts, and never think for themselves. It's just an echo chamber. They --"

"I know what you're saying," Mortimer interrupted. "Probably less than five percent of art critics know what they're talking about. The rest are idiots."

JD nodded and continued. "Take a closer look at the chart – the early part. You need to look at history."

Mortimer took another look at the graph. "I think I see what you mean. There was a big drop just before 1920. House prices fell by almost half. And it looks like they didn't start recovering until maybe 1945."

JD smiled. "That's right. That's what got me started into doing my own research. I asked myself a very simple question -- what would happen if the housing market were to collapse as it did in the 1920's? What could I invest in and profit from?"

JD moved to the next slide, which showed the structure of a typical mortgage bond. Mortimer followed the discussion closely, interrupting with incisive questions. Mortimer had clearly been thinking about all of this, and was surprisingly familiar with many of the concepts and terms. JD was almost beginning to enjoy himself as he explained his past success.

Mortimer interrupted him. "You know, Dr. Dionne, your history lesson is interesting. But we all know that past performance is not necessarily an indicator of future success. What are you going to do now that the markets are collapsing?"

JD took a deep breath, and opened the next slide in his deck. It was a graph showing the results of his mathematical modeling, focused on the effects of the housing crash on the stock market. It was a straight line turning down.

"There's your answer. There's going to be panic in the streets. Or more specifically, on Wall Street. My strategy is very simple. I can state it in one word - wait."

Mortimer frowned as he looked at the chart. He took a sip of his Laphroaig,. "So you would do nothing."

"That's right. I would put your money in Treasury Bonds and wait until the time is right to get back in."

"But I don't need *you* for that. I could do it myself."

JD leaned back. "That's very true. But when the time comes, you'd have to know what to buy, and when to buy it. Some big companies will probably go bankrupt, and you'd have to know which ones are most vulnerable. Banks and financials will be hardest hit initially, but they will recover quickly, so you'd have to be nimble."

"How will *you* know which to buy? And when?"

"I look at free cash flow, the earnings multiple, the debt ratio." JD paused, still looking at Mortimer. "It takes a lot of detail and a lot of hours. Maybe like your sculptures."

Mortimer folded his hands under his chin and gazed at the paintings on the wall. "I guess I wouldn't expect you to make one of my sculptures, Dr. Dionne. We each have our own areas of expertise."

"That's assuming you and I are in the five percent who know what we're doing."

Mortimer turned to JD and smiled slightly. JD realized that Mortimer had probably been testing him, and he felt that he had passed the test.

Mortimer took a sip of his Laphroaig and looked at the chart on JD's laptop, the one with the line turning down. "Go on. Let's see the rest of your presentation."

JD realized that he'd hooked Mortimer, and was now reeling him in. He proceeded through the twelve remaining slides with more confidence, and had only a few further questions from Mortimer. Finally, he closed his laptop. "That's it. That's why you should invest with me."

Mortimer smiled, reached into the breast pocket of his blue banker suit, and pulled out a checkbook. He opened it and put it on the marble table, and then drew out a black Montblanc fountain pen. He wrote out a check for ten million dollars, and then looked up at JD.

"To whom should I make this payable, Dr. Dionne?"

JD didn't have an answer. In the past, all checks had been made out to his investment funds, but his new one didn't exist yet. He cursed himself for not thinking far enough ahead. The devil was always in the details.

"Just make it out to me. Joshua Dionne. It'll take me a couple of weeks to set up the new investment fund, and I'll move it in there as soon as I can. You can post-date the check if you'd like."

""There's no need to post-date. I know I can trust you with my money."

"I'll put it in Treasuries before the end of the day. We're losing interest as we speak."

Mortimer wrote JD's name on the check and signed it, *Yelberten A. Mortimer*. He held the check in front of him to let the ink dry, and then handed it to JD with a chuckle. "So now you know. That's my legal name."

JD was careful not to laugh in response. "Your parents were fans of Y.A. Tittle, right? And your middle name must be Abraham."

Mortimer grinned. "Very clever, Doctor. You're an expert in more than economics. I'm impressed. You are definitely in the five percent."

JD started to feel more relaxed after Mortimer's flattery, and looked down at the check. It was the largest single investment anyone had made in his funds, with maybe a lot more to come. He smiled and said, "Thank you. You won't regret this, Y.A."

Mortimer's eyes studied him as they clicked glasses. "Do you have a few minutes? Perhaps you'd like to see my private sculpture collection now."

"I don't know. I really should be getting back to the office to get your money working right away."

"Don't worry about it. I know you'll do well with it. There's no hurry."

Mortimer's response was abrupt, and his face was starting to change. The smile was gone, and his eyes were unwavering and very intense. Mortimer obviously didn't want JD to leave. JD thought about the Glock at his side, leaned forward, and rubbed his hands up and down his thighs. He thought about the police cars at Harriman's place, and his call to Puccini. Puccini hadn't replied yet.

"I'm not sure I would fully appreciate your collection, Mortimer. I don't know much about art. And I really should be going."

Mortimer stood up and started buttoning up his suit jacket. "Doctor Dionne, I have just invested ten million in your fund, and I would really like to show you my special collection. Very few people have had that privilege, and since we'll be working together for many years, it's important to me. It won't take long." JD thought he saw a bulge under the lapel of Mortimer's jacket. "Later on, I'd also like to introduce you to some of my other friends and collectors. I'm sure they'd also be interested in making some investments with you – major investments."

This was becoming a contest of wills, and JD knew that Mortimer held all the cards. Why was he so insistent on showing JD his private collection? And was that a pistol under his jacket? JD could feel his pulse quickening.

Mortimer's voice became very quiet. "You're an economist, Doctor Dionne, and I think you'll very much appreciate my latest piece. I call it *The Visible Hand.* It's an allusion to Adam Smith's 'invisible hand,' a term you must be familiar with."

Mortimer's face relaxed a little, and he smiled slightly. JD realized he was probably being paranoid again in imagining that Mortimer had a gun under his jacket. It was nothing but an awkward social situation, and he'd make the best of it. And Mortimer was right – it wouldn't take long. He'd take a look at this special collection, and then leave quickly. He had to be polite. After all, Mortimer *had* just given him a ten-million-dollar check.

JD forced a chuckle. "*The Visible Hand.* That's very clever."

Mortimer seemed to relax a little further, although he never seemed to blink, and JD remembered Annie's comment about his eyes. "Well, in fact this hand is quite visible. That's my little joke on Adam Smith. Come along, and I'll show you."

JD started to get up from the couch, but was startled when he heard someone approaching from behind. He had thought they were alone in the house. He turned around, and saw that it was a dark-haired woman, probably in her mid-thirties. Her features were Asian, and she was quite tall, with a solid, athletic build. She was dressed completely in black.

Mortimer looked toward the woman and smiled. "Doctor Dionne, I'd like you to meet my wife, Abigail Chong. She also assists me in my work."

There was something about the woman that made JD uneasy. And he remembered Annie's comment about the mysterious assistant that no one had ever seen. But Annie had thought it was a man. Mortimer obviously kept his private life very private.

"It's nice to meet you, Ms. Chong," JD said, shaking her hand. "I must have missed you at Stuart Cole's party."

"I did not attend, Doctor Dionne." She looked over at Mortimer, who nodded, and she continued, "You see, I suffer from agoraphobia. I cannot deal with social situations and crowds very well."

Mortimer turned to Chong. "Abigail, dear, Doctor Dionne will be investing some of our capital for us. He has an excellent strategy and will do very well for us."

"I hope he does better than Winthrop Harriman."

"I'm sure he will, dear."

Chong smiled, but said nothing further.

Mortimer motioned JD to walk across the living area toward a hallway leading to the right. JD's unease started to intensify. Something didn't smell right. He wondered again why the police were in the neighborhood. And his research on Mortimer had disclosed nothing about a wife. Were there other surprises in store?

They continued down the hallway toward Mortimer's special collection, and JD glanced out a side window at the courtyard behind the house. What he saw triggered a sudden flash of recognition, and he felt a slug of adrenaline shoot down his arms. His breathing stopped for a few seconds, and he sensed time slowing to a crawl. The last time he'd felt this way was when he'd been careening down Round Hill Road, trying desperately to stay alive.

There were two black Cadillac SUVs in the courtyard, very low slung, with big tires.

JD jolted himself into the present. He turned toward Mortimer and Chong, reaching for his Glock. But he froze. It was too late. Mortimer and Chong were both holding pistols, pointed at his chest.

Mortimer smiled very slightly. "Abigail, I think our genius economist has finally figured out his profits and losses."

JD's mind was reeling, trying to figure out what clues he had missed. There was the white speedboat, but there were lots of those around. And then he remembered. He should have checked out that black

SUV in Cole's courtyard the night of the party. It was probably a Cadillac with big tires, not a Mercedes. And now Mortimer had seduced him with his ten million. He had let his guard down. And most of all, he'd been obsessed with John Smith. Mortimer had been hiding in plain sight all the time, and Annie had been right. Maybe she couldn't express exactly why, but she'd been right.

Mortimer stepped closer. "Just relax, JD, the show's about to begin. Please raise your hands, very slowly, and put them up against the wall, with your feet apart. Abigail will relieve you of your hardware. We have a metal detector at the door."

JD did as he was told, and Chong, still keeping her gun trained on JD's back, removed his Glock from the holster. She held it up and examined it. "Very nice piece, Doctor Dionne. We'll be sure to take good care of it. Please put your hands behind your back." She clipped some plastic snap-ties over his wrists and pulled them tight.

Mortimer waved his gun down the hallway. "Okay, it's not much farther. Be careful, we don't want you to fall and hurt yourself."

They reached an ornate carved oak door with a keypad beside it. Chong entered a code to open the door, and they entered a small room. There were no windows, and very dim indirect lighting. JD could hardly see. Nothing was in the room except a lighted keypad on the left wall. Mortimer entered a code, and JD saw parts of the floor slide back, revealing small glass boxes mounted under the floor. The boxes rose slowly on black pedestals, and locked into place at waist-height. The floor closed again, leaving the boxes seemingly floating in mid-air.

JD counted nine glass boxes.

There was not enough light to see what was inside the boxes, but JD had a nauseous feeling about Mortimer's need for all this security. What could he be hiding? He knew it had to be something bad.

Mortimer manipulated the keypad to increase the lighting.

JD had to blink hard, because he couldn't believe what he was seeing. Each box contained a human hand, floating in some kind of liquid. *Mortimer was a collector of severed human hands*. This was sicker than he could have imagined. The scene was unreal, something from a parallel universe. He closed his eyes for a few seconds, but when he opened them, the display was still there.

Mortimer motioned JD closer to the glass boxes with his pistol. He was smiling. "That's my special collection. How do you like it?"

JD could only make a weak croak. He couldn't get a word out, and he could feel his knees getting weak. He was starting to think he must be dreaming. Or maybe he was hallucinating. He dug his fingernails into his palm, hard. He could feel the pain, so this was real.

Mortimer moved over to the side, and entered another code in the keypad. An opening appeared in the middle of the floor, and a tenth glass box rose and locked into place on its pedestal. Mortimer made a grand sweeping gesture toward this tenth box.

"And now for my *pièce de résistance*, Doctor Dionne. Behold . . . *The Visible Hand.*"

Another spotlight turned on, highlighting the glass box. Inside the box was another human hand. JD felt a queasy sensation welling up inside his gut. Something about the hand looked very familiar. There was some sort of marking on it.

Mortimer motioned JD to move closer to the box. JD steeled himself and stepped over, trying to keep his balance and stay on his feet. He was feeling very dizzy. Then he saw it. There was a tattoo on the severed hand, and one finger was missing.

The tattoo was a black belt – a karate black belt.

JD started screaming. "Jesus Christ. That's Rich's fucking tattoo. It's Rich's hand."

JD legs collapsed and he fell to his knees, his chest heaving and his heart pounding. He let out a loud moan. He got hold of himself after a few seconds, and tried to stand up, but he felt Chong grab him from behind.

Then he felt a needle prick in his arm.

JD fell over sideways and his head hit the floor. His next vision was of swimming back to Christian Island from Penetanguishene. The waves were very high. He kept struggling, but he was getting weaker and weaker. He could hardly raise his arms to stroke, and finally one big wave swept over him, and he went down, down and down.

CHAPTER 21

Annie was sitting at her easel, unable to paint. She was too worried about JD and his meeting with Mortimer. The more she thought about the sculptor, the more it made her skin crawl. She stared at the half-finished painting, holding her brush, but she could not move her hand to the canvas. The cobalt blue and cadmium yellow-orange she had squeezed onto her palette half an hour earlier were starting to harden, and would soon be useless. She gave up, and put down her brush. With a sigh of resignation, she started to clean up.

When she was finished, she picked up her phone and texted JD. It was an act of compulsion, but she couldn't help it. He'd be annoyed, because he was probably still in his meeting, but he'd take a look at his phone, make excuses to Mortimer about the interruption, and text her back to say that everything was okay. It would take only a few seconds, and he'd do it. He always did. He knew that her imagination was sometimes too vivid and too dark, and when she went over to that dark side, he could bring her out of it.

But this time there was no answer. Now she was becoming even more concerned and wished she hadn't sent the text at all. Then she remembered the message on their land line. JD hadn't checked it because he thought it was another irate client. She picked up the phone, punched in the voicemail password, and listened to the message.

"It's Puccini calling, pal. I just wanted to give you a heads-up that Bucky Harriman has disappeared, probably taken off because his fund is blowing up. You were dead right about that one. Give me a call, and I'll bring you up to date."

Annie could feel her heart hammering in her chest. *Another disappearance, just like Richard's.* And Harriman was connected to Mortimer. Was Mortimer involved in Harriman's disappearance?

Unable to paint, she went to the kitchen and prepared a cappuccino. She sat down at the island counter to try to figure out why she was so strongly obsessed with Mortimer. She was becoming more and more convinced that Mortimer was somehow evil – evil in a way she could sense and yet couldn't pin down. She took a sip of her cappuccino, and visualized that first meeting with Mortimer at Kosnowski's gallery. What was it that bothered her so much? At first, Mortimer had just seemed rude and indifferent. But when it became clear that she and JD were interested in spending three million on one of his sculptures, he became charming and attentive. In retrospect, it was a remarkable transformation, almost a new personality. She remembered his intensity when he turned on the charm, the way he listened, focusing one hundred percent on her face, his eyes never wavering—and never changing. It was flattering, almost hypnotic. He made her feel like the most important person in the world, but she couldn't quite figure out how he did it. Maybe that was what bothered her – that extraordinary charisma. It didn't seem real, somehow. But why would she have negative feelings about someone who made her feel good about herself? It didn't make sense.

Dark thoughts were reeling in her mind, and she couldn't turn them off. She needed more facts about him, more about his background, more details. She had heard some of the rumors about him, like the mysterious assistant, but she needed more. Her thoughts turned to her New York network of artist friends, so she went back to her studio, and got out the dog-eared book of phone numbers she had been using since the early days with JD at Oxford. She flipped through the pages, looking for someone who might help her quest, and stopped when she came on the name Sandra Whitlock.

She hadn't talked to Sandy in over a year, even though she was a fellow Brit. They'd been friends in Boston almost fifteen years earlier, both involved in the art scene, and Sandy had been a regular at the Charles River Playboys gigs. But their paths had diverged, as Sandy had dedicated herself totally to her painting. She was now one of the rising stars on the

Manhattan art scene, with connections to a number of influential galleries and artist co-ops. Her work had been featured in solo gallery shows in both New York and London, and her pieces were selling well into six figures. Annie knew that if there was anyone who had the inside scoop on Mortimer, it would be Sandy.

Annie punched in her number. Her call went to voicemail, but the voicemail greeting was interrupted as Sandy picked up her phone.

"Hey, Ms. Annie R, of Connecticut. I saw your name on the phone, and it was *so* exciting. It's been much too long, *mon amie*. And how is the Greenwich scene? You know, I think it's about time you moved into the fast lane. You need to blossom, dear, leave the hinterland. And hey, I heard about your new show. Are the juices flowing?"

Annie had to take a deep breath before responding. Sandy had been a good friend at one time, but she was now certainly travelling in that fast lane. That was one of the reasons Annie hadn't spoken to her in over a year. She could be overwhelming, and Annie liked to take her in small doses.

"The creative juices have dried up a bit, Sandy. I don't know if you've been following events outside the center of the universe in Manhattan, but we've had some serious trouble over here recently. Our old friend Richard Bridger disappeared a week ago, and Fareed Ghanem was shot and wounded. It's been kind of crazy. That's sort of why I'm calling."

Sandy's voice increased in pitch and volume. "Disappeared? And shot? Are you serious? That sounds more like New York. Greenwich is supposed to be a peaceful little village. What in Hades happened?"

"That's what we're trying to figure out."

Annie heard Sandy take a deep breath. "How are Dot and what's-her-name coping? And is Fareed going to be okay? We're talking original Charles River Playboys here."

"What's-her-name is Heema," Annie said, slightly annoyed that Sandra couldn't remember the name. "And Fareed will be okay. But it's a dangerous time here –too many knives and guns. And at the moment, I'm very worried about JD. He went to a meeting with Mortimer this morning, and I have a weird feeling about that bloke. I think there's something off about him. He makes my stomach churn, and I don't really know why. I've heard rumors, but nothing really concrete. He just gives me the chills. What do you know about him?"

There was silence on the phone for a few seconds, which was unusual for Sandy. "Not a whole lot, to tell you the truth. His pieces sell in the millions, as I'm sure you know. The only strange thing I can think of is that he lives and works in Greenwich. And that's *your* Greenwich, dear, not the Village. With all due respect, that's not exactly the throbbing heart of the art world. The question everyone asks is . . . how can his pieces sell for New York prices in that artistic desert? And the critics don't like his work, but that doesn't seem to have any effect on his stratospheric prices either. No one can understand it. He has some very, very dedicated patrons, apparently from all over the world. Rich patrons."

Annie closed her eyes and rubbed her forehead in thought. "Do you think he may have a sideline of some sort . . . maybe drugs? JD says his assets are greater than his income."

"Hey, girl, I think your imagination is working overtime. Yes. . . maybe he's doing money laundering for Nicaraguan rebels, or arms trading." Sandy hadn't lost any of her Brit sarcasm.

Then her voice became quieter and more serious. "But wait a minute, there *is* one thing I just thought of. It goes way, way back. But it's probably nothing."

Annie remembered that Sandy loved to dramatize, so she waited patiently without comment.

"Mortimer had some sort of hand fetish when he was starting out," Sandy said at last. "You know, the way some people have a foot fetish. Not that there's anything wrong with that, you understand, but it's unusual, don't you think? At one point early in his career, he did a series of hand sculptures. And I mean, just the hands, kind of disconnected from everything . . . and with perfect detail. You couldn't tell them from the real thing unless you picked them up."

Annie glanced at her own hands, and started twisting her wedding ring. She remembered reading somewhere that an obsession with details, not seeing the whole of something, could be a symptom of obsessive/compulsive disorder. She hoped that was why Mortimer made her uncomfortable. Lots of artists were OCD.

"Is that all? That's pretty tame compared to some of the things I've seen in New York."

Sandy's voice was still very quiet and dramatic. "Ah, but there's more to it. One of the galleries I work with still has one of those hand sculptures. There are rumors about how Mortimer was able to make them. How did he get all those details so correct – the colors, the texture, the veins, the fingernails?"

"That's easy." Annie laughed, trying to relax. "He used live models, same as in art school. There are professional hand models in advertising, you know." Annie was doing her deliberate best to dissolve any dark thoughts.

Sandy paused, and her voice became even more deliberate and serious. "No, the rumor was that he used dead hands . . . body parts. These sculptures didn't look like living hands. They looked like something you'd see in a funeral home . . . white and blue, with a covering of powder. I saw one, and it totally freaked me out."

Annie felt her chest tighten, and her breathing became almost a gasp. *If the rumor was true, how did Mortimer get access to body parts?* This was truly macabre. Annie was starting to regret having called Sandy. Her worries about JD were now increasing exponentially, and she decided she didn't need any more detail about Mortimer's hand fetish.

"I hope they're only rumors." Her voice was a whisper.

"Maybe. But that's the nature of rumors. They may or may not be true."

They disconnected. Annie was now working herself into a frenzy about Mortimer. She had to get hold of herself. It was still well before noon, and she thought she might be able to calm herself by preparing lunch. Keeping busy might get her mind off Mortimer. She forced herself to walk over to the fridge. And forced herself to believe that JD would be home soon.

She decided on a quiche Lorraine, and started to rummage for ingredients. She found some eggs, bacon, cream, some Swiss cheese, and plenty of onions. That would work. Then she realized that there was still some left-over cold salmon, and added that to the ingredients. When everything was set, she checked the time. Half past eleven. JD would be home soon, she said to herself, only half believing it.

She finished frying the bacon, and put the slices on paper towels to absorb the fat, still waiting for the sound of JD's car in the driveway.

Half an hour passed, then forty-five minutes. She put the quiche ingredients back in the fridge, picked up her cell phone, and texted JD again. Still no damn answer. What the hell was going on? She finally called, but the call went directly to voicemail. She left a message, and now her mind started reeling again with visions of Mortimer - and his persuasive voice and piercing eyes.

Then she felt a sudden shock coursing through her whole nervous system, a visceral sensation that something awful had just happened to JD. These telepathic incidents had occurred before. When her father had died suddenly five years earlier, she'd awoken from a deep sleep halfway around the world, and when the phone rang a few hours later, she had known instinctively what the call would be about. She now had that same feeling. She knew JD was in serious trouble, maybe fighting for his life.

She couldn't sit still. The only help she could think of was Puccini. He had agreed a few days earlier that Annie and JD might both be in danger, and had even suggested a bodyguard. But she didn't have his cell number, so she went to her computer to find a number for the Greenwich Police. If she called the 9-1-1 emergency number, they'd think she was being hysterical, so she dialed general information.

A man's voice said, "Greenwich Police Department. How can we help you?"

"I need to speak to Detective Puccini."

"What would you like to talk to him about?"

"My husband has disappeared."

"Disappeared? How long has he been gone? When did you last see him?"

Annie started tapping her foot impatiently. "I don't want to discuss it. I need to talk to Puccini. My husband knows him. He's a friend."

There was a pause on the phone. "I'm afraid that the best I can do is give Detective Puccini a message, ma'am, and he'll call you when he has a moment. It may take a while."

Annie's voice became louder. "Just give him the message." She almost said *fucking* message but caught herself. She had to be patient. All she needed now was for the officer to hang up. "My name is Anne

Rutherford, and my husband's name is Joshua Dionne. *Doctor* Joshua Dionne. Please ask Detective Puccini to call as soon as possible." She gave the officer her cell phone number.

"Anne Rutherford and Doctor Joshua Dionne. Yes, ma'am. Will do."

"Thank you."

Annie disconnected, and sat down to think. She called JD's number again, but still no answer. There was only one solution. She'd have to drive out to Belle Plains herself to find JD. She patted the Sig Sauer under her belt, and headed for the garage. Her cell phone rang, and it was Puccini.

"Hi, Annie, what's up? The dispatcher said JD has disappeared." He sounded concerned. "What happened? How long's he been gone?"

"He went to meet Mortimer at his house in Belle Plains about three hours ago, and he was supposed to be home for lunch an hour ago. I have a bad feeling about Mortimer, and I think something's happened to JD. He always calls or texts when he's going to be late. I can't reach him, and this just is not like him at all. I'm very worried. And he knows I worry."

Annie could sense the skepticism in Puccini's voice as he said, "So it's only been an hour. Maybe his cell phone died. Wait a while. He'll turn up."

"But I'm sure something's happened. Can't you go out there to check on him?"

Annie could hear Puccini take a deep breath before responding. "Try to relax. I'm sure he's fine. Anyway, there's nothing we can do. I can't send out a patrol car unless there's been a complaint of some sort."

Annie's voice became more strident. "Listen to me, detective. I'm making a complaint right now. Get someone out there and make sure he's okay." She regretted her outburst immediately. She needed Puccini's help, and she knew that getting angry was not the way to convince him.

"And tell the dispatcher what? That JD's an hour late for lunch? I'd like to do it, believe me, but it won't wash. And anyway, why are you so worried about Mortimer?"

Annie paused. It was a good question, and she had no answer that a detective would understand. "He's just weird. He gives me a very bad vibe. I don't know any other way to put it."

"Weird? Okay. . . I'll keep that in mind. Let me know if JD calls. I'll give you my cell number."

Fuck, thought Annie. *He's not going to do anything.* Her voice grew cold. "Fine. I'll let you know when he calls." She wrote down Puccini's cell number.

She disconnected abruptly, and headed for the garage. If Puccini wouldn't do it, she'd have to check up on JD herself. She sat down in her white Suburban and started pulling out of the garage but suddenly realized she'd need Mortimer's address. She stopped the SUV, and pulled out her iPhone to search for it, but no luck. She concluded that the address must be unlisted, but decided to head for Belle Plains anyway. She would just ask at the gate.

She turned down Field Point Road, and ten minutes later, she was at the Belle Plains gatehouse. She rolled down her window as the guard left his desk inside and walked over to the door.

"Good morning, madam. Can I help you?"

"I need to see Mortimer, the artist. My husband is at his house for a meeting, and I need to talk to him. It's urgent."

The guard stretched over toward his computer screen, and then swiveled back to Annie. "Mortimer does not seem to have any further appointments this afternoon. Did you call ahead to inform him that you were coming?"

"No, I didn't have time. It's urgent. I can't reach my husband on his cell phone."

The guard pursed his lips, and then nodded. "Very well. I shall call Mortimer to provide clearance. I'm afraid I can't let you proceed without his approval."

Annie shook her head in disbelief at the bureaucratic procedures. But she tried to remain polite. "All right. I'll wait."

"What is your name, madam?"

"Anne Rutherford."

"Thank you, Ms. Rutherford."

The guard went back to his desk and picked up the phone. Annie heard him explain the situation to someone on his phone, finally saying, "Yes, madam." He then turned back to Annie with a slight smile. "I am so sorry, Ms. Rutherford, but Mortimer does not want to be disturbed at the moment."

Annie sighed in disgust, and then turned back to the guard. "Fine. But could you at least tell me whether you've seen my husband leave here? His name is Doctor Joshua Dionne, and he's driving a silver Mercedes AMG."

The guard raised his eyebrows. "My most sincere apologies, madam, but I cannot discuss the comings and goings of our residents and guests. I am obliged to follow our privacy policy." The guard pointed back up the road with a fake smile. "You shall have to turn around and drive back."

A few choice expletives ran through Annie's mind, but she said nothing, rolled up her window, and backed up. She made a U-turn, and ten minutes later she was back at the house. As she parked her SUV, she started thinking about her next steps. She looked at her watch. It was now half past one. JD had been missing for an hour and a half.

How could she get in touch with him? A plan started crystallizing, but she would need some help. She picked up her cell phone, and texted Junior at school, asking her to call back as soon as possible. Since she'd never called Junior at school before, she was certain that Junior would know this was important.

Junior called back in less than five minutes. "What's happening, Mom? What's wrong? Are you okay?"

"I don't want to worry you, but Dad went to a meeting with that artist Mortimer. He was supposed to be home for lunch an hour and a half ago, and there's no sign of him. I'd like you to come home and hack into his cell phone to find out where he is. Can you do that? I have a bad feeling about Mortimer."

"Bad feeling?" Junior sounded both skeptical and a bit worried. "Have you tried calling Dad? Or maybe Mortimer?"

"Of course. I tried calling Dad three times, but no answer. I don't have Mortimer's number, and I tried to go to his house, but the bloody gate-keeper wouldn't let me into Belle Plains. And I called Detective Puccini, but he won't help. We're on our own."

"I'm sure Dad's okay. Maybe he's just caught up in the meeting."

"Maybe, but please come home. Let's see if we can at least confirm where Dad is."

"Okay, I'll be right there. Dad always leaves his phone on, so we'll be able to find him."

"Thanks, love. It may be nothing, but with all the weird stuff happening lately, we can't sit around and wait. Drive carefully."

"You'll have to call Mrs. Campbell to let me leave school."

More damn bureaucracy, thought Annie. "I'll give her a call right now."

They disconnected, and Annie called Mrs. Campbell, the principal of the school. She wasn't available, and it took five minutes to convince her assistant that Junior needed to come home due to a family emergency. The assistant wanted more detail, and Annie refused to provide it. Annie could hear Junior in the background, arguing with the assistant, but finally she prevailed and Junior was on her way home. Annie felt a little better. Any action would be better than sitting around. With each passing minute, she was more and more certain that something bad had happened to JD.

Ten minutes later, Annie heard Junior's car pull into the garage, and then Junior rushed in. Her face was slightly flushed, and she gave Annie a hug. As she pulled away, Junior said, "I've contacted some of my hacker friends, and I can get right to work."

They headed up to Junior's room, and as Annie sat down on the bed, Junior plopped into the chair in front of her computer.

"Dad has an iPhone 3G. It's the latest thing, and guess what? It has built-in GPS. Steve Jobs really did it with this one. I've already given Dad's phone number to Otto over in New Haven, and he's working on a hack to pick up its location."

"How long will this take?"

"It shouldn't take too long, less than half an hour, and then he can patch me in. In the old days, without the GPS, we had to triangulate, and that could take a while. It required a lot of calculation, and the best we could do was place the phone within maybe a hundred feet. And it depended on where the cell towers were located. But with the new GPS phones, we just need to ping the phone, and we can get the latitude and longitude within a few feet."

Annie looked at her daughter with renewed respect. "So we can find JD's phone, and locate it within a few feet." She paused. "But won't Mortimer hear the ping?"

"No, it's a silent electronic signal. No one will hear this ping." Junior smiled, looking very proud of herself. "And there's more. We can completely bypass the operating system and the antivirus software, and hack directly into the radio processor. The iPhone then becomes a microphone. We'll be able to hear any conversation in the vicinity of the phone."

"What about Otto? Can he listen in?"

"He won't. We have an honor code. He'll make the connection, and patch me in. Then he's gone."

Annie frowned slightly. "Is this legal?"

Junior pushed her chair back from the computer and faced her mother, crossing her arms. "Not by a long shot." Her eyes narrowed. "Do you still want me to go ahead?"

"Damn right. I was just curious. Do it."

CHAPTER 22

JD could hear the gentle call of seagulls. The calls were faint and muffled, but the sound was unmistakable. It was definitely seagulls. He tried to concentrate on the sound, because he wasn't sure whether he was awake or dreaming, and then he heard surf breaking on a shore somewhere nearby. The steady rhythm of the waves was very peaceful, and he started drifting off to sleep again. And then he finally recognized the sound. It was his alarm clock. He'd gotten tired of being jolted awake by the twin fiddles of Bob Wills, especially with a hangover, and he'd inserted one of those relaxation CDs, something called *Songs of the Ocean.* He rolled over on his side, and suddenly noticed that his head hurt. His temple was throbbing, his throat felt dry, and he had a touch of nausea. He opened his eyes.

He wasn't in his bed at home. He was in a big room that he'd never seen before, lying on a strange bed and still wearing his clothes. Annie was nowhere to be seen. Sunlight was streaming in, and he had to squint in the bright glare. As his eyes gradually adjusted, he saw that the far wall consisted mostly of a floor-to-ceiling window, with a spectacular view of the ocean. He checked his watch. It was two o'clock. Where was he and how had he gotten here? He felt for his iPhone, but it was gone. Then he noticed some congealed bloodstains on his shirt. He'd been in some sort of accident, but he wasn't in a hospital.

He looked around the large room. Nothing was familiar. There was a fully stocked bar, a small fridge, and a cappuccino machine on the counter. He noticed a video monitor on the far wall, and he got up and went to check the door. It was locked.

And then it hit him. With a jolt, he remembered *The Visible Hand*, and the needle prick in his arm. He recalled falling to the floor, and the feeling of drowning.

Mortimer and Chong had drugged him, and had obviously taken him somewhere. But at least he was still alive. Then the shock of recognizing Rich's black-belt tattoo came back to him, and he felt the wave of nausea all over again. Was Rich still alive? Then the vision of those glass boxes sliced into his thoughts. He could see that dark little room, and that sudden flash of the spotlight focused on *The Visible Hand.*

JD sat down on the bed, feeling ill as the sickening scene ran through his mind again.

He still couldn't comprehend the depravity of it. Mortimer seemed to be more monster than human, cutting off Rich's hand and putting it in that box. He tried to avoid the thought of Rich with a missing hand. But despite his efforts, his consciousness flowed back to that dark room.

In his mind's eye, JD could see those nine other boxes on their black stands. Each of those glass boxes contained the result of some sadistic ritual carried out by Mortimer and Chong.

JD involuntarily looked down at his own right hand, and he could feel the sweat running down the side of his face. He started to shiver uncontrollably. He realized there was only one possible conclusion from what he had seen in that little locked room. He tried to avoid it, dreaming up other possible scenarios, but it was no use. The truth was too obvious.

Mortimer was a serial killer. He had murdered ten people, and JD was about to become victim number eleven.

JD wiped his face with his sleeve and squeezed his eyes shut. He mustn't panic. He took ten deep breaths, exhaling very slowly each time, and focused on his diaphragm, just as his mother had taught him when he was very young and afraid of something. He opened his eyes. Then he sat down cross-legged in front of the window to meditate. He began to feel calmer, and as he looked out on the ocean, he suddenly realized that the land on the other side was Long Island. He was on Mortimer's private island, the one he had read about in his research.

He looked down the cliff in front of the window, and the view was distorted. The glass was probably an inch thick. The waves were breaking a hundred feet below. There were seagulls gliding on the air currents, and he felt he could almost reach out and touch them.

JD closed his eyes again. If he was going to stay alive, he had to think clearly. But as he tried to concentrate, overwhelming feelings of regret coursed through him. How had he been so stupid as to allow Mortimer to capture him without any struggle? He hadn't even drawn his Glock. He's been blind-sided completely. Why had he been so vulnerable? Annie had known there was something off about Mortimer, but JD himself had not sensed it, hadn't taken her concern seriously. Mortimer had met JD only once for about half an hour at Kosnowski's gallery, and had figured out his most basic weakness – his pride in his investing acumen. Mortimer had played him like a Stradivarius.

JD relaxed a little more as he continued to meditate. He could feel his memory drifting back to his undergraduate days at Princeton. He was in psychology class, listening to one of his favorite professors discuss the latest edition of the *Diagnostic and Statistical Manual of Mental Disorders*, commonly known as the DSM. It was 886 pages long, and contained 374 psychological disorders. The professor was focusing on an aberrant personality type in this particular lecture, talking about what he called "the warrior gene." Individuals with this gene – called psychopaths – had brains that were wired differently. Mostly men, they had no sense of fear, and also lacked a moral compass. They tended to be very intelligent and master-manipulators. Some of these psychopaths went on to become successful CEOs, investment bankers, and lawyers. Others became criminals. Among these criminals, a small number took to extreme violence, often undergoing their initiation by abusing animals at a very young age. These outlier psychopaths grew up to become serial killers, and JD remembered reading about three of them in that psychology course: Jeffrey Dahmer, Ted Bundy, and John Wayne Gacy.

JD continued his deep breathing, concentrating on that lecture. He knew there was a reason for this particular memory to be rising to his consciousness. Mortimer was clearly a psychopath, maybe even on a par with Dahmer, Bundy and Gacy. He recalled that Gacy had been a father and a family man with a successful business, well respected in his Chicago neighborhood. But he had also raped and murdered 33 men and teenage boys, burying most of them under his house and in his backyard. His neighbors were completely unaware of his murderous activities, even though they had heard muffled screams and sobs from the house late at night. Sometimes, true unmitigated evil can hide in plain sight. JD remembered that one of his Princeton professor's colleagues had interviewed a number of serial killers in prison, and said that after spending several hours talking to them, he felt as though he'd been hypnotized. Psychopaths could be very charming and charismatic, and sometimes even truly talented. Mortimer seemed to fit that pattern.

Then the knot in JD's stomach began to tighten again as the past drifted away and his current reality intervened. The bottom line was very simple - Mortimer intended to kill him. The only questions were when and how. JD had exactly one hope for survival — he had to delay the inevitable until he could escape or be rescued.

His thoughts then turned to Annie. She was already suspicious of Mortimer, and when JD failed to show up for lunch, she would have known that something serious had happened. But Annie would not be able to get instant results. It would take time to convince Puccini that Mortimer had captured JD, and to search for him. JD knew he had to stay alive until they got here. To do that, he had to do his own analysis of what Mortimer's weaknesses might be - and how to manipulate him, instead of vice versa. JD had no weapons, so it would have to be a mind game. But how? What were Mortimer's weaknesses?

He concentrated again on that Princeton lecture about psychopathy. He remembered studying for the psychology exam, and could visualize the list of criteria that defined the disorder. JD realized that threats would have no effect on Mortimer. He had no fear, and, in fact, he might enjoy the excitement. Looking for any vulnerability he might be able to exploit, JD began to make a mental list of the classic psychopath's characteristics:

- Charming and entertaining
- Grandiose self-perception, arrogance
- Constant need for stimulation
- Dishonest
- Manipulative

JD knew there were other criteria, but he couldn't remember them all. No matter - those five characteristics were dangerous enough. He mulled them over, and realized that there was one aspect of Mortimer's personality he might be able to exploit: his grandiose self-perception and arrogance. The most interesting person in Mortimer's world was Mortimer, and JD needed to get him talking about that subject. He'd become the most attentive listener Mortimer had ever met, fascinated by every aspect of Mortimer's life, achievements, and personality. To stay alive, JD would become the perfect mirror to Mortimer's grandiose view of himself. It was a gamble, and the odds were certainly against him, but he couldn't think of any other strategy. He was sure as hell not going to roll over and let Mortimer kill him without pushing back. He was going to fight to stay alive – not through physical force, but by deflecting Mortimer's mind games and hopefully, outmaneuvering him somehow.

But Mortimer wasn't the only one he had to worry about. Abigail Chong was the other half of the team. Female psychopaths were rare, but they certainly existed. He remembered a serial killer couple from Canada where the woman had seemed to be the leader and instigator in a series of brutal murders of young women, including the psychopathic woman's own sister. And even if Chong was not a psychopath, she certainly was deadly. He'd have to find out more about her.

JD got up, yawned and stretched, and walked over to the bar. He figured that Mortimer would have left some Sazerac for him, and he was right. He grabbed two ice cubes from the fridge, put them in a small glass, and poured himself two fingers of his favorite rye. Then he sat down in the lounge chair overlooking the water, and took a sip. The drink would help him become an attentive listener. He walked back to the mirror over the bar, and practiced his you-don't-say expression, raising one eyebrow in surprise. Too much, he decided. It had to be subtle, or Mortimer would figure out what he was up to.

* * *

Half an hour later, the door to JD's room opened, and Mortimer walked in, accompanied by Chong. She was holding a small chrome pistol, and remained standing by the door, pointing it in JD's direction. Mortimer sat down on the sofa near JD. The blue banker suit was gone, and he was dressed in blue jeans, a grey sweatshirt, and white sneakers. The outfit reminded JD of pictures he'd seen of Picasso, except no beret.

"It's a beautiful view, isn't it?" Mortimer said. "I know my other guests rather enjoyed it in their last few hours. It's so peaceful here."

JD didn't answer. He got up, found more ice in the fridge, and poured himself another splash of Sazerac, pleased that his hand was steady. Chong tracked him with the pistol as he crossed the room, but JD's face remained impassive. He turned to Mortimer, wanting to put him off balance and take control of the situation.

"Could I fix you a drink, Mortimer? Laphroaig, I believe. We have a lot to talk about. And how about you, Ms. Chong?"

Chong didn't respond, but Mortimer said, "I'll take a splash, no ice, please."

JD couldn't tell if he had surprised Mortimer with his request. Mortimer acted as if having a person he was about to kill offering him a drink was nothing new. Or maybe he just didn't care. JD now recalled that a flat affect – no show of emotion – was a characteristic of psychopaths. That's what Annie had seen in his eyes, JD realized. Then again, at least Mortimer didn't look bored. Boredom could be deadly. Psychopaths needed constant stimulation.

Chong glanced at Mortimer, and he motioned her toward the door with a nod. She left and closed the door. JD fixed Mortimer's drink, and turned toward him. For a fleeting moment, he thought about throwing the drink in Mortimer's face and trying to overpower him, but as he approached Mortimer, JD saw him pull up his sweatshirt and withdraw a black pistol from the holster under his belt. He pointed it at JD.

"I hate shooting bartenders. Just put the drink down very slowly."

JD did as he was ordered and sat down in the lounge chair near the window, still holding his own glass. Mortimer put the gun down on the table and picked up his Laphroaig.

JD forced a smile, and raised his Sazerac in a toast. "To your beautiful view. And to the memory of the ten guests who have passed through here. And passed on."

Mortimer smiled back. "Ahhh, the man with the doctorate. It certainly didn't take you long to put two and two together."

"Two and two only makes four, and you've done ten so far. I guess I'll be number eleven. But you know, you have a long way to go. Dahmer did seventeen, Gacy did thirty-three, and Bundy did over forty."

Mortimer frowned. "Maybe. But I don't kill prostitutes or teenage boys. I kill prominent people, important people. So there's no comparison. My targets have security and bodyguards. It takes much more creativity and skill. Killing prostitutes is easy. There's no challenge. And anyway, it's a lot more than eleven. I started early. Those ten you mentioned are just the most recent. And these were done professionally, not for pleasure alone."

"Professionally? Were these some other artists who were threatening your sales? Were you eliminating competition?"

Mortimer sighed, but his face was expressionless. "No, no. My art stands on its own merits. That part of my life is what you might call normal. But my main profession is contract killing, and my fees are very high." Mortimer paused for dramatic effect. "Of course, I don't do it just for the money. I do enjoy it." Mortimer smiled slightly.

JD shook his head slowly, his eyes wide but never leaving Mortimer's face. "My God, a professional assassin? So how many have you actually killed? And when did you get started?" He was curious about the fees Mortimer had mentioned. Maybe that would explain his wealth. But JD wanted to approach each facet of this psychopathic personality slowly, giving due attention to each aspect of Mortimer's bizarre worldview. The more complicated he could make it, the longer he would survive.

Mortimer gave him a charming smile. "I'm glad you asked. I don't get to talk about this very often, except with Abigail. She understands my drive. In fact, she gets the same sort of charge from killing as I do. It's like Ted Bundy said . . . 'You feel the last bit of breath leaving their body. You're looking into their eyes. A person in that situation is God.'"

JD knew he had Mortimer on a roll now. He was boasting about his killings, and comparing himself to his peer group. He could even quote them word for word. But JD didn't know how to respond in a way that would seem "normal" to a psychopath. What Mortimer said was revolting, but JD knew he couldn't show his revulsion. He decided to take a neutral approach, pretending to himself that he was a historian or a journalist, documenting the exploits of this serial killer. It would also help him keep his mind off the memories of Rich, and his own probable demise. He had to be patient, stay calm. And look for an opening.

"So you've studied a lot of other serial killers. And you compare yourself with them?"

"It's sort of inevitable. I like keeping score, and I believe the press should consider the degree of difficulty when they cover these cases."

Mortimer seemed to be describing a sporting event rather than cold-blooded murders. JD could see no sign of empathy, guilt, or regret. There was a hypnotic quality to the bizarre way the artist described his actions, and a certain outlandish logic to his claims.

JD tried to keep his voice as cool and neutral as Mortimer's. "Maybe someone will write a book about you, and make a movie. But how will it end? Do you think you'll ever get caught?"

"I don't know. They never caught the Zodiac Killer. But it doesn't matter to me. I can't stop. After the first one, it became an obsession. And I turned it into a very lucrative profession."

"Who was your first one?" JD found he was genuinely curious.

"It was a rival artist in New York. I was competing with him for my first solo exhibition, and I wanted him out of the way. I'd killed animals before, but this was different. It gave me a lot of pleasure. Not real sexual pleasure, but a feeling of power. I proved that I could do it. And when you think about it, I'm not really that unusual. Everyone is capable of killing. Look at what happens during wartime. People like me win medals. But very few people are willing to act on these impulses unless they're sanctioned by the government. Abigail and I are among the select few."

"So Abigail . . . is like you?"

Mortimer's his lips creased in a very slight smile. "That's why I love her. That's why I married her. We make a great team. We both take real pleasure in killing. She discovered it when she was an MP in Iraq, and was caught in a firefight. They were in a convoy, and she killed four Iraqi soldiers. Got a medal for it. The aftermath was PTSD and agoraphobia, which is why she doesn't go out much, but she never had any regrets. And by the way, don't get any ideas about trying to escape. She's fully trained in hand-to-hand combat, and I have a black belt in taekwondo. Your colleague Professor Bridger found out about that, and he died sooner than necessary. I think we could have had some very pleasant conversations about economics, but he was determined to fight. So I had to use my knife." Mortimer looked directly at JD. "I did get a great deal of pleasure watching his face lose its color. When they bleed out, they become very pale. Have you ever seen a person bleed to death, Doctor Dionne?"

JD felt his heart rate increasing, and a small bead of sweat started trickling down his back as Mortimer described how he had murdered Rich. So that confirmed it. Rich was dead. JD felt an overwhelming sense of grief, and he closed his eyes tightly to hold back tears. Then he forced his mind away from the grief. Rich was gone, and there was nothing he could do about it now. He had to get back on track with his strategy. And he was going to get as much information as he could. If he survived this, he swore that Mortimer would pay for Rich's death. JD noticed that his hand was shaking very slightly.

Mortimer smiled as he looked at JD. "Are you getting nervous? I'm sorry if I upset you by talking about killing your friend."

Fake empathy, another classic sign of a psychopath, thought JD. He knew that Mortimer was probing for weakness. He was clearly a sadist, and if JD showed any sign of pain, Mortimer would continue putting pressure on him, squeezing him. He got up to look out the window to gather his thoughts and calm down.

He turned back to face Mortimer. "How did you get rid of the bodies?"

"Come, come, Doctor. Don't play stupid. It's unbecoming. You know how I did it. I burned them."

"In your ceramics kiln? So that's why it's so big."

"That extra size is coincidence. The oversize sculptures came first, in fact. But you must admit it was serendipitous. Corpses fit easily. I have a glass door so I can watch."

"You say corpses. That means your victims were dead when you burned them."

"Most of them. Sometimes they weren't quite dead yet. Those were the difficult cases, the ones who refused to cooperate. Sometimes my clients require specific information from the targets before I kill them, and that can take a lot of time if people are stubborn. I get very angry about that. I mean, they're going to die anyway. You'd think they'd want to cooperate and make it easier for all concerned. Sometimes I just don't understand people. They can be very irrational."

JD walked back to his chair and sat down, taking another sip of his Sazerac. It sounded as if Mortimer had tortured his victims to extract information. JD had no intention of being tortured. He smiled at Mortimer. "Well, I'd certainly like to cooperate. What is it you'd like to know from me?"

Mortimer paused. "I would like to discover your investment secrets, Dr. Dionne. Bucky was running a fraud, so his advice was obviously useless. But you actually made a lot of money for your clients, and for yourself. I'd like to learn from you, and continue building my capital after you're gone."

JD was stunned. This psychopath was about to kill him, but first, he wanted investment advice. Then he realized that this could be a great opportunity to prolong his life – giving a lecture on investment. "I'd be very pleased to provide that advice." He [illegible] another smile. "But remember – past performance is not necessarily indicative of future returns. By the way, who was the client that wanted to get *me* out of the way?"

"Client? There's no one right now in your case. You're just a loose end. You know too much, and you've become a problem."

"But why did you try to kill me by running me off the road last week? That happened right after I met with Winthrop Harriman . . . and threatened to expose his Ponzi scheme. I was sure back then that he was behind that stunt, or maybe his two sons. But after I saw your two black Cadillac SUVs, I knew it was you. Why did you try to kill me? I'd never even met you at the time."

"Well, it's complicated. And by the way, that was excellent driving. A bootleg turn . . . very clever. Abigail just didn't react quickly enough. If I'd been behind you, you'd be dead. But anyway, yes, Harriman was my client at the time. He was going to pay my usual five million to get rid of you. But I asked him to explain why he wanted you dead, and unfortunately for him, he told me. We go back a long way, and he thought he could trust me. He told me about the Ponzi, and I'll tell you, I had no idea. *Nada*. It was a complete surprise. How did you figure it out?"

JD rubbed his cheek with his fingers, thinking of his analysis and hacking. He decided not to go into too much detail yet; he wanted to keep Mortimer asking questions. "I did some simple calculations, and the numbers didn't make sense. And then I found out that Harriman had never actually done any trading. All his client reports were fakes. He'd just spent the money."

Mortimer nodded thoughtfully. "I was very surprised by his blatant dishonesty. I asked for my money back, and . . . can you believe it . . . he said he couldn't pay it right away. It would take time. I asked him to come to my house to discuss it, and convinced him to be honest with me. I can be very persuasive when the need arises." Mortimer smiled at his little understatement. "Bucky finally told me all the money was gone. Let me tell you, Doctor Dionne, when a good friend betrays you like that, it's very, very disappointing. He begged and he pleaded, but I found him to be very manipulative. He actually started crying, trying to make me feel sorry for him. So I had to kill him. I must say it made me feel especially good when I killed him, because he betrayed me. It was personal, and I got a great buzz from doing it. It wasn't quick."

JD didn't want to imagine Harriman's slow death. He changed the subject. "And who were the clients in Rich and Fareed's cases?"

Mortimer scowled and put his glass down on the coffee table. "JD, you're cute when you pretend to be slow, but it's getting to be a little irritating. The clients you're asking about were at Stuart's party and you talked to them. I watched you. So cut the bullshit."

JD realized he'd pushed Mortimer a little too far with his fake naiveté. He had to be careful. He decided to backtrack.

"I had my suspicions, but as you can see, I was wrong about Harriman. I thought he was your client in my case. It's clear that John Maynard Yates had a motive to get rid of Rich, because Rich had discovered that Yates was also running a financial fraud. In fact, I confirmed that myself. Yates's scheme was more sophisticated than Harriman's. And in Fareed's case, I assume it had to do with the lawsuit he started against you on *Tricolor One.* It would have tied up the work in court for years, and Cole would have been upset. So your clients were Yates and Cole, right?"

"That's right. They paid the full fee for my services, no friendship discounts. I would have been happy to go to court against Fareed on my own, because I would have prevailed. No money had changed hands, and there was nothing on paper. But Stuart was in a hurry . . . and willing to pay my five million."

So if Mortimer was telling the truth, then Dot had not been involved. JD felt some relief over that, but he knew he had to keep the conversation going. "But why did you try to shoot Fareed from such a long distance, and almost in full public view? It was very risky. And who did the shooting?"

Mortimer helped himself to more Laphroaig. "You're right. It was very risky. We couldn't get closer because he had a bodyguard, and that guard knew what he was doing. Fareed was never alone. But the main reason we did it that way was for the thrill . . . the challenge, if you will. Abigail and I got a huge kick out of it. And Abigail did the shooting. It's a pity she had time for only one shot. I can't believe she missed."

JD realized that Chong must be a trained sniper, and that Annie had been right all along. Smith and Cole were not the ones. It had been Mortimer – and Chong.

"She didn't miss by much. The boat hit a wave, and that was the difference."

Mortimer looked very closely at JD and nodded. "That's good to know. I'll tell her it wasn't her fault. She felt very bad about it. She ––"

Mortimer was interrupted as the door opened, and Chong walked into the room. Her pistol was gone. "Mortimer, I need some help in the kitchen. I'm making the bouillabaisse, but we should also have a salad. We want our guest to enjoy his last meal."

Mortimer turned to JD. "You'll have to excuse me. I didn't have a chance to check on your culinary preferences, but I hope you like fish. Abigail is an excellent cook. I thought this was the least we could do for you. It's sort of our tradition."

"I love fish," JD said, unable to believe how bizarre this entire conversation was becoming.

"Good. We can continue our discussion later. Just relax and enjoy yourself, and we'll come and get you when dinner is ready."

But as his captors left the room, JD's mind wasn't on food. His plan for interim survival was in place, and it seemed to be working.

Now he had to figure out how to escape.

CHAPTER 23

Annie was sitting in Junior's bedroom, watching her daughter applying her skills at the computer, and trying not to fidget impatiently as she waited for the results. It was now half past two, and she was now certain that JD was in serious trouble. The situation reminded her of Rich's disappearance, and her gut feeling was that she shouldn't waste any time. She could sense her heart rate increasing, but all she could do was wait. She did not want to disturb Junior's concentration.

Junior kept typing very quickly, occasionally moving the mouse. Annie's tension kept mounting, and finally, Junior leaned back and said, "Take a look. I've got the coordinates for Dad's phone. It's out in the middle of Long Island Sound."

Annie jumped up and stared at the monitor. "Wha-a-a-t? What do you mean? Is it on a boat or something?"

Junior pointed to a map on the screen. "It's on an island, about five miles out from Greenwich."

Annie looked more closely at the screen. "We can pinpoint it on the marine chart. There's one in JD's office."

Junior grinned. "Don't need it. I can just use Google Earth. Watch this."

Junior zoomed in on the coordinates, and Annie could see a fairly large island with two buildings on it, plus a dock and a boathouse. Three smaller wooded islands were nearby, and looked to be uninhabited. A small dot in the middle of the larger building indicated JD's cell phone.

Annie stared at the image on the screen. "I think that's Mortimer's studio island. JD told me about it when he was doing the financial research on Mortimer. They must have taken JD out there. Why else would his phone be there?"

Junior zoomed in further, focusing on the building, and it became clear that it was a very large house. "His phone is turned on, but he can't answer it. Someone must have taken it. The screen on the iPhone goes blank after it hasn't been used for a while, so they probably don't know it's on. But why did you say 'they' took him out there? Is someone else there with Mortimer?"

"I'm not sure"- Annie stopped to think -"but JD would not have gone out to the island voluntarily, certainly not without calling me to tell me he'd be late. So he must have been captured somehow. It's possible that Mortimer did it by himself, but JD had his Glock." Annie paused again, and looked intently at Junior. "So I think someone must have helped Mortimer. And there's another thing. When I drove out to Belle Plains to find Mortimer's house, the gate-keeper wouldn't let me in without calling the house. When he did, I heard him say, 'Yes, madam.' So there was a woman at Mortimer's house. It might have been a housekeeper, but if so, she's probably in on it."

Junior started rubbing her upper arms with her hands, and rocking back and forth slowly. "Do you think it was the same people who kidnapped Rich?"

Annie shifted in her seat and bit her lip. "I don't know. But it's very possible. The one thing we do know is that Dad is in serious trouble, so let's get moving on this. You said you can turn his iPhone into a microphone, and listen in on what's happening nearby. Can you do that now?"

"That's the next step. It'll only take a minute." Junior turned back to the computer and got busy with the mouse and keyboard. Annie heard a crackling noise, and then clear as a bell, she could hear kitchen sounds coming from the speakers. Junior turned up the volume. It was unmistakable – pots and pans clanging, an exhaust fan, and the sound of footsteps as someone moved around.

Annie was puzzled. "It sounds like someone's cooking something." She looked up abruptly. "They can't hear *us*, can they?"

"No, Mom, it's only one way. Don't worry."

They continued to listen in, but aside from occasional quiet gurgles of a liquid being poured, and some humming, there were no sounds except that of someone cooking. From the variety of sounds, the recipe seemed quite complicated. Annie and Junior continued to listen silently for a few minutes, and finally they heard a door opening and a second set of footsteps, heavier than those of whoever was in the kitchen cooking.

A male voice said, 'How's the bouillabaisse coming along? I'm getting hungry." Annie thought the voice sounded familiar, and realized it was Mortimer.

A female voice answered, "It will be another hour or so. I like to cook it slowly and let it simmer. I need to draw out the fish juices."

"Well, make it good. I want him to enjoy it."

"Is he ready yet? When should we start the final steps?"

"After dinner. After it gets dark."

Junior and Annie could make out the sound of footsteps, and a door closing. Then it was only the cooking sounds again.

Annie took a deep breath and clenched her hands to stop them from shaking. "There's a woman out there with Mortimer, and they're going to kill him. They've got him, and they're going to kill him. After it gets dark. That's what they meant by 'final steps.' I need to call Puccini. We have to save him."

Junior's face had turned white, and she seemed to be on the edge of tears. Her hand was trembling as she clicked the mouse. "I recorded that last part. You can play it for the detective."

* * *

Puccini was sitting at his desk poring over the list of evidence on Smith and Cole. He hadn't gotten much further in seeking grounds for an arrest, and he was getting frustrated. He was certain that Smith had shot Ghanem, but he still couldn't prove it. His cell phone rang, and he saw that it was Anne Rutherford. He considered letting it go to voicemail, but finally picked up.

"Hi, Annie. So did JD turn up, full of apologies?"

"No, he bloody well didn't. And he's not going to, unless you do something." Her voice was loud and angry. "Mortimer's captured him, and he's going to kill him tonight."

Puccini moved the phone away from his ear. "Whoa, whoa, lady, hold on. Captured him? And killing him? What's going on? Slow down and back up. Last time we talked he was late for lunch." Puccini glanced over at Brown across his desk, shaking his head.

Annie's voice got louder. "JD's on Mortimer's island out in the Sound. I overheard Mortimer and someone else say that they were going to kill JD." She was almost screaming, "You have to get out there."

Puccini started listening more carefully. "Okay, slow down. First off, how do you know he's out there?"

"My daughter hacked JD's phone and located it. And that's how we overheard them talking."

"Your daughter? Hacked a phone? How old is she?"

"Why does that matter? I heard the conversation myself, and she recorded it. You can listen."

"I thought pinging cell phones was restricted to law enforcement. But okay, I'll listen to the recording. Have her put it on."

Puccini heard a muffled discussion, and then the recording of the conversation came on. He listened carefully, and then said, "Play it again. I want to hear every word." He listened to the recording a second time.

A male voice said, 'How's the bouillabaisse coming along? I'm getting hungry."

A female voice answered, "It will be another hour or so. I like to cook it slowly and let it simmer. I need to draw out the fish juices."

"Well, make it good. I want him to enjoy it."

"Is he ready yet? When should we start the final steps?"

"After dinner. After it gets dark."

Puccini considered the precise words for a while, and then said, "There's nothing there about killing anyone. They're cooking dinner, and it sounds like they're in the middle of some sort of negotiation. What was JD meeting with Mortimer about?"

"It was about an investment in JD's fund. But didn't you hear the part about 'final step'? That means they're going to kill JD. That's what 'final step' means. They're going to kill him after it gets dark."

"Maybe. But the 'final step' could be the signing of some sort of contract. There's nothing there about an imminent murder. I think you're worried over nothing."

"Good God! Can't you see it?" Annie screamed. "You're caught up in semantics. It's bloody well obvious. *They've got JD and they're going to kill him.*"

Puccini did not respond to Annie's angry outburst at first. He didn't think Mortimer was any sort of problem – Smith was the problem. But he owed JD for protecting his life savings, and decided he should humor his wife. Puccini kept his voice very calm. "Okay, tell you what I'll do. I'll go and check out the island, see if JD is there and see if he's all right."

"You have to search the whole island. I'm sure they won't have him sitting in the living room."

Puccini ignored Annie's sarcasm. "I'll try, but I won't have a search warrant. I have no probable cause. The recording you made is illegal and inadmissible."

There was a pause on the phone, and Puccini heard some more muffled conversation. Then Annie came back on, her voice still very loud. "My daughter says it's perfectly legal. We hacked into JD's own phone, and that's our property, so it's perfectly legal."

Puccini had to think about that one. "Maybe, but it would still take time to get a warrant. I could wait and get one, or head out there right now. The Marine Section has some boats that could run me out there. It's up to you. How far out is the island?"

"It's about five miles from Greenwich. I can give you the coordinates. My daughter has them right here."

"Okay, our boat can get out there in maybe fifteen minutes from the harbor. Give me those co-ords and I'll get right on it, see if a boat's available."

Annie gave him the numbers, and her voice was a little calmer. "Please get out there right away. You'll be saving JD's life."

"Roger that. I'll call you as soon as I learn anything."

Puccini disconnected and turned to Brown. "That was Joshua Dionne's wife. She's convinced that he's been kidnapped by that artist Mortimer and . . . get this . . . is about to be murdered. I know it sounds a little crazy, but I have to go check it out. I owe him. You want to come along?" He shrugged. "It's probably a wild goose chase."

"Murdered? I thought Smith was the perp."

"It's a long story. You in or out?" The words of the recording started running through Puccini's mind again. What if there was something to it? What if it wasn't a wild goose chase?

Puccini's voice grew quiet. "I wouldn't mind some backup, just in case."

Brown still seemed reluctant. "How long will it take?'

"You'll be away an hour, maybe hour and a half. Depends on whether a boat's available. I'll have you back at your desk by four-thirty, guaranteed. Home for dinner."

Brown shrugged. "All right. I'm in. But what about Harriman? That's supposed to be our main case."

"I think Harriman's skipped town for someplace with no extradition. Listen, he's sleaze and JD's a friend. I've got to check this out."

Puccini called Sergeant Bonner, the officer in charge of the Marine Section, and was told that PB 124 was at the dock and fully fueled. Puccini explained the situation, and gave him the coordinates to Mortimer's island. The Sergeant confirmed that the crew could take Puccini and Brown out there right away. The two detectives rushed down to the police garage, jumped in their Crown Vic, and ten minutes later were parked at the Marine Section dock in Greenwich Harbor.

As they were walking toward the boat, Puccini started thinking again about Mortimer. He was still certain that Smith was responsible for shooting Ghanem, but what if Mortimer *was* somehow involved? Mortimer was actually the one who would have had to go to court in the *Tricolor One* lawsuit, so maybe Smith was working for Mortimer – and not for Cole –

when he shot Ghanem. So if JD *had* actually been kidnapped, Smith could be involved. He might even be on that island with Mortimer.

Puccini was now glad that Brown had agreed to come along. He instinctively felt for the Glock under his armpit.

Brown gave him a quizzical glance. "Feeling a little nervous, Tony?"

"Nothing I can't handle. Don't worry about it."

Two Marine Officers greeted Puccini and Brown as they clambered aboard. One was older, with lots of grey hair, obviously the captain. The other one was taller and younger. Puccini had met them before, but their paths hadn't crossed very often. The Marine Unit had its own rhythm and culture.

The PB 124 was underway within minutes. The boat first proceeded slowly through the harbor to minimize its wake, but as soon as they reached open water, the captain opened the engines to full power. The grey-haired man grinned. "We've got jet drive and 960 horsepower. It won't take long."

The shoreline receded, and soon Puccini could see a large island, with three smaller ones nearby. Within minutes, the boat was settling down off its plane, and heading slowly toward the dock off the larger island. Puccini's cell phone buzzed, and he looked at the caller ID. It was the Chief's office, probably harassing him about Harriman. He let it got to voicemail.

Puccini looked up at the buildings on the island, and turned toward Brown. "Quite the spread Mortimer's got here. Look at that house up there . . . must be five thousand square feet. And dig this fancy boathouse."

"Mortimer must be doing okay. But what's that shiny smokestack about?"

Puccini turned toward the second building on the island, and saw the smoke coming from its gleaming stack. Something was definitely going on here. His skin started to tingle.

The boat pulled up to the dock, and the two detectives disembarked as the Marine Patrol officers tied up behind a large barge-like vessel. As Puccini and Brown walked along the dock to the shore, Puccini tried to figure out what the hell that smoke meant. What was Mortimer burning?

And what was that barge for? His thoughts were interrupted when he saw a moving shape in one of the lower windows of the main house way up the steep hill.

It looked like a tall dark-haired woman, dressed in black. She was in the window for only a few seconds, and then she disappeared. Why was she hiding? Puccini unbuttoned his jacket to free up his Glock as they started walking up the path toward the house.

Brown said, very quietly, "What's going on, partner?"

"I'm not sure, but stay close. This may not be a picnic."

CHAPTER 24

Mortimer and Chong had left JD in his prison-like room, locking the door behind them. He was still sitting in the lounge chair by the window, looking out at the Sound, but he didn't know whether to laugh or cry. Two serial killers were cooking a very fine meal for him – and then they were going to kill him, either before or after cutting off his hand. Had all their other victims had the dubious pleasure of this final meal? And was it always bouillabaisse, or did Mortimer and Chong vary the menu? And if they did, what were the criteria for determining what the meal would be? He felt as if he were lost in a very deadly funhouse.

His thoughts turned to what he had learned about Mortimer so far. Despite his own skewed moral code, Mortimer expected honesty in his victims and became incensed when anyone lied to him. JD wondered if he might be able to build some weird sort of trust relationship with Mortimer by being brutally honest.

Then JD remembered that Mortimer wanted more investment advice. That might prove to be JD's most immediate means of staying alive. He started developing the lecture in his mind, making it as long as possible, while still hoping to retain Mortimer's interest. He would try to exploit Mortimer's tilted morals by showing how most investment managers act in their own interest rather than their clients' interest.

No, that wouldn't work. Telling Mortimer that he'd been a fool to invest with Harriman would backfire. It would just remind him of how Harriman had bamboozled him. JD needed another angle, and he finally figured out the most promising one–he'd explain the critical importance of incentives. Follow the money, or more importantly, check out how the broker was making his own money.

He went over to the bar to pour himself a little more Sazerac, and then sat down in front of the window, swirling the ice cubes. He wanted to be relaxed but still sober enough to think straight and to take action if the opportunity presented itself. He looked out on the Sound, and noticed something odd about the clouds. It was a pattern he'd seen before, and he remembered it as if it were yesterday – a combination of cirrus and cirro-cumulus. The sailors had an old saying about this cloud pattern: *Mackerel skies and mares' tails make tall ships wear short sails.* A storm was approaching.

This specific cloud pattern had changed his life many years before, had put him on a path from Christian Island to Princeton and Oxford. It was that knowledge of weather patterns that had led him to save that banker when he was in high school.

He looked up at the sky again, and he could also see a few cumulonimbus clouds – anvil-shaped thunderheads – forming over Long Island. The storm would hit in two or three hours. He started thinking about how he might use that information. All he had to do was live that long.

JD's thoughts were interrupted as he heard a key in the door. Mortimer opened the door so hard that it hit the doorstop with a bang. His face was impassive, and he was holding his black automatic pistol.

"There's been a change in plans. We have to put you on ice for a while. And don't try anything. Shooting you would be an inconvenience, but it would also give me a great deal of pleasure. Get moving."

JD got up and started easing toward the door. Mortimer stayed six feet behind him, still pointing the gun, and they walked out the door.

"Keep moving," Mortimer snapped.

JD realized there was no way he could turn to grab the gun and overpower Mortimer - the psychopath was carefully staying out of reach. They proceeded down a hallway at a fast pace until they came to a walkway overlooking a large room. They turned to the right along the walkway, which was lined by a marble balustrade. The walls of the room below were painted white, and they were covered with artwork. A polished wood dining table sat in the middle, bordered by eight chairs done in dark wood and black leather. Chong was waiting down below at the table, holding her chrome automatic. Mortimer motioned JD to go down the stairs at the end of the walkway, and when they reached the floor below, Mortimer said to Chong, "We'll put him down in the basement for now. We need to tie him up and keep him quiet."

Chong waved her pistol at JD. "Move. They're almost here."

JD felt some relief at the instructions. At least they weren't about to kill him yet. But he wondered who was coming – and why. They obviously didn't want these visitors to see him. He thought about shouting for help, but looked at the two guns, and realized that it might be the last sound he ever made. Chong opened a door on the far wall, and Mortimer said to JD, "Just keep walking. And keep quiet."

They went down to the basement, and while Mortimer continued to point his gun at JD, Chong very quickly bound his hands and feet with thick snap-ties, and taped his mouth shut with duct tape. They lifted him up brusquely, carried him over to a large closet, and dropped him on the floor. Then they tied his hands and feet behind his back so he could hardly move. They were obviously in a hurry, but JD was surprised by how effortlessly they had carried him. Chong was much stronger than she looked.

JD lay on his side in the dark after Mortimer and Chong left, and tried to pull his hands free of the snap-ties, but it was no use. He tried to shout, but with the tape over his mouth, his cries came out as muffled moans. A few minutes later, he heard the door open upstairs, no more than fifty feet away, and some footsteps. He couldn't quite make out what was being said, but he thought he recognized one voice.

It sounded like Puccini.

* * *

Puccini and Brown were only a few steps from the house when the front door opened, and Mortimer greeted them. Puccini remembered the artist from his visit to Cole's house the night before. He looked different now, wearing blue jeans, a grey sweatshirt, and white sneakers instead of the all-black artist's getup; and his hair was slicked back instead of spiky.

"And what brings you fine gentlemen out here? I saw you only yesterday at my friend Stuart Cole's party. You made quite the entrance."

Puccini paused to catch his breath from the long walk up the hill. "We're looking for Doctor Joshua Dionne. His wife said you had a meeting with him, and he seems to have disappeared. He was supposed to be home hours ago, and she can't reach him."

Mortimer smiled. "He was in fine shape when I last saw him. We met at my house in Belle Plains this morning. I was thinking of investing with him. He came out to the island here to look at some art, and I took him back to the mainland about an hour ago. Unfortunately, we couldn't make a deal. He's probably home by now."

Puccini narrowed his eyes as he looked at Mortimer's face closely. Something was off. How could Mortimer have come out here, back to town with JD, and back to the island so quickly?

"That was a pretty speedy trip. You say you came out here with Doctor Dionne, took him back to Greenwich, and got back here yourself. Did you travel in that barge you have down by the dock?"

"Don't be silly, detective, of course not. I have a Donzi 22 with a 450 horsepower Mercruiser. When the water's calm, it's very quick. I can get back to my house in Belle Plains in fifteen minutes."

At the mention of the speedboat, Puccini suddenly remembered something about the Ghanem shooting. A witness had seen a speedboat leaving the island near the yacht club where Ghanem was shot– with two people aboard.

"What color's your Donzi?"

"That's an odd question, detective. What does that have to do with Joshua Dionne? Anyway, it's white. I admire purity."

Puccini's sixth sense started twitching. A white speedboat. Maybe Anne Rutherford's instincts were on the mark. But he wanted to keep moving with his questions.

"His wife couldn't reach him on his cell phone. That's why she got worried." Puccini decided not to mention the hacking part.

Mortimer's smile was relentless. "You know how it is with cell phones. Maybe the battery ran down, or he didn't have reception. There are some dead zones out here."

Puccini looked at Brown, and toward the second building. Puccini pointed toward the building with his thumb. "Maybe he forgot it here. Do you mind if we look around a bit? Won't take long, and we'll be gone. I just want to tell his wife we tried."

"I'm afraid I'm rather busy right now. My kiln is at operating temperature, and I was just about to start firing a large sculpture. It can't wait, and I'd be nervous about having you wandering around here by yourself. There's an open cliff over on that side."

Firing a sculpture – that explained the smoke, thought Puccini. Now he wanted to know about the woman in the window.

"Is there anyone else here? Maybe they could show us around."

"I'm here by myself. I like to be alone when I'm working on my sculptures."

Puccini paused. He knew Mortimer was lying, and that piqued his interest further. Why would he lie about something so apparently innocuous? "My partner and I really need to look around. It would be in your interest to give us fifteen minutes of your time."

Puccini started moving toward Mortimer, and Brown did the same, trying to intimidate him. Mortimer just kept smiling. "If you'd like to look around, you'll need a warrant. You know that and I know that. So let's just stop wasting our time. Please leave, and come back with a warrant if you wish. Without it, you have no right to search my property."

Puccini realized his bluff had fallen through, and now he was becoming more and more suspicious. What was Mortimer hiding? Anne Rutherford was probably right. JD might be here. But he and Brown had no cards left to play.

"Okay, we'll go. But we'll be back very soon."

"Take your time. I'm not going anywhere. I have to fire my sculpture."

Puccini took a deep breath and shrugged. He just wished the goddam asshole would stop smiling. He nodded to Brown, and they turned to walk back down the path to the dock. He took a quick look through the window of the boathouse, and confirmed that there was a white Donzi inside. They boarded the Marine Section boat, and as they pulled away, Puccini wondered what the large barge was for.

The twin turbo diesels changed in pitch as the Marine Section boat accelerated, and within half a minute it was on a fast plane, heading back to Greenwich Harbor. Puccini picked up his cell phone to call Annie and bring her up to speed on his visit. He looked at his watch. It was half past three.

"Hello, Annie. I was out at the island, but there's no sign of JD. Mortimer claims he met with him and brought him out to the island to look at some artwork, but then took him back to the mainland."

"That's balderdash. JD would never go look at art without me. He doesn't know anything about art. He's out there and Mortimer's hiding him. He's going to kill him."

Puccini had to reflect for a few seconds. Mortimer had lied to him about being alone on the island, and had that white speedboat with a possible connection to Ghanem. Puccini was becoming more and more convinced that Annie's concerns might be justified. But there was nothing he could legally do at the moment without a search warrant. He decided not to tell Anne about his suspicions yet. There was no need to get her even more worried. He'd get the warrant and go back as soon as possible. If JD was there, he'd find him.

"Annie, I did my best. I tried to bluff Mortimer and search the place, but he went all legal on me, wouldn't let us in. I'll have to get a warrant, and I'll need a copy of your recording. I also need a statement from you. Could you come down to PSC? I'm going to do everything I can to find JD."

Annie's response was immediate and furious. "Look, JD will be dead before I have time to sign that statement. Isn't there some way to go out there and save him? I can't believe this. Do you have to have a dead body before you can act?"

Puccini did his best to keep his cool. "I'm sorry, Annie. My hands are tied. Meet me at the PSC and I'll see what we can do."

"That will be too late. I'll talk to you later."

Puccini's phone went dead. Annie had disconnected. Puccini felt a knot in the pit of his stomach. His instincts were telling him that Annie was right, that JD was somewhere on that island, but he couldn't move on it yet. This was one of those times when being a cop was crap.

* * *

The voices that JD had heard upstairs had stopped. The house had been silent for what seemed like five or ten minutes. His hands and wrists were raw from his attempts to attract Puccini's attention by bouncing his fists against the wall to make noise, but he hadn't been successful, and now he could hear the bass rumble of a powerful boat growing quieter, probably on its way back to Greenwich. JD guessed that Annie must have contacted Puccini, and Puccini had acted quickly, gotten a boat out here to look for him. Annie must have somehow figured out where he was. Puccini had been so close. But now he was gone, and JD was stuck here, with two murderous psychopaths. Mortimer had outsmarted them all somehow.

JD's shirt was drenched with sweat, and his eyes stung, but he couldn't reach up to wipe his face. A feeling of total dread overwhelmed him. Then he heard footsteps outside the closet, and the door opened. JD couldn't see anything at first in the suddenly bright light, but as his eyes adjusted, he could make out a shape in the doorway.

It was Mortimer, and in his right hand was a large black knife.

CHAPTER 25

Mortimer squatted next to JD, and showed him the knife. "This is an Ontario Mark 3 Navy, the one used by the SEALS. You know the reason they carry these knives? The SEALS need to be able to kill effortlessly. I had to use it on your friend Bridger . . . and they were right. Effortless."

JD stared at the knife and felt the muscles in his chest contract. His heart started hammering. The vision of Rich's severed finger in that hotel room became vivid in his mind again. And he knew he was next.

Mortimer touched the tip of the knife gently to JD's throat. "And now I may have to use it on you." Mortimer traced a line across JD's throat with the knife. JD froze in fear but he didn't flinch. He tried to force himself to keep his breathing steady, but he could do nothing about the sweat beading on his forehead. Mortimer was playing God and might plunge the knife into his throat at any second.

But then Mortimer pulled back the knife and rested the blade gently on his knee. "Your friend Puccini came here, asking for you. Said you were missing. He asked if he could look around, but I declined. It'll take him a few hours to get a search warrant, and by that time there'll be nothing to find. Ashes to ashes, and dust to dust."

Mortimer moved around to JD's back and started slicing through the snap-ties on JD's wrists and ankles. If he noticed the bloody damage to JD's wrists and hands, he made no comment. He finished cutting off the bindings, and said, "But first we must have some early dinner. You must be starving, and the bouillabaisse is done to perfection."

The whole scene again became totally surreal to JD. In the blink of an eye, Mortimer had changed from a cold-blooded hit man with a knife at JD's throat to a gracious host announcing a gourmet dinner. Seemingly sensing JD's confusion, and probably reveling in it, Mortimer smiled and said, "It would be very ungracious of us to let you go to your final reward without a worthy last supper."

JD sat up and started gently pulling the duct tape off his mouth. Then he shook his hands vigorously to get the circulation back. They were badly scratched and bloody, and there was a sharp pain where his watch had dug into his skin. He stood up, but his feet were numb from the snap-ties, and he almost fell down again. He steadied himself with a hand on the wall of the closet.

Mortimer stepped out into the adjoining room, pointing toward the stairs with his knife. JD stumbled toward the stairs and started climbing up to the main floor. Still in a daze, he vaguely considered turning and attacking Mortimer, but he sensed that the encounter would not end well. He knew that Mortimer was very skilled with that Mark 3 Navy Knife, and would be expecting the attack. JD would have to wait for another opportunity. He didn't want to end up like Rich just yet.

They arrived in the large dining room with the art on the walls. Chong was waiting for them. The table was set with china and crystal, and the bouillabaisse was steaming in the middle of the table in a large glass bowl. A fresh salad was in another ceramic bowl beside it. JD sensed that Mortimer and Chong had done this ritual with some of their other victims. They seemed to be very relaxed about it.

JD's place setting was across the table from Mortimer and Chong. Her chrome pistol sat on the table next to her bowl and wineglass, well out of JD's reach. They sat down. JD unfolded his white linen napkin and placed it carefully on his lap. Chong started ladling out the bouillabaisse while Mortimer poured the wine. "This is a '98 Screaming Eagle cab. We like red with fish, but we have white if you prefer."

JD took a sip. "This is fine."

Chong smiled, the first time JD had seen her smile. "At thirteen hundred a bottle, it better be fine. Please enjoy."

Please enjoy? The polite suggestion was so absurd that JD wanted to scream. Instead, he reminded himself that he had to play along. He focused on the wine and had to admit that the Screaming Eagle was probably the best wine he'd ever tasted. It had layers of fruit, a hint of smoke, and a long, seductive finish. He swirled the dark red liquid in his glass, looking at it with a sigh. "This wine is more than fine. It is insanely delightful."

Mortimer raised his own glass in a toast. "Well said, Doctor Dionne. Abigail and I like to share our pleasures. We don't receive many visitors out here."

JD swirled the wine again to savor the bouquet, and took another sip. He felt the wine on his tongue, then swirled it inside his mouth, and swallowed. It really was remarkable that something so simple could provide so much pleasure. Their bizarre ritual - and the feel of the wine inside him - were having their effect. He was almost starting to relax a little. He took another sip and closed his eyes. When he opened them, Mortimer and Chong were both looking at him, their faces beaming with pleasure. *This is truly nuts,* thought JD. *It's a killer meal – literally.*

Chong smiled and said, "Please try my bouillabaisse. It's one of my specialties."

JD picked up his spoon and dipped it into his bowl of bouillabaisse. He chose a large piece of fish, and started to put it in his mouth, but it was too hot. He blew on it to cool it, and then took a taste.

Chong was looking on expectantly, eyes wide. "It's red snapper, striped bass, and lobster."

JD breathed slowly through his nose as he let his taste buds do their work. There was no question – it tasted delicious. JD smiled. "It's wonderful. Certainly the best bouillabaisse I've ever tasted outside Marseilles."

JD looked down at his hot soup. His compliments seemed to be working, buying him time. He took another liberal mouthful of the Screaming Eagle, and continued eating his bouillabaisse as he tried to predict what the bizarre couple would do next.

Mortimer swallowed a little of his own wine and then looked carefully at JD. "You're going to have to work for your dinner, Doctor. Our agreement was that you would share some of your investing secrets." He took another sip. "But that can wait. We don't want your soup to get cold."

Chong frowned. "It's not soup, dear. It's bouillabaisse."

"Whatever," said Mortimer, and shrugged, directing a see-what-I-have-to-put-up-with half-smile at JD. JD rolled his eyes in understanding, and turned to his bouillabaisse. They continued eating quietly, and despite the underlying tension in the room, JD found he was hungry. He asked for a second helping. The wine was flowing freely, and Mortimer opened another bottle. JD didn't want to drink too much, but Mortimer kept pouring, and he decided that keeping up was the safest course. He wasn't going to do anything to shorten this dinner.

When they had finished their bouillabaisse, Chong got up and turned to Mortimer. "I better check the kiln. You and Doctor Dionne can have your salad now and talk about your investment strategy."

Mortimer nodded. "Of course, dear. We'll be out there shortly."

JD felt a jolt of adrenaline shoot down his chest again at the mention of the kiln. While they'd been enjoying the exquisite food and wine, Mortimer and Chong had also been heating up the kiln for him. They'd been setting him up for the kill all along. He could feel the blood draining from his face as he tried to remain calm.

Chong picked up her pistol and smiled at JD. "I'm so pleased that you enjoyed my bouillabaisse." She turned and left the room.

Now Mortimer placed his own gun on the table. He put some salad on his plate, and then passed the salad bowl across the table to JD, who pushed the bowl away, and put down his fork, mumbling, "I guess my time has come. I don't think I'm hungry anymore."

Mortimer looked up from his salad, and frowned. "What do you mean, your time has come?" Then he seemed to comprehend what JD was worried about. "No, no, you misunderstand. We've prepared the kiln for Bucky. Cremation takes place at fourteen hundred degrees, which is lower than I need for the ceramic pieces, but it still takes some time to heat up. So don't worry, we're not preparing it for you. I still want to have our conversation about your investment strategy. So please do have some salad."

JD was still in shock. He'd just gone from enjoying their fine dinner despite himself, to contemplating his imminent death by fire when Chong mentioned the kiln. Now he was facing this damned lunatic again, wanting a lecture on investment strategy. JD took a deep breath and looked at the salad bowl. He wasn't hungry at all, but eating a little salad would keep things moving while he gathered his thoughts. His mind was circling aimlessly, and he had to get it back on track – to be capable of talking coherently about investment strategy, if he wanted to stay alive. He took some salad and started eating.

Mortimer looked up from his salad and turned to JD. "So what's the best way of preserving and growing my capital – that is, what I have left after Bucky stole half of it?"

JD took another sip of wine. "It's as I told you back at your house. You have to buy low and sell high, or invest like Warren Buffet does, buy smart and hold forever."

Mortimer scowled. "That's just a bullshit cliché . . . buy low and sell high. There's got to be more to it, some secret formula. There's no need to hide that secret from me, because soon it won't be any use to you."

JD shrugged. "There's no secret formula. What you need is an advisor who actually lives that cliché, someone who doesn't follow the herd. The herd panics when prices drop and sells at the wrong time, and become giddy when there's a bubble, and buys more, exactly at the worst time. Making money requires an even keel and nerves of steel."

"Maybe I should let you live so you can advise me." Mortimer paused, and then gave a little laugh. "Just kidding . . . but where can I find one of these magic advisors?"

"Fareed Ghanem is one, but he may be reluctant to handle your money after you shot him. What you want is someone who invests their own capital successfully and then advises you to do exactly what he's doing."

Mortimer smiled. "You mean someone who eats their own cooking?"

"Precisely."

Mortimer seemed to be contemplating this new idea when the door opened again. Chong walked in. "The kiln is ready, dear." Mortimer picked up his gun and stood up. "The seminar is over, professor. We've got work to do. Get up . . . very slowly."

Mortimer motioned JD toward the door with his gun as he walked around the table. Chong held the door open and JD proceeded through, followed by Mortimer, still holding the gun. They passed through a living room with a huge picture window overlooking the Sound, walked through a wide hallway lined with art, and came to an entry hall lit by a skylight. Chong opened the front door, and they went outside.

JD could see a path toward a second building, and as they moved toward it, he had a chance to look at his surroundings. Mortimer's island looked to be oblong in shape, and about a quarter of a mile wide. The land surrounding the buildings consisted of manicured lawns and winding pathways around a small Zen garden, but the rest of the island had been left wild. The ground sloped down sharply from one side of the island to the other. The main house was built on the highest part, overlooking Long Island Sound and the hundred foot cliff that JD had seen from his window. On the other side of the island, which faced Greenwich about five miles away, the land met the water at a gentle slope, and a road had been built down to a dock and a boathouse. Tied up at the dock was a large, barge-like vessel, but he couldn't see what was in the boathouse.

JD looked out at the three small islands that he remembered from his research on Mortimer. The islands were three or four hundred yards out in the direction of Greenwich – an easy swimming distance for him, if he could somehow break free. He had picnicked on those islands with his family aboard the *Ojiway*, and he knew they were wild and uninhabited with excellent places to hide.

JD glanced the other way, toward Long Island, and could see two cumulonimbus clouds, maybe ten miles out now, moving across the water toward them. Their anvil-shaped heads meant that the storm was not far away. He saw a flash of lightning in the cloud on the left and heard a very faint rumble of thunder.

JD's thoughts were interrupted as Mortimer said, "Keep moving."

They were walking toward a large two-story building with full-height windows facing south toward the Sound. The north side of the building had an industrial door that reached almost to the roof, and above the door towered a gleaming stainless-steel exhaust stack. A very large cylindrical propane tank rested on a frame beside the building. JD realized this was where Mortimer carried out both his artistry and the macabre finishing touches to his killings. He felt that familiar gnawing in the pit of his stomach as Mortimer said, "Open the door, and don't try anything heroic."

They entered the building and walked down a hallway past some closed doors. Chong opened the door at the end of the hallway, and as they entered, JD stopped abruptly. It was the kiln room, at least fifty feet wide and two stories tall. Three six-foot-tall ceramic sculptures were sitting on pallets in various stages of completion, but the reason JD had stopped abruptly was directly in front of the kiln - a body lying on a gurney. Even from a distance, JD could tell that it was Winthrop Harriman. The corpse was still dressed in a very fine Italian suit, dark blue, and JD noticed something else as he looked more closely.

Harriman's right hand was missing.

There was a blood-soaked bandage on the stump of Harriman's forearm. JD stared at the body, totally transfixed. He knew he was looking at his own future. Unconsciously, he put his own right hand deep in his pocket, as if to hide it. He couldn't move - his feet felt glued to the floor. His stomach was starting to rumble. He could taste the bouillabaisse welling up, and the retching response was almost overwhelming, but he held his breath, and kept it down. He closed his eyes for a few seconds, but when he opened them, the body on the gurney was still there, the face still bloodless and pale. Harriman's eyes were closed, thankfully, and he wore a very peaceful expression, almost a smile.

JD felt a gun in his back, and managed to slowly put one foot in front of the other, moving toward the kiln. He forced himself to turn his gaze from the body, and looked at the rectangular box-like unit that dominated the room. It reached almost to the ceiling, and a large steel beam ran across the room just above the top of the kiln. Attached to the beam via rollers was an electric chain hoist, and sitting next to the ceramic statues was a small yellow front-end loader. Mortimer and Chong, strong as they were, obviously required mechanical assistance around the shop. It occurred to JD that the hoist and the front-end loader also helped move bodies.

JD looked to his left, and saw two wooden boxes lined up against the wall, each about seven feet long and three feet wide. The boxes had small holes on the top. JD realized they were air holes. He had probably arrived at the island in one of those boxes. His knees started to buckle, and he had to pause to steady himself. He felt like a condemned man walking down the corridor to the gallows. He tried to focus, because he knew he needed to gather as much information as he could about his surroundings, to figure out if there were any cracks in Mortimer's fortress.

He observed that the kiln itself had heat-resistant slabs on three sides, reinforced by a lattice of narrow steel beams. The entire fourth side of the kiln seemed to consist of a door that could swing open and expose the full interior of the kiln. That was the only way JD could imagine that those large sculptures could be moved in for firing.

This large door had a smaller door built into it near the bottom, complete with a small viewing window. JD realized what this small door was for. The gurney with Harriman's body was lined up right in front of it.

Mortimer waved his gun toward the sculptures over to the side. "These have to dry before I can fire them." JD looked at them, and thought, *And I'm supposed to give a shit?* Then Mortimer turned toward Harriman's body. "But a corpse needs to be dealt with immediately, or the results are not very pleasant. We have no expertise in embalming, unfortunately." He looked at Chong. "Are we ready, Abigail?"

Chong smiled expectantly. "We're at fourteen hundred degrees, ready to go."

Harriman's body was just another inanimate object to these bastards, thought JD. No different from one of those sculptures over there. They had nothing in the way of normal human feelings. These two were another species.

Mortimer nodded at JD, pointing the gun. "Go over and help Abigail put Bucky in the kiln."

JD's first thought was, *Fuck you, asshole, do it yourself,* but he caught himself quickly, and moved over to one side of the gurney. Abigail rolled the gurney right against the kiln, just below the small door. She put on some thick gloves, and quickly opened the door. A blast of hot air hit the side of JD's face as Chong shouted, "Now! Pick up your side and push."

JD fought back nausea as he bent to the task. Harriman was surprisingly heavy, but in a few seconds his body slid off the gurney into the kiln. Chong shut the door with a loud bang, and locked it. JD felt his knees start to buckle again, but he closed his eyes and recovered without falling.

Mortimer watched the kiln for a few seconds, and then smiled. "It's very efficient, don't you think? And the cremations become part of my art. That black and grey color in *Blood and Bone* is from your friend Professor Bridger."

CHAPTER 26

Puccini had been silent on the drive back to PSC from the Marine Section dock. He was trying to outline the main points of a search warrant for Mortimer's island in his mind. He was also running through a list of sympathetic judges. He wanted to get back to the island as soon as possible. Fortunately, Brown seemed to know his moods and had the good sense to leave him alone.

Puccini parked the Crown Vic in the PSC garage, and he and his partner went upstairs. Puccini sat down at his desk, turned on his computer, and opened the template for a search warrant request. He had just started typing his first point in the probable cause section when Brown said, “”Don't look now, Tony, but the LT just left his office. He's heading this way, and he's not happy.”

Puccini glanced left and saw Lieutenant Argus striding quickly toward his cubicle. His mouth was turned down in an angry scowl, and his hands were balled up in fists. Argus stopped abruptly in front of Puccini's cubicle. The three other detectives in the squad room were trying to look busy, keeping track of the coming drama while pretending not to be watching. Brown started typing and manipulating his mouse. Argus opened his left hand and started rubbing his right fist in it, looking as if he was thinking of landing a punch on the side of Puccini's face.

Puccini gave a big sigh. “What's up, lieutenant?”

Argus looked directly at Puccini, not even glancing at his partner. “You know fucking well what's up,” he began, his voice low and guttural. “Where the hell have you been? The Chief is all over my ass on the

Harriman disappearance, and you're supposed to be in charge. He's been trying to reach you. Why the hell didn't you pick up? Harriman's sons got their lawyers involved, and the media's all over it now."

Puccini stood up. "You know, Jim, that's kind of between me and the Chief. He asked me to look into it, and I'm doing that. Harriman is a crook and a thief. And if you sit back and think about it, we've got three possibilities - maybe he's taken the wind, maybe one of his unhappy clients kidnapped him, or you know what? Maybe he's dead. If he's gone, it's not a Greenwich PD problem anymore. If he's been kidnapped, we'll hear about a ransom note. And if he's dead, we'll find a body and take it from there. Anyway, the Bureau is all over it, Jim. Didn't the Chief tell you that?"

By Argus's silence and befuddled expression, Puccini could tell that he was unaware of the FBI involvement. But he had to be cool. He needed Argus's help in getting the search warrant. He knew he had very weak probable cause, and a little political pull from Argus could go a long way.

Puccini smiled at Argus. "Can I get you a cup of coffee? I've got another disappearance I'm working on, and this guy's not a crook."

Argus looked as if he had to decide whether to continue dressing down Puccini, or accept the peace offering. He had an audience, and making a scene would not be in anyone's best interest. His scowl disappeared, and he said in a quiet tone, "No need for coffee. Let's go to my office and talk."

Puccini looked at his partner, who was still busily typing away. "What about Brown? You want him in there too?"

"It's okay. Looks like he's got something on his plate."

Puccini and Argus walked over to the lieutenant's glass-walled office, and Argus sat down behind his desk. He glanced at the three detectives in the squad room. Before Puccini could sit down, Argus said, "Better close the door."

Puccini closed the door and sat down.

"So you're saying the Bureau was brought in on the Harriman case?"

Puccini shrugged, palms facing the ceiling. "The Chief should have told you. I was out of the office."

"Doing what? And what's this other disappearance about?"

"It's Joshua Dionne. He's the one who got my money out from Harriman's Ponzi scheme, and I think that's what got the Chief to get his money out as well. I haven't talked to the Chief about Dionne's disappearance, but I'm sure he'd be heated up about it."

Argus showed no surprise. Puccini guessed that Argus was probably seething inside about his mention of the Chief again. But for Puccini, finding JD was far more important than finding Harriman, so he continued putting pressure on the LT.

"Dionne went for a meeting with that artist Mortimer this morning, and he never returned. His wife called, and I went out to look for him out on Mortimer's island studio."

"What made you think Dionne was out there?" The LT's voice became softer, and he leaned forward.

"Just a hunch." Puccini didn't want to tell Argus about the hacking. "I tried to bluff Mortimer into a search, but he wouldn't bite. I need a warrant."

Argus smiled. Puccini couldn't tell whether it was from disdain or encouragement. "A hunch, huh? What's your PC?"

"Not much. Mortimer lied to me about something, and he has a white speedboat that meets the description of the one seen leaving the site of the Ghanem shooting. I think he may have been involved in that too."

The info about Ghanem seemed to glide right past the lieutenant. "So he lied to you. What about?"

"He said he was alone on the island, and I saw a woman in the window."

Argus put his hands on the edge of his desk and leaned back in his chair, gazing at the ceiling. Then he turned to Puccini, looking very lieutenant-like. "That won't get you a warrant, and if it did, the results would never stand up in court. It won't work. There are lots of reasons for lying about a woman in the house. That's not probable cause."

Puccini thought about going directly to the Chief on the warrant, but he knew that the Chief would probably support the chain of command on this one. He knew he'd played it wrong. He'd asked for the warrant, and gotten an answer he didn't want - and all because the LT was pissed that the Chief hadn't kept him in the loop about the Bureau.

Puccini stood up. "Anything else?"

"No. Just get back on the Harriman case, and this time, keep me informed."

Puccini nodded, and walked back to his cubicle. He briefed Brown on the encounter with Argus, and then with a deep sigh, picked up his cell phone to call Anne Rutherford. Puccini told her he wasn't be able to get the search warrant, and listened to her angry reaction to this news. He had to hold the phone away from his ear, grimacing as he looked at his partner.

After he disconnected, he turned to Brown. "She didn't take the news well, and I can't blame her. I think she may go out and do something."

"Like what? What can she do?"

"She's pissed off enough to go out to the island on her own." Puccini rubbed his chin slowly. "I need a drink. I have to get the hell out of here and think about my career options. Sometimes I hate this job."

Brown made no move to accompany his partner.

Puccini shut down the computer, put on his jacket, and went downstairs. It took him fifteen minutes to walk down to the Sundown Saloon on Greenwich Avenue.

He sat at the near-empty bar and ordered a double Bulleit on the rocks, trying to figure out what to do next. He looked at his phone, deciding whether to call Annie again to tell her to sit tight and not try anything, but then he put it back in his pocket. He felt in his gut that the ship had sailed, and there was nothing he could do to stop it.

He knew she would to go out to the island on her own.

* * *

Annie had to restrain herself from throwing the phone against the kitchen wall. Puccini had actually been to the island where JD was being held captive, and he had done nothing. Absolutely bloody nothing! And now he couldn't even get a search warrant. She had to take some deep breaths to get her pulse rate down. Puccini was just going to let JD die. She had to do something. She put the cell phone down to think

Junior was sitting across the kitchen island with a concerned look on her face. “Not good, huh?”

“Puccini can’t get the search warrant, and he’s damn well not going to do anything. This leaves us with exactly one option. We’re going to have to do it ourselves. We’re going to have to rescue Dad.”

“Rescue him? How? You said these are dangerous people.”

Annie closed her eyes and rubbed her forehead. “Yes, they are, and I don’t know how we’re going to do it. We have only a few hours before it gets dark. I’m sure they’re armed, and it’s five miles to get out there from Greenwich. We would have to surprise them somehow.” It sounded impossible to her even as she said it. She checked her watch. “It’s almost four o’clock. What time is sunset tonight? Could you check on your computer?” She knew they needed to keep moving. If she stopped to think about what they were about to do, doubts would start creeping in, and her resolve would vanish. And then JD would be dead. They had to move quickly.

Annie and Junior went back up to Junior’s bedroom to use her computer. Junior turned it on, and half a minute later she said, “Sunset is at 7:02.”

“So, we have about three hours.”

“Why don’t we wait until dark? It’ll be easier to sneak up on them.”

Annie glared at her daughter. “Don’t you remember what they said? They’re going to kill Dad when it gets dark. Maybe we could get on the island then, but Dad will be dead. We don’t have any time.” She paused and checked the holster under her belt. “I have my Sig Sauer, but we can’t get close enough to use it unless we surprise them somehow.” She put the pistol on the counter.

Junior recoiled from the gun – but then seemed to calm herself. “We could get to the island on the *Ojibway*.”

“We can’t exactly sneak up in a boat that size. They’d be waiting for us. There’s got to be another way. Let’s look at the layout of those islands again. And thanks for finding out where Dad is. That was brilliant.”

Junior opened the Google Earth view of Mortimer's island, and Annie took a closer look at the layout. "It will take over half an hour for us to get out there on the *Ojibway.* We can anchor near one of the smaller islands, and use the dinghy to get ashore."

"Then maybe we could get to Mortimer's island on the dinghy without being spotted."

Annie took a closer look at the computer screen. "Could you zoom in on that first small island? I want to see how far it is from Mortimer's island."

Junior adjusted the screen, and said, "It looks like it's about three hundred yards."

Annie shook her head. "Then they'd see us for sure if it's daylight. We'll have to think of something else."

Annie tried to visualize some approach to catch Mortimer and that woman by surprise, but it seemed impossible. The big island was surrounded on all sides by too much open water. Even a diversion of some sort would be too risky. But if they waited until dark, JD would be dead. She felt her neck tighten as she realized there might actually be one possible way to rescue JD. It would be extremely violent - probably deadly - and highly illegal, and would also place her children and herself in great jeopardy. At the very least, they might all go to jail for a very long time. But what choice did she have? If they did nothing, JD would be dead within three hours. It was the only way - she knew they had to try it. As she made her decision, she could feel beads of sweat breaking out on her back.

"Junior, do you know how to get into B's gun safe?" Her voice was almost a whisper.

Junior shook her head vigorously. "No way. B wouldn't give me the combination. He knows I hate guns." Her eyes narrowed as she seemed to realize what Annie was considering. "Mother, what are you thinking?"

"I have to call B and get him back here. He has to help us. It's the only way."

Annie ignored Junior's piercing stare, picked up her cell phone, and left both a voicemail and text message for B, asking him to call as soon as possible, saying it was a family emergency. Then she sat down to wait.

Junior's face had turned very pale. "Are you going to get B to shoot someone?"

Annie hesitated. She wasn't sure she wanted to put it into words yet. "I don't know. I need to talk to him. He's the only one who knows about that Winchester."

Junior's eyes grew very wide, but Annie turned away to think. She had to approach B very carefully. She'd need to convince him to do something that a week ago would have sounded totally insane. In many ways, it sounded insane even now. But she knew that, given the circumstances, B was the only one who had the ability to save JD. She also knew that the idea she was about to propose to B would probably shock him more than anything he'd ever heard in his life.

Her phone rang, and it was B. "I called as soon as I could. What happened? What's wrong?"

"Are you sitting down, B? I have some very bad news."

There was a long silence, and Annie could hear a deep intake of breath and the scraping of a chair on the floor. "Okay, I'm sitting down. What's going on? Did something happen to Dad or Junior? Are you okay?"

"It's Dad. He's been kidnapped."

B's voice rose in pitch, almost in panic. "Kidnapped? That's crazy. Are you sure? What happened?"

"He went to a meeting with that artist Mortimer about an investment this morning, and he was supposed to come home for lunch. That was four hours ago. Junior hacked Dad's phone, and we located it on Mortimer's island studio out in the Sound. Dad never answered any of my calls, and he's disappeared. He's being held on that island."

"That sounds like what happened to Dad's friend Rich."

"It does, and that's what terrifies me. But at least we know that Dad's still alive. We were able to listen in on some conversation by the kidnappers. Mortimer has a woman helping him. They're going to kill Dad tonight . . . as soon as it gets dark."

B's voice became louder. "*Kill him*? But what about the police? They should be right on it, especially after Rich's disappearance and Fareed's shooting. They should have a SWAT team out there."

Annie kept her voice steady. "Detective Puccini went out to the island, but Mortimer bluffed him. Puccini can't go out again until he has a search warrant, and he just called to say that he can't get one tonight. No probable cause, whatever that means. So we're on our own, B."

"That's crazy. If Dad's in trouble, the police should rescue him. It's their job." B was obviously in denial, and Annie knew she had to bring him around. There was no other way, even though part of her said her plan was crazy. She realized deep down that she could lose JD *and* her son. But she also knew she had to go ahead.

"You're not listening to me, B. It's not going to happen. The police won't do anything. We're on our own. Unless we do something, Dad will be dead before the ten o'clock news."

There was another long silence on the phone, and then B said, "What can we do? You say these people are killers."

"We need to go out in the *Ojibway* and rescue him. And you have to help."

"Do you think Mortimer had something to do with Rich's disappearance?" B was avoiding the issue, dancing around the obvious reason for Annie's call. Annie decided to let him dance.

"Yes, I think that's possible. There's some sort of pattern here. I think it's all connected."

"So these people have done it before, and they have guns."

Annie decided to get right to the point of the call. "Yes, B, and that's why I called you. We need your Winchester and all your equipment. And your skill. There are three small islands near Mortimer's island where they're holding Dad, but there's no way to cross that water without being seen. We wouldn't be able to surprise them until it gets dark, and by then Dad would be dead. The only way we can rescue him is from a distance. We're talking three hundred yards, B. And you are the only one with the skill to cover those three hundred yards - with your Winchester."

B's voice grew so quiet that Annie could barely hear him. "You want me to shoot someone?" He couldn't avoid it any longer.

Annie didn't want to push him too hard, so she decided to leave it vague. "I don't know, but there may not be any other way. Maybe we can try to bluff them somehow. But listen, B, here's how it is . . . we have three hours before they kill Dad. We can meet you at the yacht club, motor the *Ojibway* out to the islands, and take it from there." She looked at her watch, and decided to force B to focus on the details. "Now, what should we bring? What sort of equipment? And where is it?"

There was silence on the phone. Annie knew her son was repulsed by the thought of using his target rifle to shoot a living person. She started to feel nauseous herself at the thought of having to kill someone, but there was absolutely no choice. It was kill or be killed now. She swallowed hard, and tried to sound calm.

"B, are you still there? If you won't help us, Dad will be dead. Don't you understand? You *have* to help."

"Okay." He sounded as if he'd made up his mind. "Bring the Winchester. It's in the gun safe, and you'll need the combination. Do you have pen and paper?"

He gave Annie the combination, and he continued, "Bring the spotting scope, the bipod for the rifle, the small ballistics laptop, some of the camo paint, and my camo jacket and pants. And there's a portable weather station with a wind indicator, and a laser range-finder. Those are all in the cabinet next to the gun safe."

Annie made a note of all the equipment. "Anything else?"

"Yeah. Don't forget the ammunition. It's in my gun safe, a little gold box marked Hornady."

Annie felt a combination of relief and fear, and had to hold back tears. B was going to help. There was now a possibility that they might save JD. The despair she had felt when Puccini told her that he couldn't get the search warrant was starting to dissipate. Her family was coming through. But then a chill ran through her again. She was putting her children in harm's way, and she could lose them both, either to jail – or something more permanent. She took a deep breath and continued, "B, you have no idea how much this means to me. We really have a chance of saving Dad."

"I love him too, Mom. I'll see you at the club in an hour."

Annie disconnected, and then looked at Junior sitting across from her. Junior's face was very pale, and her mouth was a thin red line. "You want B to shoot someone? I can't believe you could even think of doing that. It's murder. You want B to commit murder."

Annie's voice was very calm, although she certainly didn't feel that way. "Look, Junior. I am *not* going to sit back and wait for Dad to die. The rules we've lived by all our lives are done, and we have no choice. Are you with me or not? You can help me, or you can spend the rest of your life without a father. It's your choice."

Junior looked down at the counter. "It's not fair. We should let the police handle it. It's their job."

"Let me be very blunt, Junior. The police are out of it. They're not going to do anything in the next three hours. Your choice is cut and dried. Are you in or out? I have to get the Winchester and head down to the club." Annie paused, and her voice grew softer. "And Junior, I need your help. You can monitor what's happening inside the house with your laptop."

Junior's head was still tilted down, and Annie saw three teardrops fall on the counter. She waited, and then Junior wiped her eyes with the back of her hand and looked up at Annie. Her voice was now steady and quiet. "Okay, I'll do it. We're family. Let's go."

Annie walked around the kitchen island and gave Junior a gentle hug. They both went upstairs to B's bedroom, and Annie opened the gun safe. She looked at her list, and they put all the equipment on B's bed. As Annie took the Winchester from the safe, she noticed Junior's sharp intake of breath, but her daughter made no comment about the rifle.

Annie checked off everything on the list, and then said, "We'll need something to carry all this through the club to the boat without attracting attention. It's not a shooting range. We can't carry a rifle through the clubhouse."

Junior thought for a moment. "We can use the sailing duffle bags, and we've got some old sail-bags and sails in the garage. The rifle should fit in one of the big sail-bags."

Junior was aboard all the way now, Annie realized. "All good ideas. Let's get going."

"There's one more thing you didn't mention, Mom. B needs a spotter."

"Spotter? What's that?"

"B explained it to me once. When he's shooting, he needs someone to look through the spotting scope to tell him where the bullets are landing. Then he can make adjustments on the rifle."

"Could I do that?"

"He said it needs young eyes." Junior looked at the Winchester on the bed. She shuddered slightly, then said, "*I* could do it."

Junior glanced at the rest of the equipment on the bed, and ran her hand over B's camouflage jacket. "And I'll need something like this if I'm going to be a spotter." She stepped over to B's closet, found a second camouflage jacket, and tried it on. The sleeves were too long, and it was obviously too big.

"I look ridiculous," she said.

"No, you look like you could help save your Dad."

They went downstairs and came back upstairs with the sail-bags and duffle bags, and packed the guns and equipment. Then they carried it all down to Annie's SUV. As Annie waited for the garage door to open, she looked at her watch. It was half past four. Two and a half hours left.

* * *

Annie parked in the yacht club parking lot, and she and Junior unloaded the equipment. As they were walking down toward the docks with the bags over their shoulders, they ran into three other members heading to the clubhouse for dinner.

One of the members, an older grey-haired woman, asked, "Are you going sailing tonight? It seems a little brisk out there."

Annie smiled. "We're not happy with our new sails, so we want to try these old ones again."

"Don't stay out too long. The forecast says there's a storm on the way."

"Thanks. We'll see you in the dining room later. Have a good dinner."

Annie and Junior continued out to the *Ojibway*. The sturdy 32-foot motor-sailer was rocking gently at the dock as they approached. Annie hadn't been on the boat for a few weeks, but she had always admired its stubby lines. It was a no-nonsense work boat, with a large pilot house in the middle, a. single mast with two furled sails, and an open cockpit at the rear. She saw the inflatable dinghy with a small outboard hanging off davits at the stern, and knew they even kept spare changes of clothes aboard. It had hot and cold running water, an electric toilet, and four berths.

Junior carefully stepped down into the cockpit, and Annie passed her the bags. As Annie stepped aboard, Junior sat on the bench that ran around the edges of the cockpit and opened her laptop. She concentrated for half a minute, looked at the screen, and then glanced at Annie. "I've hooked up to Dad's phone again, but nothing seems to be happening."

Annie listened but there was only silence. "Maybe they're finally having that bouillabaisse."

"Or maybe they've moved the phone." Junior answered nervously.

"Let's not worry about that right now. We need to unpack."

Junior placed the laptop on the bench so they could continue to listen for any activity near JD's cell phone, and carried the sail-bags into the pilot-house. Junior unpacked the smaller bag and took out the spotting scope and small ballistics laptop. She examined them and said, "I'll have to wait until B gets here to figure out what these are all about."

Annie nodded but didn't respond. She was becoming concerned about B. It was almost five o'clock, and there was no sign of him. She watched Junior unpacking more equipment, and then anxiously went back to the cockpit to keep an eye on the parking lot, hoping to see B's car pull in. She was starting to become fearful that there had been an accident on the Turnpike and a major traffic jam. She was too nervous to sit down, so she went back into the pilot-house and stood behind the wheel, twirling it absent-mindedly as Junior continued to examine the sniper gear – all except for the Winchester rifle. Junior had left that in the bag without touching it.

Five minutes later, Annie glanced through the window of the pilot-house, and was relieved to see B hurrying down the dock toward them. She started the diesel engine, and shouted to him, "Throw on your bag, and untie the lines. Let's go!"

B threw the lines on the deck, jumped aboard, and the *Ojibway* started moving slowly out of the harbor with Annie at the wheel. B greeted his sister quickly, but his eyes narrowed when he noticed her outfit. “You’re wearing my camo jacket. What’s going on here?”

Junior stretched out her arms to the side and looked down at the jacket she was wearing. “You like? I’m going to be your spotter.”

“But you hate guns, and you’ve never done anything like this before.”

“We’ve never had to save Dad before, bro. As Mom said, all the rules have changed. I’m going to be your spotter, so you better teach me what to do.”

The *Ojibway* was now up to its top speed of nine knots, and its small diesel was throbbing quietly as the boat slipped through the waves. Annie kept a close eye on their course as B started showing Junior the fine details of the various pieces of equipment. First was the spotting scope. Junior looked through it, aiming back at the harbor. “It’s jiggling too much. I can’t really focus on anything.”

B nodded. “The boat’s bouncing up and down. We’ll test the scope when we have a steady shooting platform. And I’ll show you how to test the wind speed and direction, and use the range-finder.” He glanced around the cabin. “I need to get the rifle ready right now.”

Junior pointed to the corner of the cockpit. “It’s in that long sail-bag - the blue and white one over there.” Junior put the spotting scope back in one of the duffel bags. “Are you really ready to shoot someone, B?”

B was silent for a few seconds. “I guess we’ll find out when the time comes. It’s all about Dad, right?”

B walked over to the blue and white sail bag and withdrew the .308 Winchester. He removed the magazine, took five rounds from the Hornady box, and loaded the magazine. Then he clicked the magazine into the rifle and activated the bolt to get a round in the chamber. When he was finished, he checked the safety, and put the rifle back in the sail-bag. “We’re ready,” he said.

Annie nodded, keeping her eyes on the waves ahead. She could see the storm clouds out on the Sound, still too far away to create a problem. But she knew it wouldn’t be long before the storm hit. She’d seen those kinds of clouds many times before out on the water. She knew the *Ojibway* could deal with the storm, but if it arrived too soon, her plans to rescue JD would have to change.

She pushed the throttle as far forward as it would go, trying to squeeze out more speed.

* * *

Half an hour later, she eased back on the throttle as they closed in on one of the three small islands. Annie checked her watch – it was quarter to six. As the boat bobbed up down with the waves, Annie called to Junior. "Can you hear anything on Dad's phone?"

"Yes, they're talking about our boat. They saw us coming."

"B, could you take the wheel? I'd like to hear what they're saying. Head for the lee of that first little island."

B moved into the pilot house and took over the wheel as the boat moved slowly toward the small island. Annie walked back to the cockpit, and Junior turned up the speaker on her laptop so Annie could hear the conversation around JD's iPhone.

A female voice said, "I noticed the boat about ten minutes ago. I thought they were heading toward the Sound, but they turned right this way. Now they're heading toward Alpha Island. She's got three people aboard."

A male voice answered. "I don't think they're on a pleasure cruise. It's a little cold for a picnic, and anyway, it'll be dark soon. Somebody may be interested in our house guest. Keep an eye on them. If they start heading this way, we'll have to speed up our schedule and put him down right away."

Annie felt a cold chill run down her spine. Mortimer and the woman sounded very skittish - ready to kill JD at a moment's notice. But at least B would have the element of surprise with the Winchester. Mortimer would know they were behind the island, but would not be expecting a bullet from three hundred yards away. She went back to the pilot house and took over the wheel from B.

As she steered toward the small island, she spoke to B, still keeping her eyes on their course. "B, it's time to fish or cut bait. We have no choice. Mortimer just said that if we approach his island, they'll kill Dad." She felt her neck muscles tighten with tension at her own words. "You are going to have to kill them first."

Annie could see B's face turning pale. Up to this point, the idea of killing someone had been an abstraction. Now it was becoming very real. B nodded slowly. "Okay. We have no choice." He seemed to repeat the phrase in order to actually believe it, to reassure himself that what he was about to do was the only option.

Annie could see how conflicted he was, and she also knew that in fact there was a choice – they could let JD die, and she and her two children would still be safe. As she looked at B, her conviction started to waver. B seemed to sense her ambivalence, and got up and went over to the blue and white sail-bag sitting on the bench. He took out the Winchester, and said, "If we let Dad die, our own lives will be over. I could never look at myself in the mirror again. We came here to rescue him, and we're going to do it."

Annie's eyes filled with tears, and she couldn't see to steer the boat. She wiped her eyes, and said, "Thank you, B. I needed to hear that."

She steered the *Ojibway* around to the back of the island, and turned off the engine as the boat's momentum carried them closer to the shore. They set the anchor, transferred the rifle and its equipment into the dinghy, and lowered the dinghy into the water. A few minutes later, they were ashore. Annie could see a few flashes of lightning a mile or so away. She watched as B set up a shooting platform on a flat piece of ground hidden by some trees. Through a gap in the trees, they had a clear view of the house and of the path down to Mortimer's dock. They sat down to wait for one of them to leave the house and present a target. The sun was low, but there was still enough light to see the island clearly. Junior set up her laptop to monitor the conversation in the house.

Annie noticed a plume of smoke rising from the second building on the island, and guessed that it was Mortimer's kiln. But it seemed very odd for Mortimer to be firing a sculpture while he was about to murder someone. Maybe the kiln had a dual purpose – and when she realized what it was she exhaled sharply.

Mortimer was heating the kiln for JD.

Annie pushed away the cold terror that threatened to paralyze her, and forced herself to deal with the present. She could sense that B was nervous as he set up the rifle on its bipod. Next he took the laser range-finder to check out various points on Mortimer's island, and then turned on his ballistics laptop. Junior found a comfortable position for viewing the island through the spotting scope.

Annie knelt down beside him. "How does it look, B? And how are you feeling?"

B's voice was quiet, but steady. "I'm okay. The distance is just over three hundred yards, so it's well within my range. My main concern is the wind."

They continued watching the house, but there was no sign of movement. Annie couldn't hear any conversation on Junior's laptop, so Mortimer and the woman were somewhere else in the house. Annie knew she had to do something while there was still daylight. They couldn't wait any longer.

"I'll take the dinghy and head toward their island. That should bring them out of the house."

Junior looked up from the spotting scope, and even through the camouflage paint on her face, Annie could see her fear. "You can't do that, Mom. You'll be an easy target." She paused and looked at the island. "And . . . they might kill Dad."

"I have to. Nothing is happening, and we can't wait. I have to take the chance."

B adjusted the scope on the Winchester, and then looked back at Annie. "You'll be okay if you don't get too close to the island. She probably only has a pistol, and she can't hit you from any distance."

Annie hoped this was true. She got in the dinghy, started the outboard, and headed around the edge of the island into the stretch of water that separated them from Mortimer's island. She'd gotten about halfway across when the door of the big house opened and the woman appeared. She started walking down the path to the dock. When she was halfway down, Annie heard a thunderous bang from the island behind her — B's first shot. The woman stopped in her tracks. Then she started running back up the path, weaving back and forth in an evasive pattern. There were two more sharp rifle reports from the island behind Annie, but the woman kept running up toward the house, zigging and zagging.

Annie gunned the motor and started heading back to the shelter of the small island as quickly as possible. She heard a very loud report from Mortimer's house, but made it to the back of the small island unharmed. She could feel her heart pounding as she checked the dinghy for damage, but the shot had missed. The gunshot sounded much louder than a pistol. She beached the dinghy and headed to where B and Junior had set up their shooting platform.

B's face was ashen. It appeared that shooting at a live target had been almost more than he could handle. "Are you all right, B?" Annie asked.

"No, I'm not all right." B's voice was shaking. "I recognized that woman. I remember her from the thousand-yard range. She was the one shooting a Lapua Magnum, and she *never* missed. I've a got a Winchester and she's got a Lapua. We are totally fucked." He shook his head and rested his cheek on the stock of his rifle, closing his eyes.

Annie's head started throbbing. She knew they were committed now, and there was no escape. Two heavily armed killers were after them, and the maximum speed of their escape vehicle – the *Ojibway* - was nine knots. There was no chance that they could get away. They would have to stand and fight. She knelt down next to B and shook him by the shoulder, her voice almost a shout. "We are *not* fucked, Balthazar! Dad told me how accurate you are with that rifle. Get up and fight back, or we're all dead."

Annie regretted her outburst immediately. She was losing control, taking on some weird new personality, someone she didn't know. B and Junior looked at her as if she were some sort of wild beast.

But after a few seconds, Annie's outburst had the desired effect. B positioned himself behind the Winchester and put the stock on his shoulder, sighting through the scope. "I missed her when she ran. I took three shots, but she was moving too quickly. The first shot was the kill shot, but it went wide right."

Kill shot? thought Annie. B was back on track, ready to do what had to be done.

Junior was now peering through the spotting scope, right beside her brother. "The wind came up just as B pulled the trigger." Her voice became a little louder and more anxious. "And now she's in an upstairs window, third from the right. Can you see her, B?"

Junior turned toward B, her face very pale. "She's got a rifle. A big rifle."

CHAPTER 27

JD was sitting in the lounge chair by the window, watching the storm approaching across the Sound. He could see flashes of lighting, and feel the rumble of thunder shaking the window. After the trauma of helping load Harriman's body into the kiln, his mind had gone blank for a while, but he remembered Mortimer ushering him back to his room. He wondered how much time he had left. The kiln was still hot, and the cremation of Harriman's corpse would soon be finished. He knew he'd be next. His heart had been pounding without respite since he'd returned to the room, and there was nothing he could do to relax. He didn't want to drink anymore, because he still had a faint hope that he'd find an opportunity to escape, and he wanted to remain at least somewhat sober in case Mortimer left him an opening. He checked his watch. The crystal had cracked when he'd pounded the wall to get Puccini's attention earlier, but it still seemed to be working. It showed a little past six o'clock.

The sky gradually darkened, and he finally started to accept that it was all over. This view of Long Island Sound and the advancing storm would be the last thing he'd ever see of the world outside. He got up, put some ice in a tumbler, and opened the bottle of Sazerac. He figured he might as well get thoroughly drunk. He filled the glass to the brim and was about to down it when he heard a loud bang. At first he thought it was thunder, but then he realized the storm was still a mile off, and this was too close. It had been a sharp crack, with almost no reverberation.

It must have been a rifle shot, he realized.

He put the full glass of rye back on the counter, and went to the door to listen. His senses were suddenly very sharp, and he felt adrenaline coursing through his body. Something was happening. Maybe there was hope after all. He heard two more echoing bangs, and then some loud voices downstairs. Maybe Puccini had come back, and brought a SWAT team.

Then JD heard someone coming upstairs. Was it his rescuers or his killers?

A booming explosion sounded, much louder than the previous ones. It had come from inside the house. JD realized what was happening - Chong must be shooting at someone. He took a sip of the Sazerac and sat down to wait. His life would now depend on who came through that door next – Mortimer, or whoever had fired those first three shots. He closed his eyes and clenched his fists, hoping it would be Puccini and a SWAT team.

* * *

Annie had heard that second loud rifle report coming from the house, similar to the one fired at her when she was in the dinghy. While the sound was still reverberating, she heard a loud thwack in the large fir tree right beside Junior's head.

It took her a second to understand: the bullet had missed her daughter by less than a foot.

Despite the danger, Annie ran toward Junior in a low crouch. "Oh my God, Junior! Are you all right?"

Junior looked up at the tree, and then pushed her face down in the pine needles beside the spotting scope. Annie could see that she was shaking, and could hear her muffled sobs. She lay down beside her daughter, and reached an arm across her shoulder, trying to comfort her.

B was still peering through the scope on the rifle. "I need you to spot this, Junior. The wind is shifting, and you have to tell me where it lands." His voice was very calm. The shot hitting the tree beside them hadn't affected his focus.

Junior slowly raised her head to the spotting scope again, wiped her eyes, and said, "Ready." Her voice was trembling.

B fired, and two seconds later, Junior said quietly, "Three feet right, elevation was good."

B adjusted his scope, and then started aiming again.

Before he could shoot, another rifle report rang from the island, and bits of metal and plastic showered the ground between B and Junior. B turned his head from the rifle. "Shit, she just took out the laptop." Junior was seemingly frozen is place, staring at the spot where her computer had been.

Annie knew that the woman with the rifle wouldn't miss with her next shot, and one of her children would be dead. "Get up!" she shouted. "We have to get the hell out of here."

B got up into a crouch, carrying the rifle, and Junior followed with the spotting scope, moving quickly but keeping low. They scrambled through the bush and trees to a spot about fifty feet to the right, and B lay down on the ground to take another shot. There was only a very small opening in the trees in front of them now, providing more cover.

Junior said, "She hasn't seen us yet. She's scanning the area over to the left."

B kept looking through his rifle scope. "I have to wait for the wind to die down."

Annie could hear the wind whistling through the trees, and a thunderclap hit nearby. Then the wind seemed to diminish, and was almost calm for a few seconds.

The blast from B's Winchester made Annie shut her eyes, and there was a slight ringing in her ears. She heard Junior shout, "You got her! She's not moving."

Annie stared at the house across the water, but it was too far for her to see anything.

B lowered the rifle after the recoil from the shot, and looked through his telescopic sight. "You're right," he said, his voice quiet. "I think I got her." He put the rifle on the ground and sat up. He took a deep breath, and let it out very slowly. "Oh, God. I think I just killed a woman."

B's anguish cut through Annie like a straight razor, and she started to reach for him, but then she caught herself. She knew that compassion would have to wait for a quieter moment. The woman was dead, but Annie had no doubt that Mortimer still wanted to kill them, and had the means to do it. She crawled over to B and shook him roughly by the shoulder. "It's not over yet, B. You have to focus. Mortimer's still over there with Dad. We have to wait for Mortimer to come outside, and you have to take him out."

B shook his head, his eyes on the ground. "I don't think I can do it. I don't feel too good right now. I think I'm going to throw up."

Junior picked up the rifle and handed it to her brother. "We're only halfway there, B. We still have to save Dad. You can do it. I know you can."

B held the rifle, and ran his hand down the barrel. "It's still warm," he said. He pulled back the bolt to eject the spent cartridge. "The gun's empty. I need to reload." His voice sounded hollow, yet a little firmer.

He removed the magazine, reached into his pocket for more cartridges, and reloaded the rifle. He lay back down on his chest, elbows out, and aimed the rifle at the house again. Junior took her place behind the spotting scope, and they waited.

Annie could see that it was getting darker. She felt a few drops of rain. The wind came up again, and the lightning bolts were more frequent. The thunder was very close.

They kept waiting, but there was no sign of Mortimer or JD.

B said, "It's getting too dark. I can't see much through the scope." The rain started coming down in sheets. Annie's clothing was soon soaked. She'd been too preoccupied with their mission to put on rain gear, and she was starting to shiver from the cold.

Junior was still on the spotting scope. "I can hardly see the house. There's too much rain."

B got up on his knees, and clicked the safety on the side of the rifle with his thumb. "That's it. I can't see enough to shoot."

Annie felt the tears mixing with the rain on her face as she looked out at the dark silhouette of the island in the teeming rain.

I'm sorry, JD, she said silently. *We did all we could. I love you.*

CHAPTER 28

JD looked out at the fierce storm that had finally hit the island. He could see the whitecaps smashing against the cliff below, and the rain streaming down the window. He'd just heard two loud rifle reports from inside the house somewhere, just before the storm hit - and one final shot from a distance. Then it had become very quiet. He knew that could mean only one thing – one of the two shooters had been hit, and the gun battle was over. But was it Chong or the other shooter who had survived?

He went to the door and listened, but there was total silence. Nothing seemed to be moving on the second floor. JD waited. If Puccini and his SWAT team had won the gun battle, they'd be here soon. There was hope, and he could feel his heartbeat slowing. He crossed the room and stared into the storm, listening to the rain beating hard on the window.

Then JD heard a key in the lock, and he spun around sharply. The door opened, but it was not Puccini. It was Mortimer. He had a trace of a smile on his face, but his eyes were flat and cold. He was wearing yellow rain gear, and he was pointing his pistol at JD.

It was all JD could do stay upright. Despair was closing in around him, and he wished he could just lose consciousness now. Mortimer and Chong had won the gun battle, which meant Puccini was probably dead. And now Mortimer was here to cut off JD's right hand and put him in that white-hot kiln with Harriman. But why was Mortimer wearing that rain gear? And where was Chong?

"There's been a slight change in plans," Mortimer said. "We're leaving now. Move!"

"I heard some shooting . . . rifle shots. What happened?"

Mortimer kept the gun on JD, and his voice grew quiet. "Nothing much. We're leaving the island. You're now my ticket out of here. Shut up and start walking. We're taking the barge. The weather's too rough for the Donzi."

JD felt a flood of relief at Mortimer's words. He might now be some sort of hostage - but Mortimer was not going to kill him yet. He still had a chance.

They walked down the corridor and headed downstairs. As they passed through the house, JD saw no sign of Chong. Questions started reeling through his mind. Did her absence mean she had been the loser in the gun battle? And if she was the loser, who was the winner? And where were they? Where the hell was Puccini?

They walked out the front door, but JD could see no sign of a police boat at the dock. He saw only the barge, rocking up and down in the waves. He glanced at a white speedboat in the boathouse, probably the Donzi that Mortimer had mentioned.

Mortimer said, "Hold still. Now put your hands up, and walk right in front of me. Very slowly." JD did as he was told. The rain was letting up a little, and he could now see the three small islands more clearly.

* * *

Annie's eyes were shut tight. They'd gotten so close, but they'd been unable to save JD. Another tear trickled down her wet cheek.

Then she heard a shout from Junior. "There's Dad. He's alive! Look."

The rain had eased a little, and Annie could see two people walking down the path from the house toward the dock – one with his hands up, the other walking close behind him.

It seemed too good to be true. "Are you sure it's Dad? I can't tell anything from this distance."

"Of course it's Dad. Who else could it be? Take a look through the scope."

Annie lay down and took a look through the spotting scope. She suddenly had a feeling of weightlessness. She couldn't see his face clearly in the mist, but she recognized his gait and saw the black ponytail.

JD was alive.

Annie looked over at B, who was still aiming at the island through his scope. "It must be Mortimer behind him," she said. "Can you get him?"

B continued sighting through the scope. "No, I can't risk it in this wind. I might hit Dad. He's too close."

Annie continued to watch in frustration through the spotting scope as JD and Mortimer continued down the path. As she watched, she felt the rain coming down in torrents again, and the path and the island disappeared in the storm. She got up and gave a loud scream.

"Mortimer, you bloody bastard! It's not over!"

* * *

JD heard the shout, but at first he couldn't believe it. It was Annie. She was out on one of the small islands with Puccini and the police sniper. He realized that was why Mortimer was using him as a human shield. He knew he'd have to get away from Mortimer somehow, to give the sniper a clear shot.

The stones on the path were becoming very slippery as JD stepped gingerly downhill. The rain was coming down in torrents again, and the smaller islands were disappearing in the rain. He deliberately stumbled and fell, hoping the sniper would have a shot at Mortimer. But instead he heard a gun go off behind him. Mortimer had shot him. He lay motionless, wondering where he'd been hit, but he felt no pain. Then he heard Mortimer. "That was just a warning. Get up, and don't try anything stupid again. The next one will be for keeps."

JD got up slowly and continued down the path. He was soaked to the skin, and was starting to shiver uncontrollably. They reached the dock, and Mortimer motioned the gun toward the barge. "Get on. We're taking a little trip."

The barge was bobbing up and down, and JD had to time his step to avoid falling overboard. Mortimer followed him, and JD looked more closely at the layout of the vessel. It was flat, with low gunwales, and a hoisting davit on one side for loading and unloading cargo. A seven-foot-long wooden box with air holes on top – just like the ones in the kiln room - sat near the front of the vessel, and there was a small pilot house at the rear, with a windshield and a peaked green roof.

Mortimer ordered JD to sit down in the middle of the deck, and went back to the pilot house, still training the gun on him. He started the engine, and then shouted over the teeming rain and wind, "Untie that line on the bow. And don't think about running. I need you as a hostage, but not that much. And I'm a very good shot."

JD moved to the front of the boat and untied the line. Mortimer said, "Now sit down in the middle again. Nice and slow."

Mortimer moved sideways over to the stern of the barge, still watching JD through the rain, and untied the line at the rear. Then he returned to the pilot house, put the engine in reverse, and the barge started backing away from the dock. JD was shivering like a leaf in the wind, and his teeth were chattering from a combination of fear and cold. "What about some life jackets? I'm freezing out here."

"We don't need life jackets. This thing is unsinkable." He threw JD a small tarp. "Here, wrap this around you. I don't want you dying from pneumonia before we get back to shore."

They were now clear of the dock, and Mortimer shifted into forward drive and gave the throttle full speed. The engine note rose in pitch, and the barge started moving. It looked to JD like they were heading back to Greenwich. He wondered why his hands hadn't been tied, and then realized that Mortimer needed his help to cast off, and maybe to tie up at the other end when they docked.

The barge was making good headway in the lee of the island, but when they rounded into open water, the waves and wind became much stronger, rocking the boat violently. Their progress slowed. JD started edging toward the pilot house, pushing himself with his feet in a sitting position, still covered by the tarp. The light was fading, and the barge's running lights were starting to give off an eerie glow in the heavy rain.

Mortimer was concentrating on keeping the lumbering craft on an even keel through the crashing waves, and in the gathering darkness, he didn't seem to notice that JD was moving closer and closer to the pilot house.

Mortimer was steering with one hand, still holding the pistol in the other, but was mostly focused on the breaking whitecaps made visible by the almost non-stop flashes of lighting. He finally seemed to notice how close JD was, but the barge then hit a huge wave, and threw him off balance. Leaning far over to one side, Mortimer grabbed at the wheel to keep from falling. With the sharp turn of the wheel, the barge headed directly into another giant wave.

It's now or never, JD realized.

He threw off the tarp and lunged at Mortimer with every ounce of his adrenaline-charged strength, grabbing the gun with one hand, and getting him in a choke hold with his other arm. But Mortimer reacted quickly, and in a lightning-fast move, flipped JD over his back and got the gun free. But JD kept his tenacious hold around Mortimer's neck, and they both fell in a tangled heap on the slippery deck behind the pilot-house. JD heard the gun go off, and felt a sharp pain in his right leg. With all his strength, he got up on his left leg, still holding Mortimer around the neck, and flipped both of them over the gunwale into the pitching waves.

They went down deep, JD still holding Mortimer in an iron grip around his neck. JD's stamina from years of competitive swimming took over as he held Mortimer under the surface. They bounced up and down under the waves, but JD kept his arm tightly under Mortimer's chin. He kept him underwater for over a minute, holding his own breath, and he could feel Mortimer's struggles slowing down. When JD felt his own lungs almost bursting, he finally came to the surface, and pushed Mortimer away with a kick of his good leg. He could see Mortimer struggling and gasping for breath, trying to spit out water. There was no sign of the gun, and the lights of the barge were already a hundred yards away, disappearing into the rain.

JD's right leg was throbbing, but he was able to keep his head above water as he continued watching Mortimer. It was clear that Mortimer had taken some water in his lungs, and he seemed to be panicking, thrashing about aimlessly and wasting his energy. JD backstroked away from him, still keeping an eye on him as he came to the top of each wave. Mortimer tried to follow him, but his head kept disappearing in the waves. He obviously wasn't a very strong swimmer. *Too fucking bad,* thought JD.

JD turned and looked for some landmarks as he bobbed up to the top of each wave, and through the lighting flashes, he could see the dark outlines of the three small islands. Mortimer's studio island was much farther away to the right, and upwind. He decided to head toward the closest small island. But his leg now felt like it was on fire, and he could hardly move it. The flood of adrenaline had dissipated. He was certain he was losing blood, and started to check for signs of shock as he struggled to keep his head above water. He found he could hold his breath and bob under the waves to rest, and then thrust his head above water to take a breath. This kept him from drowning, but he was not making much headway toward the small islands. He finally tried a weak backstroke, using his arms and his one good leg, and also letting the waves carry him. This way, he could make a little progress, but only very slowly.

He tried to keep track of Mortimer. It was now almost pitch black, and the only visibility came with the lightning flashes. As he struggled toward the island, JD could see Mortimer occasionally at the top of a wave, but his flailing arms were falling farther and farther behind. Another lightning strike hit, this one brighter than the others, but all JD could see were the crashing whitecaps behind him. Mortimer was gone.

JD felt a small pang of guilt, but he knew it was a question of kill or be killed. And now he had to concentrate on his own survival. He was feeling very cold, his entire body shivering – the first signs of shock. His arms were starting to feel like lead weights, and all the strength was ebbing from his body. He was still losing blood from the leg wound, and his stamina was oozing away with every minute he spent in that cold water. Maybe he and Mortimer were going to meet the same lousy fate, drowned in the waters of the Sound. The cold seemed to affect his thinking, and a voice inside was starting to say, "Give up . . . it's no use."

But after another long interval of slow progress, the island was getting closer, and the rain was letting up. He could now see the dark outlines of trees, and hear waves breaking on the shore. Then he remembered the shout he'd heard from Annie when he was walking down the path in front of Mortimer, and he felt a reserve of energy jolt through his muscles. That shout had been real. He hadn't dreamt it. He kept struggling, moving his leaden arms. The trees were almost over his head now, darkening the sky.

Then he finally felt something solid under his feet. He swam a few more strokes, and realized he could stand up. He ignored the searing pain in his right leg. He'd done it. He was ashore, and still alive. He staggered onto the beach, and fell down on his knees. He was feeling very dizzy, but he swore he could hear some voices. But then he knew he was dreaming, because the voices sounded like B and Junior.

He took a deep breath, and a surge of warmth overwhelmed him. He closed his eyes, and a vision of Christian Island floated by. The sun was shining, and he was paddling his canoe over to Penetanguishene. His whole life lay before him.

It felt good.

CHAPTER 29

JD was dreaming about Christian Island and the calm waters of Georgian Bay. In his dream, he had beached his canoe and tried to walk ashore, but his leg hurt, and he had to stop and rest. He wondered what the pain was about, and then he saw a bright flash of light. He opened his eyes, and realized he was now awake. He wasn't dreaming. It was dark all around him, and the bright light forced him to squint. He could just make out a figure leaning over him, and he tried to get up. But he was wrapped in a blanket, and his arms were pinned, so he could hardly move. His leg still hurt, so that must have been what wakened him from his pleasant dream. Where was he? What was going on?

Then he heard a voice that he recognized instantly. It was Annie. "We thought we'd lost you, JD. Welcome back."

JD's eyes adjusted to the light, and he could see Annie kneeling beside him. He struggled and got his arms free from the blanket, and then reached up to pull her down into a hug. He could feel the warmth of her body against him, and her breath on his cheek. She gave him a gentle kiss, and then they held each other silently for a long time. JD just relaxed and listened to her breathing. He could feel her tears wetting his cheek, and he closed his eyes. He knew he was safe at last.

It seemed only moments later that it all started coming back to him – the struggle with Mortimer, seeing him disappear beneath the waves, and the long swim to the island.

"Where am I?"

Annie got back on her knees, and aimed her flashlight to the side. "You're on the little island where we used to picnic. I bandaged your leg to stop the bleeding, and tried to keep you warm. I thought you'd never wake up."

JD paused a few seconds to think. "I knew you were here, Annie. I heard you shout when Mortimer had the gun on me." JD smiled. "And such language. . ."

"That was I," she admitted with a soft laugh. "But what happened to Mortimer? Is he still out there?"

JD shook his head. "I think he drowned. I saw him go down in the waves. I tackled him on the barge, and that's when he shot me. We both went down . . . under water."

"So that's why that barge was going around in circles. We knew something had happened. We took the dinghy out there, but we couldn't find you in the dark."

"Mortimer wasn't a very good swimmer." JD paused. He couldn't quite admit that he'd held Mortimer in a choke hold, doing his best to ensure that Mortimer had no breath left to fight the waves. "But you just said 'we'. Where's Puccini? I heard his voice out on the island earlier, and then I heard some shooting. Where's the SWAT team?"

"Puccini's not here, JD. He couldn't do anything because of legal red tape . . . he couldn't get a search warrant. It was B and Junior. They're the ones who saved you."

Annie shined her flashlight over to the side. JD could now see B and Junior standing a few feet away, looking down at him silently. They were dressed in camouflage gear, and their faces were painted with streaks of dark grease. JD thought they looked very tired.

B came and squatted at his side, and Junior knelt down by his feet. JD still had a hard time understanding what had occurred, how they had saved him. He'd heard the rifle shots from a distance, and those must have come from this island. Then he looked again at their outfits and streaked face paint. He took a deep breath, and exhaled very slowly before he spoke.

"B, tell me something. I heard some shooting. Was that you with your .308?"

B looked down, closed his eyes, and started rubbing his forehead with the tips of his fingers. His voice was so quiet that JD could hardly hear him. "Yes, Dad, that was me. I shot that woman. We had no choice."

His son had shot someone. JD's mind started to race with the implications. JD knew he was alive as a result of B's action, but his son could be in trouble, maybe in jail for a long time. And Junior and Annie, his accomplices, would be in nearly as much trouble.

Junior broke the silence. "I hacked your phone, Dad, and we were able to hear some of their conversation. They said they were going to kill you when it got dark."

JD felt Annie squeeze his hand. "It was the only way we could save you."

JD started to put the pieces together. He hadn't seen Chong after that last rifle shot, and Mortimer hadn't mentioned her. She'd just disappeared. "So Chong is dead," he said quietly.

"If you mean that woman on the island, yeah, I think she's dead," Junior answered. "I saw her through the spotting scope after B's last shot, and she wasn't moving. She's in one of the upstairs rooms, by the window. That's where she was shooting from."

B finally spoke. "She had a Lapua Magnum, Dad. Remember the woman I told you about at the thousand-yard range? That was her. She almost killed us before we got her."

"She missed Junior by less than a foot, hit the tree right beside her head," Annie added.

The reality of what B and Junior had done was slowly sinking in, and he knew there was only one way to keep them out of jail. They had to get rid of Chong's body. And he knew how they were going to do it - Mortimer and Chong had showed him.

"You all did what you had to do, and I'm incredibly proud of you," JD said. "But now we have to keep B and Junior out of jail. We have to go back to the island."

Annie shook her head. "You want to go back to Mortimer's island? Why? We need to get you to the hospital, and then get the police out here."

"The hospital can wait. We need to clean up some things first."

Then Annie seemed to get it. She helped JD get up, and he could see that she had cut his pants leg to bandage the bullet wound on his thigh, and then taped the pants around his leg so he could move. His leg was no longer bleeding. It all looked awkward, but it seemed to work. He started limping slowly along an overgrown path toward the other side of the island, following Annie's flashlight. The rain had stopped, and the skies were clearing. The full moon was showing through the fleeting clouds, and when they stepped out of the woods onto the beach, JD could see the *Ojibway* bobbing up and down in the waves about a hundred feet out. The dinghy was resting on the beach.

Annie pushed the dinghy into the water, and JD stepped carefully into the bobbing vessel. Annie started the motor and steered it out to the *Ojibway*. JD climbed aboard gingerly, and sat down while Annie found some dry clothes. He changed with her help, and then sat down to wait while she went back to get B and Junior.

JD noticed the .308 Winchester lying on the floor of the cabin, along with the spotting scope and the other sniper equipment. They'd have to take care of that, too.

When all the others were back aboard the *Ojibway*, JD said, "We need to wear gloves when we go up to the house. No fingerprints. Our hunting gloves will work. And B and Junior, you need to change your clothes now, and take those camo outfits with you. We have to get rid of them. They have gunpowder residue."

* * *

Annie expertly brought the *Ojibway* next to Mortimer's dock, and B and Junior jumped out to tie up. Annie then helped JD climb out, and they started up the path to Mortimer's big house, with JD using one of the dinghy paddles for support. The lights from the three flashlights were bobbing up and down in front of him, and the moon was creating shadows as it occasionally slid out from behind the clouds. When they reached the front door, Annie said, "We'll have to break in somehow. We can use my Sig Sauer." She pulled the gun out of her belt.

JD hobbled up to the door and tried the handle. It opened easily. "Mortimer didn't lock the door. We left in a hurry."

They walked into the house, and Annie turned on the lights. JD remembered the layout, and the first thing he wanted to do was find his iPhone. "Do you know where my phone was when you heard Mortimer's conversation? Any idea what room it was in?"

Junior said, "It was in a kitchen. We heard cooking sounds, and they were talking about some fancy dish. Boula-something."

"Bouillabaisse. It's a fish stew. I think I know where the kitchen is – just off the dining room."

Annie shook her head. "That's really odd, Mortimer feeding you a fancy dinner."

"Believe me, you don't know the half of it. But let's keep moving. We have to find my phone."

JD led them to the dining room with all the artwork, and Annie had to stop, wide-eyed. "There are millions of dollars on this wall. What a bizarre place."

JD nodded and kept moving. He opened the door to the kitchen, and found his phone on the counter by the fridge. He picked it up, and checked it out. It seemed to work fine. *So this was how Junior found me*, he thought. *Thank you, Mr. Jobs.*

JD headed back to the dining room, where Annie was still admiring the artwork, and B and Junior were waiting impatiently. "I found my phone. Let's get upstairs," he said.

He retraced their route back to the front hall and then led them to the stairs. He didn't want B or Junior to be the first ones to see Chong's body, and he grimaced in pain as he lurched up the stairs, one step at a time. He moved down the hallway to an open door, and looked in, turning on the light. He could see Chong's body on the bed, her head still facing the little island. She looked almost asleep, except for the big rifle cradled in her arms, pointing out the open window. The rain had created puddles on the floor, and the curtains were swaying in the wind.

JD turned and put his arm out to stop B and Junior. "There's no need for you to come in here. Your mother and I will handle this. Just stay in the hallway."

B's face was contorted in anguish. "She's dead, isn't she?"

JD didn't answer, just beckoned Annie to come into the room. Then he closed the door and walked over to the bed. The back of Chong's head was a mass of blood and hair, but the exit wound wasn't very big. He looked back at the wall on the far side of the room, and could see a small hole about four feet from the floor. B had used a target round, so the bullet hadn't mushroomed. Then he turned back to Chong, and with his gloved hand, reached and turned her body over so he could see her face. Her eyes were open, and he could see that the bullet had hit just below her right eye. As he looked down at the body and the rifle, he couldn't help thinking how easily it could have been B's body that he would have had to turn over. He had to stop and sit down on the edge of the bed. That familiar feeling of nausea was starting to overcome him.

Annie shook his shoulder. "We have to get this all cleaned up. It's almost nine o'clock. Somebody will find that barge and send the Coast Guard out here."

JD nodded. "Let's wrap the body in these bed sheets and blankets and get it downstairs. We're going to burn it."

"In Mortimer's kiln? That's how he got rid of the bodies, isn't it? I saw it smoking earlier."

JD nodded, the sick feeling still with him. "They forced me to help load Harriman's body into that kiln. And Rich is dead too. Mortimer and Chong killed at least ten people."

Annie's mouth fell wide open. "Ten people?" She shook her head. "And Rich is dead?"

"All the evidence is in Mortimer's house in Belle Plains. He showed it to me when he captured me. He has a trophy room . . . Mortimer was a professional hit man."

Annie was silent for a few long seconds. "I told you there was something off about him," she said. "And this afternoon, I was sure you were in danger, but *ten people* . . ." She looked at the lifeless figure on the bed. "So why would B be in trouble for shooting a serial killer? The law ought to thank him."

"The law is an ass. Look at what happened to Puccini. He couldn't help because he couldn't get a damn search warrant. Now help me wrap the body, and then we'll clean up the room."

They pulled out the bed sheets and blankets from the mattress, and started wrapping Chong's body. When they were done, JD opened the door and asked B and Junior to come in. "We need to find some fresh sheets and blankets. Check along the hall – there must be some closets."

B and Junior looked at the mummy-like shape on the bed, and left quickly without comment. They returned a few minutes later with sheets and blankets, plus two pillows, and stood there holding them, all the while staring at the shape on the bed.

JD said, "We need to move the body off here so we can make the bed, and then move it downstairs and to the studio. That's where the kiln is."

"The kiln?" Junior's face turned white. "You mean, you're going to burn it? Like, cremate it?"

"Yes. We have to get rid of it. That's how Mortimer and Chong got rid of at least ten bodies." Annie turned to B. "So there's no reason for you to regret what you did, B. Those two were serial killers."

JD walked over to B and put his hand on his shoulder. "That's right, son. Now let's do what we have to do. There's a gurney over at the studio. Let's go get it while Mom and Junior finish making the bed."

* * *

Twenty minutes later, JD could see his plan moving along. Chong's body was on the gurney right next to the kiln, along with all the bedding and the camouflage outfits that B and Junior had been wearing. JD knew they had to burn everything. He waited patiently while Annie examined the control panel, with B and Junior standing off to the side. Their faces were drawn, and Junior looked as if she was about to cry. Annie's brow was furrowed as she ran a finger along the bottom of the control panel.

"It all looks pretty standard. It's the biggest kiln I've ever seen, but all the controls are similar to the ones I used in art school. I just need to figure out the correct cone number and fire it up."

JD glanced up at the kiln. "Cone number? What the hell is that?"

Annie kept studying the panel. "It's a temperature measure for pottery and ceramics."

JD peered over Annie's shoulder. "Chong said it was set it at about fourteen hundred degrees for cremation."

Annie looked as if she wanted to ask why JD had been discussing cremation temperatures with Chong, but she let it pass. “That would be a cone setting of oh-fifteen, if I remember right.” Annie pushed some buttons, and JD could hear a low roar starting in the kiln. It sounded about the same as when he had helped load Harriman’s corpse into the lower door, and a yellow-orange glow lit up the room.

JD said, “I think the kiln was already hot.” He decided not to mention that he was the one that Mortimer and Chong had been heating it for, or that all the victims had lost their right hands before they were cremated. B and Junior had enough to deal with at the moment.

“B, if you open that lower door quickly, Mom and I can push the body off the gurney into the kiln.” It was hard for him to bend forward with his leg so stiff and painful, but he couldn’t ask Junior or B to do this. They’d have nightmares enough.

The little door opened, and JD and Annie averted their faces from the blast of hot air as they pushed, and Chong’s body and all the other material disappeared into the orange-yellow glow inside. B closed the door, and stepped back. Annie pushed the gurney off to the side, and everyone was silent as they filed out of the room. JD turned off the lights and closed the door.

“I’d like to take a last look at that room upstairs, and make sure we’ve done everything we can to clean it up. And we have to get rid of Chong’s rifle . . . and B, also your rifle.”

As they walked back to the house, JD thought about loose ends in the story he was going to tell Puccini. He wondered if Puccini had seen Chong out on the island. If so, her disappearance would have to be explained. In any case, he’d say that Mortimer had taken him out on the barge into the storm, and he’d overpowered Mortimer and escaped. Then Mortimer had drowned – that was easy to explain. But what about Chong? Puccini would want to know why Mortimer had left by himself – without Chong. The only possible explanation was that Chong had left earlier for some reason. JD wouldn’t have to know the reason she left, but how did she get off the island? That would have to be explained.

JD looked down at the boathouse, dimly visible in the moonlight. That was it. He would say that Chong had left earlier in the Donzi, had been caught in the storm, and had also drowned. That story would be a stretch, but it was plausible. And the best one he could come up with.

They reached the house and went back upstairs to the bedroom where Chong had died. The window was closed, and the rain water had been wiped off the floor. The bed looked like a Swiss chamber-maid had just finished it. All it needed was a little chocolate piece on the pillow.

"You've done a great job. Let's pick up the Lapua, and get out of here." JD looked around the room again. "Where are the shell casings? She took at least three shots."

B dug into his pocket. "Right here."

"Good. We have to get rid of them. And when you and Junior get home, you have to take long showers to get rid of the gunpowder residue."

Annie picked up the rifle, JD turned off the lights after one last glance around the room, and they went downstairs. JD stopped at the bottom of the stairs. "We have one more item on the agenda. We have to sink that white speedboat in the boathouse. That will be our story on how Chong left the island. We need to find the key for that boat."

They started searching in the front hallway and the kitchen, and after five minutes, Junior found a box on the wall with a number of keys. She pulled one out, and JD could see the big Donzi logo on the side. "That's the one. Let's get down to the boathouse."

JD's leg was starting to throb painfully again, but he knew they were almost done, and he picked his way carefully down the path to the dock, following the others. He stopped in front of the boathouse.

"My leg is bad. B and Junior, you'll have to take the Donzi and sink it. Just shoot some holes in the hull, and it'll be gone in half an hour. Annie, could you follow them in the dinghy? I'll wait here until you get done."

Annie frowned. "Do you think all this will work, JD? You're writing quite a script here."

"It'll work if Puccini kind of looks the other way a little. We'll see, but right now, it's all I can think of. We don't have much time, so let's get on with it. I need to have this leg looked at."

B and Junior entered the boathouse, and in less than a minute, JD heard the rumble of the Donzi's engine. B backed the speedboat out of the boathouse, and Junior jumped in. Annie had already lowered the dinghy into the water, and was getting ready to retrieve them after they had put the holes in the bottom of the Donzi to sink it.

B nudged the white speedboat closer to the dock. "I forgot something. I need a gun to make the holes. Mom, could I borrow your Sig?"

JD said, "Don't forget the two rifles. We need to get rid of those. And the shell casings."

Annie went aboard the *Ojibway* to get the two rifles, and passed them to B, along with her Sig Sauer automatic. B looked at the Winchester silently as he put it in the bottom of the boat. He stepped behind the wheel, and the Donzi's engine rose in pitch as it started moving toward open water. JD watched briefly, and then went aboard the *Ojibway* to wait. The rumble of the Donzi and the whine of the dinghy outboard grew quieter, and then became silent. The waves were still rolling from the recent storm, and he could see the silhouettes of the two boats in the intermittent moonlight, about half a mile away. Then he heard seven gun reports in rapid succession. He'd emptied the magazine, thought JD. Good. It wouldn't take long now, and the Donzi would soon be history.

JD started rehearsing in his mind again what he was going to tell Puccini when he called him. He went through his entire story, testing it for flaws and trying to anticipate any awkward questions. His train of thought was interrupted by the sound of the dinghy's outboard as Annie pulled up beside the dock. B and Junior disembarked, and then climbed aboard the *Ojibway* while Annie steered the dinghy around to the stern. They set the davit lines, and hoisted it clear of the water. Annie got behind the wheel of the *Ojibway*, and they headed for Greenwich.

JD checked the time on his iPhone. It was ten o'clock. Time to call Puccini.

CHAPTER 30

Puccini was home in his den, watching the Yankees and the White Sox. He was angry because he'd missed the first inning. Dinner had been late, because his four-year-old daughter, Isabella, had been frightened by the fierce storm, and he'd read some stories to her and her six-year-old brother Angelo to calm them down. The storm had passed, and they were finally asleep. The nanny had retired to her apartment downstairs, and was probably watching one of the reality show series, so he'd finally been able to kick back with the ball game. But he'd missed the big milestone - that single in the first inning by Derek Jeter when he passed Lou Gehrig's record of 1,270 hits for the Yankees. And even worse, the Yankees were losing 6 to 2. He'd thought the game would help him forget the day's events for a while, but that hadn't worked. The politics of the search warrant was still eating away at him. His gut feeling was that JD was on that island. What else would Mortimer have been hiding? It must have been JD.

He hadn't heard from Annie again, so he knew JD must still be missing. She'd said she'd call if there was any news. He was dreading that next call – it would either be word that JD had turned up safe, or that something very bad had happened to him. Puccini didn't want to go to sleep yet, so at least the baseball game gave him a little bit of relaxation. It would be even more relaxing, he thought, if the Yankees were winning.

He heard his cell phone vibrate on the coffee table, and looked at it without answering. Then he gave a start. *The name on the screen was Joshua Dionne.* He put the baseball game on mute, still watching the phone vibrate, and then ran his fingers through his hair, closing his eyes. Was it JD, or was it Mortimer using JD's phone? Maybe it was a call for ransom. He picked up the phone and answered it. "Hello, Puccini here."

"Hi, Tony. It's me . . . JD. I hope I didn't wake you. Sorry to call so late."

Puccini realized he'd been holding his breath, and let it out slowly. He felt a shock wave of relief on hearing JD's voice. "No, no problem. We've been very worried about you, pal. Annie thought you'd been kidnapped. Are you okay? What's that noise in the background? I can hardly hear you."

"I'm aboard our boat, on the way back to Greenwich from the island. And I'm alive, but not by much. I was shot in the leg, so I have to get to the hospital. And Annie was right about Mortimer. He kidnapped me, but I got away. I think he's dead . . . drowned. Annie saved me."

Puccini thought that JD sounded almost cheerful, considering what he'd been through. But he knew that JD must be thankful to be alive. He leaned back, trying to piece together what had happened.

"So Mortimer drowned? And you're shot? What the hell happened?"

"I went to Mortimer's house at White Plains for a meeting this morning, and they drugged me and took me out to the island. They were going to kill me tonight. It was – "

"You said 'they,'" Puccini interrupted. "Was there a woman involved? Annie got me to go out to the island, and I saw a woman in one of the windows."

"That's Mortimer's wife, Abigail Ch[illegible]ng. She's in on it. And I could hear you when you were out on the island, but they'd tied and gagged me, so I couldn't get your attention." JD was silent for a couple of beats. "And Annie told me about your problems with the search warrant."

"Sometimes being a cop is shit, pal. I'm sorry I couldn't get out there again myself."

"It gets worse. These two have killed at least ten people. Rich is dead, and they were the ones who killed him. They also killed Harriman. Harriman is dead."

Puccini was silent for a few long seconds, letting the words sink in. He was starting to think that JD was in shock from the wound, and maybe imagining things. Finally, he said, "What about Smith and Cole? They must've been involved. And ten murders? Is there any evidence of that?" He paused. "Let me ask you something, JD. Did you hit your head? Are you feeling okay?"

JD's voice became quieter and more serious. "I'm okay, Tony, and trust me, this is all very real." Puccini heard JD draw a deep breath. "Here's how it is, detective . . . Mortimer was a very expensive hit man, five million per. Cole was Mortimer's client, so was Yates. And many others. And I saw Harriman's body myself . . . before they burned it in Mortimer's big ceramics kiln. That's how they got rid of the bodies. There's evidence of ten other victims in Mortimer's house in Belle Plains."

Puccini felt his back muscles tighten, and he had to stand up and walk around, tilting his head back to ease the tension. Ten murders . . . five million per . . . bodies burned in a ceramics kiln. It sounded crazy. He still wasn't convinced. It had to be Smith and Cole. Mortimer was an artist, for fuck's sake.

"What sort of evidence was at Mortimer's house?"

JD hesitated. "It's not something I can talk about right now. I can give you all the details if you meet me at the hospital. I need to get this leg looked at. It hurts like hell."

Puccini could tell that JD probably didn't want to discuss the evidence in front of Annie. It must be very graphic and repulsive. But he still wanted to determine if JD's story was real, or the result of a shock-induced imagination.

"Okay, I'll meet you at the hospital to get the details, but tell me something . . . how the hell did you get away from Mortimer? And how did you get shot?"

"For some bizarre reason, he wanted to go back to Greenwich on his freight barge just as that storm hit. The barge hit a big wave, and I tackled him. He shot me in the leg, and then I pushed us both overboard. He didn't last long in those waves. He wasn't a very good swimmer, and he went down. I was able to swim to one of those smaller islands, and that's where Annie found me."

Puccini decided not to ask JD why he hadn't tried to save Mortimer. And how could he swim with a gunshot wound? Then he remembered that JD had been a varsity swimmer.

"And what about that woman . . . Chong? Where is she?"

"I don't know. She must have left in their speedboat before the storm hit."

JD's story was starting to bother Puccini. Why would the woman have left Mortimer alone when they were holding JD as a prisoner? And why did Mortimer want to leave in the middle of the huge storm? But his main feeling was still one of relief that his friend was alive.

"I'll go to the house in Belle Plains and see if she's there. But I'll need a warrant to search the place."

"Meet me at the hospital, and I'll give you all the probable cause you need for a warrant. I know this all seems way out there, but you'll understand when you get into Mortimer's house. I'll give you the details about where to look. I should be there in an hour."

"Roger that. Give me a call when you get to the hospital."

They disconnected, and Puccini turned off the TV. He went to his home office, took out his small note-pad, and summarized everything he had just heard from JD. Then he looked at his notes, and realized there was still one piece missing. What about Fareed Ghanem? He'd been shot from a distance by a high-powered rifle, and John Smith was the obvious perp in that case. Mortimer and Chong didn't fit that scenario, and Smith was still the main suspect. Puccini had to get to work, and decided to call Brown at home.

Brown picked up on the [illegible] ring. "Hey, partner, what's happening? Did you see Jeter's hit? Too bad we're losing." Puccini could hear the baseball game in the background.

"I missed it. That's not why I'm calling. It looks like there may be a break in the Bridger and Harriman cases. We need to get to work right away."

"A break? We've been chasing our tails on that for over a week. What happened? And how come in the middle of the night?"

"Anne Rutherford was right. Joshua [illegible]onne was captured by Mortimer, and he escaped. And get this . . . he's convinced that Mortimer's a serial killer, says he has all the evidence. And he says Mortimer's dead."

As Puccini expected, there was a long silence on the phone. Then Brown said, "So Mortimer's a serial killer? No fucking way, man. What I think is that Dionne's been hit on the head . . . real hard. That's cloud-cuckoo land. I don't believe it."

"Maybe, but let me give you the details." Puccini proceeded to read from his notes for a few minutes, summarizing what JD had told him. Brown asked some questions, and then finally said, "It's ten-thirty. What do you want to do?"

"Meet me at the PSC, and we'll get to work on it. If Dionne is right, there's a barge running around with no one aboard, and I'll get on that right now. Then I have to find out more about this woman Chong, and get started on writing up probable cause for some search warrants."

They disconnected, and Puccini called Sergeant Bonner of the Marine Patrol at home to tell him about the unmanned barge motoring around the Sound. Puccini thought about mentioning the white Donzi 22 somewhere out there, but decided he'd check on it first at Mortimer's house in Belle Plains. Then he headed downstairs, and told the nanny that he had to go back to work.

As he was driving down to the PSC, Puccini started thinking about what he had just heard from JD. The whole case had been turned upside down, and he tried to figure out what he'd missed. Everything pointed to Smith, and he still wasn't totally convinced about Mortimer. He'd have to sit down with JD, and determine if he was telling the truth.

* * *

When Puccini arrived at the PSC, Brown was already waiting at his own cubicle, with two coffees at the ready. He handed one to Puccini. "Looks like it'll be a long night."

"Yeah, and we're just getting started. First thing is to draft up those search warrants and get them ready to fax to our favorite judge. I've got to fill in some blanks, but I'll get that info from Dionne. Meantime, you can start on the paperwork with these notes. And I should call Delvecchio and tell him about Harriman, save him a lot of effort. Dionne said that Harriman's not missing . . . he's dead."

"Are you sure about all of this? Sure enough to get a warrant? How well do you know this guy Dionne?"

"I thought about that. I know him. He was rattled, but I think he's solid. I'm going with it. The missing piece is this woman Chong. We need to find out more about her. I'll do that while you type out those search warrant requests. But first, I've got to let the Bureau know about Harriman. They're still looking for him."

Puccini called Delvecchio, and the FBI agent picked up right away. "Hey, sport, what's happening? We missed you at the poker table tonight."

"I had a rough day, needed a break. But it's turning around. I've got some news about Harriman. Harriman's dead, and so is the perp."

There was silence for a few seconds. "No shit. So his clients caught up with him. I didn't think it would be so quick. But did you find the body? He'd have every reason to fake it and disappear some place with no extradition treaty."

"No, we don't have the body. It's a long story, and I have to confirm it all. But I wanted to give you a heads-up. I'm pretty sure he's dead."

Puccini outlined the call from JD, and the next steps he was planning to take to gather evidence. When he was finished, he said, "I think Harriman's a GPD homicide case. The Bureau can look after Harriman's financial fraud, figure out who else was involved. I'd bet on the accountant and one of the sons. And we'll do the homicide angle."

"Let's talk tomorrow. If there really are ten murders involved, it's probably interstate, maybe international. You'll need some help. The Bureau should probably take the lead."

Puccini agreed. No point in fighting it. Wouldn't be his call anyway. They disconnected, and he turned to his computer to do some research on Abigail Chong. He first did a search of media reports and articles, but the only clue he found was an old story about a woman with the same name who had won a medal for an incident in Iraq. She was an MP, and had killed four insurgents when her convoy was ambushed. But there was no mention of any marriage to Mortimer. It was almost as if this Abigail Chong had fallen off the map after her stint in the army. He checked the NCIC criminal records database, but her name did not pop up. He did find a mention on a taekwondo website, but that was from five years earlier. How could a woman married to a prominent artist leave such a faint trail in the digital forest? JD hadn't mentioned weapons, but Puccini decided to check the Connecticut gun registration records. It took a few minutes, but then he finally found something big. He had to take a very deep breath. Then he pushed his chair back and swung it around to think. The pieces were starting to fit.

Puccini saw that Chong owned a number of guns, but what floored him was the Remington 700 Tactical Rifle chambered for a .338 Lapua Magnum. This was a top sniper rifle, similar to the one used by Chris Kyle, the Navy SEAL who had 255 kills in the Iraq war. So Smith wasn't the only trained sniper in Greenwich.

This put the Ghanem case in an entirely new light. Chong was capable of killing a target from a mile away. Even if Mortimer was dead, there was still a problem. Chong was on the loose with a Lapua Magnum.

In a white speedboat.

* * *

JD was exhausted. He'd fallen asleep in the cabin of the *Ojibway*, only to be awakened by a bump as the boat reached the dock at the yacht club. He could feel the throbbing pain in his leg again. He raised himself to a sitting position and looked up the open double doorway toward the cockpit. Annie was still at the wheel, and she smiled down at him. He got up slowly, and climbed the three steps up to the cockpit. B and Junior were already on the dock, chocking the lines to make the *Ojibway* secure. Then the reality hit him again – B had killed someone, Junior and Annie had helped, and JD needed to keep them all out of jail.

JD climbed up to the deck, and leaned against the lifelines, but there was still a foot-wide gap between the boat and the dock. Junior walked over and offered her hand to help him, and he stepped on the dock. There was nothing much to unload, JD realized, because they had dumped or burned almost everything. The yacht club seemed to be deserted. He pulled out his iPhone and checked the time. It was past eleven P.M. It was a weeknight, so everyone had already gone home. That was good – he wouldn't have to explain their late-night sail to other members – or his wounded leg.

With Annie holding his arm, JD hobbled along the dock and they made their way to the parking lot. Annie's SUV was at one end, and B's car was parked halfway across the lot. JD said to Annie, "Why don't we let the kids drive home and get some sleep, and you can take me to the hospital?"

B shook his head. "No, Dad, we're coming with you. I want to make sure you're okay."

"I'll be fine. They'll put on a new bandage, and maybe give me some antibiotics and a painkiller. You and Junior have had a very rough day, and you should really get some rest. I won't be long." JD didn't want Puccini to meet or talk to B at the hospital. He also wanted to help B and Junior rehearse their stories before being subjected to any police interviews. And the sooner B left for Yale, the better.

B finally agreed and Junior joined him to head home. JD and Annie watched as they pulled away from the parking lot. Annie said, "You're really worried about them, aren't you?"

"I don't know how Puccini's going to handle this. We've done all we can for now, but I think we're just getting started."

* * *

Annie and JD checked in at the Greenwich Hospital emergency room. The triage nurse did a quick interview, and sent JD to one of the examining rooms within minutes. Annie accompanied him and sat on a chair while JD climbed up on the examining table, his feet dangling over the edge. He pulled out his phone. "I told Puccini I'd call him as soon as I got here."

"Don't you think you should talk to the doctor first, get some X-rays or something?"

"I want to get going on this while it's all fresh in my mind."

He punched in Puccini's number, and Puccini picked up right away. JD told him he was at the hospital, and the detective said he'd be right over. JD was just disconnecting when the doctor walked in, introducing himself as Doctor Aggrawala. He seemed young for a doctor, maybe early thirties, and JD wondered whether he might be a resident or intern. He was tall and thin, with dark brown skin and black hair.

He cut through the tape job that Annie had done on JD's pants leg, checking the gauze that was wrapped around the wound. "This was well done . . . it stopped the bleeding. It looks like an Israeli combat dressing."

Annie nodded. "We always keep a few in the medical kit on the boat. My husband insists on it."

The doctor removed the blood-stained compression bandage. "It looks like the bullet went through and through, mostly hitting muscle. The entry is here," he indicated, and then pointing to a second red puncture wound on the other side, said, "The exit is here. They're close together, so the trajectory is not very deep. We'll take some X-rays to check for fragmentation, but I don't think you'll need surgery. Looking at that clean exit wound, I'd say the bullet didn't mushroom or tumble. And no arteries or veins . . . you were very lucky. So I'll wash it and disinfect it, and then we'll send you over to X-ray. If it's all clear, I'll sew you up." He turned to Annie. "You may wish to wait outside."

Annie shook her head. "I'll stay. We've come this far together."

Dr. Aggrawala nodded, and then went to the medicine cabinet for a syringe. "This is a local anesthetic. Close your eyes and grit your teeth, because this is going to hurt like hell . . . just kidding." He swabbed an area near the wound with alcohol and injected the local. "We'll let that work a bit, and I'll come back in a few minutes." He left the room and closed the door.

* * *

An hour later, JD was back in the examining room, getting ready to go home. The X-rays had shown no fragmentation of the bullet, so the doctor had sewed up the wounds and bandaged them.

As he sat on the edge of the exam table, JD realized how tired he was. The morning seemed like a month ago. It had been one hell of a day, and it wasn't over yet. He closed his eyes for a few seconds, and then heard the door open. It was Puccini. The detective also looked very tired; he had a half-day's growth of beard. He sat down on the chair beside Annie .

"Looks like they're taking good care of you. How're you feeling?"

JD grimaced as he moved his leg slightly. "They cleaned me up and patched me. It went through and through."

Puccini smiled. "Through and through, huh? You're starting to get the lingo, sport."

JD leaned forward and rubbed his forehead. He had no interest in Puccini's jokes at the moment. "So what's happening? Any sign of Mortimer's body?"

Puccini's face became more serious. "Not yet. The Coast Guard found the barge, but no sign of Mortimer. And no sign of that white speedboat. We're working on the warrants, but it's close to midnight, and we have to find a judge who's a nighthawk. Once I give her all the info, Brown should have them within an hour. Then we can search the house and the island."

JD nodded. Puccini turned to Annie. "And it looks like you were right all along, Annie. Mortimer was the one. I'd like to get all the details from JD now. I can take him home afterward."

Annie frowned. "No, I need to make sure he's okay."

JD leaned forward from the examining table and took Annie's hand. "I'll be fine. You should go check on Junior." He decided not to mention B's presence to Puccini just yet.

Annie was silent for a few seconds, and then gave a deep sigh. "Okay, I'll go home. But I'll be waiting up for you." She leaned over and gave JD a kiss on the cheek and left the room. Puccini closed the door after her. Then he then put a small recorder on the counter beside him. He turned it on, and pivoted toward JD.

"Okay, JD, tell me exactly what really happened. How did you kill Mortimer?"

CHAPTER 31

JD stared at Puccini, alarmed by his question and hard tone of voice. This was the Puccini that JD had first met ten days earlier, the one who considered JD a suspect in Rich's disappearance. And JD was too exhausted to have the patience for it.

"I told you I didn't kill Mortimer. He drowned after he tried to kill *me*. What the hell is going on here, detective? Am I a suspect or something? Do I need a lawyer?"

Puccini shrugged. "Don't take it so personal, sport. It's been a long day for both of us." He took a deep breath, and let it out slowly. "And no, you don't need a lawyer . . . I was just pushing a little. And the reason is, buddy, your whole story seems a little out of kilter, if you want to know the truth. What is this evidence at Mortimer's house you were talking about? I mean . . . *ten* murders? Come on, this is Greenwich, Connecticut, not Chicago or the Bronx. And what was it you didn't want to tell me over the phone?"

"You want to know about the evidence? Look, here's how it is, detective . . . Mortimer was a fucking psychopath, a stone-cold killer. He cut the right hand off each of his victims, probably *before* he killed them, and kept these as some sort of sick trophies. He preserved them, and called them his – quote – special sculptures. I counted ten of them in a locked room in his house, just before he knocked me out with a needle. And here's the surprise, detective . . . I didn't want to damn well explain all that in front of my family. They were upset enough already."

Especially after what B and Junior did to Chong, JD thought silently.

Puccini scratched his forehead. "You say 'my family,' JD. Was your son Balthazar there as well? I thought he was away at college."

JD started to feel more nervous about Puccini's questioning. "He's here. He came to help Annie find me."

Puccini nodded. "Okay, so tell me more about those special sculptures. You say there were ten."

"The first one I saw was Richard Bridger's severed right hand." JD's voice faltered, and he had to steady himself. "I recognized his black belt tattoo. And the missing finger. That's when I realized what was going on, and that Rich was dead."

"How do you know that Rich is dead?"

"Inference," JD said, his tone bleak at having to outline the obvious. "They forced me to help them load Harriman's body into that kiln, and his right hand was missing. There was just a bandaged stump. Rich has now been missing for over a week, and I saw his severed right hand in that room. So . . ." JD forced his voice to stop shaking, forced himself to sound rational. ". . . *ipso facto,* Rich's body must also have been burned in that kiln. And further logic dictates that the ten severed hands imply ten bodies cremated in that kiln. Can you think of any other explanation?"

"Yes, in fact, I can think of a few. But that's not the point here. I have to see all of this for myself because, frankly, JD, your story is just too fucking bizarre."

JD clenched his fists and took a deep breath, "Those severed hands are all in the back room of Mortimer's house in Belle Plains, and the kiln is on the island. And I'll bet the farm that each of those hand sculptures correlates with a missing person . . . someone that Mortimer and Chong killed for a fee of five million dollars."

"Five million? So that explains all his money and the island. And we all thought he was just an artist." Puccini shook his head and looked intensely at JD. "But this still all sounds like pure bullshit."

"He was an artist," JD said, ignoring Puccini's skepticism. "And according to Annie, a genuinely good one. But also a killer. And his two identities actually meshed. Remember those billionaires at Cole's party? They were probably invoiced for both services – bespoke murder and great sculpture." The weariness was catching up with JD. He wasn't sure how much longer he could keep talking or even stay upright. "From what Mortimer said to me, there were more than ten. His killing didn't just start recently. But I can tell you about two of the hands in his collection. They belonged to Richard Bridger and Bucky Harriman. You'll have to figure out the rest yourself. All I know is what I saw."

Puccini's eyes narrowed. "Okay, I'll check it out as soon as we get the warrants. But tell me one thing . . . what happened to Chong? Where is she?"

JD frowned and shook his head. "I told you, I don't know. I was locked in an upstairs room, waiting for them to kill me. My only view from the window was the Sound. I couldn't see what was happening on the other side where the dock was. She must have left in the speedboat."

Puccini was silent, still looking intently at JD, and apparently trying to decide whether to believe him. JD could feel his heart rate increase, and was glad that he was not connected to a lie detector at the moment. Puccini took a deep breath, and JD started anticipating another question, but then the detective reached over, turned off the recorder, and got up.

"When we confirm that Bridger is dead, I'll have to inform Mrs. Bridger. And if what you're saying checks out, this clears her as well."

JD sighed in relief, although Puccini probably thought it was exasperation. "Don't do it tonight. It's too late. And anyway, Annie and I could talk to her first. It might be gentler that way."

"No, as detective in charge of Bridger's case, it's my job. The worst part of my job," Puccini admitted. "When she sees my car pulling up in front of the house, she'll know what it's about. They always know."

"Okay, do it the official way. But wait until tomorrow morning, at least."

"Let's go. I'll take you home. Brown and I have a lot of work to do."

Puccini called for a nurse, who brought the discharge papers and the requisite wheelchair. JD signed the papers, and a nurse wheeled him to the door. She waited with JD while Puccini got his car.

"Thanks," JD said, gingerly lowering himself into the front seat.

"No problem. Let's get you home." Puccini's voice was gruff, and he almost spun the tires as they pulled away. Ten minutes later, they were in front of JD's house. Puccini turned to JD. "Take it easy, sport, and we'll talk tomorrow. In the meantime, keep all this under your hat. We want to go through all the evidence before we make any announcements about anything. Including Mrs. Bridger."

And I know you also want to find Abigail Chong before you make any announcements, JD thought as he got out of the car.

* * *

When JD walked into the house, the whole family was waiting for him in the kitchen. They were all sitting around the island counter, looking wide awake and very worried, even though it was almost one in the morning.

Annie helped JD sit down on one of the counter stools. "Would you like some coffee – or maybe something stronger?"

JD tilted back his head and closed his eyes. "A little coffee would be good. The doc said to take it easy on the liquor."

Annie set a cup on the counter. "So what did Puccini want? Are we okay?"

JD took a sip of the black coffee. "He wanted more detail on what happened. I haven't told you the whole story. Everybody please take a deep breath and listen, because I'm going to tell you what Mortimer and Chong were really up to." He looked at B. "I think you'll feel a lot better after you hear the whole thing."

"The part I didn't mention earlier was what I saw in Mortimer's house in Belle Plains, a room he called his 'special gallery.' It was . . . horrific. If I hadn't seen it myself, I wouldn't have believed it." He hesitated and took a deep breath. "Mortimer had cut off the right hands of each of his victims, and preserved them as some sort of sick sculptures . . . there were ten of them."

JD saw the color drain from Junior's face. She looked as if she was about to be sick. "They're like people from another planet. They're not human."

B's face was impassive, but his jaw muscle was twitching slightly. "So Mortimer was a psychopath. Like Ted Bundy and Jeffrey Dahmer."

JD's voice was very quiet. "A lot like them. He compared himself to them. And remember one other thing . . . Chong was in that same sick league. She marched step-in-step with Mortimer in everything he did. She was the one who shot Fareed, and helped capture Rich. She was just as evil as Mortimer."

Annie had been silent to this point. "I can't say I knew he was a serial murderer, but Mortimer's persona always seemed like a façade to me. I sensed there was something evil inside and underneath." She looked at her son. "You did the right thing, B. You saved Dad's life and probably many others. If you hadn't stopped them, Mortimer and Chong would have just kept doing what they were doing. And they would have killed all of us."

JD got off his stool and hobbled over behind B and Junior. He put his arms around their shoulders, and gave them both a hug. "Thank you, both. I owe you my life, and I love you both very much."

"But what about Chong?" Annie said. "Did Puccini mention anything about her? What did you tell him?"

JD returned to his stool and coffee. "I told him she must have left in the speedboat. I don't think he bought it at first. He started off pretty aggressive, the hard-ass detective. But he finally backed off. I'm sure he's found out about her Lapua and the sniper training by now, but he didn't mention it. But the important thing is: there's nothing to find, so there's nothing to worry about."

B got up and then sat down again, biting his lip. "I sure hope so. I'm the one that pulled the trigger."

Annie tried a weak smile. "There's no evidence, B, and we're the only witnesses. We'll just all say the same thing as Dad – we have absolutely no idea what happened to Chong."

Junior got up. She wasn't quite as pale anymore, and looked almost relieved. "I'm really tired. I need to get some sleep if I'm going to school tomorrow. Or at least, I have to *try* to get some sleep."

B got up as well. "I think I may stay home tomorrow, get some rest. It's been a helluva day."

JD shook his head. "No, B, you have to get back to Yale right away. You have to behave as if nothing unusual has happened, and act as normally as possible. And if Puccini wants to question you, you want to be far away. He'll have to interview us all eventually, but we should put that off as long as possible. I want him to see Mortimer's special sculptures before he talks to any of you. That will put him in the correct mind-set."

B nodded. "Okay, got it. I was just a bystander, right?"

JD said, "And there's one more thing everyone should know and remember. B's Winchester was stolen from his car last week, but he didn't realize it until today. We'll put in an insurance claim as soon as we can. Everyone got that?"

They all agreed, and B and Junior went upstairs to their bedrooms to try to sleep. Annie and JD stayed in the kitchen, trying to make sense of what had happened over that very long day.

JD said, "Well, you were absolutely right about Mortimer. How did you know?"

"I just knew, that's all. Some things can't be expressed in words. How's your leg, by the way?"

JD gave a fake grimace. "It hurts . . . but I think we can still fool around a little."

Annie smiled and they went upstairs.

* * *

When Puccini arrived back at the PSC, Brown had the search warrants ready. Puccini added the details about Mortimer's "special gallery," and they faxed the requests to Judge Rothman. Twenty minutes later, she faxed the warrants back, duly signed.

"It's nice to see a judge working overtime," Puccini noted. "Let's get over to the house and take a look at that back room."

"If it's a crime scene, we should have forensics there as well. And a couple of patrol officers."

"It's two in the morning. That can wait until tomorrow. I just want to see those so-called sculptures and confirm Dionne's story. We'll make sure we don't disturb anything. I just need to know if it's all bullshit or not."

"What if this woman Chong is at the house?"

"She won't be there. She'll be long gone. If she's still alive." Puccini's gut feeling was that they'd never find her. He wasn't sure why, but he wasn't worried about Chong any more.

"Okay," said Brown. "But if we're on our own, we need the entry ram."

They took the elevator downstairs to the police garage, and requisitioned a special operations entry ram. It was a Blackhawk Zoro – a two-foot-long black cylinder weighing about thirty pounds, with handles on the top and sides. Brown put it in the trunk. "If the door is locked, we won't need a key."

They drove along Greenwich Avenue, turned at Railroad, and headed down Field Point into Belle Plains. It took them less than ten minutes, because there was almost no traffic, but Puccini figured it would take almost as long to get past the guard at the gatehouse.

He rolled down his window as they pulled up to the Belle Plains gate, and the guard turned from his computer screen. "Do you have an appointment, sir? It's rather late."

Puccini had never seen this guard before. He was much younger than the one he had met previously, and with his crew cut, he looked almost military. *They keep their Ivy Leaguers for the days shift*, he thought.

He badged the guard. "I'm Detective Antonio Puccini, and this is my partner Garry Brown. We don't have an appointment. We're here to serve a search warrant at the Mortimer residence."

"It's very late. Why don't you come back tomorrow? They're probably all asleep."

"No. We're going in right now. The judge just signed it, and it's urgent."

The guard frowned. "Let's see that warrant."

Puccini handed it up to the guard. His eyes widened as he read, and he shook his head slowly. When he finished, he handed the document back to Puccini. "I have to call ahead. I'll get fired if I don't."

Puccini gave him the full cop glare. "Look, sport, you just read that warrant, so you know what's going on. We're talking murder here, and I'm sure Belle Plains doesn't want reporters all over the place. We'll do it very quietly tonight, but the full enchilada arrives tomorrow. You can bet on it. If I were you, I'd call someone very discreetly right now to give them a heads-up on what to expect tomorrow, and then get back to watching your move. If you don't want to do that, I'll have six black-and-whites here in ten minutes, and we'll play it your way."

The guard hesitated for a moment. Then he pushed the button releasing the gate without changing his expression.

Puccini headed toward Quarry Point, driving slowly. When they reached the address, he stopped in front of a six-foot wall.

Brown leaned forward. "That's weird. Someone left the gate open."

"Strange," Puccini agreed, slowly driving onto the grounds. In the moonlight, he could see the outline of a very large mansion, partly hidden by tall trees. Puccini's eyes widened at the size and grandeur. "Holy shit, what a place," he said. "No wonder Dionne said Mortimer was living beyond his means. That house is bigger than Harriman's."

As they drew closer, the headlights showed a yellow two-story house with a circular drive in front, a second driveway leading around the right side of the house, and a wide stairway leading to a massive wooden front door.

Puccini said, "If Dionne was telling the truth, his car must be around the back somewhere." He parked the Crown Vic in the circular driveway, and they got out. He couldn't see any lights on inside the house. "Looks like no one's home, but let's do a quick walk-around before we go in."

"You sure we shouldn't call for backup?" Brown's voice was almost a whisper.

"No, we'll be fine . . . but let's put on the vests, just in case."

They walked to the trunk and grabbed their Kevlar vests and latex gloves, and then drew their guns. Puccini led the way around the right side of the house, holding his Glock in his right hand, and his flashlight in his left, well away from his body. He heard a dog barking, probably at the neighboring house a hundred yards away. They stood still for half a minute, and the barking stopped. They continued around the side of the house, following the driveway, and as they rounded the corner, Puccini could see three vehicles in the moonlight. He shined his light toward them, and recognized JD's Mercedes, plus two black SUVs - Cadillacs. Probably the ones that tried to run JD off Round Hill Road, Puccini realized. His hand tightened around the Glock.

They continued around the perimeter of the house, but Puccini could see no lights, no signs of life. They reached the front door again, and tried the doorbell, but there was no answer. They rang three more times with the same result. Puccini shrugged. "I guess Chong's not here."

Brown went to their car to get the battering ram. He carried it up the entryway stairs to the landing, and lifted the cylinder into a horizontal position, ready to break down the door. "Give me a hand here, Tony, and we'll get inside and take a look."

"Wait a minute. This place has an alarm system. Look at the sign in that window over there." Puccini nodded toward a security company decal on the window to the right of the door. "I'll give them a call first, get them to turn it off. We don't want to wake up that dog again." He called the alarm company, and after a brief discussion, the alarm system was turned off.

Puccini sidestepped the battering ram. "Let's try it the easy way. The front gate was open, remember." He turned the door handle and pulled gently, and the heavy door slowly swung open. "I guess they really trust their super-rich neighbors."

Brown put down the battering ram. "Or maybe Chong left in a real big hurry."

"Maybe. But if Chong left, there'd be only one SUV behind the house, right? Keep your head up."

They walked in carefully, guns still drawn, and Puccini groped for a light switch on the wall. He turned on the lights, and saw the two-story open plan living area with the two-sided brick fireplace in the middle. "You could play touch football in here."

They moved past the black leather couches and marble coffee tables, and headed toward the back of the house. Puccini turned on lights as they walked down a hallway, opening the doors and looking in as they passed. "The whole place looks empty." He started to relax.

At the end of the hallway, they came to an ornate oak door with a keypad beside it. Puccini tried the polished brass doorknob, but the door was locked. Brown stepped back and lined up the battering ram just below the knob. "Give me a hand here, Tony, and we'll see what we've got."

Puccini grabbed the handles on the right side of the ram, and they started swinging it back and forth. Brown said, "On three," and counted out. On "three" they both put all their weight behind the ram and crashed it into the door. Puccini winced in pain from the impact, and the ram rebounded quickly. Part of the oak paneling had shattered and dropped away. A solid sheet of dull grey metal shone beneath the wood.

"Great, a fucking solid steel door," Brown said. "This ram's not going to do it. We need a drill or a torch."

"Yeah, there's no way we're getting in there tonight. We'll come back in the morning with a full crew. But at least the room that Dionne described is right here."

They started walking back to the front of the house, and Puccini stopped by a window that looked out on the back parking area. "There's just one more thing to check. Let's go look at the dock."

They went out by the front door and headed down the driveway again, toward the rear of the house. Puccini could see a stone path leading toward the water, and they followed it to a dock and a boathouse. He could hear the waves from the recent storm splashing onto the piers of the dock as they approached. They walked onto the dock and checked the boathouse. Nothing.

Puccini stood in the moonlight looking out at the Sound. "No sign of a speedboat. If Chong was here, she's gone."

Brown said, "We'll put out an APB for the boat. It should be easy to find."

Puccini didn't respond right away. The speedboat bothered him. "I'm not so sure we'll find it."

CHAPTER 32

Wednesday, September 17, 2008

JD was sweating as if he'd just run five miles. He opened his eyes, took a deep breath, and let it out very slowly. He took another breath, and he could feel his chest rising and falling as he looked up at the ceiling. He opened his eyes, turned to the side, and realized that he was at home, in his own bed. The sheets around him were rumpled and damp, but he saw no sign of Annie. He moved to get up, but an electric charge of pain coursed through his right leg, and he decided to lie still for a while. He'd been sleeping for a long time, it seemed, but he was still tired. He moved his head to look at the alarm clock, and saw that it was nearly noon.

He sat up on the side of the bed and looked around. He was in no hurry to get up. He wanted to sit still for a while, and savor being alive.

After a few minutes, he finally got to his feet and limped downstairs. He could smell coffee brewing, and as he entered the kitchen he saw Annie at the stove, preparing what looked like a quiche. The eggs shells, sliced peppers, and mushrooms on the cutting board confirmed it. The sights and smells suddenly made him very hungry. Annie turned to him and smiled. "Well, well, well. Perfect timing. How'd you sleep? It's almost afternoon."

JD shook his head. "I'm still really tired. I had a lot of nightmares."

Annie walked over and gave JD a long hug. "You've been through an awful lot." She stepped back and looked at his face. "You look really worn out. Maybe we need to watch for PTSD."

JD took a deep breath. He was not interested in talking to a therapist at this point – he was more worried about his family. "What about B and Junior? Are they awake yet?"

"They're awake and gone. B took your advice and left for Yale. He seemed to be feeling better after finding out what Mortimer and Chong had been up to, all those murders. And Junior was proud of what she had done. Saving your life, that is. I think they'll be fine. I hope so, anyway."

JD could tell that Annie was being more optimistic than she really felt. There was still good reason to worry. Their nightmare was not over.

"Puccini's pretty tenacious, and he's going to look at all the loose ends. I didn't want to get into the details with B and Junior last night, but the legal stuff will have to play out. They may have to go through some hard questioning."

Annie returned to the stove. "Let's not worry about that right now. You must be hungry." She cut out a quadrant of the quiche, scooped it on a plate, and handed it to JD. "Sit down and eat. Would you like a cappuccino?"

"Yes, please, even though it's a little late in the day. Puccini would not approve. He says no cappuccinos after eleven."

Annie sat down at the counter. "So you're still looking for his approval. Are you meeting with him again today?"

JD had to stop and think. Was he actually seeking Puccini's approval? Yes, he decided, in a way he was. He wanted Puccini to approve of what his family had done in killing Chong and letting Mortimer die. Morally, JD knew they had absolutely done the right thing, but Puccini would have to deal with the right and wrong of their actions in the eyes of the law. One thing was for sure – he did not want to piss off Puccini at this point, even in a matter as trivial as the proper timing for a cappuccino. So Annie was right, but he decided to let her comment pass.

"He was supposed to give me a call when he'd checked out Mortimer's trophies. And he was going to go see Dot to tell her that Rich is dead."

"Shouldn't we do that? It would be much gentler."

"I offered, but Puccini insisted on doing it himself. It's part of his job – he has to notify next of kin in a murder case before it goes public. We can talk to Dot afterward, after the initial shock, and then provide some support. Besides, I really don't want to talk to her about Rich's severed hand unless I absolutely have to."

"At least she's no longer a suspect," Annie said.

JD ate his quiche in silence. Then he looked up and wiped off his cappuccino mustache. "What are you up to today?"

Annie started clearing the dishes. "I'm going to try to paint again. I mixed some colors this morning, but nothing happened, just a couple of brush strokes. What about you?"

"I better check the markets and answer some emails. I'm sure a lot has happened over the past twenty-four hours."

"Junior watched CNBC this morning and said the markets were still going down. Are you really going to start a new fund after your experience with Mortimer?"

"I don't know. Greed led me into his trap. I may wait a while, get to know myself a little better, and figure out what I really want to do. I feel like I've come to some sort of fork in the road. And as Yogi Berra said, when you come to a fork in the road, take it. And I have to visit Fareed at the hospital. Maybe he can help me decide." JD gave Annie a wry half-smile. "We can compare gunshot wounds."

JD got up, kissed Annie gently on the cheek, and headed down the hall to his office. He looked around the familiar room, checked out his guitar on its stand, and sat down in front of the computer. It felt like a very long time since he had last been here. As the computer booted up, he looked out the window at the backyard. The storm from last night had been followed by a strong northwest wind that was still blowing, and he could see the big oak tree waving in the breeze. Then he saw that the little circle on his screen had stopped spinning, and he went to the Bloomberg financial website.

He could tell that the market panic was getting worse. The government's $85 billion bailout of AIG the previous day had not stopped the financial meltdown. Morgan Stanley had dropped another 24% to a ten-year low, and was in merger talks with Wachovia, another major bank. The Dow Jones was in a 449-point sell-off, and Russia had halted all trading. One broker was quoted by the Wall Street Journal as saying, "Forget about retail investors, all the pros are scared."

A week ago JD would have been pursuing these stories in detail, but something had changed. He just wasn't that interested. In fact, he was almost bored. After the confrontation with Mortimer, his swim through the storm, and his efforts to keep B and Junior out of jail, the financial graphs and talking heads on his monitor now seemed like a juvenile soap opera. He thought that maybe after a few days, the fascination would return, but if not, he'd have to think about his future. As a result of his hugely successful bet on the market downturn, the family's financial future was secure. He didn't really need any more money. And if the game no longer held his interest, why play it?

He checked his emails. There were only two and he read them slowly. Both were from former colleagues at MIT, thanking him for making them rich. He answered them in a formal manner – his heart wasn't in it. He saw no messages of thanks from his many other clients. That made him more sad than angry.

JD shut down the computer, got up, and limped over to Annie's studio. She had started another painting, but JD could tell that she was still in a dark mood. The painting was mostly shades of black and grey. He could see no bright colors on her palette as he sat down to watch.

Annie put down her brush and sat down beside JD, staring at the somber painting. "I can't help it. It's something I have to do – to purge the darkness, I guess. I don't like the world much right now. I always thought we were safe, JD . . . that we had an oasis of calm and reason here. But we don't, really, do we?"

JD had no answer. He just sat for a few minutes silently as a few tears trickled down Annie's cheeks. She didn't bother to wipe them away. JD gently put his arm around her.

"At least we have each other." He knew it was trite, but it was all he could come up with.

Annie wiped her eyes with a clean rag. "I know you're right, and that's what's important. I'll get over it. I should be feeling relief, but I just feel very sad."

JD walked over to the easel, removed the bleak half-finished painting, and replaced it with a stretched canvas already prepared with gesso. Then he took her palette, wiped it clean, and squeezed out a daub of yellow and a daub of light blue.

"Every painting starts with the first brush stroke," he said.

Annie looked at the dark canvas sitting off to the side, and stood up before the new blank canvas. She stared at it a moment, put the tip of a clean brush into the yellow pigment, and then placed a small streak of the bright color near the middle of the off-white canvas.

She turned around, brush in the air. "So what do you think, Dr. Dionne?"

"It's a start. It'll get better."

JD's phone buzzed, and he thought about turning it off, but Annie looked at him and sighed. "Better answer it. It's probably Puccini."

JD glanced at the screen on his phone. "You're right. Bad timing, but I better take it." He pushed the answer button and got up, nodding to Annie as he started walking back to his office.

"So what's happening, detective?"

"We found the 'special' sculptures, just like you described. Forensics is in there right now, and they're doing the whole house. With ten murders, I've also called in the Bureau for some help."

"The bureau?"

"The FBI. This thing will go big and go international. Mortimer was a global celebrity, and most of his clients were probably high profile as well, some of them likely from Europe – those guys at the party. This is going to stir things up in both the art world and high finance. And here's the thing, JD - we want to keep it quiet as long as possible, because the perps involved in hiring Mortimer will start destroying evidence. There's a lot of money and power at stake here. Lucky that it all started in Belle Plains – they don't want any publicity, so they'll keep it quiet for now. We've got a team in there and another team out on Mortimer's island. And oh, by the way, your Mercedes is still at the house. We'll pick it up for you. You'll have a hard time getting into Belle Plains right now."

"I appreciate that, but I'm sure Annie could drive me to retrieve it."

"Just let us handle it, pal. What I want right now is for you to come down to the PSC. I've got a few more questions, and we need to do a proper interview. I need it all on the record before we go public."

"Will I be part of the publicity?"

"I guess that depends on our interview. I'll see you in half an hour."

Puccini disconnected, leaving JD hanging on his last words. It didn't sound good. He could feel his leg throbbing again. It sounded as if Puccini had some new information, something he didn't want to discuss over the phone. JD got up and walked back to Annie's studio. Her new painting had the yellow and blue, but JD could also see some grey on the palette. His ploy to improve her mood had only half-worked.

She was gazing out the window with her hands folded on her lap. "So what did Puccini want?"

"He wants me down at the station for an interview. It's probably just a formality." JD knew he was being overly optimistic, but if the news was going to be bad, he wanted to put it off as long as possible. He squeezed her shoulder gently. "I need to borrow your car."

"Okay, good luck. Fingers crossed."

I'll need it, thought JD as he hobbled out to the garage.

* * *

JD told the desk sergeant at the PSC that Detective Puccini was expecting him, and a few minutes later Puccini opened the door to the left of the glass enclosure and ushered him up the stairs to the detective squad room. When they got to his desk, Puccini said, "If you give me your car keys, I'll get someone to drive your Mercedes home. It's the least I can do." JD handed over his keys, wondering if the detective was being especially friendly now because he knew they were headed for a difficult interview – probably about his and Junior's whereabouts yesterday. Puccini took the keys, and thanked him.

"Let's go to the Case Cracker room. I need to record your statement. Please follow me." Puccini's face was now more serious. JD felt his heart rate increasing, and his hands started to sweat.

Puccini led JD into the small room he remembered from a week earlier. He saw the square table in the middle with a chair on either side, and the camera lens on the wall. He knew the drill, so he sat down in the chair opposite the camera. Puccini sat down in the other chair, and put his notepad, cell phone, and laptop on the table in front of him.

"You remember this set-up from last week. Garry Brown is watching us on the monitor, and we're going to record the interview. Just relax, and tell us what happened yesterday."

JD could not relax. His mouth felt dry, but he didn't want to ask for a glass of water. It would make him look nervous, and he wanted to appear calm, make Puccini think it was just a walk in the park, rather than a conversation that would determine the future of his family. JD cleared his throat, and then immediately regretted doing so.

"Where would you like me to start? We went over all this yesterday."

"I know we did, but we need your statement now as formal recorded testimony. The next step will then be to track down all of Mortimer's clients, the ones who paid him to kill those ten victims. Your testimony will allow us to expedite the warrants and get the Bureau aboard. You can help us, JD."

"So I'm not some sort of suspect again? This room makes me nervous."

"No, no, JD, just relax. Just tell us exactly what happened, what you saw and heard."

JD did start to relax a little, although he was still wary. He knew he would have to dance around some of the facts to protect B and Junior, so he had to concentrate on keeping his story straight. He started by again describing his arrival at Mortimer's house for an investment pitch, enticed by the promise of a ten-million-dollar check, and related how the scales had fallen from his eyes when he saw those two black Cadillac SUVs behind the house. Puccini listened keenly as the story progressed, interjecting questions from time to time. Over the next hour, JD described how Mortimer and Chong had captured him, his imprisonment on the island, and his escape by swimming. Puccini asked a few additional questions about Yates and Cole, and as JD was responding, Puccini's cell phone started vibrating. He looked at the screen, and picked it up. He listened for a while, nodded, then said "Okay," and disconnected.

"They found Mortimer's body. That should put the case to rest, except for a few loose ends like the individuals who commissioned the killings. And of course, Abigail Chong. There's still no sign of her, and no sign of the speedboat. We put out an APB, and the Bureau will put it on their system. Anyway, that's all the questions for now." He turned and looked at the camera lens behind him. "Garry, you can turn it off. We've got all we need."

JD felt a wave of relief. Puccini had not asked the awkward questions he'd been so afraid of. The comments about Chong's disappearance seemed almost an afterthought.

Puccini stood up. "Let's go have a cup of coffee, sport. There's something else I want to talk to you about."

* * *

The lunchtime crowd was mostly back at work, and Starbuck's was half-empty when they nabbed the corner table. Puccini put the two double espresso down in front of them, and they sat down. JD's leg hurt from the walk, and he thought about taking one of the little pills the doctor had given him, but he held off.

Puccini took a sip of his espresso. "Here's the lay of the land, JD. I need some help with putting the collar on Yates and Cole. If they each paid five million to Mortimer like you said, there's got to be a record of it, and you're the one who can find it, help us get those bastards off the street. You can trace the payments, and maybe get at some of their emails. I can get warrants to do that legally. How about it? You want to help us nail those guys?"

JD was stunned by the offer. He'd been expecting more grilling about Chong and B, and had to change gears. He was silent for a few seconds.

Puccini continued, "Look, you saved my bacon with Harriman's fund. You're good at what you do, and we could use your help."

JD took a sip of his espresso, still playing for time. "I don't know. I should get back to running my fund. Forensic accounting isn't exactly my specialty. Besides, this can be a dangerous business. I'm lucky to be alive after yesterday."

"We can provide protection and even training if you want. It won't be the same as being a sworn officer, but you could be a consultant. And look at it this way . . . you could help collar the guy who paid to get your friend Bridger killed."

Yeah, thought JD, *you can provide protection as long as you can get a search warrant in time.* But the thought of putting Yates in jail for a long time grabbed him, and his voice grew softer. "I want to help. But I have to talk to Annie about this. She'd almost be married to a cop, and that's not what she signed up for. I don't want her sitting by the phone again, wondering where I am. Plus it's not what I worked for at Oxford and MIT . . . I'll think about it and get back to you."

"That's all I ask . . . just think about it. But not too long. There are ten people out there who belong in jail."

JD nodded in agreement. "You're damn right about that. I wonder what the motive was in each case . . . for the clients, I mean. What reason could someone possibly have to commission a murder?" He shook his head. "Those billionaire visitors from Germany and England at Cole's party were probably Mortimer's clients in this murder business, so that's your starting point. But there's at least one saving grace . . . Yates's Ponzi scheme will collapse in the coming financial crash, so the FBI will get him for fraud in any case. He'll go to jail. But that's not quite as good as getting him as an accessory to murder. And then there's Cole . . ."

Puccini smiled, and waved his espresso cup, almost spilling it. "Exactly. So you'll do it? I want to tie those bastards to the murders. That would be justice. They're as guilty as Mortimer."

"I said I'd think about it."

Puccini pushed his chair back and rubbed the back of his neck. Then he looked intently at JD. "There's just one more thing I wanted to talk about, JD, and that's Abigail Chong. I'm missing a few pieces of that puzzle. Tell me again exactly what happened. Just between you and me, something doesn't smell right."

JD almost froze and he hoped Puccini could not see his face going pale in the dim light. It was now clear that Puccini had been softening him up with that request for help, and now he was coming in for the kill. Puccini had figured out what had happened. JD would have to duck and weave to keep B and Junior safe. He decided to feign anger and impatience.

"I've told you three times already . . . I don't know what happened to her! She just disappeared. Mortimer came and got me from the room where I was being held and she was no longer around. And that's it." JD was starting to wonder why Puccini hadn't asked all these questions in the Case Cracker room.

"Did you see Chong before that? On the island, I mean?" Puccini was giving nothing away with his facial expression.

"Yeah, I saw her. If you can believe it, she prepared this fabulous dinner for me . . . bouillabaisse, with Screaming Eagle cabernet. Thirteen hundred a bottle, they said. It was the most bizarre performance you've ever seen. Here they were about to kill me, and she cooked me this gourmet meal. They said they'd done it for the other victims." JD shook his head, still mystified. "It was like . . . some sort of ritual with them."

"Yeah, they'd make an interesting study in criminal deviancy – if we ever find Chong. Mortimer's done talking. But what about the speedboat? There's no sign of it at the island or their dock in Belle Plains."

"Maybe she got out before the storm and made it across to Long Island. Or maybe the boat sank. Mortimer said it wasn't very stable in rough water. That's why he took the barge. And she looked to me like an athlete, so she might have made it ashore even if the boat sank. *I* did."

"That boat could be anywhere in a hundred square miles, and the water's mostly a hundred feet deep, so if it sank, we'll never find it. But if she made it to shore, we *will* find her. Anyway, weren't you curious about where she was? It doesn't make sense that Mortimer took you off the island by himself."

"I was concentrating on only one thing – the gun Mortimer had at my back. That was all I could think about."

Puccini started tapping his finger in the table. "Gun at your back . . . yeah, that would do it. Kind of throws off your concentration. But there's some other stuff that doesn't make sense. We found some bullet holes in the wall of the house on the island, and some traces of blood in one of the bedrooms. Any ideas on how they got there?"

"I really don't have a clue, Tony. Look, you've got the evidence. They killed at least ten people on that island. That might explain the blood." JD heard the sarcasm in his own voice and knew he had to dial it down a notch. The last thing he wanted to do was rile up Puccini. When he spoke again, it was in a calmer tone. "And the bullet holes? I don't know. Maybe Chong was doing some target practice. Mortimer said she'd been in the army, an MP."

Puccini hesitated, and his voice became very quiet. "We got a bullet out of that wall." *Oh shit*, JD thought, *here it comes. He's going to nail B.* Puccini continued, "This is a very awkward question, Joshua, but could we have a look at your son Balthazar's Winchester .308? We need to do some tests on it."

JD tried to calm his racing heart by taking a deep breath, and he hoped his blinking wouldn't give away his nervousness.

"B doesn't have it anymore. It was stolen from his car last week."

Puccini's eyebrows came together as he frowned and rubbed his chin. "Stolen, huh? That's a real shame." He looked up at JD. "Did he report it?"

JD shook his head nervously. He realized he wasn't very adept at lying. "No, I don't think he did. He only noticed it was missing this morning."

Puccini looked up at the ceiling and drew a big breath. He seemed to be thinking about how he was going to handle this. It was clear to JD that Puccini didn't believe his story about the theft of the Winchester. JD literally held his breath. He knew that Puccini's decision over the next few seconds would seal the fate of his family.

Puccini was silent for a few more beats, and then he finally looked directly at JD. He shrugged his Sicilian shrug, and said, "Well, JD, I guess you better put in a theft report when we get back to the PSC. He'll want to claim the insurance on it and get a new one. I understand he's on the Yale rifle team." He shook his head. "It's a real shame how you can't trust anyone these days. Some people will steal anything."

JD nodded, hoping he had an I-agree expression on his face. He took a deep breath, and then a sip of his espresso. His hand was shaking a little.

"Thank you, Tony, for everything. That will be very helpful."

Puccini smiled. "We're not going to find Chong's body, are we, JD? The kiln was still hot this morning."

JD hesitated, trying to think of a response. Was Puccini playing him? "I guess Mortimer forgot to turn it off after they cremated Harriman."

"I guess. We figured out how to turn it off, but there sure were a lot of ashes in the kiln."

JD knew better than to respond to that. He was almost certain that Puccini knew what had happened on the island. Puccini knew that B had killed Chong, and that they had burned her body in the kiln. That's what the "lots of ashes" and "we're not going to find Chong's body" comments were about. But it also seemed clear that Puccini was not going to do anything with that knowledge. Yes, Puccini was an officer of the law, but he also seemed to believe in justice, and JD liked to think that the detective - like JD himself - knew that everything that had happened on that island was justified. The bad guys were dead, the good guys lived, and that was all that mattered.

Or maybe it wasn't that complicated. Maybe Puccini had realized that he could never get enough evidence to prove what had happened to Chong, even though in his gut he knew the truth. If there was no evidence, it didn't happen.

Puccini finished his espresso. "Let's get back to the PSC and fill out that theft report. And I want you to think about my offer. And there's one more thing. The only announcement we're making this afternoon is that Mortimer drowned in the storm, but only after we've notified next of kin. So keep all this other stuff under your hat for now."

JD nodded and they stood up and started heading back to the PSC. It was only a long block away, but it was slow going with his bad leg. They went upstairs to Puccini's desk and filled in the theft report, and then JD went back down to the SUV.

He sat in the front seat for a few minutes, thinking about what had just happened. B seemed to be in the clear, and JD had a decision to make about his future. He knew he'd have to discuss it with Annie. But first, he wanted to visit his old friend Fareed.

* * *

Fareed was fast asleep when JD walked into his hospital room. He had an IV bottle hooked up to his left arm, and the bandages on his right shoulder seemed to have diminished in size compared to JD's last visit. JD watched his friend sleep for a while. His thoughts drifted back to MIT and the Charles River Playboys. Rich was gone, but Fareed would be okay, and JD himself was still alive. Maybe they could get back to playing music again someday. Rich would have liked that.

JD could see Fareed starting to stir, gradually waking up. His friend let out a quiet moan and slowly opened his eyes.

"Joshua. My goodness, it is so nice to see you. How are you? I missed you yesterday. I had my surgery this morning, and I'm told it went splendidly."

"I'm sorry I couldn't visit yesterday, but it was quite a day. We have something in common now. I was shot in the leg. And I found out who shot you."

Fareed frowned and shook his head. "You cannot be serious, Joshua. You say that you have been shot as well. That would be a remarkable coincidence. And we already know who shot me. It was John Smith. And Stuart Cole was --"

Fareed was interrupted as the surgeon walked in. Fareed smiled, and said, "Good afternoon, Doctor Craig. I'd like you to meet my friend Joshua Dionne."

The doctor nodded to JD, checked out his ponytail, and said, "Hello, Mr. Dionne. I heard you were well taken care of last night in the ER. We don't get many gunshot wounds at this hospital. You two are keeping us busy." She looked down at the medical chart in her hand and then turned to Fareed. "How are you feeling, Mr. Ghanem?"

"I feel fine. There is no pain, which is surprising, frankly."

"There will be some pain after the anesthetic wears off, but the surgery went well. We've given you some antibiotics to fight any possible infection, and you're familiar with the morphine pump. You'll be able to eat some solid food tomorrow, and we'll have you home in a couple of days. You'll need help at home for the first week, and you won't be able to drive for at least two or three weeks. We'll provide you with a sling, but I don't want you lifting anything . . . nothing at all." A smile passed fleetingly over her lips. "Any questions?"

Fareed looked at JD; then he grinned as he turned back to the doctor. "When will I be able to play the drums again?"

Doctor Craig still looked very serious. "That will take about three months . . . if you do all your physical therapy and exercise conscientiously."

The doctor waited for a few seconds, and when there were no more questions, she turned and left the room.

"Well, she was certainly a ray of sunshine," JD observed.

Fareed shifted his shoulder slightly, and raised the back of the bed with the control button. "Do not mind her, Joshua. She is one of the superior orthopedic surgeons in Connecticut. I carried out some research on her." He reached his left hand over to the table beside him. "You see, they allowed me to finally have my laptop. I can get back to work soon. But please tell me how you managed to get shot, Joshua. Greenwich is becoming very dangerous. Was it an attempted robbery?"

"No. I know it may be hard to believe, Fareed, but I was shot by Mortimer, your favorite artist."

Fareed shook his head "That is absolutely and categorically impossible. Mortimer is one of the greatest artists of our time. You are mistaken. It cannot be."

JD's voice became very quiet, and he spoke quickly, wanting to get it all out. "No, I'm afraid it's true. And there's more. I saw the evidence. Mortimer was a serial killer, and his wife Abigail Chong was the one who shot you. They kidnapped me and took me to his island studio, and they were about to kill me. I escaped, but he shot me in the leg." JD paused and leaned forward. "Mortimer is dead, and probably so is Chong. They killed at least ten people. He was a high-end paid assassin. Five million per assignment."

Fareed started to laugh and then stopped abruptly. "Surely you are joshing, my friend. I think perhaps I am hallucinating from the morphine. Mortimer cannot be a killer. He is one of the greatest artists in the world, a truly wonderful talent. I love his work. Stuart Cole and John Smith are the felons. Mr. Smith killed Raji and then shot me. He tried to kill me because I started the lawsuit over *Tricolor One.*"

JD looked intently at his friend and then rubbed his fingers across his forehead slowly. "Maybe we should talk about this later. You're just recovering from the surgery. This can wait until you get home."

Fareed reached his left hand over to pinch his right hand. He winced, and shook his head slowly. "You sound very serious, Joshua. And this is not a morphine hallucination after all. You are here, and I can see you and hear you. But what you are telling me cannot be true."

JD started to get up. "You're too upset, Fareed. I shouldn't have started telling you about this now. It can wait."

Fareed reached out for JD with his left hand, almost tipping over the IV stand. "I want to hear it. I must hear it."

JD sat down again. "Okay. I'll tell you the worst part." JD took a deep breath. "Rich is dead. He's gone. I'm sorry."

Fareed's eyes closed, and one tear slid down his cheek. It was clear to JD that Fareed now believed him. It had been difficult to tell him, but he certainly didn't want his friend to hear the bad news from anyone else.

Fareed sighed, and opened his eyes. He looked as if he wanted to ask something, but then he seemed to change his mind. He gazed out the window. JD sat silently for half a minute, and finally took Fareed's left hand to say good-bye.

"I'll be back tomorrow, Fareed. And I'm sorry, but I thought you should know."

"I am very sorry too, Joshua. Thank you for telling me."

JD walked out, closing the door behind him. He limped down to the SUV, and as he started the engine, he thought again about Puccini's offer. He had a big decision to make. He pulled out of the parking lot and headed for home.

CHAPTER 33

When JD got home, he headed straight to Annie's studio. He saw that her latest painting had seen a great deal of progress, and he was pleased that it was mostly bright colors. There was that slash of grey across one corner, but the predominant hues were yellow and blue, just as he had suggested earlier. Annie did not acknowledge him as he sat down, and he watched patiently for a few minutes. He finally realized that she was in the zone and did not want to be disturbed. She looked almost as if she were in a trance. He got up without a sound and retreated to his office. His conversation with Annie would have to wait.

JD sat down at his computer and started typing a letter to his investors, announcing that he was shutting down his fund. The letter was not very long, but it took him about an hour to compose. He wanted to make it concise, but he also wanted to explain why he was doing it. He knew he had placed a big bet, and despite his confidence in his own judgment, he also knew it had been risky. He decided to make the letter very diplomatic. He thanked his investors for their confidence in him, though he knew that many of them had been unhappy with his strategy over the previous months. The main reason he gave for closing the fund and giving his clients their six-fold return on their investments was simply that he had achieved everything he wanted to achieve. He also knew, though he didn't say it, that repeating this stellar performance would be difficult.

But he did not include in the letter the *real* reason he was closing it down. JD had fought the devil and won. Collateralized debt obligations no longer held the interest they had a week earlier.

He read over the draft of the letter one final time, but he couldn't quite push the "send" button. He printed off a copy for Annie to review. He still wanted to discuss it with her, so he walked back to the studio. Annie was sitting back in a chair in front of the easel, looking at the painting, a brush in hand. To JD, the painting looked finished.

"It sort of reminds me of *Blood and Bone*," he said.

Annie looked at the painting, and nodded. "I guess that sculpture had some influence on me. Mortimer was a genius, a genuinely great artist. I can't get away from that. I just can't fathom how he was capable of all that evil when he was also capable of creating all that beauty."

"It's a crazy contradiction," JD agreed. "Mortimer was a psychopath. A wonderful artist with world-class talent, but still a psychopath. Maybe he had a special deal with the devil."

Annie put down her brush. "We'll never know, and I'm glad it's over. We did what we had to do, but I don't feel good about it. I guess that's what's in that painting. Joy that you're alive, but sorrow about what we did. Mortimer and Chong deserved to die, but I still feel guilty about it."

JD had a brief flashback of Mortimer struggling in the crashing waves during the storm. He'd had no remorse at the time and now — when his own life was no longer in danger — he was still glad that the bastard was gone. But that wouldn't be the right thing to say to Annie.

"I know what you're saying," he told her. "But if you hadn't saved me, I think that painting would be very different."

Annie reached back and put her hand on JD's knee. "I'll take what we have now, any day of the week. But how did your interview with Puccini go? Is B going to be okay, or is he in trouble?"

"Puccini did a complicated dance with me. I'm sure he's figured out what happened . . . maybe not all the details, but he knows that Chong wound up in the kiln. And he suspects that B shot her. But the weird thing is, it looks like he's going to let it rest."

"Let it rest?" Annie's eyes widened. "Is that for real? Can you trust him?"

"I think so. First, he knows we did the right thing. We had no choice. I would have been dead, the eleventh victim. And besides, he has no evidence. And as he once told me, if there's no evidence, it didn't happen. He knows that without the rifle they can't do ballistics tests, and we were the only witnesses to what actually happened. And there's no body. And no rifle. So he doesn't have a case."

"Still," Annie said, "I'd hate to have either B or Junior grilled by the police. It would be rough on them, especially B. And what if one of them slipped up?"

"I know," JD agreed. "I've worried about that myself. But Puccini got me to fill out a theft report on B's rifle. I think that's his signal that he's not going to pursue B's role in Chong's disappearance."

Annie's face relaxed. "So B and Junior are in the clear? They won't be questioned?"

JD gently took Annie's hand. "I think they're in the clear. And there's more. Puccini wants me to help him track down and convict the people who paid Mortimer for those ten killings. He wants me to use my forensic accounting to track the payments."

Annie still seemed skeptical. "Is that some sort of quid pro quo to keep B out of jail?"

"No. B's innocence is signed, sealed and delivered with the theft report. We don't need to worry about it. But I do have a decision to make about Puccini's offer."

"So Puccini wants you to help catch the bad chaps?"

"Yes, although he seems to prefer the term 'collar the perps.'"

Annie smiled. "You're starting to sound like a detective, JD."

"Well, we already know two of the perps – Yates and Cole. We just need to prove it."

"You say 'we' . . . as if you're part of the team already."

"I'm moving toward it, but it's complicated. I have something here I'd like you to read first. It's a letter to my clients announcing that I'm closing the fund, giving them all their money back, plus about a 600 percent return. I haven't sent it yet. I wanted you to read it first."

"So you've made up your mind?"

"Almost, but please read it. It would be a big step."

Annie took the sheet of paper and started reading. JD got up and headed back to his office, but as he was heading down the hall, he heard the doorbell ring. As he walked toward the door, he saw a woman in a police uniform through the window.

"Special delivery from Detective Puccini," she said as he opened the door. She turned and pointed to the silver Mercedes AMG sitting by the curb. A black-and-white police cruiser was parked behind it. The officer gave JD the keys, and waved as she walked down the steps to the cruiser. JD shouted thanks after her, and went back inside. It was good to have the Mercedes back, but he now also realized how much he missed his Porsche Turbo. It had been in the shop for almost a week, and the repairs should be done. After all, it was just a matter of a few bullet holes, with no other serious damage.

He called the body shop and found out that his car was ready to go, so he jumped in the Mercedes and headed down to the shop. Walter, the shop owner, greeted him with a smile. His hands were greasy, and he was wiping them as he ushered JD over to his car. One of the workers was buffing the paint on the hood as they approached, and he stepped back. Walter led JD around the car, pointing out the new paint finish with a wave of his hand.

"Some of my customers want *fake* bullet holes on their cars," he said with a grin. "These are the first real ones I've had to remove. It took a lot of work to get it right."

JD thanked Walter, and signed the insurance paperwork. Then he gave the Mercedes keys to Walter for return to the rental agency, and took his own Porsche keys. He sat down in the black leather bucket seat, and inserted the key to the left of the steering wheel. He turned the key, and closed his eyes as he listened to the sweet thrum of the flat six turbo engine coming to life. He had enjoyed the Mercedes, but he now realized how right the Porsche felt. He drove home.

* * *

Back home again, JD went straight to Annie's studio. The finished yellow, blue and grey painting was sitting against the wall, and a clean canvas was on the easel – clean except for one black slash of paint.

"Don't worry," she said, "I'm rationing myself to that one black mark on this painting. I just wanted to get the bad news out of the way first. How's your car? I heard you drive in."

"It's great to have it back. It helped me make up my mind. How did you like my resignation letter?"

"It's good. Just a hint of the pain they caused you, without burning all your bridges in case you want to go back sometime."

"I'm going to accept Puccini offer, and then just run our own money. And maybe run Puccini's, if he wants."

"Not a good idea. Never sell a used car to a friend, or invest their money for them."

"It was just a thought. But are you okay with this new direction after what we've been through? "

"We did get through it, dear, and I know it sounds trite, but you could make the world a better place. We have enough money."

JD sat down beside Annie, and took her hand. "Thank you. I'll bet this is something you never bargained for when you said 'I do' back at Oxford."

"Not exactly," she admitted. "But it would be a very dull marriage if we didn't surprise each other now and then." She looked at him, a bit worried. "Do I still surprise you?"

JD laughed. "Well, you did head up a commando mission to rescue me yesterday. I don't think I foresaw that back at Oxford."

He got up and hobbled to his office, brought up the resignation letter on his computer, attached it to an email to his clients, and pushed "send." It felt good. Then he swiveled in his chair to look at the picture of The Charles River Playboys on the wall.

He went out to the living room and poured himself a drink, added some ice, and returned to his office. He put on a Playboys CD, and closed his eyes to listen. Rich was dead, but he was going to make sure the person behind his murder would pay for it. And that would be just a start. There would be nine more cases. And who knows how many others after that?

Then his mind filled with the vision of crashing through the storm while Mortimer held the gun on him, and the mixture of terror and anticipation he felt at the time. He took a large gulp of the Sazerac to quell the chill that ran down his back.

His cell phone buzzed and he picked it up. It was B.

"Hi, sport, what's happening? Did you get to class today?" JD did his best to sound cheerful.

"I did, but I was way too nervous to concentrate. I tried to act as natural as possible, but it was hard. I thought about talking to Vivian about it, just to share it with someone . . . and this is going to sound weird, considering I'm in the middle of a campus with nearly twelve thousand students, but . . . I feel very alone."

"We're on cell phones, so keep it vague, son. Maybe you can talk about it with her later, but not yet. I had a good meeting with Detective Puccini, and you have nothing to worry about. He helped me fill in a report about your stolen Winchester. You'll be able to collect the insurance on it."

There was a long silence on the phone, and JD could sense the wave of relief in B's voice when he finally spoke. "That's great news, Dad. And insurance . . . that's a bonus. But I may not get another rifle for a while."

"There's no hurry, B. You can think about it. But if you do get one, you probably shouldn't leave it in the car. As Puccini said, you never know what people will steal these days. Even in Greenwich."

"I'll see you on the weekend, Dad. Thanks for everything. I love you."

"I love you too, son. And thank *you* for all your help. If you need anything, be sure to call."

* * *

By mid-afternoon, JD was feeling very hungry, and for some strange reason, he had a strong craving for bouillabaisse. He wondered if maybe it was an indirect form of Stockholm syndrome – he hadn't fallen in love with his captors, but he had fallen in love with their food. He drove down to Whole Foods and bought the ingredients: a live lobster, some red snapper, cockles, mussels, shrimp, a variety of spices, and a fresh baguette.

When he got home, he laid out everything on the counter. He checked the time – four o'clock. He knew it would take about an hour and a half to prepare the dish, and he started with the lobster, first boiling it and then cutting the tail meat into two inch slices. Then he started the main pot, first with tomatoes, onions and garlic, and then added fennel fronds, bay leaf, saffron, sea salt, and pepper. After ten minutes, he added the lobster, snapper, and shellfish. The aroma from the cooking was making him even hungrier, and he cut a slice off the baguette and buttered it. It disappeared into his mouth as he placed the rest of the sliced baguette into the oven.

As the pot simmered, he opened a bottle of Stag's Leap cabernet, poured himself a glass, and swirled it before taking a sip. "Not quite Screaming Eagle, but it will do," he said to himself.

JD heard the front door open, and Junior walked in. She stopped, took a slow deep breath through her nose, and smiled. "Wow, Dad, that smells great. What is it?"

"It's bouillabaisse, my secret recipe from Boston. That's what we're having for dinner tonight."

Junior frowned. "Isn't that the same stuff that Abigail Chong was cooking yesterday? We could hear her banging around in the kitchen."

"Her bouillabaisse was delicious, so I thought I'd try mine today to compare. How was school?"

Junior still seemed puzzled by JD's choice of recipe, and hesitated. "That's pretty strange, Dad, cooking that stuff they forced you to eat yesterday. I guess I'd want to forget all about it if someone had tried to kill me. Anyway, school, yeah . . . I got through it, but that's about all I can say. I could not concentrate. I was worried about B. Have the police come for him yet?"

JD went over to check the baguette slices in the oven. "The police aren't coming for him. I told Detective Puccini that his rifle was stolen, and I believe that part of the case is closed. You and B are in the clear."

"So our plan worked." Her face was serious, as if the worry had only partly dissipated.

JD stirred the soup. "Puccini is a smart cop. I think he may have guessed what happened . . . or at least part of it . . . but there's no proof. We just have to stick to our story. And I mean, forever."

Junior nodded, and JD continued, "And there's one more thing you should know – I'm shutting down the fund, and I'm going to help Puccini track down Mortimer's clients in his murder-for-hire business."

Junior squinted. "So you're going to become a detective?"

"Not quite. More like a consultant."

Junior was quiet, and seemed to be thinking about this new development. "Will you need any help?" she asked at last.

JD smiled at his daughter, who looked much more mature than she had a week earlier. "I'll need all the help I can get."

* * *

"I spoke to Dot this afternoon," Annie said that night. She and JD were sitting out on the back deck. It was cool, and she had wrapped her blue wool shawl around her shoulders. The moon was almost full, and the clouds were flitting by overhead, covering and then revealing great white swaths of stars.

"Puccini came to see her and told her about Rich," Annie went on.

"How did she take it?"

"She sounded sad, but not devastated. It wasn't much of a surprise, I guess. On some level, she must have known. It's been eleven days since he went to that conference."

"Eleven days," JD echoed, shaking his head. "It seems more like a lifetime." He looked up at the moon and the stars, and took a deep breath, letting it out very slowly. "It's beautiful out here. What a great night to be alive."

Annie nodded and took a sip of her port. "We were very lucky yesterday."

"It wasn't luck, Annie. You and the kids were amazing."

They sat in silence for a while, still holding hands. Annie turned and looked at JD. "There's just one more thing, JD. John Smith is still around. Are you sure it was Chong who shot Fareed?"

"That's what Mortimer said."

"But Mortimer was a psychopath . . . a pathological liar."

JD leaned back and looked up at the moon again. A small cloud moved across, and the moon disappeared. He felt the familiar chill run down his back. He took a sip of the Sazerac, and closed his eyes in thought.

His voice was very quiet as he said, "I guess we're going to have to find out."

JD felt Annie squeeze his hand, and they looked up in silence as the moon came out from behind the cloud again and shone down on them. The wind whispered through the trees, and JD could feel Annie's calm breathing as she leaned against him.

It felt good.

Made in the USA
Columbia, SC
11 September 2024

42090227R00209